U0034425

張翔／編著

英文袋著聊 口語慣用句5,000

聊天神句放口袋，隨手翻，就能說！

Daily English in Pocket!

Best

絕讚 1　6大情境完全制霸

絕讚 2　5,000絕讚精華句

絕讚 3　單字解析一目了然

聊天神句放口袋，隨手翻，就能說！

1 道地發音靠MP3就通

收錄每一句的完整英語發音，不只學會詞彙怎麼說，還能兼學老外的道地語調。

2 豐富多元的單元主題

每一個 Part 之下分出數個單元，多元主題齊發，架構最完善，聊天絕不冷場。

Daily English in Pocket!

UNIT 6

日常雜貨哪裡逛 Shopping For Groceries

1479 My **fridge** is nearly **empty**.
我的冰箱幾乎空無一物了。fridge 名(口)冰箱 empty 形 空的

1480 We need to go **grocery** shopping.
我們得去買菜了。grocery 名 食品雜貨

1481 Where are you going? I believe the market is closed today.
你要去哪裡買？超市今天不是沒開嗎？

1482 There's a new grocery store that has just **opened**.
有一家新開的雜貨店。open 動 使開張

1483 The supermarket is having a **grand** opening sale this weekend.
那間超市這個週末有舉辦開幕特賣。grand 形 盛大的

1484 How often do you go grocery shopping?

3 句句精華的 5,000必備句

只教用得上＆最順口的精華句。除此之外，5,000英文句經過嚴謹編排，學習更省力。

4 關鍵單字／片語好好記

每一句英文裡的關鍵單字＆片語，都會標注在中文翻譯後面，學句子兼擴充詞彙量。

5 6大生活主題無一遺漏

一本囊括六大熱門領域，日常生活、旅遊走跳、公司點滴，全都能用英文順口溜。

Part 2 從早到晚的日常

1488 Also, the price is **negotiable**. That's my favorite part.
而且，還可以殺價，這是傳統市場最吸引我的地方。
negotiable 形 可協商的

1489 She usually gets free **green onions** or chili peppers when buying other items.
她採買時經常能拿到店家送的蔥或辣椒。 green onion 片 蔥

1490 I don't like shopping at traditional markets because of the **crowds**.
我不喜歡上傳統市場，因為人擠人太可怕了。 crowd 名 人群

1491 I like going to the **farmer's** market very much.
我很喜歡去逛農貿市場。 farmer 名 農夫

1492 The one I usually go to is a **chain** grocery store.
我常去的那家是連鎖超市。 chain 名 連鎖店

1493 It **offers** a wide variety of food and **household** items.

聊天神句帶著走，走到哪、聊到哪！

對許多華人學子而言，開口說有時是學習的一大罩門。這其實是個很普遍，卻也讓人憂心的情況。以我們的母語為例，「說」往往比「寫」還要更早發展，小孩子也許還寫不出字，但他們很快就能夠學會說。如果把聽、說、讀、寫化成學習階梯圖的話，「說」這一層階梯肯定是比「寫」還要容易跨的，可惜的是，在我們學習英文的過程中，往往忽略了「說」的訓練，長久下來，竟讓學習者在面對外國人時，感到無從開口，這真的是非常可惜的一件事。

記得有一次在搭乘火車時，我看見一名外國人用英文詢問兩名年輕人「某某站到了沒」。看年輕人的表情就知道，兩個人都聽懂外國人在問什麼，也知道要回答NO，但接下來……就完全愣住，兩人面面相覷，幾度張口欲言，最後還是沉默。

其實，日常英文並非遙不可及，甚至有很多只是用大家熟知的單字重新排列組合而已，學習者所缺乏的，是「句子」。因為不熟悉句

子，所以臨場用不出來，就算腦中浮現幾個 key words，往往也因為混亂，而不知該如何回答。

也因為如此，我開始著手於本書的編寫。想透過本書達成的目的，是希望能讓大家熟悉生活必備的英文句，記得愈熟，臨場的反應自然就愈快，而當大家發現自己能開口說出一句英文時，就能從中得到成就感，這個才是能推動人繼續學習的動力。

類似的工具書，坊間也很多，但那些動輒上萬的英文句，卻不一定適合大眾。首先，那些書籍往往過於重視「句子數量」，導致讀者花了時間記憶之後，才發現很多句子根本都在表達同一個意思。在我們時間、記憶力有限的情況下，這種只看中數量的書籍，反而會增加學習者的負擔，讓人望之卻步。因此，在本書中，我剔除了那些雖然許多語言書上有教，但母語人士幾乎不會講的句子，以「精煉」、「實用」為兩大主軸，把那些「學了真的用得上」的句子介紹給大家。

張翔

目錄 CONTENTS

我的人際關係

MAKING FRIENDS

▸001

開啟對話的第一步
Starting A Conversation

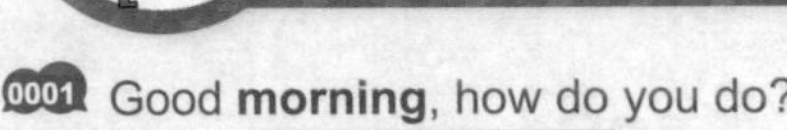

0001 Good **morning**, how do you do?
早安，你好。 morning 名 早晨；上午

0002 Nice to meet you. My name is Tommy. / I'm Tommy.
很高興認識你，我的名字是湯米。

0003 Hello. You can call me Vicky. I am a friend of the **hostess's**.
你好，你可以叫我薇琪，我是女主人的朋友。 hostess 名 女主人

0004 My Chinese name is Chia-yi Lee, but people call me Victoria.
我的中文名字是李佳儀，大家都叫我維多利亞。

0005 Most of my friends call me Alex, but my given name is Alexander.
大部分的朋友都叫我艾力克斯，但我完整的名字是亞歷山大。

0006 I don't think I've met you before. I'm Richard Yang.
我覺得我們應該沒見過面，我是楊查理。

0007 I think I should introduce myself first. I am Dr. Wang from Taiwan.
我想我得先自我介紹，我是台灣來的王醫師。

0008 I'm sorry, but I didn't **catch** your name.
抱歉，我沒聽清楚你的名字。 catch 動 聽清楚

0009 Could you please spell your name for me?
可以告訴我，你的名字怎麼拼嗎？

0010 Say, have we met somewhere before?

嗨！我們是不是在哪裡見過面？

0011 You look very **familiar**. Do I know you?
你看起來很眼熟，我們是不是認識？ familiar 形 熟悉的

0012 What a **surprise** to meet you here! / What a **coincidence** to meet you here!
好巧，竟然在這裡碰到你！
surprise 名 令人驚訝的事 coincidence 名 巧合

0013 What brings you here today? / Why are you here?
是什麼風把你吹來的？

0014 I haven't seen you for ages. / Long time no see! How are you?
好久不見了，你好嗎？

0015 What's up? / What's new? / What's going on? / How's it going?
最近過得好嗎？

0016 Couldn't be better. Yourself?
好到不能再好了，你呢？

0017 Same here.
我也一樣。

0018 I am doing just great. How's it going so far?
我一切都好，你呢？最近還好嗎？

0019 Not much.
馬馬虎虎啦。

0020 Not too bad. / No **complaints**. How about you?
還過得去，你呢？ complaint 名 怨言

0021 I was occupied with work. / I was **engaged in** work.
我都在忙工作。 engage in 片 忙於

0022 How's everybody? Have you **kept in touch with** our **classmates**?
大家都還好嗎？你有和同學保持聯絡嗎？
keep in touch with 片 與…保持聯絡 classmate 名 同學

0023 How's your family? Do your parents still live in Tainan?
你的家人好嗎？你爸媽還住在台南嗎？

0024 You're Julia, right? I've wanted to meet you for quite some time.
你就是茱莉亞吧，我一直想認識你。

0025 I believe you're Mrs. Wilson, aren't you?
我想你就是威爾森太太吧？

0026 I think I know you. You're one of Polly's friends, aren't you?
我應該認識你，你是波莉的朋友，對吧？

0027 Hello. You may not remember me; I'm Allen Lee from Anderson Co.
你好，你也許不記得我了，我是安德森公司的李亞倫。

0028 You don't remember me! I am one of your high school classmates.
你竟然不認得我了！我是你的高中同學。

0029 Nice to meet you. And I **assume** this is your son?
很高興認識你，我想這是你的兒子吧？ assume 動 假定為

0030 Do you happen to know the man in the dark suit talking to the host?
你認識那位穿著深色西裝，在跟主人講話的男士嗎？

0031 Could you introduce me to your cousin?
你能把我介紹給你的堂姊嗎？

0032 Is Ms. Chang an **acquaintance** of yours?
你和張小姐認識嗎？ acquaintance 名 認識的人；熟人

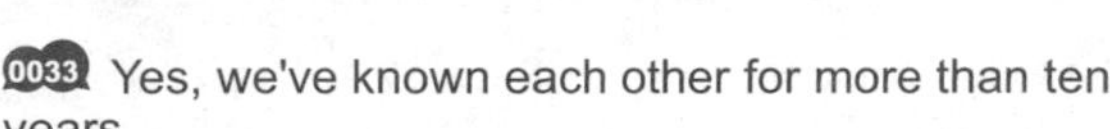

0033 Yes, we've known each other for more than ten years.
是的，我們已經認識超過十年了。

0034 I don't think I know him. That name doesn't **ring a bell**.
我應該不認識他，我對這個名字毫無印象。
ring a bell 片 令人想起某事

0035 Dad, this is my friend Jack. Jack, my father.
爸，這是我的朋友傑克。傑克，這是我爸爸。

0036 It's a sight for sore eyes.
見到你真好！（見到老朋友或看到能幫助自己的人）

0037 It's my honor to meet you here. / I'm honored to know you. / It's been my **pleasure** to meet you.
很榮幸認識你！ pleasure 名 愉快；高興

UNIT 2 我的城市與住處 The Place I Live

0038 Where are you from? / Where is your **hometown**?
你是哪裡人呢？ hometown 名 故鄉

0039 I am from Taiwan, a beautiful island in East Asia.
我來自台灣，一個位於東亞的美麗小島。

0040 Taiwan has a **population** of 23 million.
台灣的人口有兩千三百萬。 population 名 人口

0041 Taiwan is an island south of Japan, near China.
台灣是位於日本南方的島國，靠近中國。

0042 Have you ever been to Taiwan?
你去過台灣嗎？

0043 Our country is famous for its **tourism**.
我們國家以旅遊業聞名。tourism 名 旅遊業

0044 What are your favorite cities in Taiwan?
你最喜歡台灣的哪幾個城市？

0045 I like Beitou and Jioufen the best.
我最喜歡北投和九份。

0046 My hometown is Kaohsiung, the second-biggest city in Taiwan.
我的家鄉在高雄，它是台灣第二大都市。

0047 Do I sound like I have a little bit of a southern **accent**?
我講話聽起來有南部口音嗎？accent 名 口音；腔調

0048 I like Taipei. The mass **transit** is very handy there.
我喜歡台北，那裡的大眾運輸系統很方便。transit 名 運輸

0049 I can't live without the nightlife and other social activities cities offer.
我的生活中不能缺少城市的夜生活與社交活動。

0050 My hometown is small and quiet, but for me, it is the best place.
我的家鄉很小，又不熱鬧，但對我而言，那是最棒的地方。

0051 To tell you the truth, I don't like big cities. There is too much noise.
老實說，我不喜歡大都市的環境，太嘈雜了。

0052 I prefer the simple and quiet life.
我比較喜歡簡單、安靜的生活。

0053 I just can't stand air **pollution** in big cities.
我完全無法忍受大都市的空氣汙染。pollution 名 汙染

0054 I was born in Taiwan, but I immigrated to America a couple of years ago.
我在台灣出生，不過幾年前我移民到美國。

0055 My **nationality** is Australian. / I'm an Australian.
我是澳大利亞籍的。 nationality 名 國籍

0056 I have both U.S. and French **citizenship**.
我有美國和法國的雙重國籍。 citizenship 名 公民身分

0057 I live in San Diego. I am Chinese American.
我住在聖地牙哥，我是華裔美國人。

0058 I was born in Hong Kong but grew up in Vancouver.
我在香港出生，在溫哥華長大。

0059 Tokyo is like my second home.
東京就像是我的第二個故鄉。

0060 I think Switzerland is the most suitable place to live because it is clean and beautiful.
我覺得瑞士最適合居住，因為那裡既乾淨又漂亮。

0061 What a coincidence! We're from the same country.
真巧！我們來自同一個國家。

0062 What **languages** do you speak?
你會說哪些語言呢？ language 名 語言

0063 My native language is Chinese. / Chinese is my **mother tongue**.
我的母語是中文。 mother tongue 片 母語

0064 I speak Chinese, English, Spanish, and some Japanese.
我會說中文、英文、西班牙文和一點日文。

0065 Do you live with your family or live **alone**?
你和家人同住還是自己一個人住？ alone 副 獨自地

0066 Are there any shopping malls near your house?
你家附近有購物中心嗎？

0067 No, but you can find several convenience stores **nearby**.
沒有，不過附近有幾家便利商店。nearby 副 在附近

0068 I have been living here for fifteen years.
我在這裡住了十五年。

0069 Is there much **traffic** in your area?
你家附近的車流量很多嗎？traffic 名 交通量

0070 Many buses go by and there is a subway near my house.
我家附近有很多公車會經過，還有地鐵站呢！

0071 I **commute** to work by subway every day.
我每天搭地鐵去上班。commute 動 通勤

0072 Guess what? Many **celebrities** live in our **community**.
你知道嗎？有很多名人住在我們的社區喔。
celebrity 名 名人；名流 community 名 社區

0073 We really need a big house, but we can't afford to buy one.
我們實在需要一間大房子，但我們買不起。

0074 The apartment is really nice, but it is out of my price range.
這間公寓真的很不錯，但超出我的預算了。

0075 If only I could have a house like that.
如果我能擁有那樣的房子就好了。

0076 We bought a new house last month. It is still under construction.
我們上個月買了棟新房子，現在還在蓋。

0077 We are going to hold a housewarming party after

getting settled in.
安頓好新家之後，我們會舉辦喬遷派對。

0078 Is your house far from here?
你家離這裡遠嗎？

0079 My house is nearby. It's just two **blocks** away.
我家就在附近，過兩條街就到了。 block 名 街區

0080 We live on the same block.
我們住在同一個街區。

0081 My house is **located** on a **hill**. It's cool in summer and warm in winter.
我家在山丘上，冬暖夏涼。 locate 動 座落於 hill 名 山丘

0082 My mother lives in the same building as me. She lives on the seventh floor.
我的母親和我住在同一棟大樓裡，她住七樓。

0083 I live on the twenty-fifth floor, the top floor of this building.
我住在這棟建築物的最高層，二十五樓。

0084 Welcome to my home!
歡迎來到我家！

0085 Come on in. Let me show you around my house.
請進，我帶你參觀一下我家。

0086 The biggest one is probably the master bedroom.
最大的一間應該是主臥室吧。

0087 Can I get you something to drink?
要喝點什麼嗎？

0088 How about a cup of coffee?
要不要喝杯咖啡？

0089 "Feng Shui" is an **ancient** Chinese art believed to promote **prosperity**.

風水是一種中國傳統文化，人們相信能用它來提升運勢。
ancient 形 古代的　prosperity 名 繁榮

0090 Most Americans don't **take off** their shoes when entering the house.
大部分的美國人進房子是不脫鞋的。take off 片 脫去

0091 Does the room get plenty of **natural** light in the **daytime**?
這個房間的採光好嗎？natural 形 自然的　daytime 名 白天

0092 My room has a gorgeous view of the ocean.
我的房間可以看到海，視野極佳。

0093 I love the Japanese-style window **frames**. How about you?
我喜歡房子裡的日式窗格，你呢？frame 名 框架

0094 Look at the crystal lamp on the **ceiling**! It looks so **luxurious**.
快看天花板上的水晶燈！看起來真豪華。
ceiling 名 天花板　luxurious 形 豪華的

0095 Where did you get the sofa and **cushions**?
你的沙發和抱枕是在哪裡買的啊？cushion 名 靠墊

0096 The **intercom** is out of order. Please call me when you get here.
對講機壞了，你到的時候請打電話給我。intercom 名 對講機

0097 I think our house needs **remodeling**.
我們的房子需要重新裝潢了。remodel 動 改造；整修

0098 The walls have got **cracks** and need painting immediately.
牆壁的油漆都剝落了，得馬上粉刷才行。crack 名 裂縫

從天南聊到地北
Getting To Know Others

0099 Look at the clear blue sky! What a lovely day!
看這晴朗的藍天，多棒的天氣啊！

0100 It's finally **cleared up**. Do you want to go **outside** with me?
終於放晴了，你想和我一起出門嗎？
clear up 片 放晴　outside 副 向外面

0101 What kind of **weather** do you like?
你喜歡什麼樣的天氣？weather 名 天氣

0102 I like cool and windy days, so autumn is my favorite season.
我喜歡涼爽有風的天氣，所以最喜歡秋天。

0103 I like warm weather because I feel weak in the cold.
我喜歡溫暖的天氣，因為我怕冷。

0104 I really don't like hot and **humid** weather.
我真的很不喜歡又熱又潮溼的天氣。humid 形 潮溼的

0105 Cold and **gloomy** weather makes me depressed.
又冷又陰暗的天氣會讓我感到鬱悶。gloomy 形 陰暗的

0106 **Actually**, I don't care much about what the weather is like.
我其實不太在乎天氣。actually 副 實際上

0107 What's your **favorite** season?
你最喜歡什麼季節？favorite 形 特別喜愛的

0108 Like most people, I like **spring** the best.
跟大多數人一樣，我最喜歡春天。spring 名 春天

0109 I love spring because it **symbolizes** the **awakening** of life.
我喜歡春天，因為它象徵萬物復甦。
symbolize 動 象徵；標誌　awakening 形 正在醒過來的

0110 The weather is warm, and we can see **blossoms** everywhere.
天氣很溫暖，到處都能看到盛開的花朵。 blossom 名 花

0111 I love summer because I can enjoy lots of water **activities**.
我喜歡夏天，因為可以享受各種水上活動。 activity 名 活動

0112 My favorite time of year is from late summer to early **autumn**.
一年當中，我最愛從夏末到初秋的這段時間。 autumn 名 秋天

0113 Autumn is the best season. It's not as hot as summer or as cold as winter.
秋天是一年之中最棒的季節，既不像夏天那麼熱，也不像冬天那麼冷。

0114 I **prefer** winter to summer.
和夏天相比，我比較喜歡冬天。 prefer 動 更喜歡

0115 Cold weather doesn't stop me from going out at all.
天氣再冷，也無法阻擋我外出。

0116 I don't think I can **pick** one **specific** season I like the best.
我選不出我最喜歡的季節。 pick 動 挑選　specific 形 明確的

0117 How old are you? / What is your age?
你今年幾歲？

0118 Would you mind telling me your age?
你介意告訴我你的年齡嗎？

0119 I am four years older than you.
我比你大四歲。

0120 I won't be a **minor** anymore, and I will have the right to vote.
我即將成年，而且就快要有投票權了。minor 名 未成年人

0121 Guess, but I won't tell you the exact answer.
猜猜看吧，不過我不會老實告訴你的。

0122 I guess you are in your early thirties.
我猜你大概三十出頭。

0123 My mother is in her late sixties.
我媽媽快七十歲了。

0124 I was born in August. I had my thirty-first birthday a few days ago.
我是八月生的，前幾天才剛過我三十一歲的生日。

0125 What a coincidence! We were born on the same date.
真巧！我們竟然同一天生日。

0126 Though I look older, I'm actually the youngest of the four.
雖然我看起來比較成熟，但我其實是四人當中年紀最小的。

0127 He looks much older than his age.
他看上去比實際年齡還大很多。

0128 You look younger than your age. / You seem younger than your age.
你看起來比實際年齡小。

0129 Lisa looks her age.
麗莎看起跟實際年齡差不多。

0130 Guess what? Kyle is going to be fifty next Saturday.
我跟你說，凱爾下週六就滿五十歲了。

0131 Are you kidding? He doesn't look like that age at all.

你在開玩笑吧？他看起來一點都不像。

0132 My grandmother is in her nineties. She is very healthy for her age.
我奶奶已經九十幾歲了，就年齡來看，她算是非常健康的。

0133 Your sister is very **mature** for her age.
就年齡來看，你的妹妹非常成熟。 mature 形 成熟的

0134 What's your **animal sign**? / What's your Chinese **zodiac**?
你是屬什麼生肖的？ animal sign 片 生肖 zodiac 名 黃道帶

0135 I was born in the Year of the Pig. / My animal sign is the pig.
我是豬年出生的。/ 我屬豬。

0136 Many parents want their children to be born in the Year of the Dragon.
很多父母都希望他們的小孩在龍年出生。

0137 What's your sign? / What's your **star sign**? / What **astrological** sign are you?
你是什麼星座的？ star sign 片 星座 astrological 形 占星學的

0138 Do you believe in **astrology**?
你相信星座嗎？ astrology 名 占星術

0139 No, I don't believe in it. I think it is **superstitious**.
一點都不相信，我覺得那是迷信。 superstitious 形 迷信的

0140 I really think there's a relationship between star sign and personality **traits**.
我真的認為星座與個性有關。 trait 名 特徵；特點

0141 My star sign is **Capricorn**. / I am a **Capricorn**.
我是摩羯座的。 Capricorn 名 摩羯座

0142 I don't know what my sign is. My birthday is on December 20.
我不知道我是什麼星座的，我的生日是十二月二十號。

0143 You are either a Capricorn or a **Sagittarian**.
你不是摩羯座就是射手座。 Sagittarian 名 射手座

0144 Aquarians don't like to be **tied down**.
水瓶座的人不喜歡受到拘束。 tie down 片 束縛

0145 My brother and I are both **Gemini**, but our **characters differ**.
我哥哥和我都是雙子座，但我們的個性差很多。
Gemini 名 雙子座　character 名 個性　differ 動 相異

0146 We are much **alike** in character. / We **resemble** each other in character.
我們的性格很相似。
alike 形 相像的　resemble 動 類似

0147 I don't think my personality traits match my star sign.
我的個性和星座不太符合。

0148 How tall are you? / What is your **height**?
你的身高多高？ height 名 身高；高度

0149 I **wonder** how tall you are.
我很想知道你有多高。 wonder 動 納悶；想知道

0150 I am a bit too short for my age.
就年紀來看，我有點太矮了。

0151 His **build** is average.
他是中等身材。 build 名 體格；體型

0152 I have thick **eyebrows** and big eyes.
我有雙濃眉大眼。 eyebrow 名 眉毛

0153 Danny is not fat but he's got a **double chin**.
丹尼並不胖，卻有雙下巴。 double chin 片 雙下巴

0154 Do you have single **eyelids** or double eyelids?
你是單眼皮還是雙眼皮？ eyelid 名 眼皮

0155 Shoulder-length hair looks good on you.
及肩的中長髮很適合你。

0156 My hair is naturally **wavy**.
我的頭髮有自然捲。wavy 形 波浪的

0157 The woman wearing a **ponytail** is my boss.
那位綁著馬尾的女士是我的老闆。ponytail 名 馬尾辮子

0158 Is your hair parted in the center or on the side?
你的頭髮是中分還是旁分？

0159 I like to make my hair into a **bun**. / I like to wear my hair in a **bun**.
我喜歡把頭髮盤起來，梳成一個髮髻。bun 名 圓髮髻

0160 She wears too much **makeup**.
她的妝太濃了。makeup 名 化妝品

0161 Although Leila has borne three children, she still has a shapely figure.
雖然生了三個小孩，莉拉的身材還是很勻稱。

0162 I've gained five pounds since last winter.
從去年冬天開始，我胖了五磅。

0163 Are you like your mother or father?
你長得像媽媽還是爸爸？

0164 Most say I look like my mother because of my long eyelashes and fair skin.
大多數人都說我長得像媽媽，因為我遺傳到她的長睫毛和白皮膚。

0165 Sharon has beautiful eyes. She takes after her father.
雪倫有雙漂亮的眼睛，遺傳自她的父親。

0166 All my siblings are good at music. It runs in the family.
我的兄弟姐妹對音樂都很在行，那是家族遺傳。

0167 I have always been happy-go-lucky.
我是個樂天派。

0168 I think I am a bit **sensitive**.
我覺得我有點敏感。 sensitive 形 易受傷害的

0169 I was rebellious when I was young, but I am not now.
我年輕的時候很叛逆，但現在不會了。

0170 Don't be so **nosy**. It's none of your business.
別那麼愛管閒事，那跟你無關。 nosy 形 好管閒事的

0171 Jerry is a shy guy. He doesn't talk much.
傑瑞的個性害羞，話不多。

0172 Her graciousness charmed everyone at the party.
她的風采令聚會上的每一個人都為之傾倒。

0173 William is a man of his word. You can totally rely on him.
威廉是一個信守諾言的人，你可以完全信賴他。

0174 He's my type. / He's my style.
他是我喜歡的類型。

0175 My co-worker Frank is a **big-head**. He likes to tell people how great he is.
我的同事法蘭克很自負，老愛向別人吹捧他自己有多棒。
big-head 名 自負的人

0176 He's a bit **stubborn** and doesn't listen to others sometimes.
他有點固執，有時不聽別人的意見。 stubborn 形 頑固的

0177 My boss can be a bit **moody**.
我的老闆有點喜怒無常。 moody 形 喜怒無常的

0178 Emily is so **vain**. I just can't stand her.
愛蜜莉很愛慕虛榮，我實在受不了她。 vain 形 虛榮的

0179 He has a double personality.
他有雙重人格。

0180 Tommy is quite **spoiled**.
湯米被寵壞了。spoiled 形 被寵壞的

0181 He is a **creature** of habit.
他是個墨守成規的人。creature 名 生物

0182 How many family **members** do you have?
你家裡有幾個人？member 名 成員

0183 There are six people in my family, including me.
把我算進去的話，我家共有六個人。

0184 I have a five-year-old girl.
我有一個五歲大的女兒。

0185 I was born into a family of five in a small **village** in Yilan.
我出生在一個宜蘭小村莊的五口之家。village 名 村莊

0186 I was born into an **ordinary** family.
我出生於一個平凡的家庭。ordinary 形 普通的

0187 I come from a family of **politicians**.
我來自政治世家。politician 名 政治家

0188 Do you come from a big family?
你來自大家庭嗎？

0189 I live with my grandparents. We are an **extended** family. / We are big family.
我跟祖父母同住，我們家是大家庭。extended 形 擴大的

0190 We are **nuclear** family.
我們家是小家庭（核心家庭）。nuclear 形 核心的

0191 I don't have many **relatives**.
我的親戚並不多。relative 名 親戚

0192 Do you have any brothers or sisters? / Do you have any **siblings**?
你有兄弟姐妹嗎？ sibling 名 兄弟姐妹

0193 I have an older brother and two younger sisters.
我有一個哥哥和兩個妹妹。

0194 My younger sister and I are three years **apart**.
我的妹妹和我差三歲。 apart 副 相間隔地

0195 I am the second child of four.
我在四個小孩中排行老二。

0196 I am the youngest child in my family.
我在家中的排行最小。

0197 I am an only child.
我是獨生子 / 女。

0198 We are twin brothers. Can you distinguish between us?
我們是雙胞胎兄弟，你分辨得出誰是誰嗎？

0199 Having twins can bring great **joy** to a family.
雙胞胎能給家裡帶來很多的歡樂。 joy 名 歡樂

0200 I come from a single-parent family.
我來自單親家庭。

0201 I'm a single mother, and I **bring up** my son on my own.
我是單親媽媽，獨立撫養兒子。 bring up 片 養育

0202 My cousin **adopted** a baby eight years ago.
我堂姊八年前領養了一個小孩。 adopt 動 領養

0203 My husband is a family-**oriented** man.
我的丈夫很顧家。 oriented 形 以…為方向的

0204 I am afraid my mother tends to **spoil** her grandchildren.

我擔心我媽媽會把孫子寵壞。spoil 動 溺愛

0205 My parents **passed away** when I was twelve.
我的父母在我十二歲時都過世了。pass away 片 過世

0206 My grandparents raised me. I was in a skipped-generation family.
我生於隔代教養的家庭，我是由祖父母帶大的。

0207 Are you **close** to your family?
你和家人的關係親密嗎？close 形 親密的

0208 I talk to my mother on the phone every day.
我每天都會和我的媽媽講電話。

0209 Have you ever **talked back** to your parents?
你曾跟父母頂嘴嗎？talk back 片 頂嘴

0210 I never talk back to my parents because it is **impolite**.
我從不跟父母頂嘴，因為那不禮貌。impolite 形 無禮的

0211 How could you talk back to your father like that?
你怎麼可以這樣跟爸爸頂嘴呢？

0212 I don't think there is a **generation gap** in my family.
我們家沒什麼代溝。generation gap 片 代溝

0213 My parents are democratic, not **tyrannical**.
我的父母很民主，不專制。tyrannical 形 專橫的

0214 Bill's parents are bossy. He was forced to live up to their expectations.
比爾的父母很霸道，他被迫要符合他們的期待。

0215 Wendy doesn't want to do whatever her parents want her to do.
只要她父母希望的，溫蒂就不想照做。

0216 Do you get along well with all your relatives?

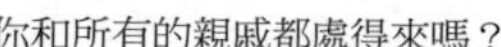

你和所有的親戚都處得來嗎？

0217 I think so. We're very close. / Yes, we get along very well.
算是吧，我們很親密。 / 嗯，我們的關係很融洽。

0218 My relatives are mostly OK. But I have two aunts I don't like very much.
我和大部分的親戚都處得不錯。不過，有兩個阿姨我不是很喜歡。

0219 Not really. I don't like most of them.
不盡然，大部分的親戚我都不喜歡。

0220 Do you live with your parents?
你與父母同住嗎？

0221 No, I share an apartment with my sister in Taipei.
不是，我和我妹妹同住在台北的一間公寓。

0222 In America, children often move out when they're eighteen.
在美國，小孩滿十八歲後，通常就會搬出家裡。

0223 Who looks after your kids while you are working?
你去上班的時候，誰照顧你的小孩？

0224 We hired a Filipina housemaid. She takes care of my kids.
我們有雇用一個菲律賓女傭，她照顧我的小孩。

0225 My mother-in-law takes care of my three-year-old daughter.
我的岳母幫我照顧我三歲大的女兒。

0226 More and more young couples don't want to have children nowadays.
現在不想生小孩的年輕夫妻愈來愈多了。

0227 Her baby is **due** next month. / She is expecting, and her **due** date is next month.
她的寶寶下個月就要出生了。 due 形 預期的

0228 My parents set a good example for us.
我的父母為我們樹立了好榜樣。

0229 That's why I have an **optimistic** attitude towards life.
所以我對人生的態度很樂觀。optimistic 形 樂觀的

0230 My father **runs** a law firm.
我的父親經營一家法律事務所。run 動 經營；管理

0231 Does your mother work, too?
你的母親也在工作嗎？

0232 You bet! She is a **secretary** in a big company.
沒錯，她在一家大公司當祕書。secretary 名 祕書

0233 In Chinese tradition, the **notion** of men being **breadwinners** and women being housewives is very common.
在中國的傳統中，「男主外，女主內」的這個觀念很常見。
notion 名 想法 breadwinner 名 負擔生計的人

0234 Your family should always come before your job.
家庭的重要性永遠都應該排在你的工作前面。

0235 Sometimes I wish I had been born into another family.
有時候我真希望出生在別人的家庭。

朋友關係與互動
Interacting With Others

0236 I have a lot of nodding acquaintances but only a few **bosom friends**.

點頭之交我有很多，但摯友只有幾個而已。
bosom friend 片 知心朋友

0237 Gina takes me to be her best friend, but I think we are just average friends.
吉娜視我為最好的朋友，但我覺得我們的交情很普通。

0238 My colleagues would be the last people I would make friends with.
我最不可能和同事交朋友了。

0239 Is it important for friends to have common interests?
和朋友擁有相同的興趣很重要嗎？

0240 It's easier to become friends if two people have similar backgrounds.
成長背景相似的人會比較容易成為朋友。

0241 I met my boyfriend at a friend's wedding.
我是在朋友的婚禮上認識我男朋友的。

0242 He's just an acquaintance. We met him through Tim at a party.
我們和他不熟，只是在派對上透過提姆認識的。

0243 Uncle Chang and my father are lifelong friends. They've been friends for over forty years.
張叔叔和我爸爸是老朋友了，他們認識的時間超過四十年。

0244 Can I introduce you to an old friend of mine?
我可以把你介紹給我的一位老朋友嗎？

0245 Do you have more friends of the same or **opposite** sex?
你的同性朋友多，還是異性朋友多？ opposite 形 對立的

0246 My best friend and I **fell out** over a boy we both liked recently.
我最好的朋友最近和我吵架了，因為我們喜歡上同一個男生。
fall out 片 吵架；失和

0247 We had a terrible **row**. / We had a terrible quarrel.
我們大吵了一架。 row 名 (口)吵架；口角

0248 Don't let arguments destroy your friendship.
別讓爭吵破壞了你們的友誼。

0249 One of my friends always **dishes the dirt** about me behind my back.
我有個朋友總是背著我散播是非。 dish the dirt 片 說壞話

0250 Don't hang around bad **company** like that.
別跟那樣的損友在一起。 company 名 朋友

0251 I don't like anyone who is **cynical**.
我不喜歡愛挖苦別人的人。 cynical 形 挖苦的；嘲諷的

0252 How often do you go out with your friends?
你多常和朋友出去玩呢？

0253 We **hang out** almost once a week.
我們幾乎每週會出去一次。 hang out 片 出去玩

0254 We seldom hang out. We usually chat on the phone or by Skype.
我們很少一起出去，通常都是講電話或上 Skype 聊天。

0255 Where do you and your friends usually go?
你通常都和朋友去哪裡啊？

0256 It depends. We go shopping together most of the time.
不一定，大多數都是一起去逛街。

0257 Sometimes we play volleyball or go to a movie.
有時候也會一起去打排球或看電影。

0258 Real friends **inspire** and push each other to achieve their goals.
真正的朋友應該要激勵彼此達成目標。 inspire 動 激勵

0259 My best friend encourages me whenever I feel depressed.
當我感到沮喪時，我最好的朋友總會鼓勵我。

0260 Can **gossip** damage a friendship?
散播八卦會不會破壞一段友誼呢？ gossip 名 閒話

0261 I am not interested in gossip.
我對八卦沒有興趣。

0262 I don't want to talk about others' **scandals**.
我不想談論其他人的流言蜚語。 scandal 名 流言蜚語

0263 Do you tell your friends secrets?
你會把祕密告訴朋友嗎？

0264 Hardly ever because I am afraid they will **spread** them.
幾乎不會，因為我怕他們會傳出去。 spread 動 散布

0265 She was the only one who knew all my secrets, but she spilled the beans.
她是唯一知道我所有祕密的人，但她把那些都講出去了。

0266 Have you ever **reunited** with a long lost friend?
你曾與失聯很久的朋友重聚嗎？ reunite 動 重聚

0267 I happened to meet a long lost friend at the cinema.
我碰巧在電影院遇見很久沒聯絡的朋友。

0268 I would like to express my **appreciation** / **gratitude**.
謹表達我的謝意。 appreciation 名 感謝 gratitude 名 感恩

0269 I cannot **express** how grateful I am.
我不知道要如何感謝你才好。 express 動 表達

0270 That's very nice of you. / That's very kind of you.
你人真好。

0271 I can never thank you enough.
感激不盡！

0272 Thanks for coming!
你能來真是太感謝了！

0273 Thank you for **dropping by**.
謝謝你順道來此拜訪。 drop by 片 順便拜訪

0274 Thank you for buying me lunch.
謝謝你請我吃午餐。

0275 A thousand thanks for giving me this chance.
萬分感謝你給我這個機會。

0276 I'll never forget what you have done for me. Thanks a million.
我永遠不會忘記你為我做的事，萬分感謝。

0277 Please convey my **hearty** thanks to your parents.
請向你的父母表達我的謝意。 hearty 形 衷心的

0278 You're welcome. It's my pleasure.
不用客氣，那是我的榮幸。

0279 I am delighted I could help. / I am glad to be of some **assistance**.
很高興我能幫上忙。 assistance 名 幫助

0280 No problem. / Not at all. / It's nothing. / Don't **mention** it.
沒什麼。 mention 動 提到；說起

0281 I'm sorry. / It's my fault. / **Pardon** me.
對不起！ pardon 動 原諒；寬恕

0282 I don't know what to say. I am so sorry.
我不知道該說什麼，真的很抱歉。

0283 I **apologize** for saying so.
我為所說的話道歉。 apologize 動 道歉；認錯

0284 Excuse me for losing my **temper**.
抱歉，我發了脾氣。 temper 名 脾氣

0285 I'm terribly sorry for being late.
真的很抱歉，我遲到了。

0286 I am extremely sorry for keeping you waiting for thirty minutes.
真的很對不起，讓你等了三十分鐘。

0287 I'm afraid that I have to leave early, sorry.
我恐怕要提早離席，抱歉。

0288 I didn't mean to start an argument.
我不是故意要引起爭吵的。

0289 Forget it. I am not angry at you anymore.
算了，我不生你的氣了。

0290 I didn't **intend** to cause you so much inconvenience.
我不是有意造成你的不便。 intend 動 想要；打算

0291 Sorry for calling you at this time. I have something **urgent**.
抱歉在這種時候打電話給你，我有急事。 urgent 形 緊急的

0292 Pardon me for my **selfishness**.
請原諒我的自私。 selfishness 名 利己主義

0293 Excuse me for **interrupting**, but the meeting is about to begin.
抱歉打斷你，不過會議要開始了。 interrupt 動 打斷

0294 I hate to bother you, but could you speak louder, please?
實在不想打斷你，但可以請你講大聲一點嗎？

0295 I hope I'm not **disturbing** you, but the bus is leaving.
希望沒有妨礙到你，但公車要開了。 disturb 動 妨礙

0296 Sorry to trouble you, but we're rather stuck here.
不好意思打擾你，但我們這裡有點狀況。

0297 I am sorry for being **neglectful**.
我對我的疏忽大意感到抱歉。 neglectful 形 疏忽的

0298 I was too **careless**. Please forgive me.
我真是太粗心了，請原諒我。 careless 形 粗心的

0299 Don't worry. I'll deal with everything.
別擔心，我會處理好所有的事。

0300 Don't **blame** yourself.
別自責了。 blame 動 責備；指責

0301 Have you **learned your lesson**?
你學到教訓了吧？ learn one's lesson 片 汲取教訓

0302 I offered Claire an apology yesterday, but she didn't accept it.
我昨天向克萊兒道歉，但她不接受。

0303 You are **at fault**, so you should apologize to him.
那是你的責任，你應該向他道歉。 at fault 片 有責任

0304 Please extend my apologies to your father.
請代我向令尊致歉。

0305 Excuse me; I just **burped**.
對不起，我剛剛打嗝了。 burp 動 打嗝

0306 It's all right. / It's OK. / It's nothing. / Never mind.
沒關係。

0307 It's all right. It could happen to anyone of us.
沒關係，這種事誰都會發生。

0308 Thanks for understanding.
謝謝你的諒解。

0309 Thank God! I'm relieved to know that.

謝天謝地，聽你這樣說，我鬆了一口氣。

0310 I'm glad you feel that way. I've been worried about it for days.
很高興你那樣想，為了這個，我擔心了好幾天。

0311 My father is so scientific that he doesn't believe in any religion.
我爸爸只信科學，任何宗教他都不信。

0312 Religious differences sometimes lead to conflict.
宗教信仰上的差異有時會導致衝突。

0313 Different faiths **coexist** harmoniously in Taiwan.
各種不同的信仰在台灣這片土地上和諧共存。 coexist 動 共存

0314 Shakyamuni Buddha is the founder of **Buddhism**.
釋迦牟尼佛是佛教的始祖。 Buddhism 名 佛教

0315 In East Asia, Buddhism has the most **followers**.
在東亞，佛教的信眾最多。 follower 名 信徒

0316 The majority of Chinese are either Buddhists or Taoists.
大多數的華人不是信仰佛教就是道教。

0317 I'm a **pious** Buddhist.
我是虔誠的佛教徒。 pious 形 虔誠的

0318 When my parents don't know what to do, they go to temples and **draw lots**.

當我父母無所適從時，會去廟裡求籤。draw lots 片 抽籤

0319 Do you believe in **reincarnation**?
你相信輪迴嗎？reincarnation 名 輪迴說；轉世

0320 My grandmother sits in **meditation** an hour every morning.
我的祖母每天早上都會靜坐冥想一小時。meditation 名 冥想

0321 I follow a vegetarian diet on the first and fifteenth day of each **lunar** month.
我農曆的初一、十五吃素。lunar 形 陰曆的；農曆的

0322 Do you find it inconvenient being a vegetarian?
你會不會覺得吃素不方便？

0323 Not at all. Most restaurants offer vegetarian food.
一點都不會，大部分的餐廳都有提供素食。

0324 Have you ever seen any religious **ceremonies**?
你有看過任何宗教儀式嗎？ceremony 名 儀式

0325 I was **baptized** a Christian when I was born.
我一出生就受洗為天主教徒。baptize 動 給…洗禮

0326 We worship and praise the Lord through singing **gospels** in the church.
我們上教堂唱誦福音來敬拜與讚頌上帝。gospel 名 福音

0327 That brings us inner peace and happiness.
那帶給我們內心的平靜與喜樂。

0328 My family members are Catholic and they go to Mass every Sunday.
我的家人都是天主教徒，每個星期天都會去望彌撒。

0329 Hinduism is a major religion in India.
印度教是印度主要的宗教信仰。

0330 Muslims kneel down and worship Allah in **mosques**.

穆斯林在清真寺跪拜阿拉真主。mosque 名 清真寺

0331 Muslims don't eat **pork**.
穆斯林不吃豬肉。pork 名 豬肉

0332 Do you think the Chinese are superstitious?
你覺得中國人迷信嗎？

0333 Seeing **magpies** is a good omen in Chinese culture.
在中國文化中，看見喜鵲是一個好預兆。magpie 名 喜鵲

0334 It is bad luck to have two room doors facing each other.
兩個房間的房門相對是不吉利的。

0335 It is bad luck if your front door directly faces a road.
如果你家大門正對著一條馬路，也會招來厄運。

0336 Four is an unlucky number as it sounds like the Chinese word for death.
四是不吉祥的數字，因為聽起來像中文的「死」。

0337 We call July in the lunar **calendar** "ghost month".
我們稱農曆七月為鬼月。calendar 名 日曆

0338 There are a lot of **taboos** related to ghost month.
鬼月有很多禁忌。taboo 名 禁忌；忌諱

0339 Westerners think that the number 13 is an unlucky number.
西方人認為十三這個數字不吉利。

0340 There are also many superstitions in America.
美國也有很多迷信的行為。

0341 Walking under a **ladder** is unlucky.
走在梯子下面是不吉利的。ladder 名 梯子

0342 Do you believe in **fortune-telling**?

你相信算命嗎？ fortune-telling 名 算命

0343 A fortune-teller told me that I would marry a rich guy in my early thirties.
有一個算命師告訴我，我在三十歲出頭時會嫁給一個有錢人。

0344 Was the **prediction accurate**?
他的預言準嗎？ prediction 名 預言 accurate 形 準確的

0345 He was wrong because I am in my late thirties and still single.
根本不準，因為我現在已經快四十了還單身。

0346 I believe in **palm** reading as it predicts our lives.
我相信看手相這回事，它能預言我們的人生。 palm 名 手掌

0347 That fortune-teller is very good at Chinese face-reading.
這位算命師對於看面相很在行。

0348 Lips **stand for** feelings.
嘴唇代表感情。 stand for 片 代表

0349 People who have thin lips are colder than those who have full ones.
和厚唇的人相比，嘴唇薄的人比較冷酷。

0350 **Moles** around the mouth mean **wealth**.
嘴邊的痣代表財富。 mole 名 痣 wealth 名 財富

0351 Many people believe that our future is determined by **fate**.
很多人相信我們的未來是命定的。 fate 名 天命

0352 I think that our future is determined by ourselves.
我覺得未來是掌握在自己手中的。

UNIT 6 結束話題與道別
Closing A Conversation

0353 May I be excused for a while? I won't be long.
我可以失陪一下嗎？不會太久的。

0354 I'm afraid I need to be excused for a moment.
我恐怕得先離席一下。

0355 Bye! / Bye for now! / See you!
再見！

0356 I've enjoyed talking to you. / I had a great time talking to you.
跟你聊天真開心。

0357 It's late. I'm afraid I have to go. / I'm afraid I have to leave.
時間太晚了，我恐怕得走了。

0358 I really hate to say goodbye, but it's so late.
實在不想說再見，但時間太晚了。

0359 I have to catch the last bus. See you around.
我得去趕末班車了，再見。

0360 See you around. / Talk to you soon. / Talk to you later.
回頭見！

0361 I'm afraid I've **taken up** too much of your time. I really must leave.
我恐怕占用了你太多時間，我真的該走了。take up 片 費時間

0362 Thank you for your time. Have a nice day!
謝謝你撥時間給我，祝你有個美好的一天！

0363 It's still quite early. Why don't you stay a little longer?
時間還很早，再待一下吧。

0364 If you don't mind, I've got another **appointment**.
希望你不介意，我另外還有約。 appointment 名 約會

0365 Let's **call it a day**. See you next time.
今天就到此結束吧，下次見。 call it a day 片 結束一天的工作

0366 I had a wonderful evening. Thanks for everything.
今晚過得很愉快，謝謝你準備的一切。

0367 I'm really glad that we **bumped into** each other. See you!
這次的巧遇實在令人開心，再見囉！ bump into 片 巧遇

0368 Here is my train. Got to go.
我的火車來了，該走了。

0369 Have a nice trip. Call me when you're home.
祝你旅途愉快，到家的時候，打通電話給我吧。

0370 See you next Monday. Have a nice weekend!
下週一見，祝你週末愉快！

0371 I am heading to class. I've got to run. Talk to you later.
我要去上課，得走了，晚點見。

0372 Is it possible for me to meet you again sometime?
我們還有可能再見面嗎？

0373 Let's stay in touch! / Let's keep in touch! You have my number, right?
保持聯絡！你有我的電話號碼吧？

0374 I'll call you. Take care!
我會再打電話給你，保重！

0375 Say hello to your parents for me.

代我向你父母問好。

0376 Remember to **drop me a line.**
記得寫信給我。drop sb. a line 片 寫信給某人

UNIT 7 愛在不明時最美
You Light Up My Life.

0377 Hey! **Look at** that girl over there.
嘿！你看那邊那個女生。look at 片 看；檢查

0378 Allen **swept me off my feet** when we first met.
亞倫讓我一見傾心。sweep sb. off one's feet 片 使某人傾心

0379 Annabelle is the most charming girl I've ever seen.
安娜貝兒是我所見過的女生當中，最有魅力的一個。

0380 The girl over there is my type.
那邊那個女生是我喜歡的類型。

0381 I want to catch her **attention**.
我想引起她的注意。attention 名 注意；注意力

0382 Let me **chat** her **up**.
我來跟她搭訕。chat up 片 與…調情；搭訕

0383 Sure! Don't miss out on your **potential date**.
好啊！不要錯失良機。potential 形 潛在的 date 名 約會對象

0384 I do **admire** your **courage**.
真是佩服你的勇氣。admire 動 欽佩 courage 名 勇氣

0385 Don't be **silly**! I **bet** she has a boyfriend.

別傻了！我賭她一定有男朋友。 silly 形 愚蠢的 bet 動 打賭

0386 I really don't know how to chat a girl up.
我真的不知道要怎麼跟女生搭訕。

0387 You have to create **opportunities**.
你應該要製造機會。 opportunity 名 機會；良機

0388 You can create a **situation** where you can start a conversation.
你可以製造聊天的機會。 situation 名 情況

0389 Be **adventurous**! Don't be **chicken**.
勇敢一點！別當膽小鬼。
adventurous 形 大膽的 chicken 形 膽怯的

0390 What **openers** are good to use?
有什麼不錯的開場白可以用嗎？ opener 名 開端；開啟工具

0391 I can show you some ice breakers.
我來教你幾招打破僵局的招數。

0392 What's a good-looking girl like you doing in a place like this?
像你這樣的美女，怎麼會出現在這種地方呢？

0393 I only **have eyes for** you.
我只注意到你。 have eyes for 片 對…感興趣；專注於

0394 You look so familiar to me. Have we met before?
你看起來好面熟，我們是不是在哪裡見過？

0395 Have we? I don't think so.
有嗎？沒有吧。

0396 This is my cell phone number and my Skype address.
這是我的手機號碼和 Skype 帳號。

0397 Please **feel free to** contact me.
隨時都可以和我聯絡。 feel free to 片 隨意

0398 May I have your number?
可以給我你的電話嗎？

0399 I don't think that's **necessary**.
沒有那個必要吧。 necessary 形 必要的

0400 When you've secured the phone number of your potential date, it's a good idea to text him or her.
如果你拿到未來約會對象的電話號碼，傳簡訊會是個不錯的方法。

0401 By **texting**, there would be less **pressure** on either side.
傳簡訊比較不會有壓力。 text 動 傳簡訊 pressure 名 壓力

0402 Is this **seat taken**?
這個位子有人坐嗎？ seat 名 座位 take 動 就(座)

0403 Do you **mind** if I sit next to you?
你介意我坐你旁邊嗎？ mind 動 介意

0404 I'm **waiting for** someone.
我在等人。 wait for 片 等候

0405 This seat is taken.
這個位子有人坐了。

0406 If possible, can I **buy you a drink**?
我能請你喝杯飲料嗎？ buy sb. a drink 片 請某人喝飲料

0407 Do you want to have a cup of **coffee**?
要不要一起喝杯咖啡？ coffee 名 咖啡

0408 Would you like to get a **bite** to eat?
要不要一起去吃點東西呢？ bite 名 咬；一口之量

0409 Are you interested in going shopping **after work**?
下班後有沒有興趣一起去逛街？ after work 片 下班後

0410 How about going to a concert with me **tomorrow** night?
明天晚上要不要和我一起去聽音樂會？ tomorrow 名 明天

0411 I have an **extra** ticket to the concert. Would you like to come?
我有多出一張演唱會的票，你想去嗎？ extra 形 額外的

0412 I'm **inviting** you to my birthday party.
我想邀請你來參加我的生日派對。 invite 動 邀請；招待

0413 We're thinking about going to KTV tonight. Do you want to come?
我們今天晚上想去唱 KTV，你想一起來嗎？

0414 Are you up for some Thai food this Friday?
這個星期五想不想去吃泰國菜？

0415 Are you **available** this **weekend**?
你這個週末有空嗎？ available 形 有空的 weekend 名 週末

0416 Maybe we can go to a movie. How does that sound?
我們也許可以去看場電影，你覺得怎麼樣？

0417 Would you allow me the pleasure of your company this evening?
不知道我今晚有沒有這個榮幸做你的伴？

0418 Is anybody taking you to the **dance** this Saturday?
星期六的舞會有人約你去了嗎？ dance 名 舞會

0419 I'd love to. I think I can make it.
好啊！我想我可以去。

0420 Great! When should I **pick** you **up**?
太好了！那我幾點去接你呢？ pick up 片 用汽車載某人

0421 Where should we **meet**?
要約在哪裡碰面呢？ meet 動 遇見；碰上

0422 I'll meet you at the **usual** place.
我們在老地方見！ usual 形 通常的；平常的

0423 Let's meet at the front gate of the **stadium** at 6:30 p.m.
我們晚上六點半在體育館的前門碰面。 stadium 名 運動場

0424 I am afraid I can't **make it**.
我恐怕去不了。 make it 片 及時趕到

0425 Sorry, I'm not **interested**.
對不起，我沒有興趣。 interested 形 感興趣的

0426 I am not in the mood to go to a KTV.
我沒有去唱 KTV 的心情。

0427 Thank you for inviting me, but I am going to work **overtime** tonight.
謝謝你的邀請，不過我晚上要加班。 overtime 副 超過地

0428 I have a **headache** and want to go home early.
我頭好痛，想早點回家休息。 headache 名 頭痛

0429 Maybe some other time! / May I take a **rain check**?
改天吧！ rain check 片 延期；改期

0430 Not on your life.
你這輩子都別想。

0431 Over my dead body!
除非我死，否則不可能！

0432 I asked Judy out and was **turned down** again.
我約了茱蒂，但又被拒絕了。 turn down 片 拒絕

0433 I think you should **pluck up** your courage.
我覺得你應該鼓起勇氣。 pluck up 片 鼓起；振作

0434 Don't be afraid of **rejection**.
不要害怕被拒絕。 rejection 名 拒絕

0435 Don't try so hard. The best things come when you least expect them to.

別太著急了，最好的總會在最不經意的時候出現。

0436 I fell in love with Camilla **at first sight**.
我對卡蜜拉一見鍾情。at first sight 片 初見

0437 You are the most **amazing** woman that I have ever met!
你是我見過最完美的女人！amazing 形 驚人的

0438 Do you have a **boyfriend**?
你有沒有男朋友？boyfriend 名 男朋友

0439 Yeah, we have been going out for more than a year.
有啊，我們在一起一年多了。

0440 **Unfortunately** not. I've got lots of male friends, though.
沒有耶，雖然我男性朋友很多。unfortunately 副 遺憾地

0441 I met the girl of my dreams today.
我今天遇見我的夢中情人。

0442 That's a good thing. How did you **feel**?
那很好啊，你感覺如何？feel 動 感覺；感知

0443 I was so **high-strung**. I couldn't even say hello to her.
我好緊張，連打招呼都不敢。high-strung 形 十分敏感的

0444 I was too **nervous** to say a word.
我緊張到一句話都說不出來。nervous 形 緊張的

0445 I want to make a good **impression** on her.
我想在她心裡留下好印象。impression 名 印象

0446 I really want to make an **advance** on her.
我真的很想追她。advance 名 發展；前進

0447 You should have showed your **fascination** with her.

你應該在她面前展現你的魅力。 fascination 名 魅力

0448 Tell you something exciting: I saw Lance again in the campus.
告訴你一件興奮的事，今天在學校，我又見到蘭斯了。

0449 I couldn't believe that he still **remembered** me.
他竟然還記得我耶，真令人不敢相信。 remember 動 記得

0450 The best part was we **chatted** for five minutes.
最棒的是，我們還聊了五分鐘。 chat 動 閒談；聊天

0451 We also **exchanged** email **addresses**.
我們還交換了電子郵件信箱。
exchange 動 交換 address 名 住址；地址

0452 Are you sure? He is nice but not **handsome**.
你確定嗎？他人是很好，但長得並不帥。 handsome 形 英俊的

0453 Most good-looking guys are **insecure**.
大部分的帥哥都讓人沒有安全感。 insecure 形 不牢靠的

0454 I've never met anyone who shares so many common interests with me.
我從來沒有碰過和我興趣這麼相投的人。

0455 I like to hang out with Matt because I feel like I can talk to him.
我喜歡跟麥特在一起，因為我們很聊得來。

0456 When I am with Emma, I feel completely fulfilled.
和艾瑪在一起的時候，我感到心滿意足。

0457 Kevin always makes me laugh. He is so **humorous**.
凱文老是惹得我發笑，他好幽默。 humorous 形 幽默的

0458 I like a **bubbly** girl in my class. Her **smile** is lovely.
我喜歡班上一名活潑開朗的女生，她的笑容很可愛。
bubbly 形 活潑的 smile 名 笑容

0459 I think that guy is **making a pass at** me.
我覺得那個男的對我有興趣。 make a pass at 片 向某人調情

0460 Do you know Zack? He seems to like you.
你認識查克嗎？他好像喜歡你。

0461 I'm singing a **torch song** for Haley.
我單戀海麗。 torch song 片 傷感的歌(描述無回報的愛情)

0462 It was love at first sight.
那就是一見鍾情。

0463 I wonder if she likes me.
不知道她喜不喜歡我。

0464 My friend fell into an **unrequited** love with her teacher.
我朋友單戀她的老師。 unrequited 形 得不到報酬的

0465 Oliver finally asked me out, and we'll have a date this weekend.
奧利佛終於約我了，我們這個週末要去約會。

0466 I heard that Jack asked you out. What do you think of him?
我聽說傑克約你出去，你覺得他怎麼樣？

0467 He is a **metrosexual**. I could see why my sister's **crazy about** him.
他是個都會型男，我能理解我妹妹為何這麼喜愛他。
metrosexual 名 都會美型男 crazy about 片 很喜歡…

0468 There's no **chemistry** between us.
我們之間不來電。 chemistry 名 男女間的「來電」

0469 That **womanizer** hits on every woman he sees.
那個花心的傢伙，見一個追一個。 womanizer 名 玩弄女性者

0470 To be honest, I am not so **enthusiastic** about him.
老實說，我對他不怎麼感興趣。 enthusiastic 形 熱情的

0471 What he did made me lose my **appetite**.
他的所作所為真讓我倒胃口。appetite 名 愛好；胃口

0472 I don't know how to turn him down.
我不知道要怎麼拒絕他。

0473 Albert is not in the same **league** as I am.
亞伯特和我是不同世界的人。league 名 範疇；等級

0474 I would never date a mommy's boy.
我絕對不會和一個媽寶交往。

0475 Maybe God wants us to meet the wrong people before meeting the right one.
在遇見真命天子之前，上天也許會安排我們先遇到錯的人。

0476 My cousin is **single**. She is on the make.
我表姊單身，她在徵男朋友。single 形 單身的

0477 I know a man with three highs; high height, high degree and high income.
我認識一個人，他具備三高的條件一身高高、學歷高、收入也高。

0478 He's 34, and he's really a nice guy.
他三十四歲，個性真的很好。

0479 I am sure your cousin will like him.
我相信你的表姊一定會喜歡他。

0480 I would love to **hook** someone **up** with my handsome brother.
我很想幫我的帥哥弟弟介紹個女朋友。hook up 片 認識

0481 He's not only tall but **good-looking**.
他不只個子高，又長得很帥。good-looking 形 好看的

0482 The only thing is that he is **aiming** too high.
只是他的眼光太高了。aim 動 瞄準；對準

0483 No wonder he doesn't have a **girlfriend** now.
難怪他現在沒有女朋友。girlfriend 名 女朋友

0484 I look for someone that I can share my life with.
我在尋找能與我共度一生的伴侶。

0485 I have a friend who might be **suitable** for you.
我有個朋友可能適合你。suitable 形 適當的

0486 Could you send me a **photo** of him?
可以寄一張他的照片給我看看嗎？photo 名 照片

0487 Don't **judge** a person from his appearance.
不要從外表去判斷一個人。judge 動 裁判；判定

0488 He got his Ph.D. **degree** last year and is teaching in a university now.
他去年拿到博士學位，現任教於大學。degree 名 學位

0489 My classmate Benson is humorous and **outgoing**.
我的同學班森的個性幽默又外向。outgoing 形 外向的

0490 Girls are **all over him**.
女孩子都很喜歡他。all over sb. 片 迷上某人

0491 You guys would definitely make a good **match**.
你們兩個人一定很速配。match 名 相配者

0492 Maybe you can try to **figure out** a way for us to meet.
安排我跟他見面吧！figure out 片 想出；理解

0493 You can start from **corresponding with** each other.
你們可以從通信開始。correspond with 片 通信

0494 **Arranged** marriages were very common in the past.
在以前，相親是很普遍的一件事。arranged 形 安排的

0495 In my grandparents' **generation**, it was common for parents to look for a **bride** or **groom** for their children.

在我祖父母那一代，由父母幫子女挑選另一半是很普遍的。
generation 名 世代　bride 名 新娘　groom 名 新郎

0496 I **support** arranged marriages.
我支持由父母安排的婚姻。support 動 支持；贊成

0497 Some arranged couples end up falling in love.
就算是由父母決定，有些人在婚後也會愛上彼此。

0498 Do you go on **blind dates**? I can arrange one for you.
你願意去相親嗎？我可以幫你安排。blind date 片 相親

0499 My parents met each other through a blind date.
我爸媽就是經由相親認識的。

0500 I don't like it, but I won't say no.
我不怎麼喜歡相親，但也不排斥。

0501 What type of girls do you like?
你喜歡什麼類型的女生啊？

0502 Do you like blondes or **brunettes**?
你喜歡金髮還是棕髮的女性？brunette 名 深髮色的女性

0503 I like cute and innocent girls with long hair.
我喜歡個性可愛又天真的長髮女孩。

0504 I don't like **fragile** girls.
我不喜歡弱不禁風的女生。

0505 When you look for a guy, what kind of things do you look for?
你找對象的時候，有什麼樣的條件呢？

0506 Nothing special, but I can't accept **sissies**.
也沒什麼特別的，但我接受不了娘娘腔。sissy 名 娘娘腔

0507 Don't immediately say no when others offer to set you up.
有人幫你安排相親時，不要急著拒絕。

0508 It might be a chance to meet your Mr. Right.
那可能就是你遇到真命天子的機會。

0509 My boyfriend and I got hooked up **through** a friend.
我和我男友就是經由朋友介紹認識的。 through 介 透過；憑藉

0510 Going for drinks or coffee is a good way to meet.
去喝飲料或咖啡是不錯的見面方式。

0511 There's less pressure because going for drinks is not as having **formal** as a **meal** together.
喝飲料比較不會帶給人壓力，因為它沒用餐那麼正式。
formal 形 正式的　meal 名 一餐

0512 If things go well, you can decide to go to dinner afterward.
如果相處起來的感覺不錯，你們之後可以再一起去吃晚餐。

0513 If you aren't feeling a spark, you can **part ways** with little fuss.
如果不來電，那就再見不聯絡囉。 part ways 片 分道揚鑣

0514 You never know what to expect on a blind date.
相親的時候，你永遠不知道會發生什麼事。

0515 I **have a crush on** you.
我喜歡上你了。 have a crush on 片 被(某人)煞到

0516 Honey, you drive me crazy. Be my **valentine**!
我如癡如狂地愛著你，做我的情人吧！ valentine 名 情人

0517 I have fallen **head over heels** for you.
我愛你愛到暈頭轉向。head over heels 片 完全地

0518 I think I'm **falling in love with** you.
我想我愛上你了。fall in love with 片 愛上

0519 I can't help loving you.
我情不自禁地愛上你了。

0520 Do you remember Suzy? She **charmed** me at the party.
你還記得蘇西嗎？她在派對上把我迷倒了。charm 動 吸引

0521 You look more **beautiful** every time I see you.
每次見到你，都覺得你變得更美了。beautiful 形 美麗的

0522 I **am infatuated with** you.
我瘋狂地迷戀著你。be infatuated with 片 熱戀；著迷

0523 Can I have my heart back?
你能否把我的心還給我？（表示「心繫於你」。）

0524 I didn't know **heaven** was sending **angels** to Earth.
我不知道天堂把天使送到凡間來了。
heaven 名 天堂 angel 名 天使

0525 My thoughts are **deep** into you.
我深深地想念著你。deep 形 深的；非常的

0526 You will never know how much I **miss** you.
你不會知道我有多想你的。miss 動 想念

0527 Would you like to **go steady with** me?
你願意和我定下來嗎？go steady with 片 有固定的情侶關係

0528 Can we start a **serious**, meaningful relationship?
我們可不可以正式交往？serious 形 認真的

0529 I want a **long-term** relationship with you.
我想要和你有穩定的發展。long-term 形 長期的

0530 My boyfriend gave me this **necklace** as a **token** of our love.
我的男朋友送我這條項鍊當作定情物。
necklace 名 項鍊　token 名 象徵；紀念品

0531 Today is our **anniversary**, so Adam is taking me out for dinner.
今天是我們的交往週年紀念日，所以亞當要帶我出去吃晚餐。
anniversary 名 週年紀念日

0532 He says he will **pamper** me till I **die**.
他說會寵愛我一輩子。pamper 動 嬌養　die 動 死亡

0533 He sent you a **bouquet** of roses? Your boyfriend is so romantic!
他送你一束玫瑰嗎？你的男朋友真浪漫！bouquet 名 花束

0534 My boyfriend and I love to wear matching clothes.
我和我的男朋友喜歡穿情侶裝。

0535 How **intimate** are you with your boyfriend?
你和你男友目前進展到什麼程度了？intimate 形 親密的

0536 Give me the **scoop** about how your date went last night.
快告訴我你昨晚約會的最新進展。scoop 名 搶先報導

0537 My boyfriend and I walked **hand in hand** on the beach.
我男友和我手牽著手，在沙灘上漫步。hand in hand 手牽手

0538 Guess what? He kissed me last night.
你知道嗎？他昨天晚上親我了。

0539 My heart **beats terribly** fast.
我的心跳得超快。beat 動 跳動　terribly 副 非常

0540 We sat on the **couch** and **cuddled**.
我們在沙發上摟摟抱抱。couch 名 沙發　cuddle 動 親熱地摟住

0541 Arthur held his girlfriend in his arms.
亞瑟抱著他的女朋友。

0542 I enjoy my boyfriend **caressing** my hair.
我很喜歡我男友撫摸我頭髮的感覺。caress 動 撫摸；愛撫

0543 I also like **snuggling** up to my boyfriend.
我也喜歡依偎在我男朋友的身旁。snuggle 動 依偎

0544 I love you not because of who you are, but because of who I am when I am with you.
我愛你，不是因為你是一個怎麼樣的人，而是因為喜歡和你在一起時的我。

0545 Thank you for being my girlfriend and being around when I need you.
謝謝你願意做我的女朋友，並在我需要時陪著我。

0546 I love you because you **bring out** the best in me.
我愛你，因為你引出了我最好的一面。bring out 動 拿出

0547 You never **give up** on me and that keeps me going.
你從不放棄我，這正是讓我持續前進的動力。give up 片 放棄

0548 You're the one who holds the key to my heart.
你擁有打開我心扉的鑰匙。

0549 I love **holding your hand**.
我喜歡牽你的手。hold one's hand 片 牽某人的手

0550 I love you **with all my heart**.
我全心全意地愛著你。with all one's heart 片 全心全意地

0551 To me, you are the **world**.
對我而言，你就代表全世界。world 名 世界；宇宙

0552 Hope our love **lasts** and never dies.
希望我們的愛永恆不變。last 動 持續；持久

0553 We're a perfect match.

我們是天生一對。

0554 They are **absolutely** made for each other.
他們根本是天造地設的一對。 absolutely 副 絕對地

0555 Love doesn't **feed** you. Grow up!
愛情不能當飯吃，成熟點吧！ feed 動 餵養

0556 I'm **canceling** our date tonight.
我們今天晚上的約會要取消了。 cancel 動 取消

0557 But we've been planning it for weeks!
可是為了這個，我們已經計劃好幾個禮拜了耶！

0558 Why are you doing this to me?
你為什麼要這樣對我？

0559 You shouldn't have done that!
你不應該那樣做！

0560 Just look at what you've done!
看看你做了什麼好事！

0561 How can you say such a thing?
你怎麼可以說這種話？

0562 How can you say that after all we've been through?
我們一起經過了那麼多大風大浪，你現在怎麼能說這種話？

0563 Don't you **dare** say that again!
你再說一次試試看！ dare 助 敢；竟敢

0564 Why not?
有什麼不敢的？

0565 No matter what you say, I'll **leave** anyway.
不管你怎麼說，我都要離開。 leave 動 離開(某人的身邊)

0566 Are you leaving? You can't leave me all alone.
你要走了？你不能丟下我一個人。

0567 You must learn to **control** your **anger**.
你必須學會控制你的怒氣。control 動 控制 anger 名 生氣

0568 Don't **bother** me.
別煩我。bother 動 使惱怒；打擾

0569 Don't bother **coming over**!
你不用來看我！come over 片 順便來訪

0570 You've **gone overboard**!
你真的太過分了！go overboard 片 做得過頭；太過分

0571 I have **been turned off** by your acting.
我對你的所作所為感到厭煩。be turned off 片 胃口；沒興致

0572 What's **wrong** with you?
你有什麼毛病啊？wrong 形 不正常的；出毛病的

0573 What's your **problem**?
你怎麼回事啊？problem 名 問題

0574 Who do you think you are?
你以為你是誰啊？

0575 Don't **pick a fight with me**.
不要挑釁我。pick a fight with sb. 片 找某人的碴

0576 Please get your hand off me.
請把你的手拿開，別碰我。

0577 Don't give me your **excuses**. / No more **excuses**.
別再找藉口了。excuse 名 辯解；藉口

0578 I've had **enough** of your **garbage**.
我聽膩了你的鬼話。enough 名 足夠 garbage 名 廢話；垃圾

0579 I'm **about to explode**!
我快要氣炸了！about to 片 即將 explode 動 爆炸

0580 I'm not going to **put up with** this!

我不會再容忍下去了！ put up with 片 容忍；忍受

0581 I'm telling you for the last time!
我最後一次警告你！

0582 I can't **stand** the **sight** of you.
多看你一眼，我都受不了。 stand 動 忍受 sight 名 看見

0583 Leave me alone.
走開！別管我。

0584 **Get out** of my sight!
滾出我的視線！ get out 片 滾開；使出去

0585 I don't want to see your face!
我不要再看到你了！

0586 Where were you last night?
你昨天晚上去哪裡了？

0587 I couldn't **reach** you all night.
我整晚都聯絡不到你。 reach 動 與…取得聯繫

0588 Oh! My cell phone **battery** went **dead**.
喔！我的手機沒電了。 battery 名 電池 dead 形 失效的

0589 Why didn't you call me? It was my birthday yesterday.
那你怎麼沒打電話給我？昨天是我的生日耶。

0590 You have been acting quite strangely recently. / You are **out of sorts**.
你最近的樣子怪怪的。 out of sorts 片 不對勁

0591 You have been **cold** to me for a while.
你最近對我很冷淡。 cold 形 冷淡的

0592 Are you dating someone else?
你是不是在跟別人交往？

0593 I heard something through **the grapevine**.

我從別人那裡聽到一些傳言。 the grapevine 片 消息途徑

0594 I would never date more than one girl.
我絕對不會腳踏兩條船。

0595 There must be some **misunderstanding** here.
一定是有誤會。 misunderstanding 名 誤解

0596 That must be a **false rumor**.
那一定是不實的謠言。 false 形 不正確的 rumor 名 謠言

0597 I can't believe you were **flirting** with my best friend!
你竟然跟我最好的朋友打情罵俏！ flirt 動 調情

0598 She is just a **nodding** acquaintance.
我和她只是點頭之交。 nodding 形 點頭的

0599 **Believe** me! I am not **cheating** on you.
相信我！我沒有背叛你。 believe 動 相信 cheat 動 表現不忠

0600 It's actually not the case.
事實不是這樣的。

0601 I **warn** you! Don't try any **tricks**!
我警告你，別跟我玩什麼花樣！ warn 動 警告 trick 名 詭計

0602 You never **tell the truth**!
你從來不說實話！ tell the truth 片 說實話

0603 Why **on Earth** didn't you tell me the truth?
你到底為什麼不跟我說實話？ on Earth 片 究竟

0604 What do you mean by **keeping silent**?
你沉默不語是什麼意思？ keep silent 片 保持沉默

0605 I **regret** leaving you.
我很後悔和你分手。 regret 動 懊悔

0606 It was just an **impulsive fling**.
那只是我衝動下的一夜風流罷了。

impulsive 形 衝動的　fling 名 一時的放縱

0607 Please come back. I want to make up. I want to be your valentine.
請回到我身邊，和我復合吧！我想和你在一起。

0608 Are you cheating on me?
你是不是劈腿？

0609 I am sorry, but I'm in love with someone else.
真的很抱歉，我愛上別人了。

0610 How can you play the field?
你怎麼能到處拈花惹草呢？

0611 Don't you feel **guilty** of the **affair**?
你外遇難道不會有罪惡感嗎？ guilty 形 內疚的　affair 名 風流韻事

0612 How could you cheat on me again and again?
你怎麼可以一而再、再而三地背著我偷腥？

0613 You are such a **jerk**. I really should **dump** you.
你真的很低級，我真該甩了你。 jerk 名 渾球　dump 動 甩掉(某人)

0614 It's **obvious** that you don't love me **anymore**.
任誰都看得出來，你已經不愛我了。
obvious 形 明顯的　anymore 副 不再；再也不

0615 I heard that handsome guy is her **paramour**.
我聽說那個帥哥是她的情夫。 paramour 名 情夫；情婦

0616 I became part of an unusual love **triangle**.
我陷入一段不正常的三角關係中。 triangle 名 三角(形)

0617 I wish I could date him **openly**.
真希望能跟他光明正大地出門約會。 openly 副 公開地

0618 He **promised** that he will **divorce** his wife.
他承諾他會和老婆離婚。 promise 動 允諾　divorce 動 離婚

0619 I don't think he can make any **commitment** with

you.
我不認為他有能力給你任何承諾。 commitment 名 承諾

0620 Wake up! He has **disrupted** your life.
醒醒吧！他已經把你的人生攪得一團亂了。 disrupt 動 使混亂

0621 My best friend is caught up in a love triangle.
我最好的朋友陷入三角戀。

0622 She can't date her boyfriend openly.
她不能和男朋友公開地約會。

0623 She doesn't want to be second best anymore.
她不想再當第二順位的女人了。

0624 You **deserve** a better man.
你值得找一個更好的人。 deserve 動 應受；該得

0625 Love should not be **one-sided**.
愛情不應該是單方面的。 one-sided 形 片面的；偏於一方的

0626 No one is **worth** your **tears**, and the one who is, won't make you cry.
沒有人值得你流淚，值得讓你這麼做的人才不會讓你哭泣。
worth 形 值得有…的價值 tear 名 眼淚

0627 You're so right. I should **end** our relationship **immediately**.
你說得對，我應該立刻結束我和他之間的關係。
end 動 結束 immediately 副 立刻

0628 It's all over. We have **broken up**.
都結束了，我們分手了。 break up 片 分手

0629 I finally realize that we are better **apart** than together.
我終於了解，我們分開會比在一起好。 apart 副 分開地

0630 I wish I had never met him.
真希望我從來沒有遇見他。

0631 Good for you. It's not too late to go back.
真為你感到高興，現在回頭還不算晚。

0632 Angela and I haven't talked to each other for over a week.
安琪拉和我已經超過一個星期沒講話了。

0633 Are you still **upset** with me?
你還在生我的氣嗎？upset 形 心煩的

0634 Let's stop the **silent treatment**.
我們停止冷戰吧！silent 形 沉默的 treatment 名 對待

0635 I think we should have a talk.
我們應該好好談一談。

0636 How can I **make** it **up** to you?
我要怎麼做才能補償你？make up 片 補償

0637 I tried so hard to make it work with Fiona.
我很努力想維持我和菲歐娜的感情。

0638 I hope these flowers will make up for me being such a fool.
我真是個大蠢蛋，希望這些花能夠讓你的心情好一點。

0639 You know that I would never hurt your feelings **on purpose**.
你知道我絕不會故意傷你的心。on purpose 片 故意地

0640 I promise that I will never get **mad** at you again.
我保證以後再也不會對你發脾氣了。mad 形 惱火的

0641 I'm begging you to **forgive** me for cheating on you.
求求你原諒我，我不該背叛你的。forgive 動 原諒

0642 Let's **start over**.
我們從頭來過吧。start over 片 重新開始

0643 Can we give it one more try?

你可不可以再給我一次機會？

0644 I should have trusted you. I am sorry.
我應該要相信你的，對不起。

0645 Let's stop **quarreling** about the **trifles**.
我們別再為小事爭吵了。quarrel 動 爭吵 trifle 名 瑣事

0646 We've talked things out. Everything was just a misunderstanding.
我們把事情講開了，一切都只是個誤會。

0647 My girlfriend and I made up last night.
我和女友昨天晚上合好了。

0648 **Communication** is an important factor in a relationship.
溝通是交往中很重要的一環。communication 名 溝通

0649 We're not right for each other.
我們並不適合彼此。

0650 I can't keep going out with you.
我不能繼續和你交往了。

0651 I think we had better **cool down** for a while.
我覺得我們應該要冷靜一陣子。cool down 片 緩和

0652 I like you as a friend.
我喜歡你當我的朋友。

0653 You've changed a lot. You **used to** be very gentle.
你變了好多，你以前很溫柔的。used to 片 過去經常

0654 You are not my type anymore.
你不再是我喜歡的類型了。

0655 I want to **make** things **clear**.
我想要把話說清楚。make clear 片 使變明白

0656 Have I made myself clear?
我講得夠清楚了吧？

0657 I see. I guess this is goodbye.
我懂了，你想和我分手對吧？

0658 Do you think I am not good enough for you?
你覺得我配不上你嗎？

0659 You are too good for me. I don't deserve you.
你太好了，是我配不上你。

0660 I still want to be your friend.
我還是想繼續和你做朋友。

0661 I need to **focus** more **on** my **career**.
我需要專注於事業。 focus on 片 專注於 career 名 職業

0662 I can't make the commitment that you want.
你想要的承諾我給不了。

0663 They will break up sooner or later. It's all a **charade**.
他們貌合神離，遲早會分手的。 charade 名 裝模作樣

0664 I find myself **no longer** loving Barbara.
我發現自己已不再愛芭芭拉了。 no longer 片 不再

0665 I **implied** that I didn't love her.
我已經暗示她，我對她沒有感覺了。 imply 動 暗示

0666 We broke up because I was **two-timed** by him.
他欺騙了我，所以我們分手了。 two-time 動 (口)欺騙

0667 There's no love left in our relationship.
我們之間已經沒有愛情了。

0668 If I were you, I wouldn't let her go.
如果我是你，我不會讓她離開。

0669 Why don't you break up with her **once and for**

all?
你們怎麼不乾脆分手呢？ once and for all 片 永遠地

0670 Don't be so **heartless**.
不要這麼無情。 heartless 形 無情的

0671 He was the hardest break up ever!
他真是我遇過最難甩的男生了！

0672 What a fool I was to have a relationship with him.
我怎麼會傻到跟他交往。

0673 You finally **turned your back on** her.
你終於甩了她。 turn one's back on 片 放棄；拒絕

0674 No, actually, she dumped me. / she left me. / she **dropped** me.
事實上，是她甩了我才對。 drop 動 丟下；扔下

0675 I need someone to **comfort** me.
我需要有人來安慰我。 comfort 動 安慰

0676 All you need is a **cooling-off** period.
你只是需要一段時間，好好冷靜。 cooling-off 形 使頭腦冷靜的

0677 There are **plenty** of fish in the **sea**.
天涯何處無芳草。 plenty 名 豐富；大量 sea 名 大海

0678 I would never hit on someone unless I thought she liked me.
除非對方對我有意思，否則我不會纏著人家不放。

0679 Sometimes I think I really **screwed up** in my last relationship.
有時候我會想，是我搞砸了上一段戀情。 screw up 片 搞砸某事

0680 Forget it. Don't **waste** time on someone who isn't **willing** to spend their time on you.
算了吧，那些不願花費時間陪你的人，根本不值得你浪費時間。
waste 動 浪費 willing 形 願意的

0681 Face **reality**. Brook is obviously **unstable**.
面對現實吧！布魯克根本就不想定下來。
reality 名 現實　unstable 形 不固定的

0682 You can do way better than her.
你一定可以找到比她更好的女孩。

0683 You shouldn't let it **get** you **down**.
你不該被這件事擊倒。 get down 片 使沮喪

0684 Don't cry because it is over; smile because it happened.
別為了結束而哭泣，對你曾經擁有的微笑吧。

0685 I'm sure you'll find your Mr. Right.
我相信你會遇到真命天子的。

0686 You never know who is falling in love with your smile.
你怎麼知道？搞不好此刻就有人愛上了你的笑容呢！

0687 Time will **heal** your **sorrows**.
時間會治癒你的傷痛。 heal 動 治癒　sorrow 名 悲痛

0688 You'll **definitely** get back on your feet.
你一定有辦法走出傷痛的。 definitely 副 肯定地

UNIT 9 婚姻的分分合合 Marriage And Divorce

0689 My boyfriend and I have been dating for over six years.
我已經和我的男朋友交往六年多了。

0690 I think we have something really **special**.
我們一起度過許多特別的時光。special 形 特別的

0691 I want to **settle down**.
我想要定下來了。settle down 片 成家立業

0692 I am thinking about **proposing to** Crystal.
我正在考慮要跟克莉絲朵求婚。propose to 片 向某人求婚

0693 My boyfriend proposed to me last night.
我的男朋友昨晚向我求婚了。

0694 I was **overjoyed** when he proposed to me.
他向我求婚時，我簡直就是欣喜若狂。overjoyed 形 狂喜的

0695 He is the person you can **lean on throughout** your life.
他是可以依靠一輩子的人。lean on 片 依賴 throughout 介 貫穿

0696 Will you **marry** me?
你願意嫁給我嗎？marry 動 和…結婚

0697 If you say "yes", I will **guarantee** that you will have a very happy life.
只要你點頭，我一定會讓你幸福快樂的。guarantee 動 保證

0698 Let's **tie the knot**!
我們結婚吧！tie the knot 片 結婚

0699 My life won't be **complete** without you.
少了你，我的生命就不完整了。complete 形 完整的

0700 You are the one I want to grow old with.
你就是我想要陪伴到老的那個人。

0701 For me, this ring is too **precious** to **accept**.
對我而言，這只戒指太貴重，我不能收。
precious 形 貴重的 accept 動 接受

0702 I don't think I am ready for **marriage**.
我還沒有結婚的心理準備。marriage 名 婚姻

0703 I am not **ready**. I think you are going too fast.
我還沒有準備好，我覺得你太心急了。 ready 形 準備好的

0704 Some couples receive **counseling** during their **engagement**.
有些訂婚的男女會在婚前接受諮詢服務。
counsel 動 商議 engagement 名 訂婚

0705 This **prepares** them for the **challenges** of married life.
這是為了讓他們準備好，能接受婚姻生活帶來的種種挑戰。
prepare 動 使…準備好 challenge 名 挑戰

0706 We've **decided** to be together because the time is right to get married.
因為時機已經成熟，所以我們決定結婚。 decide 動 決定

0707 I have to discuss with my fiancé the **formality** and style of our wedding.
關於婚禮的形式，我得和未婚夫討論一下。 formality 名 禮節

0708 I **am dying for** a dream wedding.
我超想要一個夢幻婚禮。 be dying for 片 極想；渴望

0709 Guam is the **perfect destination** for my dream wedding.
關島是我夢想中的結婚地點。
perfect 形 理想的 destination 名 目的地

0710 Why don't you find a wedding planning **firm**?
你可以去找專門規劃婚禮的公司啊！ firm 名 公司

0711 My wedding **coordinator** is **fantastic**.
我的婚禮顧問很棒。 coordinator 名 協調者 fantastic 形 極好的

0712 She is not only **professional** but **considerate**.
她既專業又細心。 professional 形 專業的 considerate 形 周到的

0713 Wedding **photography** provides a **lifetime** memory.

婚紗照是一輩子的紀念。 photography 名 攝影 lifetime 形 終生的

0714 Look at your wedding photos. You are **gorgeous** in them.
快看你的婚紗照，你拍起來美極了！ gorgeous 形 極好的

0715 These photos were taken in Kenting.
這些照片是在墾丁拍的。

0716 I will choose a **designer bridal** gown for my big day.
我婚禮那天要穿由設計師特別設計的婚紗。
designer 形 專門設計的 bridal 形 新娘的；婚禮的

0717 That **handmade** wedding **gown** matches you.
那件手工製的婚紗很適合你。
handmade 形 手工的 gown 名 女禮服

0718 The classic style of wedding dress really fits the **elegant** bride.
這件典雅款的婚紗很適合那位氣質優雅的新娘。 elegant 形 優雅的

0719 The deep-V wedding dress is very **stylish**.
這件深 V 款的婚紗很時髦。 stylish 形 時髦的

0720 Are you going to send out Chinese wedding **invitations** or Western ones?
你要寄中式喜帖還是西式的？ invitation 名 請帖

0721 We sent out over 200 invitations to our wedding.
我們發了超過兩百張的喜帖。

0722 Don't forget to pick your wedding **favors**.
別忘了去挑你們的婚禮小物。 favor 名 小禮物

0723 Wedding favors are small gifts to show your appreciation to guests.
婚禮小物是為了表達對賓客的感謝，而準備的小禮物。

0724 Elizabeth and I chose candles for our wedding favors.

伊莉莎白和我選了蠟燭當婚禮小物。

0725 You must be very **tired** because of all the **preparation** for the wedding.
為了準備婚禮，你應該很累吧。 tired 形 疲累的 preparation 名 準備

0726 My parents hope that our wedding can **follow** long-held **traditions**.
我父母希望我們的婚禮可以沿襲長久以來的傳統。
follow 動 跟隨；跟從 tradition 名 傳統

0727 How much do you know about traditional Chinese wedding **customs**?
你對於中式婚禮的傳統習俗了解多少？ custom 名 習俗

0728 The usual place for a **Western** wedding is in a **church**.
西式婚禮通常會在教堂舉行。 Western 形 西方的 church 名 教堂

0729 Who is going to **pay** for the wedding?
誰會負擔婚禮的費用？ pay 動 支付

0730 In Taiwan, the groom and his family are responsible for the wedding.
在台灣，新郎和他的家人要負責婚禮的費用。

0731 I really hope you can come to our wedding.
我真的很希望你能來參加我們的婚禮。

0732 Would you be my **maid** of honor?
你願意當我的伴娘嗎？ maid 名 未婚的年輕女子

0733 Who is the **best man**? Is he the groom's friend?
伴郎是誰？是新郎的朋友嗎？ best man 片 伴郎

0734 My **niece** will be our flower girl.
我的姪女會擔任我們的花童。 niece 名 姪女；外甥女

0735 I can't wait for the bouquet **toss**.
我迫不及待要接新娘捧花了。 toss 名 拋；扔；投

0736 Please accept my **sincere congratulations**.
請接受我最誠摯的祝福。
sincere 形 衷心的　congratulation 名 祝賀

0737 I have never seen such a **pretty** bride.
這個新娘真是我見過最美的了。pretty 形 漂亮的

0738 May you be happy in your marriage.
祝你婚後幸福快樂。

0739 How lucky you are to marry such a nice girl.
能娶到這麼棒的女孩，你可真幸運。

0740 The **newlyweds** are really suited for each other.
這對新人真速配。newlywed 名 新婚夫婦

0741 How long have you been married?
你結婚多久了？

0742 It has been over a **decade**.
已經十幾年囉。decade 名 十年

0743 I married my **husband** when I was 24.
我在二十四歲那年嫁給我先生。husband 名 丈夫

0744 We **overcame** a lot of **difficulties** to get married.
我們克服了很多困難才結婚。overcome 動 克服　difficulty 名 困難

0745 After 20 years, our love is even stronger than before.
過了二十個年頭，我們的感情比以前更加堅定了。

0746 Danny and his wife have been **separated** for a year.
丹尼和他太太已經分居一年了。separate 動 使分居

0747 He has **applied for** a divorce.
他已經申請離婚了。apply for 片 申請；請求

0748 I was **shocked** when I heard the news.
剛聽到這個消息時，我真是嚇了一跳。shocked 形 震驚的

0749 I think that they'd better leave it at that.
我覺得他們最好到此為止。

0750 I am trying to comfort her.
我試著要安慰她。

0751 My ex-wife and I are fighting for **custody**.
我的前妻和我正在爭孩子的監護權。 custody 名 監護

0752 It must be **hard** for you.
你一定很難熬。 hard 形 艱難的；難受的

0753 I'll be **on your side**.
我會支持你的。 on one's side 片 支持某人

0754 You have to **keep your chin up**.
你必須振作起來。 keep your chin up 片 振作起來

0755 How much **alimony** did your ex-husband pay you?
你的前夫給了你多少贍養費呢？ alimony 名 贍養費

0756 The separation agreement was one **million** dollars.
離婚協議書上寫的是一百萬。 million 名 百萬

0757 I felt like dying when I realized that she would never come back.
當我知道她不會再回頭時，我難受得像快死掉了。

0758 We all know that this relationship isn't going to work out.
你和我都明白，這段關係無法再維持下去了。

0759 My wife broke my heart when we divorced.
我太太和我離婚時，我的心都碎了。

0760 There's no way to **fix** our problems.
我們之間的問題，沒有任何方法可以解決。 fix 動 修理

0761 All that work was for nothing.

花了那麼多的心力，到頭來，卻什麼也沒有。

0762 I don't **hold out** much **hope** for making up with her.
我們復合的希望不大。hold out hope 片 抱有希望

0763 I've been feeling **down in the dumps** lately.
我最近情緒低落。down in the dumps 片 沮喪的

0764 I don't want to talk to anyone, so leave me alone.
我不想跟任何人講話，讓我一個人靜一靜。

0765 I can't help crying whenever I **think of** him.
一想到他，我就忍不住落淚。think of 片 想到

0766 I just can't seem to be happy.
我無法讓自己看起來快樂。

0767 How could this **happen** to me?
這種事怎麼會發生在我身上？happen 動 發生

0768 I **can't help but** wait.
我忍不住想要等待。can't help but 片 不由得

0769 I have to accept the decision.
我必須接受這個決定。

0770 To be honest, I still miss my ex-wife.
老實說，我還是很想念我的前妻。

0771 Don't be silly. She would never forgive you.
別傻了，她絕不可能原諒你的。

0772 You must be feeling very sad.
你一定很難過。

0773 It's all over. Don't **dwell on** that.
你們已經結束了，不要再一直掛念那件事。dwell on 片 老是在想

0774 It'll **work out** anyway.
總會有辦法解決的。work out 片 能夠解決

0775 You'll just have to **cross** that **bridge** when you come to it.
船到橋頭自然直。 cross 動 越過 bridge 名 橋梁

0776 You are **surrounded** by people who love you and **care about** you.
你周圍有許多愛你、關心你的人。
surround 動 圍繞 care about 片 關心

0777 I have no words to **mend** your broken heart.
我不知道該說些什麼，才能讓你不這麼難過。 mend 動 使癒合

0778 It could be worse.
這樣的結果已經算不錯了。

0779 Some couples **split up** because their **personalities** are too different.
有些夫妻之所以會分手，是因為彼此的個性南轅北轍。
split up 片 分離 personality 名 個性

0780 Not every couple is a pair.
不是每一對夫妻都適合彼此的。

0781 Love cannot be **forced**.
愛情不能強求。 force 動 強迫

0782 If it comes back, it's yours.
屬於你的，想躲都躲不掉。

0783 If it doesn't **belong to** you, set it free.
不屬於你的，就讓他走吧。 belong to 片 屬於

0784 Don't try to **get even** after the **breakup**.
分手後，不要想去報復對方。 get even 片 報復 breakup 名 分手

Part 2

從早到晚的日常

DAILY LIFE

▶035

前往郵局與銀行
The Post Office And Bank

0785 Excuse me; where is the **nearest** post office?
不好意思，請問最近的郵局在哪裡？ near 形 近的

0786 You can find one on the **corner** of Zhongzheng Road and First Street.
中正路跟第一街的轉角那邊有一間。 corner 名 街角

0787 The post office is **open** from Monday to Saturday.
郵局從週一到週六都有營業。 open 形 營業的；辦公的

0788 It's open during normal business hours, from 8:30 a.m. to 5:00 p.m.
從早上八點半到下午五點的營業時間內都有開。

0789 It's closed on all the **national** holidays.
國定假日不營業。 national 形 全國性的

0790 What **services** does a post office **offer**?
郵局提供哪些服務呢？ service 名 服務 offer 動 提供

0791 As I know, post offices offer **postal** and banking services.
據我所知，郵局提供郵政及儲匯服務。 postal 形 郵政的

0792 You can buy **stamps**, and mail letters and packages at a post office.
你可以在郵局買郵票、寄信和寄包裹。 stamp 名 郵票

0793 You can also deposit money and buy **money orders** there.
你也可以在那裡存錢和購買匯票。 money order 片 匯票

0794 How much does it cost to send a **domestic** letter?

寄國內信件要多少錢呢？ domestic 形 國內的

0795 It costs NT$5 for regular mail if the letter weighs below twenty grams.
寄平信的話，重量在二十公克以下的信件要新台幣五元。

0796 Could you **weigh** the letter for me?
你可以幫我秤一下信件的重量嗎？ weigh 動 秤…的重量

0797 It's 25g, and it will cost NT$10 because it's a bit over the weight limit.
是二十五克，因為有一點超重，所以要新台幣十元。

0798 You can send these books as **printed** matter. It'll be much cheaper.
這些書你可以寄印刷品，會便宜很多。 printed 形 印刷的

0799 How would you like to send this mail? Regular or **registered**?
請問你想寄平信還是掛號呢？ registered 形 已掛號的

0800 What's the **quickest** way to send this?
最快的寄送方式是哪一種呢？ quick 形 快的；迅速的

0801 It takes three or four days at the most by **surface mail**.
寄平信大概要三到四天。 surface mail 片 平信郵件

0802 Sending letters by **express** mail saves a lot of time.
寄限時專送可以節省很多時間。 express 形 快遞的

0803 I want to **register** this letter.
我要寄掛號。 register 動 掛號郵寄

0804 Is there anything **valuable** in it?
裡面裝有什麼貴重物品嗎？ valuable 形 貴重的

0805 There are some **important documents**.
裡面有一些重要文件。 important 形 重要的 document 名 文件

0806 You need to **put** stamps **on envelopes** before you mail them.
寄信前須貼上郵票。put on 片 增加 envelope 名 信封

0807 You can buy stamps at a stamp **vending machine**.
你可以用郵票販賣機買郵票。vending machine 片 自動販賣機

0808 I want to buy some stamps. Which line should I be in?
我想要買郵票，應該排哪一列呢？

0809 I'd like to buy ten NT$5 dollar stamps, please.
我想要買十張五元的郵票。

0810 Do you need a **receipt**?
你需要收據嗎？receipt 名 收據

0811 Yes, please. I need a receipt to **claim expenses**.
是的，謝謝，我需要拿收據報帳。claim 動 主張 expense 名 開支

0812 I want to send this letter to the U.S. How long will it take?
我想要寄信去美國，請問多久後會送達？

0813 I don't know how to **write** my address in English.
我不知道要怎麼把地址寫成英文。write 動 書寫

0814 You can go to the Taiwan Post Website and click on "English-Chinese Address **Translation**" and **key in** your Chinese address.
你可以上中華郵政的網站，點選「中文地址英譯」，再輸入中文地址。translation 名 翻譯 key in 片 輸入

0815 Could you show me how to address a **horizontal** envelope?
你可以教我怎麼寫橫式信封嗎？horizontal 形 橫的

0816 Please type or print the address clearly in the **middle** of the envelope.

請打字或以正楷將收件人地址填寫在信封中間。middle 名 中央

0817 On the top left corner, write the **return** address.
在信封的左上角填上寄件人地址。return 形 返回的

0818 Return addresses should include a sender's full name and address.
寄件人地址要包含寄件人的全名和地址。

0819 Where should I **place** the stamps?
郵票要貼在哪裡？place 動 放置

0820 You can place a **postage** stamp on the top right corner of the envelope.
你可以把郵票貼在信封的右上角。postage 名 郵資

0821 If you want to know the delivery date, you could check the **postmark**.
如果你想確認郵件的寄送日期，可以看郵戳。postmark 名 郵戳

0822 I'd like to send this **package** to **England**.
我想要寄這個包裹到英國。package 名 包裹 England 名 英國

0823 Sir, you have to **fill out** this form first if you want to mail the **parcel**.
先生，你如果要寄包裹，必須先填寫這張表格。
fill out 片 填寫 parcel 名 (小)包裹

0824 Let me weigh the package to make sure how much you need to pay.
我先幫你秤一下包裹的重量，以確認你要付多少錢。

0825 It is NT$1,020 by air and only NT$368 by sea.
空運要新台幣 1,020 元，海運則只需新台幣 368 元。

0826 Do you want to mail it **by** sea or by air?
你要寄海運還是空運？by 介 用；透過

0827 I'd like to send it by air because it is much faster.
我要寄空運，因為快多了。

0828 How much is that by air mail?
寄空運要多少錢呢？

0829 It **depends on** the weight.
依信件的重量而定。depend on 片 取決於

0830 I'll mail it by sea. It'll be much **cheaper**.
我要寄海運，比較便宜。cheap 形 便宜的

0831 It will **probably** take two and a half months.
大概要花兩個半月才會送達。probably 副 或許

0832 That's too slow! My sister is **expecting** it.
那太慢了！我姐姐等著收呢。expect 動 期待；盼望

0833 What should I do to let the mail **carrier** know that he should be careful?
我要如何讓郵差知道要小心輕放呢？carrier 名 送信人

0834 Add the "**Fragile**" **stickers** on the outside of your package.
在包裹外面貼上「易碎品」的貼紙。
fragile 形 易碎的 sticker 名 貼紙

0835 If you don't have stickers, write "Fragile!" in big **letters** on your package.
如果沒有貼紙，就在包裹外寫上大大的「易碎品」。letter 名 字母

0836 I suggest you **wrap** the package with some bubble wrap and tape it.
我建議你用氣泡紙包好，再用膠帶固定。wrap 動 包

0837 I used to send my friends greeting cards before Christmas, New Year's, or their birthdays.
我以前會在聖誕節、新年或朋友生日前寄賀卡給他們。

0838 Nowadays, people send e-greeting cards instead of regular mail.
現在，大家都用電子賀卡來取代傳統郵件了。

0839 I'd like to open an **account**, please.

麻煩你，我想要開戶。 account 名 帳戶

0840 What type of account do you want to open? A savings account or checking account?
您想開什麼類型的戶頭？儲蓄帳戶或支票帳戶？

0841 Savings account, please.
我想要開儲蓄帳戶。

0842 Checking accounts don't pay any **interest**.
支票帳戶不會有任何利息。 interest 名 利息

0843 Please fill out the form. Do you have a **chop** and two pieces of ID with you?
請填寫這張表格，您有帶印章和雙證件嗎？ chop 名 印章

0844 How much cash do you wish to **deposit** in your account, madam?
女士，您想在戶頭裡存多少錢呢？ deposit 動 存(錢)

0845 I want to deposit some money in a foreign **currency** account.
我想要存錢到國外的帳戶。 currency 名 通貨

0846 Here is my **passport** and the necessary information.
這是我的護照和所需的資料。 passport 名 護照

0847 I want to **withdraw** some money from my account.
我想要從我的帳戶提領一些錢。 withdraw 動 提取

0848 **Bankbooks** are used to record banking **transactions**.
存摺用以記錄所有的銀行交易。
bankbook 名 銀行存摺 transaction 名 交易

0849 Could you help me check the **balance** on my account?
你可以幫我查一下帳戶餘額嗎？ balance 名 結餘

0850 The balance **remaining** in your account is $2,000.
您的帳戶餘額為兩千元。 remain 動 餘留；剩下

0851 I have a four-year **deposit** about to **expire**. May I **renew** it for another year?
我有個四年期的定存即將到期，我可以再續約一年嗎？
deposit 名 存款 expire 動 屆期 renew 動 使更新

0852 May I see your C.D.? In other words, your **certificate** of deposit.
我可以看一下您的 C.D. 嗎？就是定存單。 certificate 名 單據

0853 Would you like it to still be a club savings account?
您還是要辦理零存整付的定期儲蓄存款嗎？

0854 I'd like to make it a non-drawing, term savings account, please.
我要辦整存整付的定期儲蓄存款。

0855 I want to take out the rest of my money and close my account.
我要領走帳戶剩下的餘額，並結清戶頭。

0856 Could you tell me which form is for **remittance**, please?
請問一下，匯款要填哪個單子才對呢？ remittance 名 匯款

0857 I need to **remit** money to my mother.
我需要匯款給我的母親。 remit 動 匯寄

0858 Please write your mother's name on the **remittee column**.
請將您母親的姓名填在收款人這個欄位。
remittee 名 (匯票的)收款人 column 名 欄位

0859 I'd like to have a money order for NT$30,000, please.
我想要買三萬元台幣的匯票。

0860 You need to pay a NT$30 **processing** fee for each money order.

買一張匯票須付三十元的處理費。 process 動 處理

0861 Is it difficult to get a **loan** from a **bank**?

向銀行申請貸款很困難嗎？ loan 名 貸款 bank 名 銀行

0862 If your credit check meets all the required conditions, you will **qualify** for a **mortgage** with this bank.

如果您的信用紀錄滿足所有條件，就能申請這家銀行的抵押貸款。

qualify 動 使具資格 mortgage 名 抵押借款

0863 It took my parents twenty-five years to **pay off** the mortgage on our house.

我爸媽花了二十五年的時間還清房貸。 pay off 片 償清債務

0864 You should **proceed** to the bank **counter** after drawing a ticket and waiting for your number to be called.

您應該先抽取號碼牌，再到銀行櫃台那邊等待叫號。

proceed 動 繼續進行 counter 名 櫃台

0865 If you don't have time to go to the bank during business hours, you can do on-line banking or telephone banking.

如果你無法於營業時間去銀行，也可以使用網路銀行或電話銀行的服務。

0866 Interest rates **vary** depending on the **individual** bank.

利率會隨著銀行不同而有所差異。

vary 動 使不同 individual 形 個別的

0867 Interest rates **fluctuate** in a **reflection** of our ever-changing economy.

利率會隨著瞬息萬變的經濟情況波動。

fluctuate 動 波動 reflection 名 反映

0868 What transactions can you **perform** at an ATM?

自動提款機能提供哪些服務呢？ perform 動 執行；完成

0869 You can withdraw, **transfer**, and deposit money. Also, you can check your account balance.
你可以領錢、轉帳和存錢，還能查詢餘額。 transfer 動 轉讓

0870 I **usually** use my ATM card to withdraw money.
我通常會用提款卡領錢。 usually 副 通常；常常

0871 Many ATMs **accept** deposits. It's very **convenient**.
許多自動提款機都能存款，很方便。
accept 動 接受 convenient 形 便利的

0872 I keep all the monthly **statements** the bank sends me.
銀行寄給我的對帳單我都會留著。 statement 名 (銀行的)結單

0873 What **currency** do you want?
您想換什麼貨幣呢？ currency 名 貨幣

0874 Could you tell me the **current** exchange rate for the U.S. dollar?
可以告訴我現在的美金匯率是多少嗎？ current 形 當前的

0875 I'll check the exchange rate between the dollar and the yen for you.
我來幫您查一下美元對日圓的兌換率。

0876 Do you want large or small **bills**?
您的現金要換大面額還是小面額的呢？ bill 名 (美)鈔票

0877 Please give me small bills. I'd like some ten dollar bills, please.
請給我小面額的鈔票，我需要換十元的美金。

來一場美食饗宴
Let's Cook A Meal!

0878 Rice and **noodles** are **staples** for most Taiwanese and Japanese.
米飯和麵是大部分台灣人與日本人的主食。
noodle 名 麵條　staple 名 主食

0879 I usually have fried **turnip cake** for breakfast.
我早餐通常會吃煎蘿蔔糕。turnip cake 片 蘿蔔糕

0880 It's made of rice and **radish**.
蘿蔔糕是由米和蘿蔔製成的。radish 名 小蘿蔔

0881 Do you know how to **fry** turnip cake?
你知道怎麼煎蘿蔔糕嗎？fry 動 油煎；油炸

0882 **Heat up** a non-stick frying pan, and then add a **drizzle** of oil.
先熱不沾鍋，再倒一點點油下去。
heat up 片 加熱　drizzle 名 一滴

0883 Then pan-fry on both sides until they are golden-brown and **crispy**.
兩面煎到表面呈金黃色，有點酥脆就可以了。crispy 形 酥脆的

0884 My mother has been cooking for us for more than thirty years.
我媽媽已經為我們煮飯超過三十年了。

0885 I enjoy cooking, and I often cook for my family.
我很喜歡烹飪，經常煮給我的家人吃。

0886 I am good at cooking. I can cook Italian and Chinese food.
我很擅長烹飪，我會煮義大利菜和中國菜。

0887 I almost never cook. I am **too** busy **to** cook.
我幾乎不下廚，根本忙到沒時間做菜。 too...to... 片 太…以至於不

0888 You can take cooking lessons or buy some cookbooks if you want to learn cooking.
如果你想學烹飪的話，可以上烹飪課或買食譜來看。

0889 Using a rice cooker is a **simple** and **effective** way to cook rice.
想煮飯，用電鍋是最簡單、也最有效率的方法了。
simple 形 簡單的 effective 形 有效的

0890 It also keeps the rice warm after it's cooked.
電鍋在飯煮熟之後還會保溫。

0891 One of the best ways to maintain our health is to eat a balanced diet.
維持健康最好的方法之一是攝取均衡的營養。

0892 Don't take too much **salt** and **sugar**.
不要攝取過多的鹽分和糖分。 salt 名 鹽 sugar 名 (食用)糖

0893 I like eggs and cheese because they **contain protein**.
我喜歡蛋和起司，因為裡頭富含蛋白質。
contain 動 包含 protein 名 蛋白質

0894 People like **organic** and **additive**-free foods.
大家都喜歡有機和不含添加物的食品。
organic 形 有機的 additive 名 添加物

0895 What's your favorite **food**?
你最喜歡什麼食物？ food 名 食物

0896 I like **spicy** and **sour** Thai food.
我喜歡又辣又酸的泰國菜。 spicy 形 辛辣的 sour 形 酸味的

0897 My favorite Thai food is green **curry** chicken.
我最喜歡的泰國菜是綠咖哩雞。 curry 名 咖哩

0898 The main ingredients of this **course** include

green curry **paste**, **coconut** milk, and chicken.
這道菜的主要食材包括綠咖哩醬、椰奶和雞肉。
course 名 一道菜 paste 名 醬 coconut 名 椰子

0899 I don't like the **flavor** of coconuts. I like green **papaya** salad better.
我不喜歡椰子的味道，我比較喜歡青木瓜沙拉。
flavor 名 味道 papaya 名 木瓜

0900 Japanese food is my favorite. I love **tempura**.
我最愛日本菜了，我喜歡天婦羅。tempura 名 日本的油炸料理

0901 Do you know how to make **shrimp** tempura?
你知道炸蝦天婦羅怎麼做嗎？shrimp 名 蝦子

0902 First, you remove the heads and **shells** from the shrimp without removing the **tails**.
首先，剝掉蝦頭和蝦殼，但尾巴要留著。shell 名 殼 tail 名 尾巴

0903 Mix eggs, ice water and flour in a bowl to make the **batter**.
將雞蛋、冰水和麵粉倒進碗裡，混合後做成麵糊。batter 名 糊狀物

0904 Flour the shrimp before frying and then fry the shrimp until it's crispy.
在炸蝦子之前，先裹上麵粉，再油炸至酥脆為止。

0905 It will taste better if you serve shrimp tempura with a **dipping sauce**.
炸蝦天婦羅搭配沾醬會更美味。dip 動 沾；浸 sauce 名 醬汁

0906 It's almost dinner time. Are you **hungry**?
晚餐時間快到了，你餓了嗎？hungry 形 飢餓的

0907 I'm **starving**! I have got to **grab** something to eat.
我快餓死了！我得找點東西吃。starving 形 飢餓的 grab 動 抓取

0908 Let's start with some **appetizers**.
先從開胃菜開始吧。appetizer 名 開胃菜

0909 I have some frozen **Buffalo** wings in my **freezer**.
冷凍庫裡有一些冷凍的水牛城辣雞翅。
Buffalo 名 水牛城　freezer 名 冷凍庫

0910 Just heat them in the **oven** or **microwave**.
只要放進烤箱或微波爐裡，加熱一下就可以吃了。
oven 名 烤箱　microwave 名 微波爐

0911 **Bamboo shoots** with **mayonnaise** is my favorite appetizer in summer.
竹筍沙拉是我最愛的夏季開胃菜。
bamboo 名 竹子　shoot 名 幼芽　mayonnaise 名 美乃滋

0912 Do you prefer **pumpkin** soup or clam **chowder**?
你喜歡南瓜湯還是蛤蜊濃湯？
pumpkin 名 南瓜　chowder 名 雜燴濃湯

0913 Pumpkins are in season. Let's make pumpkin soup.
現在盛產南瓜，來煮南瓜湯吧！

0914 First, chop the pumpkin into small **chunks** and cook in boiling water until soft.
首先，把南瓜切成塊狀，放到滾水中煮軟。chunk 名 大塊

0915 When the pumpkin is soft, put it into the **blender** with the **seasoning mix** and blend.
等南瓜變軟了，再放到攪拌器中，加入調味料攪拌。
blender 名 攪拌器　seasoning mix 片 混和香料

0916 Put the **mixture** back into a **saucepan**, and add some milk.
把攪拌過的南瓜泥放進有深度的鍋子中，加入牛奶。
mixture 名 混合物　saucepan 名 平底深鍋

0917 If it is too **thick**, you can **add** some water.
如果太濃稠，你可以加水。thick 形 濃厚的　add 動 添加

0918 Can you pass me the **ladle**, please?
可以麻煩你把那個大湯杓拿給我嗎？ladle 名 長柄杓

0919 I suggest we'd better have some **spaghetti**.
我們最好吃義大利麵。 spaghetti 名 義大利麵

0920 How about a Caesar salad to **go with** it?
再搭配一些凱撒沙拉，怎麼樣？ go with 片 和…相配

0921 Could you **tear** the **lettuce** into bite-sized pieces while I make the dressing?
我調沙拉醬的時候，你可以把生菜撕成方便一口吃下去的大小嗎？
tear 動 撕開　lettuce 名 萵苣

0922 Would you **peel** the **potatoes** for me?
你可以幫我削馬鈴薯皮嗎？ peel 動 削去…的皮　potato 名 馬鈴薯

0923 Be **careful** with that **knife**. Don't cut your fingers.
小心使用刀子，不要切到手指了。 careful 形 小心的　knife 名 刀子

0924 I would use **garlic**, **olive** oil, **mustard** and cheese to make salad dressing.
我會用蒜頭、橄欖油、黃芥末和起司來製作沙拉醬。
garlic 名 大蒜　olive 名 橄欖　mustard 名 黃芥末

0925 Don't forget to add garlic **croutons** and crispy **bacon** just before serving.
上桌前別忘了加入蒜味麵包丁和酥脆的培根。
crouton 名 麵包丁　bacon 名 培根

0926 You will need a **wok** if you want to make Chinese food.
如果你想做中國菜，就需要一個中式炒鍋。 wok 名 中式鐵鍋

0927 Traditional Chinese woks have rounded **bottoms** and two side **handles**.
傳統中式炒鍋的鍋底是圓的，兩邊有柄。
bottom 名 底部　handle 名 把手

0928 Do you know how to make **braised** pork rice?
你知道滷肉飯怎麼做嗎？ braise 動 以文火燉煮

0929 I **have no idea**, but I can find a recipe for you.

我不知道，不過我可以幫你找食譜。 have no idea 片 不知道

0930 I'm afraid the **recipe** will not help me that much.
這食譜對我的幫助恐怕不大。 recipe 名 食譜

0931 I will show you how to make **dumplings** next time.
我下次教你怎麼包水餃。 dumpling 名 水餃

0932 I like dumplings with **leek** and **ground pork** filling.
我喜歡包韭菜和豬肉的水餃。 leek 名 韭菜 ground pork 片 豬絞肉

0933 I am going to **stir-fry** the **cabbage**.
我要炒高麗菜了。 stir-fry 動 炒 cabbage 名 高麗菜

0934 Please turn on the **extractor fan** for me.
請幫我打開抽油煙機。 extractor fan 片 排氣扇

0935 Also, I need an **apron**. Can you hand it to me?
我還需要一條圍裙，你可以拿給我嗎？ apron 名 圍裙

0936 Wait until the **pot** is hot and stir-fry it over a high **flame**.
熱鍋後用大火快炒。 pot 名 鍋 flame 名 火焰

0937 Would you like a second helping of fried rice?
你要不要再來一點炒飯？

0938 No, thanks. I've had plenty.
不用了，謝謝你，我已經吃很多了。

0939 **Stinky tofu** is too much for most foreigners.
大部分的外國人都不能接受臭豆腐。 stinky tofu 片 臭豆腐

0940 I buy ground beef for making **hamburgers** once a week.
我一星期會買一次做漢堡用的牛絞肉。 hamburger 名 漢堡

0941 We are going to eat spicy hotpot tonight. I need some **sliced** meat.

我們晚上要吃麻辣火鍋，我需要一些肉片。 slice 動 切薄片

0942 Did you see the cutting **board**? I can't find it anywhere.
你有看到切菜板嗎？我找了半天都沒找到。 board 名 木板

0943 The **cleaver** is not sharp enough. I can't cut up the beef.
這把菜刀不夠利，我切不斷牛肉。 cleaver 名 切肉刀

0944 What's in the pot? I smell something **burning**.
鍋子裡在煮什麼？我聞到燒焦味。 burn 動 燒焦

0945 Oh! I burnt the chicken. What should I do now?
喔！慘了，我把雞肉煮焦了，現在該怎麼辦？

0946 My roommate sometimes **mixes up** salt and sugar.
我的室友有時候會把鹽和糖搞混。 mix up 片 弄混

0947 Should I use vegetable oil or **sesame** oil?
我應該加植物油還是麻油？ sesame 名 芝麻

0948 **Turn** the gas **down** a little. Let it **simmer** longer and it will taste better.
把火關小，用小火燉久一點會更美味。
turn down 片 關小　simmer 動 煨；燉

0949 The **roast** beef melts in my mouth. It's really **tasty**.
這個烤牛肉入口即化，真的很美味。
roast 形 烘烤的　tasty 形 美味的

0950 Should I **marinate** the pork **chops** before **deep-frying** them?
我在炸豬排前要先醃豬肉嗎？
marinate 動 浸在滷汁中　chop 名 排骨　deep-fry 動 油炸

0951 You didn't add MSG, did you? I'm **allergic** to it.
你沒有加味精吧？我對味精過敏。 allergic 形 過敏的

0952 No. I just added some black **pepper**.
沒有，我只加了一些黑胡椒。pepper 名 胡椒粉

0953 Don't **push** me. It just needs ten more minutes.
別催我，再十分鐘就好了。push 動 催促

0954 The dinner is almost ready. Could you **set the table** for me?
晚餐快好了，你能幫我擺碗筷嗎？set the table 片 擺飯桌

0955 Sure. Should every place setting have a dinner plate, glass, and **napkin**?
沒問題，每個位子都要擺餐盤、玻璃杯和餐巾嗎？napkin 名 餐巾

0956 Please arrange them **neatly** on **place mats**. Don't forget the knives, spoons, and forks.
請把那些都整齊地擺在餐墊上，別忘了放餐刀、湯匙和叉子。
neatly 副 整齊地 place mat 片 餐墊

0957 Try the sweet soup. It keeps you young and beautiful.
這個甜湯有養顏美容的功效喔，嚐嚐吧。

0958 It consists of white **fungus**, lotus seeds and **red dates**.
裡面有白木耳、蓮子和紅棗。fungus 名 真菌 red date 片 紅棗

0959 **Brownies** are a **classic** American dessert. They are great for snacks.
布朗尼是很經典的美國甜點，拿來當點心最棒了。
brownie 名 布朗尼蛋糕 classic 形 經典的

0960 This brownie is **out of this world**!
這布朗尼是最棒的！out of this world 片 無與倫比的

0961 The first step is to melt butter and chocolate in a saucepan.
首先，把奶油和巧克力放進有深度的平底鍋中，加熱融化。

0962 **Preheat** the oven before you **bake** it.

在烤之前，先預熱烤箱。 preheat 動 預先加熱 bake 動 烤

0963 I am really **full**, but I'd love to try a **bite**.
我真的很飽，但還是想嚐一口。 full 形 吃飽的 bite 名 一口的量

0964 We can share the **dessert**. How's that sound?
甜點我們可以分著吃，你覺得怎麼樣？ dessert 名 甜點

0965 It's **yummy**! I'm **giving it a thumbs up**.
太美味了！讓人忍不住豎起拇指的好吃。
yummy 形 美味的 give sth. a thumbs up 片 讚揚

0966 Want some coffee or tea to go with the dessert?
要不要來杯咖啡或茶配甜點呢？

0967 Let me find my **kettle** and **boil** the water first.
我得先找出水壺，再煮開水。 kettle 名 水壺 boil 動 煮沸

0968 Can you give me a hand in the kitchen? I can't finish everything by myself.
你可以到廚房幫我嗎？我一個人沒辦法包辦所有的事。

0969 Could you help me with the dishes?
你可以幫我洗盤子嗎？

0970 Put the **plates** in the **cupboard** after you finish them.
洗完之後，把盤子放到櫥櫃裡。 plate 名 盤子 cupboard 名 碗櫃

狂歡派對嗨一下
It's Party Time!

0971 Have you ever been to a **party**?
你有參加過派對嗎？ party 名 派對；舞會

0972 Of course! I love parties.
當然有！我超愛參加派對的。

0973 I've never been to a party. I am not a **sociable** person.
我從來不參加派對，我不擅長社交。sociable 形 好交際的

0974 Why do people **throw parties**?
人們為什麼會舉辦派對？throw a party 片 舉辦派對

0975 Usually, they celebrate something like birthdays, weddings, housewarmings, graduations, and so on.
通常是為了慶祝一些事宜，像是生日、結婚、喬遷和畢業等等。

0976 Our school holds a dance party for **freshmen** after **orientation** every year.
我們學校每年都會在校園導覽結束之後，為新生舉辦舞會。
freshman 名 大一新生 orientation 名 校園導覽

0977 Don't you feel it's embarrassing to dance with someone you don't know?
你不覺得和不認識的人跳舞很尷尬嗎？

0978 Come on! How can you miss the **opportunity** to meet girls?
拜託！你怎麼能錯過認識女生的機會呢？opportunity 名 機會

0979 Who else is going to the party?
還有誰會去參加這場派對啊？

0980 Most of the guests are my friends from school and work.
大部分都是我的同學和同事。

0981 Do you know any of the guests Mr. and Mrs. Baker invited?
貝克夫婦所邀請的客人當中，有你認識的人嗎？

0982 No, the only one I know is the hostess.
沒有，我只認識女主人。

0983 Are you interested in coming over to the party with me?
你有沒有興趣和我一起去參加派對？

0984 I was not **invited**.
我沒有被邀請。 invite 動 邀請

0985 I'd love to, but I have other stuff to do on that day.
我很想去，不過我那天有別的事要忙。

0986 Can I bring my roommate, Christine, to the party?
我可以帶我的室友克莉絲汀一起去嗎？

0987 You are **welcome** to **bring** your friends.
歡迎帶你的朋友一起參加。 welcome 形 受允許的 bring 動 帶來

0988 What should I bring to Bella's birthday party?
我應該帶什麼去貝拉的生日派對呢？

0989 I will bring a bouquet of flowers to her house.
我會帶一束花去她家。

0990 I don't know what to wear to the party. Do you have any good suggestions?
我不知道要穿什麼去派對，你有什麼好建議嗎？

0991 Check out the **invitation**. They have a dress code.
看看邀請函吧，他們有服裝要求。 invitation 名 邀請函

0992 The **dress code** is "smart **casual**". What does that mean?
上面寫著「請著半正式服裝」，那是什麼意思啊？
dress code 名 著裝標準 casual 名 便裝

0993 It means you can wear smart but **informal** clothing, like a long-sleeve shirt and no tie.
意思是，你可以穿休閒又不失禮的衣服，例如穿長袖襯衫，但不

打領帶。informal 形 非正式的

0994 If you are coming to the party, please **confirm** by Next Tuesday.
如果你要參加派對，請於下週二之前確認。confirm 動 確認

0995 What does "R.S.V.P." **mean**?
R.S.V.P 是什麼意思？mean 動 表示…的意思

0996 R.S.V.P. is a French phrase, and it means "please reply."
R.S.V.P. 是一個法文片語，意思是「請回覆」。

0997 Put "BYOB" on the invitation if you want the guests to bring their own drinks.
如果你希望客人自備飲料，就在邀請函上寫 BYOB。

0998 Birthdays only **come around** once a year.
生日一年只有一次。come around 片 來到；發生

0999 I've **reached** the age where birthdays aren't that big of a deal.
我已經到了一個不怎麼重視生日的年紀了。reach 動 到達

1000 A housewarming party is held when someone has moved into a new house.
所謂的喬遷派對，是搬到新家後所舉辦的。

1001 I would like to invite you and your husband to our housewarming party.
我想邀請你和你的先生來參加我們的喬遷派對。

1002 Andrew invited us to his new **apartment**. I can't wait!
安德魯邀請我們去參觀他的新公寓，真令人期待！
apartment 名 公寓

1003 We're throwing a **farewell** party for Dana. Do you have any **ideas**?
我們要替黛娜辦歡送會，你有沒有什麼好點子？
farewell 形 告別的 idea 名 主意；點子

1004 Why don't we have a **potluck** party?
我們來辦個百樂餐派對好了。 potluck 名 百樂餐

1005 Each **guest** should bring a dish to share with everybody.
每位客人要帶一道菜和大家分享。 guest 名 賓客

1006 What are you going to bring? We have three appetizers and two desserts so far.
你要帶什麼？到目前為止已經有三道開胃菜和兩道甜點了。

1007 I **am** not **good at** cooking. Can I bring some **chips** and salsa?
我不太會煮菜，我可以帶洋芋片和莎莎醬嗎？
be good at 片 擅長 chip 名 洋芋片

1008 Who made the **wonton** soup? It's yummy!
這餛飩湯是誰做的？好好吃！ wonton 名 餛飩

1009 I love all the dishes. They are too much to my **liking**, though!
這些菜我全都喜歡，都太合我的口味了！ liking 名 愛好

1010 A baby shower is an American **tradition** to **celebrate** the future birth of a child.
新生兒派對是美國的一項傳統，是為了即將出生的寶寶而舉辦的慶祝會。 tradition 名 傳統 celebrate 動 慶祝

1011 A baby shower is usually held by the mother-to-be's best friend before the baby is born.
新生兒派對通常會在寶寶出生前，由母親最好的朋友幫她舉辦。

1012 It is normally one to two months before the **delivery** date.
通常會選在預產期前的一到兩個月舉辦。 delivery 名 分娩

1013 Guests will bring **gifts** for the expected child.
客人會帶禮物來送給即將出生的寶寶。 gift 名 禮物

1014 Guessing the baby's size and sex are common games played at a baby shower.

猜寶寶的大小和性別是新生兒派對上常見的遊戲。

1015 Here are some tips to host a successful party.
這裡提供一些成功辦派對的技巧。

1016 First of all, you need to **choose** the date and time for your party.
首先，你必須選定派對的日期與時間。 choose 動 選擇

1017 You might also need to set a **budget** for the party.
也必須設定舉辦派對的預算。 budget 名 預算

1018 Why don't we pick a **theme** for the party?
我們來決定派對的主題吧。 theme 名 主題

1019 Do you want an **outdoor** barbecue or a formal, sit-down dinner?
你想要辦戶外烤肉會，還是正式的晚宴？ outdoor 形 戶外的

1020 I'd prefer a **cocktail** party. What do you think?
我比較想要辦雞尾酒派對，你覺得呢？ cocktail 名 雞尾酒

1021 If you're hosting the party at home, guests may expect a **tour** of your house.
如果你要在家辦派對，客人可能會想參觀你家。 tour 名 遊覽

1022 We had better **clean up** the house before the party.
我們最好在派對前，把家裡打掃乾淨。 clean up 片 打掃

1023 I think we should give the house a good cleaning.
我覺得我們需要大掃除了。

1024 The house needs to be cleaned **from top to bottom**.
這房子需要一次徹底的清掃。 from top to bottom 片 完全地

1025 Could you **tidy up** my bedroom for me?
你可以幫我整理臥室嗎？ tidy up 片 收拾東西

1026 Stop leaving things lying around!
不要再亂放東西了！

1027 Where is the **broom** and **dustpan**? I can't find them.
掃帚和畚箕在哪裡？我找不到。 broom 名 掃帚 dustpan 名 畚箕

1028 We've **run out of toilet paper**. Could you buy some on your way home?
衛生紙用完了，你回來的時候可以順便去買嗎？
run out of 片 用完 toilet paper 片 衛生紙

1029 I usually plan my food list and shop a few days **ahead of time**.
我通常會先規劃好食物清單，並於幾天前採買好。
ahead of time 片 提前

1030 Some dishes can be prepared in advance, like **beef stew**.
燉牛肉等菜餚是可以事先準備好的。 beef stew 片 燉牛肉

1031 Please **help** yourself!
請自便，不用客氣！ help 動 取用(食物等)

1032 I hope you guys **enjoy** the party.
希望你們在派對中玩得開心。 enjoy 動 享受

1033 What's your favorite **holiday**?
你最喜歡的節日是什麼？ holiday 名 節日

1034 Chinese New Year is my favorite. It's the most important holiday for the Chinese.
我最喜歡農曆新年。對中國人來說，那是最重要的節日。

1035 At New Year's, most Chinese families would post signs on the front door of their houses.
過年的時候，大多數的家庭都會在大門上貼春聯。

1036 Red is a **lucky** color during Chinese New Year.
紅色是過年期間的幸運色。 lucky 形 幸運的

1037 People go moon-**gazing** during the Mid-Autumn **Festival**.
人們會在中秋節的時候去賞月。gaze 動 凝視 festival 名 節日

1038 I like moon cakes, especially the ones with **green bean** paste.
我喜歡吃月餅，尤其是包綠豆沙餡的。green bean 片 綠豆

1039 Although it's not a traditional activity, almost every **Taiwanese** family has a **barbecue** on that day.
雖然並非傳統活動，但幾乎每個台灣家庭都會在中秋節當天烤肉。
Taiwanese 形 台灣的 barbecue 名 烤肉野餐

1040 What should we **prepare** for the barbecue party?
烤肉派對要準備些什麼呢？prepare 動 準備

1041 I'll bring barbecue sauce, brushes, **grill**, **corn**, sausages, and some **mushrooms**.
我會準備烤肉醬、刷子、烤肉架、玉米、香腸和香菇。
grill 名 烤架 corn 名 玉米 mushroom 名 香菇

1042 Besides the food, don't forget **charcoal** and **tongs**.
除了吃的，別忘了準備木炭和烤肉夾。
charcoal 名 木炭 tongs 名 夾具

1043 Kids always love **Lantern** Festival.
小孩子都愛元宵節。lantern 名 燈籠

1044 How about we make our own lanterns this year?
不如我們今年自己做燈籠，怎麼樣？

1045 Is **Tomb-Sweeping** Day a national holiday, too?
清明節也是國定假日嗎？tomb 名 墳墓 sweep 動 打掃

1046 Yes. But do you know why we sweep tombs on Tomb-Sweeping Day?
是的，但你知道為什麼清明節要掃墓嗎？

1047 Tomb-Sweeping Day is a time to **pay respect to** our deceased relatives and to tidy their **gravesites**.

清明節是對祖先表示追思之情，以及打掃他們安息之地的日子。

pay respect to 片 憑弔死者　gravesite 名 墓地

1048 The whole family goes to the gravesite of **deceased** family members to burn **incense**.

清明節那一天，全家人都會到過世親人的墓園燒香祭拜。

deceased 形 已故的　incense 名 香

1049 On New Year's Eve, will you guys join the final countdown at Taipei 101?

跨年那天晚上，你們要不要一起去台北 101 倒數？

1050 We can watch the final **countdown fireworks** show together.

我們可以一起看倒數的煙火秀。

countdown 名 倒數計時　firework 名 煙火

1051 Don't count me in. It's too **crowded**. I'd rather stay home and watch it on TV.

我不參加，那裡太擠了，我寧願回家看電視。crowded 形 擁擠的

1052 It's already **December**. Do you and your family celebrate **Christmas**?

已經十二月了，你們家有沒有慶祝聖誕節的習慣啊？

December 名 十二月　Christmas 名 聖誕節

1053 I am going Christmas shopping today. Have you done that, yet?

我今天要去逛街買聖誕節禮物，你的禮物都買好了嗎？

1054 I did my **last-minute** Christmas shopping yesterday.

我昨天已經完成聖誕禮物的最後採買。last-minute 形 最後的

1055 Let's plan a Christmas gift-exchange game. It would be fun.

我們來設計一個交換禮物的遊戲吧，一定會很有趣的！

1056 People **decorate** their Christmas trees with **ornaments** and lights.

人們會在聖誕樹上掛滿裝飾品和燈泡。

decorate 動 裝飾 ornament 名 裝飾品

1057 Have a Merry Christmas and a Happy New Year!
祝大家聖誕快樂、新年快樂！

1058 Please send my Christmas greetings to your family.
請代我向你家人傳達我的聖誕祝福。

1059 **Halloween** is coming! Should we get some **costumes**?
萬聖節快到了，我們要不要去買萬聖節的特殊服裝呢？
Halloween 名 萬聖節 costume 名 服裝

1060 My daughter is going to dress up as either a **witch** or a **zombie**.
我女兒想要裝扮成巫婆或殭屍。 witch 名 巫婆 zombie 名 殭屍

1061 My friends and I usually **carve** a jack-o'-lantern together.
我和朋友通常會一起雕刻空心南瓜燈。 carve 動 雕刻

1062 We'd better buy more candy for all the kids in the **neighborhood**.
我們最好多準備一點糖果給附近的小孩子。 neighborhood 名 近鄰

1063 Trick-or-treating is the funniest Halloween activity for kids.
對小孩子來說，「不給糖就搗蛋」是萬聖節最有趣的活動。

1064 **Thanksgiving** is a day for family **gatherings** for Americans.
對美國人而言，感恩節是家庭團聚日。
Thanksgiving 名 感恩節 gathering 名 聚會

1065 Thanksgiving Day is celebrated on the fourth Thursday in November.
十一月的第四個星期四，就是慶祝感恩節的日子。

1066 **Turkey** and pumpkin pie are common foods on Thanksgiving Day.

火雞和南瓜派都是常見的感恩節食物。turkey 名 火雞

1067 It usually takes more than five hours to roast a whole turkey.
烤一整隻火雞通常要花費五個小時以上。

1068 I **guess** I like Valentine's Day the best.
我想我最喜歡的節日是情人節吧。guess 動 (口)想；認為

1069 April Fool's Day is **truly** a time for **fun**.
愚人節確實是一個能玩鬧的有趣節日。truly 副 確切地 fun 名 樂趣

1070 Shall we head for the Easter event at the church?
我們要出發前往教堂參加復活節的活動了嗎？

1071 St. Patrick's Day is celebrated on March 17 by the Irish.
愛爾蘭人在三月十七日那天慶祝聖派翠克節。

1072 Everybody is **supposed** to wear green on St. Patrick's Day.
在聖派翠克節這一天，大家都得穿綠色的衣物。
suppose 動 認為必須

1073 It's common on most holidays to have **parades** and fireworks.
大部分的節日通常都會有遊行與放煙火這兩項活動。
parade 名 遊行

UNIT 4 打理我的外在美
At A Hair / Beauty Salon

1074 I really want a new **hairstyle**.
真想要換個新髮型。hairstyle 名 髮型

1075 I **am tired of** my **hairdo**.
我已經對這個髮型感到厭煩了。
be tired of 片 對…感到厭倦 hairdo 名 髮型

1076 I think you need a new look.
我覺得你需要一個新造型。

1077 I like my hair the way it is.
我喜歡我現在的髮型。

1078 Come on! Your hair has looked the **same** for years.
拜託！你的髮型幾年來都一樣。 same 形 同樣的

1079 You can get a **perm**, and you will look so much different.
你可以燙頭髮，這樣你看起來會很不一樣。 perm 名 燙髮

1080 My **aunt** has her hair dyed and permed every six months.
我的阿姨每半年染燙一次頭髮。 aunt 名 阿姨；姑姑；嬸嬸

1081 My sister has her hair **trimmed** every three months.
我妹妹每三個月剪一次頭髮。 trim 動 修剪

1082 I think long, **curly** hair would look good on you.
我覺得你留長捲髮會很好看。 curly 形 捲髮的

1083 You look gorgeous with shoulder-length hair.
你留及肩的長髮很美。

1084 Erin looks **younger** with short hair.
艾琳留短髮看起來比較年輕。 young 形 年輕的

1085 I like to wear ponytails.
我喜歡綁馬尾。

1086 I prefer **straight**, long hair.
我比較喜歡長直髮。 straight 形 筆直的

1087 I am starting to grow my hair out, and it's at the difficult, in-between stage.
我開始留長髮了，但現在的長度正好是過渡期，真難熬。

1088 Should I keep my hair straight?
我應該繼續留直髮嗎？

1089 Could you **recommend** a nice beauty **salon** for me?
你有推薦的美髮院嗎？ recommend 動 推薦 salon 名 沙龍

1090 I know a **professional hairstylist**.
我認識一位專業的髮型設計師。
professional 形 專業的 hairstylist 名 髮型師

1091 She always knows what hairstyles are in.
她對於時下流行的髮型瞭若執掌。

1092 Why don't you check out some celebrities' hairstyles in the magazine and decide what you want?
你何不參考雜誌，看看名人的髮型再做決定？

1093 Welcome to Fashion Hair. Do you have a **reservation**?
歡迎光臨時尚髮廊，請問有預約嗎？ reservation 名 預約

1094 Do you have an **appointed hairdresser**?
請問您有指定的設計師嗎？
appointed 形 指定的 hairdresser 名 美髮師

1095 Yes, I made an appointment with Frank for a perm at three o'clock.
有的，我有跟法蘭克約好，三點要燙頭髮。

1096 Oh, are you Ms. Lin? Please have a seat here. I'll get Frank right away.
喔！是林小姐嗎？這邊請坐，我馬上去叫法蘭克

1097 No, I don't have a **preference**. Anyone would be fine.

我沒有指定設計師，任何一位都可以。 preference 名 偏愛的人事物

1098 May I recommend Ivy to you? She's one of our best stylists.
我推薦艾薇，她是我們店裡最好的髮型師之一。

1099 All of our **stylists are tied up** now. Do you mind waiting for a while?
目前我們所有的設計師都在忙，您介意等一下嗎？
stylist 名 設計師　be tied up 片 忙得不可開交的

1100 I'm sorry, sir. We're closing in ten minutes. Could you come back tomorrow?
很抱歉，先生，我們再十分鐘就要打烊了，您可以明天再來嗎？

1101 How do you want your hair done today, madam?
女士，您今天想要做什麼樣的服務呢？

1102 How much do you **charge** for a **shampoo**?
洗髮的價格是多少呢？ charge 動 要價　shampoo 名 洗頭

1103 A shampoo and set, please.
請幫我洗頭和做造型。

1104 Could you blow-dry my hair and **part** it on the side?
可以幫我把頭髮吹乾，並旁分嗎？ part 動 使分開

1105 I used to part my hair on the left, but I'd like it parted in the middle today.
我以前頭髮都旁分在左邊，不過今天我想要中分。

1106 I have **dandruff**. Could you use anti-dandruff shampoo?
我有頭皮屑，你可以使用抗屑洗髮精嗎？ dandruff 名 頭皮屑

1107 Your hair is a bit **dry**. Would you like to try our new **treatment**?
您的頭髮有點乾燥，要不要試試我們最新的護髮服務呢？
dry 形 乾燥的　treatment 名 治療法

1108 Do you need a **rinse**?
請問要潤絲嗎？rinse 名 潤絲

1109 How much does a **haircut cost**?
剪頭髮要多少錢？haircut 名 剪髮 cost 動 花費

1110 Would you like your trim **as usual**?
您想要剪和之前一樣的髮型嗎？as usual 片 像往常一樣

1111 I would like to keep the same style. Just **trim** a bit **off** the back.
我想要維持原來的髮型，稍微修一下後面就好了。trim off 片 修剪

1112 Do you want your hair **layered**?
您的頭髮要打層次嗎？layer 動 把…堆積成層

1113 I'd like my hair thinned. **Shave** the sides, and I don't want too much at the back.
我想要打薄，兩邊修薄一點，但後面不要剪太多。shave 動 修剪

1114 I'd like a haircut. Do you have any pictures of the latest hairstyles?
我想要剪頭髮，請問有最新髮型的圖片能參考嗎？

1115 Would you like any **magazines** or hairstyle books?
請問您要看雜誌或髮型書嗎？magazine 名 雜誌

1116 The hairstyle **trend** this season is short hair with heavy **bangs**.
這一季流行短髮加厚瀏海的髮型。trend 名 潮流 bangs 名 瀏海

1117 I think you would look good with a **pixie cut**.
我覺得你剪赫本頭會很好看。pixie cut 片 赫本頭；精靈系短髮

1118 I'll put this **cape** on you before your haircut.
剪髮前，我會先幫您披上剪髮斗篷。cape 名 斗篷

1119 I'd like to get my hair dyed **auburn** with blond **highlights**.
我想要染赭紅色，再挑染一點金色。

auburn 形 赭色的 highlight 名 明亮處

1120 Would you like to try **chestnut brown**? Here is a picture of a model's hair of that color.
您要不要試試栗褐色？看起會像這張圖片裡的模特兒。
chestnut 名 栗子 brown 名 褐色；棕色

1121 You can choose color-**protecting** shampoo for your dyed hair.
您有染髮，可以選用護色洗髮精。protect 動 保護

1122 It **brings out** the **tints** in your hair.
護色洗髮精會讓您染的髮色更顯色。
bring out 片 拿出 tint 名 色彩

1123 How much does a perm cost?
燙髮要多少錢？

1124 It's NT$2,000 for a **basic** perm.
最基本的燙髮是兩千元。basic 形 基礎的；基本的

1125 I'd like my hair permed. Could it be **finished** within two hours?
我想要燙頭髮，兩個小時會好嗎？finish 動 結束

1126 I'm **afraid** not. Usually, it takes **at least** three hours.
恐怕不行，燙髮至少要花三個小時以上。
afraid 形 恐怕 at least 片 至少

1127 I think I had better have it permed next time. I am **in a hurry**.
那我還是下次再燙好了，我趕時間。in a hurry 片 匆忙地

1128 I really don't know how to deal with my **natural** curly hair.
我真的不知道該拿我這頭自然捲怎麼辦。natural 形 自然的

1129 Most women don't like natural curly hair because it is hard to **tame** and style.
大部分的女生都不喜歡自然捲，因為很難打理，也不好做造型。

tame 動 馴化

1130 I **suggest** you try a straight perm.
我建議您試試離子燙。 suggest 動 建議；提議

1131 My hair is **flat** and straight. What can I do?
我的頭髮又塌又直，該怎麼辦才好？ flat 形 平坦的

1132 If you don't want a perm, I'd suggest using a **curler** every morning.
如果不想燙頭髮，我會建議您每天早上用捲髮器整理。
curler 名 捲髮器

1133 I bought a flat, **ceramic** hairstyling iron on the Internet. It's really amazing.
我在網路上買了一個陶瓷離子夾，真的很好用。 ceramic 形 陶器的

1134 Digital perms are very **popular** in Asia nowadays.
亞洲現在很流行熱塑燙／溫塑燙。 popular 形 流行的

1135 Dry hair creates **split** ends and is always **coarse** in **texture**.
乾燥的頭髮末端會分叉，而且髮質會很粗糙。
split 形 分裂的 coarse 形 粗糙的 texture 名 質地

1136 It needs **frequent** deep **conditioning** and treatment.
需要經常做深層的滋潤和護理。
frequent 形 屢次的 condition 動 使健康

1137 Oily hair is usually caused by **hormonal imbalance**.
油性髮質常因荷爾蒙失調而起。
hormonal 形 荷爾蒙的 imbalance 名 不均衡

1138 Never blow-dry your hair **completely**.
頭髮不要吹全乾。 completely 副 完全地

1139 It's always better to leave some **moisture**.
留點水分會比較好。 moisture 名 溼氣；水分

1140 Use the **mousse** before you blow-dry your hair.
吹頭髮之前，先抹上一點慕絲。 mousse 名 慕絲

1141 You can use moisturizing shampoo and **conditioner**, too.
你也可以用含滋潤成分的洗髮精和潤髮乳。 conditioner 名 護髮乳

1142 It will help **restore** moisture, so your hair won't be so **brittle**.
護髮能滋潤頭髮，使其不那麼容易斷裂。
restore 動 恢復；使復原 brittle 形 易損壞的

1143 My hair is a bit **thin**.
我的頭髮有點稀少。 thin 形 稀少的；稀疏的

1144 He's going a bit thin on top. In fact, he's going **bald**.
他頭頂的髮量有點少，實際上，他快禿頭了。 bald 形 禿頭的

1145 I am afraid that he is going to have to wear a **toupee** soon.
他恐怕快要必須戴假髮了。 toupee 名 (男性的)假髮

1146 Would you like to take a look in the **mirror**?
你想要照個鏡子嗎？ mirror 名 鏡子

1147 Actually, I would like the waves set a little **looser**.
事實上，我希望可以把捲度再弄大一點。 loose 形 鬆的

1148 Using wax or mousse should make your waves last longer.
使用髮蠟或慕絲可以讓頭髮的捲度維持久一點。

1149 Could you introduce some **products** to me?
你可以介紹一些產品給我嗎？ product 名 產品

1150 Try the **revitalizing** shampoo. It's really nice.
試試這罐豐盈洗髮精，真的很好用。 revitalize 動 使恢復生氣

1151 It's the best product for thinning hair I've ever used.

這是我用過最棒的產品，專治髮量稀疏。

1152 It helps your hair **become** fuller and stronger.
這個產品能增進頭髮生長，髮質也會變強韌。 become 動 變成

1153 Would you like a **shave**?
您想要修個臉嗎？ shave 名 修面；刮臉

1154 Please shave off my **beard**.
請幫我剃掉落腮鬍。 beard 名 (下巴的)鬍子

1155 Sir, do you want to leave the **sideburns**?
先生，您要保留兩邊的鬢角嗎？ sideburn 名 鬢角

1156 Do you like your new hairstyle?
你喜歡你的新髮型嗎？

1157 This is the perfect style for me. I couldn't like it more.
這是最完美的髮型了，我超喜歡的。

1158 I like your new haircut. You look so cute and **stylish**.
我喜歡你的新髮型，看起來可愛又時髦。 stylish 形 時髦的

1159 What's **wrong** with your hair?
你這個髮型是怎麼回事？ wrong 形 不正常的

1160 I really find my new hairstyle **strange**. I think I need a hat.
我的新髮型怪極了，我得戴個帽子。 strange 形 奇怪的

1161 It's not too bad. You are just not used to it.
沒那麼糟啦，你只是還沒習慣而已。

1162 You just used too much hair **spray** and **gel**.
你只是用了太多造型液和髮膠而已。 spray 名 噴液 gel 名 凝膠

1163 I usually **tip** the person who shampoos my hair and the stylist.
我通常會付小費給幫我洗頭髮的人和造型師。 tip 動 給…小費

1164 Should I leave the tip at the **front desk** or give it directly to the service **provider**?
我應該把小費放在櫃台，還是直接給幫我服務的人？
front desk 片 服務台　provider 名 提供者

1165 Either way, whatever makes you feel more **comfortable**.
都可以，只要你覺得方便就好。comfortable 形 自在的

1166 Welcome to Beauty World Spa. Do you have a reservation?
歡迎光臨「美麗世界美容中心」，請問有預約嗎？

1167 Yes, I am Kathy Wang. I called this morning.
有的，我是王凱西，我今天早上有打電話來。

1168 Sure, Ms. Wang. You've reserved our **massage** service, haven't you?
王小姐您好，您預約了我們的按摩服務，對吧？massage 名 按摩

1169 Yes, I want to have a massage. My **muscles** have been pretty **stiff** lately.
是的，我想要按摩，我最近肌肉十分僵硬。
muscle 名 肌肉　stiff 形 僵硬的

1170 My neck is stiff and **aching**. I need a good massage.
我的脖子很僵硬且痠痛，我需要好好地按摩放鬆。
aching 形 疼痛的

1171 This way, please. This is your **masseuse**, Ella.
這邊請，這位是您的按摩師，艾拉。masseuse 名 女按摩師

1172 I suggest you have a **full-body** massage
我推薦您做全身按摩。full-body 形 全身的

1173 It would help you **get rid of** the aching in your muscles.
這能幫助您消除肌肉痠痛的現象。get rid of 片 擺脫

1174 The **therapeutic** effects of massage promote

wellness.
按摩的療效能促進健康。therapeutic 形 治療的 wellness 名 健康

1175 You can put your **personal belongings** in the **locker.**
您可以將個人的隨身物品放在置物櫃中。
personal 形 私人的 belongings 名 財產 locker 名 衣物櫃

1176 After a **shower**, put on the **robe.**
淋浴之後，穿上浴袍。shower 名 淋浴 robe 名 長袍

1177 You can **hang** your clothes here.
您可以把衣服掛在這裡。hang 動 把…掛起

1178 Please **lie** on the massage table.
請躺在按摩床上。lie 動 躺；臥

1179 Your **shoulders** are really **tense.**
您的肩膀真的很僵硬。shoulder 名 肩膀 tense 形 緊繃的

1180 Relax! You can **take a nap** if you feel sleepy.
放輕鬆，想睡的話，您可以小睡一下。take a nap 片 小睡

1181 Have you ever tried a **Thai** massage?
你有體驗過泰式按摩嗎？Thai 形 泰國的

1182 I've heard about it, but never tried it. What's a Thai massage like?
有聽過，但我從沒試過，什麼是泰式按摩？

1183 The masseuse massages you with her feet and her hands.
按摩師不僅會用手，還會用腳來幫你按摩。

1184 Do they usually **press** hard? It sounds **painful!**
他們會按得很大力嗎？聽起來好痛！
press 動 按；壓 painful 形 疼痛的

1185 You can also try our **aromatherapy.**
您也可以試試我們的芳香療法。aromatherapy 名 芳香療法

1186 It costs $1,200 per treatment. But if you **purchase** ten **sessions** today, you will get a discount.
一次一千兩百元，如果你今天購買十次的芳香療程，就能享有優惠的折扣。 purchase 動 購買 session 名 (活動等的)時間

1187 What's aromatherapy like?
什麼是芳香療法？

1188 We massage your body with **essential** oil.
我們會用精油來按摩身體。 essential 形 提煉的

1189 Aromatherapy has a lot of **benefits**.
芳香療法有很多好處。 benefit 名 利益；好處

1190 It can not only reduce your **anxiety** but also improve **circulation**.
它不只能消除焦慮感，讓您放鬆，還能增進血液循環。
anxiety 名 焦慮 circulation 名 循環

1191 We offer a **variety** of essential oil **scents**.
我們提供各種香味的精油。 variety 名 種種 scent 名 香味

1192 I'd like something **flowery**, like **lavender** or rose.
我喜歡花香味，例如薰衣草和玫瑰的味道。
flowery 形 花的 lavender 名 薰衣草

1193 How often do you go for a **facial**?
你多久去做一次臉？ facial 名 美容；臉部按摩

1194 I found the **pores** on my face are really huge, and I have some pimples.
我發現我臉上的毛孔好大，還長了痘痘。 pore 名 毛孔

1195 I'm wondering if you do facial care. What are the prices like?
請問你們有幫人做臉嗎？價格大概是多少呢？

1196 Our service **ranges** from 800 to 2,000 dollars.
我們的服務從八百元到兩千元的都有。 range 動 (範圍)涉及

1197 The basic facial skin care includes **exfoliation**

and mask treatment.
基礎的臉部保養包含去角質和敷臉。 exfoliation 名 剝落

1198 After facial cleaning, I will exfoliate the dead skin **cells** on your face.
做完臉部清潔後，我會幫您去除臉上老化的角質。 cell 名 細胞

1199 The facial **steamer** is used to clean the skin thoroughly by opening the pores.
這台蒸臉器會讓毛孔打開，以徹底清潔您的皮膚。
steamer 名 蒸氣機

1200 After that, I'll clear your **blackheads** and small **pimples**.
接著，我會替您清除黑頭粉刺和痘痘。
blackhead 名 黑頭粉刺 pimple 名 青春痘

1201 Thank you very much! I hope you are **satisfied** with our service.
非常感謝！希望您滿意我們的服務。 satisfied 形 感到滿意的

UNIT 5 到百貨公司一遊 At The Department Store

1202 Bloomingdale's is having an **annual sale**.
布魯明黛百貨週年慶正在打折。 annual sale 片 週年慶

1203 Sounds great! I haven't gone shopping for a long time.
聽起來很棒！我好久沒有逛街了。

1204 Why don't we **head** to the shopping mall after work?
那我們乾脆下班就殺去購物中心吧！ head 動 前往

1205 The Estée Lauder **compact** makeup **kit** is really worth buying.
雅詩蘭黛的化妝品組合真的很值得買。
compact 形 小型的　kit 名 成套工具

1206 I'll get it. I think it's the best deal of their annual sale.
我要買，我覺得那是週年慶最划算的商品了。

1207 It is **indeed** a good quality **brand**.
它確實是個代表高品質的牌子。indeed 副 確實　brand 名 品牌

1208 I want to buy a **moisturizer**.
我想看潤膚霜。moisturizer 名 潤膚霜

1209 Would you like to try this **hydration** active moisture boost?
您要不要試試這罐深層速效保溼霜？hydration 名 保溼

1210 This is our latest product. It was just **released** a few weeks ago.
這是我們的最新產品，幾週前才剛上市。release 動 發表

1211 It works very well because it **nourishes** the skin.
它能滋潤肌膚，效果很棒。nourish 動 滋養

1212 I also recommend the moisture **lotion**. It is one of our **bestsellers**.
我也推薦這瓶保溼乳液，是我們家的熱賣商品之一。
lotion 名 乳液　bestseller 名 暢銷商品

1213 It contains **soy extract** and vitamin E.
它富含大豆萃取精華和維他命 E。soy 名 大豆　extract 名 提取物

1214 I'm worried that it's too **oily**.
我怕這個用起來會太油。oily 形 多油的

1215 It's very **light** and doesn't **clog** pores.
它的質地很清爽，不會阻塞毛孔。light 形 清爽的　clog 動 堵塞

1216 I have **combination** skin. My T-zone gets oily

during the day.
我是混合性肌膚，我的 T 字部位白天會出油。
combination 名 混合體

1217 My skin is oily. Do you know how to clear up **bothersome** blackheads?
我是油性肌膚，你知道要怎麼去除這些惱人的黑頭粉刺嗎？
bothersome 形 令人討厭的

1218 Our green tea face **scrub** can be used for removing blackheads.
我們的綠茶臉部磨砂膏可以用來去除黑頭粉刺。 scrub 名 擦洗

1219 It is one of our best-selling products and the most effective treatment for pimples.
它是我們的熱銷商品，也是最有效的治痘產品。

1220 It would work better if you use the **toner** after washing your face.
洗完臉後擦化妝水，效果會更好。 toner 名 化妝水

1221 The toner does not contain **alcohol**, so it is good for sensitive skin.
這款化妝水不含酒精，適用於敏感性肌膚。 alcohol 名 酒精

1222 Can I **sample** the toner?
我可以試擦這罐化妝水嗎？ sample 動 體驗

1223 You can get a travel pack if you purchase three items.
只要購買三件以上的商品，我們就免費送您一套旅行組。

1224 It comes with a small amount of face wash, toner, lotion, and face cream.
裡面包含小包裝的洗面乳、化妝水、乳液和面霜。

1225 If you buy the night cream and day cream together, you will get three whitening face masks for free.
如果您晚霜和日霜一起買，就免費送您三片美白面膜。

1226 That's over my budget. I'll just take the day cream.
那超出我的預算了，我只要買日霜就好。

1227 Are you sure? These face masks are worth more than NT$700.
您確定嗎？這些面膜的價值超過新台幣七百元。

1228 You can take part in our lucky draw if you purchase over NT$3,000.
如果您的購買金額超過新台幣三千元，就能參加我們的抽獎活動。

1229 Could you recommend the best eye cream for my **dark circles**?
你可以推薦最能消除黑眼圈的眼霜嗎？ dark circles 片 黑眼圈

1230 I've been bothered by dark circles **for ages**.
我已經被黑眼圈困擾很久了。 for ages 片 長久地

1231 This new eye gel is the best **remedy** for dark circles.
這款新眼膠是用來挽救黑眼圈的聖品。 remedy 名 藥物

1232 It can **reduce** your **wrinkles**, dark circles and **puffiness** around your eyes.
它能減少眼周的皺紋、黑眼圈和浮腫。
reduce 動 減少 wrinkle 名 皺紋 puffiness 名 腫脹

1233 You can also use our eye **concealer**.
你也可以用我的們的眼部遮瑕膏。 concealer 名 遮瑕膏

1234 The **creamy** concealer is favored by the **majority** of women.
這種乳狀的遮瑕膏很受大多數女性的喜愛。
creamy 形 乳狀的 majority 名 多數

1235 Could you show me how to apply a concealer for my dark circles?
你可以示範怎麼用遮瑕膏來遮黑眼圈嗎？

1236 Sure. Do you want me to apply it to your face?

當然可以，您要我直接擦在您的臉上嗎？

1237 The first step is to apply your **foundation** after using pre-makeup cream.
第一個步驟是在擦完妝前乳後，上粉底。 foundation 名 粉底

1238 Use your ring finger to gently **tap** the concealer under your eyes.
用您的無名指輕壓，把眼睛下方的遮瑕膏推勻。 tap 動 輕拍

1239 Don't apply thick foundation and concealer to get a more natural look.
粉底和遮瑕膏不要塗得太厚，這樣妝感會比較自然。

1240 It covers **freckles** and pimples, too.
它也可以用來遮雀斑和痘痘。 freckle 名 雀斑

1241 The perfect **liquid** foundation protects you from **ultraviolet rays**.
這瓶完美的粉底液能抵擋紫外線。
liquid 形 液體的 ultraviolet 形 紫外線的 ray 名 光線

1242 It makes me look great even when I'm not wearing any foundation or powder.
擦上它之後，即使我沒上粉底或蜜粉，氣色也很好。

1243 The best thing is that it's not **greasy** and it keeps my skin hydrated.
最棒的是它一點也不油膩，還有很好的保溼效果。
greasy 形 油膩的

1244 The powder matches your **complexion** perfectly.
這款蜜粉和您的膚色很搭。 complexion 名 膚色

1245 This counter girl can show you how to do that.
這位專櫃小姐可以教您怎麼使用。

1246 Apply the **blush** on the apples of your cheeks using the blush brush.
利用腮紅刷，在顴骨的位置刷上腮紅。 blush 名 腮紅

1247 Do you use **mascara**?
您有使用睫毛膏的習慣嗎？ mascara 名 睫毛膏

1248 Applying mascara makes **eyelashes** long, thick and extremely volumed.
擦睫毛膏能讓睫毛變得又長又濃密。 eyelash 名 睫毛

1249 I would recommend waterproof mascara if you wear **contact** lenses.
如果有戴隱形眼鏡，我推薦您用防水睫毛膏。 contact 形 接觸的

1250 I don't use mascara much because I don't know how to **remove** it.
我不常擦睫毛膏，因為我不知道要怎麼卸。 remove 動 去掉

1251 I don't know how to **curl** my lashes and apply mascara.
我不知道怎麼弄翹睫毛，也不會用睫毛膏。 curl 動 使捲曲

1252 I usually use an eyelash curler before applying mascara.
在上睫毛膏之前，我會先使用睫毛夾。

1253 I am not used to wearing **false** eyelashes.
我不習慣戴假睫毛。 false 形 假的；人造的

1254 Your eyes will **stand out** much more with eye shadow.
用了眼影，你的眼睛會更引人注目。 stand out 片 突出

1255 Every woman **dreams of** having sexy, full lips.
每個女人都想擁有性感的豐唇。 dream of 片 夢想

1256 I sometimes use lip **gloss** to add some **glamour**.
我有時候會塗唇蜜，以增加魅力。 gloss 名 光澤 glamour 名 魅力

1257 Check out this **lipstick**. I love the color.
看一下這支口紅，我喜歡這個顏色。 lipstick 名 口紅

1258 I use lip balm before applying lipstick. It prevents cracked lips.

我在畫口紅前會先擦護唇膏，以防嘴唇乾裂。

1259 The lipstick contains vitamin E to keep your lips healthy and soft.
這支口紅含有維他命 E，能維持嘴唇的健康和柔軟。

1260 If you buy the new lipstick, you can get a free lip **balm**.
如果您購買新款口紅，我們就免費送一支護唇膏。 balm 名 香膏

1261 Makeup remover is a product any woman who wears makeup needs.
對會上妝的女人來說，卸妝乳是必備產品。

1262 Many women enjoy wearing makeup to **enhance** their beauty.
很多女人都喜歡化妝，讓自己更加閃閃動人。 enhance 動 增加

1263 Eva looks **totally** different after putting on makeup.
伊娃化妝前和化妝後判若兩人。 totally 副 完全

1264 Too much makeup makes you look older.
太濃的妝反而會顯老。

1265 That's why I prefer a **natural** to wearing makeup.
那就是我之所以喜歡裸妝的原因。 natural 名 天然物

1266 Let's shop around and find some special **jewelry** for Mom!
我們去逛逛，幫媽媽找個別緻的首飾吧！ jewelry 名 首飾

1267 My mother has been hoping to get a nice **brooch** for a long time.
我媽媽一直想要一個好看的胸針。 brooch 名 女用胸針

1268 All our brooches are **on sale** during our Mother's Day sale.
所有的胸針現在都有母親節特惠。 on sale 片 特價的

1269 Are you looking for any **specific patterns**?

您有沒有特別要找什麼款式的？
specific 形 特定的 pattern 名 樣式

1270 What is your budget?
您的預算是多少呢？

1271 I only have a **limited** budget.
我沒有太多預算。limited 形 有限的

1272 My budget has **constraints**.
我的預算很少。constraint 名 限制

1273 Would you like to **try on** the brooch?
您要試戴一下這只胸針嗎？try on 片 試穿；試戴

1274 What is the **stone** on it?
上面鑲的是什麼寶石？stone 名 寶石；石頭

1275 It's a **sapphire**. It will make you look more **elegant**.
是藍寶石，更能襯托出您的優雅。
sapphire 名 藍寶石 elegant 形 優雅的

1276 May I take a look at the brooch with three **pearls** on it?
我能看看那只上面鑲有三顆珍珠的胸針嗎？pearl 名 珍珠

1277 The **ivory luster** of the pearl looks very pretty.
珍珠的象牙色光澤看起來真美。ivory 形 象牙色的 luster 名 光澤

1278 **Surfaces** with a **lustrous** mirror-like reflection **indicate** a high quality pearl.
品質好的珍珠，表面會有像鏡子般反射的光澤。
surface 名 表面 lustrous 形 有光澤的 indicate 動 表明

1279 These are the finest natural pearls in the world.
這些珍珠是世界上品質最好的天然珍珠。

1280 Here comes another pearl brooch in a different color.
這裡有別款顏色的珍珠胸針。

1281 The white pearl can **complement** most of your **wardrobe**.
白色的珍珠和大部分的衣服都很搭。
complement 動 補足　wardrobe 名 全部服裝

1282 A pink pearl will **flatter** your skin.
粉紅色的珍珠能襯托您的膚色。flatter 動 顯得更吸引人

1283 A suitable necklace can draw attention to your beautiful neckline.
合適的項鍊能讓人一眼就注意到你漂亮的頸部線條。

1284 Is the **chain adjustable**?
鍊子的長度可以調整嗎？chain 名 鍊條　adjustable 形 可調整的

1285 Long necklaces look nice on women with **broad** shoulders.
肩膀寬的女生戴長項鍊會很好看。broad 形 寬的

1286 The **knotted** necklace looks very **feminine**.
這條蝴蝶結項鍊看起來很有女人味。
knotted 形 打結的　feminine 形 女性的

1287 Wearing a **diamond** necklace is the perfect way to **accent** a V-neck dress.
鑽石項鍊和 V 領洋裝很搭，配在一起非常好看。
diamond 名 鑽石　accent 動 強調；著重

1288 The simple **silver** chain with a **butterfly pendant** looks cute.
這條簡單的銀鍊配蝴蝶樣式的墜子很可愛。
silver 形 銀的　butterfly 名 蝴蝶　pendant 名 垂飾

1289 Face shape should be **considered** when **selecting** jewelry.
挑珠寶時要考慮臉型。consider 動 考慮　select 動 挑選

1290 The gold necklace is flattering on both square and **rectangular** faces.
方形或長方形臉的人帶這條金項鍊會很好看。

rectangular 形 長方形的

1291 I only wear **earrings** on special **occasions**.
有特別的場合我才會戴耳環。earring 名 耳環 occasion 名 場合

1292 I like wearing earrings. I even have a **jewelry box** for my **collection**.
我喜歡戴耳環，我還有一個專門放收藏品的珠寶盒呢！
jewelry box 片 珠寶盒 collection 名 收藏品

1293 Should I choose clip-on earrings or pierced ones?
我應該選夾式耳環還是穿洞式耳環呢？

1294 I think clip-on earrings are better. Everyone can wear them.
我覺得選夾式耳環比較好，因為所有人都能戴。

1295 I don't want to have my ears **pierced**.
我不想穿耳洞。pierce 動 穿孔

1296 I can only choose **clip-on** earrings.
我只能選擇夾式耳環。clip-on 形 (用夾子)夾住的

1297 We offer free ear-piercing **service**.
我們免費提供穿耳洞的服務。service 名 服務

1298 I've had problems with piercings. I get **infections** sometimes.
我沒辦法穿耳洞，因為有時候會感染。infection 名 傳染病

1299 Clip-on earrings **styles** are limited.
夾式耳環的款式不多。style 名 種類；樣式

1300 Wedding accessories include necklaces, **bracelets** and earrings.
婚禮的首飾配件包含項鍊、手環和耳環。bracelet 名 手環

1301 I'd like to take a look at that diamond ring.
我想看一下那只鑽戒。

1302 We are looking for some thing in the way of a

wedding ring.
我們想找結婚戒指。

1303 Do you prefer **platinum** rings or gold rings?
你們比較喜歡白金戒指還是黃金戒指？ platinum 名 白金

1304 I like platinum rings with diamonds on them.
我喜歡有鑲鑽的白金戒指。

1305 Platinum is a better **value** than gold.
白金的價值比黃金高。 value 名 價值

1306 There are a lot of new patterns for diamond rings you can choose from.
有很多新款式的鑽石戒指可以挑選。

1307 I want to buy a diamond over half a **carat** in size.
我想要買五十分以上的鑽石。 carat 名 克拉

1308 Do you know how to **distinguish** a **genuine** diamond?
你知道要怎麼辨別鑽石的真偽嗎？
distinguish 動 辨別；區別 genuine 形 真的

1309 Does it come with a certificate from the GIA?
這顆鑽石有附 GIA 的寶石鑑定證書嗎？

1310 A diamond's value is based on the 4 Cs.
鑽石的價值是依 4C 去評斷的。

1311 What do the 4 Cs **stand for**?
4C 是什麼意思？ stand for 片 代表

1312 The 4 Cs are a diamond's color, cut, **clarity**, and carat.
4C 代表鑽石的顏色、切工、純度及克拉。 clarity 名 清澈

1313 White pearls always complement white **wedding gowns**.
白色的珍珠和純白的婚紗是絕配。 wedding gown 片 婚紗

1314 The larger the pearl, the more **valuable** the jewelry is.
珍珠的尺寸愈大，首飾的價值就愈高。 valuable 形 貴重的

1315 If I were you, I would pick pearl wedding jewelry.
如果我是你，我會選珍珠的結婚飾品。

1316 Pearl jewelry is very popular among women of all ages.
所有年齡的女人都喜歡珍珠首飾。

1317 **Simplicity** is the **main** key to looking elegant.
簡單的設計比較典雅。 simplicity 名 簡樸 main 形 主要的

1318 The **string** of pearls looks gorgeous on you.
這條珍珠項鍊你戴起來美極了。 string 名 串線

1319 Do you have any Mother's Day **promotions** going on?
現在有什麼母親節的促銷活動嗎？ promotion 名 促銷

1320 Can you **lower** the price if I buy two sets?
如果我買兩組，可以算便宜一點嗎？ lower 動 減低

1321 If you buy two gift sets, I can give you an extra ten **percent** off.
如果買兩套禮盒組，可以再打九折。 percent 名 百分比

1322 Besides that, you can get this **crystal** brooch for free.
另外，這個水晶別針也免費贈送。 crystal 形 水晶的

1323 It is on sale for up to 50% off.
最高的折扣可到五折。

1324 The **price** is only for you.
這種低價，我只給你喔！ price 名 價格

1325 OK! It's a **deal**!
好吧！就這樣說定，成交！ deal 名 交易

1326 You've really got **unique taste** and great personal qualities.
您的眼光和品味真好。 unique 形 獨特的 taste 名 品味

1327 I think I'll get it. Could you put it in a gift box?
我要買這個，可以幫我用禮盒裝嗎？

1328 Sure! I'll put the **necklace** in a pink gift box.
沒問題！我會把項鍊用粉紅色禮盒裝起來。 necklace 名 項鍊

1329 The **sportswear** department is on the seventh floor.
運動休閒服飾在七樓。 sportswear 名 運動服；休閒服飾

1330 Excuse me. Where can I find women's wear?
不好意思，請問女裝部在哪裡？

1331 Are you **looking for** anything **particular**?
您在找什麼商品嗎？ look for 片 尋找 particular 形 特定的

1332 No, thanks. I'm just looking.
沒關係，我只是隨便看看。

1333 I love the **striped** shirt in the **window**.
我很喜歡櫥窗裡的那件條紋襯衫。
striped 形 條紋的 window 名 櫥窗

1334 I'm looking for something **in season**.
我正在找當季商品。 in season 片 當季的

1335 I've already found a coat that was **marked down** 30%.
我已經看上一件打七折的外套。 mark down 片 減價

1336 Is the **jacket** made of real **leather**?
這件夾克是真皮的嗎？ jacket 名 外套 leather 名 皮革

1337 Do you have some **warm** and light **sweaters**?
你們有保暖、質地又輕的毛衣嗎？
warm 形 溫暖的 sweater 名 毛衣

1338 That **acrylic** sweater is cheaper, but the **wool** one is much warmer.
那件壓克力纖維的毛衣比較便宜，不過羊毛的這件比較暖和。
acrylic 形 壓克力的　wool 名 羊毛

1339 Great! It's **exactly** what I want.
太棒了！這正是我想要的。exactly 副 恰好地

1340 I really like it, but I have no idea how it will look on me.
我真的很喜歡這件，但我不知道穿起來好不好看。

1341 I think this polo shirt **suits** you well.
我覺得這件 polo 衫很適合你。suit 動 適合

1342 It's nice, but I don't know what I'd wear it with.
是很好看沒錯，但我不知道要穿什麼來搭。

1343 The **floral** top and the boot-cut jeans match perfectly.
這件碎花上衣和靴型牛仔褲的搭配真是完美。floral 形 花的

1344 You can wear it **almost** on every occasion.
不管是什麼場合，幾乎都能穿。almost 副 幾乎

1345 You can try this **pair** of jeans if you don't like a too feminine style. It is **unisex**.
如果你不喜歡太女性化的款式，試試這條牛仔褲吧，它的設計很中性。pair 名 一對　unisex 形 不分男女的

1346 I thought the jeans were on sale. Aren't they?
牛仔褲不是有特價嗎？

1347 I'm sorry, Miss. The discount applies only to those **off-season** jeans.
小姐，很抱歉，過季的牛仔褲才有打折。off-season 形 過季的

1348 Is there any **discount**?
有沒有什麼折扣？discount 名 折扣

1349 Sorry, these are all **clearance items**.

抱歉，這些都是清倉商品了。clearance 名 清除　item 名 項目

1350 I'm looking for a **suit** for **business** occasions.
我想找上班穿的套裝。suit 名 套裝　business 名 職業

1351 Do you want a suit-dress or a **pantsuit**?
您想要找裙裝還是褲裝呢？pantsuit 名 女式褲裝

1352 I prefer a suit-dress in white or **beige**.
我想找白色或米色的裙裝。beige 形 米色的

1353 What about this one? It's **impeccably** cut.
這件如何？它的剪裁很合身。impeccably 副 無可挑剔地

1354 It's designed by a Japanese **designer**.
這件是由一位日本設計師所設計的。designer 名 設計師

1355 These are all made of natural materials, not **synthetic**.
這些都是天然材質製成的，不是合成纖維。synthetic 形 合成的

1356 It looks nice. Do you have any **blouses** to go with it?
看起來不錯，有襯衫可以搭配嗎？blouse 名 女襯衫

1357 Try this! The **solid** blue blouse goes nicely with the suit-dress.
試試這款！這件素色的藍襯衫和套裝很搭。solid 形 素色的

1358 Does it come in **plaid**?
這件有格子圖案的嗎？plaid 名 格子圖案

1359 The floral **wraparound** skirt suits you. Try it on!
這件印花的一片裙很適合你，試穿看看吧！wraparound 形 捲上的

1360 I'd like to check out this **pencil skirt**, too.
我也想看一下這件窄裙。pencil skirt 片 鉛筆裙(及膝/過膝的窄裙)

1361 You have a very good taste, Ms. It's **in style**.
小姐，您的品味很不錯呢，這個現正流行。in style 片 時髦地

1362 I think this kind of skirt will stay in **fashion** for a few more years.
我想這種款式的裙子還會再流行好幾年。 fashion 名 時尚

1363 **Teal blue** is still fashionable this season, and many **stars** wear it.
本季還是很流行藍綠色，很多明星都穿藍綠色的衣服。
teal blue 片 藍綠色 star 名 明星

1364 I need a **dress** for a wedding party.
我想找件婚禮能穿的洋裝。 dress 名 洋裝

1365 The **chiffon** dress looks very elegant. Is it **lined**?
這件雪紡洋裝看起來很優雅，它有內襯嗎？
chiffon 形 雪紡綢的 lined 形 有襯裡的

1366 Yes, it has a **silk lining**.
有的，是絲質內襯。 silk 形 絲質的 lining 名 內襯

1367 The dress will make you look tall and **slim**.
這件洋裝會讓您看起來又高又瘦。 slim 形 苗條的

1368 I feel like the dress was made for you.
這件洋裝簡直像是為您量身訂做的。

1369 Does it come in any other **colors**?
有沒有別的顏色可選？ color 名 顏色

1370 Is this the only color?
它只有這個顏色嗎？

1371 Do you have the **shorts** in pink?
這款短褲有粉紅色的嗎？ shorts 名 短褲

1372 I am sorry, but that color is **out of stock**.
很抱歉，那個顏色缺貨。 out of stock 片 無庫存

1373 Let me get you the blue one. You'll look great in blue.
我拿藍色的過來，藍色會很適合您的。

1374 I can place an **order** for you. Please fill out this form.
我可以幫您調貨，請填這張單子。 order 名 訂購

1375 You need to leave a 10% **deposit**.
您必須先付百分之十的訂金。 deposit 名 訂金

1376 Excuse me. Where's the **fitting room**?
不好意思，請問試衣間在哪裡？ fitting room 片 試衣間

1377 Can I try the **turtleneck** on?
我可以試穿這件高領衫嗎？ turtleneck 名 高領衫

1378 You can bring a **maximum** of six pieces in the dressing room.
您最多可以帶六件進去試穿。 maximum 名 最大量

1379 Sorry, all the rooms are **occupied**. I'll let you know when one **opens up**.
抱歉，試衣間客滿了，有人出來我再通知您。
occupied 形 在使用的 open up 片 開門

1380 The three-quarter **sleeve** blouse is too **tight**.
這件七分袖襯衫太小了。 sleeve 名 袖子 tight 形 緊的

1381 Do you have a larger size?
你們有大一點的尺寸嗎？

1382 I am sorry, but all the larger-size blouses are **sold out**.
抱歉，所有大尺寸的襯衫都賣完了。 sold out 片 銷售一空的

1383 What size do you **usually** wear?
您平常都穿什麼尺碼的衣服呢？ usually 副 通常

1384 I usually wear a **medium**.
我通常都穿 M 號的尺寸。 medium 名 中間

1385 Could you find this in a size 4, please?
麻煩你幫我找這件的四號。

1386 Do you know your **chest measurement**?
您知道您的胸圍嗎？ chest 名 胸 measurement 名 尺寸

1387 Would you like me to take your measurements?
需要我幫您量尺寸嗎？

1388 It's a little tight around the **hips**.
臀部的地方有點緊。 hip 名 臀部；髖部

1389 It doesn't **fit**. Do you do **alterations**?
不太合身，你們能幫忙修改嗎？ fit 動 合身 alteration 名 修改

1390 Could you make it **knee-length**?
你可以把長度改到膝蓋這裡嗎？ knee-length 形 長及膝蓋的

1391 It's too **loose**. I'd like the **waist** altered to a smaller size.
穿起來太鬆了，我想把腰圍改小一點。 loose 形 鬆的 waist 名 腰

1392 I'm sorry, but the T-shirt is on sale, and we don't offer alteration service.
抱歉，這件 T 恤是特價品，我們不提供修改服務。

1393 It's on sale. You have to pay for alterations, though, Madam.
女士，因為這件是特價品，所以您必須支付修改的費用。

1394 Is this **cardigan machine washable**?
這件羊毛衫能用洗衣機洗嗎？
cardigan 名 羊毛衫 machine 名 機器 washable 形 可洗的

1395 The T-shirts and pants are machine washable.
T 恤和長褲是可以用洗衣機洗的。

1396 This business suit should be **dry-cleaned**.
這套西裝必須乾洗。 dry-clean 動 乾洗

1397 I'd suggest you wash it by hand.
我會建議您用手洗。

1398 **Make sure** you use cold water while washing it.

洗滌時，請確定您用的是冷水。 make sure 片 確定

1399 Do not hang it on a **hanger**.
收納時不要掛在衣架上。 hanger 名 衣架

1400 Be sure to **lay** the cardigan flat.
羊毛衫請務必平放。 lay 動 放；擱

1401 No worries. The coat is **preshrunk**.
不用擔心，這件大衣已經做過防縮水的處理了。
preshrunk 形 防縮水的

1402 Are you ready to proceed to the **checkout**?
您準備要結帳了嗎？ checkout 名 結帳櫃台

1403 Will these be all for you today?
今天就買這些嗎？

1404 I need to buy some accessories, too. Can I leave these clothes at the counter?
我還想買一些配件，能先把衣服放在櫃台嗎？

1405 We're offering 25% off on all purchases over NT$4,000 today.
今天購物滿四千元可享七五折優惠。

1406 No, I won't buy that **maxi coat**. It's over my budget.
那件風衣就算了，它超出我的預算。 maxi coat 片 風衣；大衣

1407 Your total is NT$3,088. Cash or credit card?
您購買的總金額是新台幣三千零八十八元，請問要付現還是刷卡？

1408 Would you like the receipt in the bag?
收據要放在袋子裡嗎？

1409 You can return it within a month if it has a **tear** or **defect**.
一個月之內若發現衣服有破損或瑕疵，可以退貨。
tear 名 撕裂處 defect 名 瑕疵

1410 The **zipper** seems broken.
這個拉鍊好像壞了。 zipper 名 拉鍊

1411 Is there another blouse like this? The sleeve is **unraveling**.
有別款類似的襯衫嗎？這件的袖子脫線了。 unravel 動 解開

1412 There's a **button** missing.
有顆鈕扣掉了。 button 名 鈕扣

1413 Tell me the truth. Do I look strange in those baggy pants?
你老實說，那幾條垮褲我穿起來是不是很奇怪？

1414 Does the **sundress** look good on me?
這件背心裙我穿起來好看嗎？ sundress 名 背心裙

1415 Sherry is surely good at **picking out** clothing. It looks **fabulous** on you.
雪莉果然很會挑衣服，你穿起來真好看。
pick out 片 挑選 fabulous 形 (口)極好的

1416 Really? Don't you think the skirt makes my hips look big?
是嗎？你不覺得這件裙子讓我的臀部看起來很大嗎？

1417 Wow! What a great **haul**!
哇！買那麼多東西喔！ haul 名 (口)一次獲得的量

1418 I have to **confess** that I'm a real **shopaholic**.
我必須坦承我是個購物狂。
confess 動 承認 shopaholic 名 購物狂

1419 However, I don't think it's a **waste**.
不過，我不覺得自己是在浪費錢。 waste 名 浪費

1420 I would say that I am a smart **shopper**.
我反而覺得我是個聰明的買家。 shopper 名 購物者

1421 Don't you think that all the items I bought are good?

你不覺得我買的東西都很不錯嗎？

1422 Actually, if you spend enough money, you can get some good **freebies**.
事實上，如果你花的錢夠多，就能得到很不錯的贈品。
freebie 名 (俚)免費贈品

1423 Ha! Another great excuse for being a shopaholic!
哈！又是另一個成為購物狂的絕妙藉口！

1424 A woman is always **in need of** a new piece of clothing.
女人的衣櫃總是少一件衣服。 in need of 片 需要

1425 Let's head to the **shoe** department.
我們去鞋子的部門逛逛吧。 shoe 名 鞋子

1426 Do you have a particular brand in mind?
你有沒有特別要找什麼品牌？

1427 I am not a **brand-name enthusiast**.
我沒有特別喜歡哪一個品牌。
brand-name 名 商標 enthusiast 名 熱衷者

1428 I hope I can find a nice pair of **high heels**.
我希望我可以找到一雙好看的高跟鞋。 high heels 片 高跟鞋

1429 Do you want **pumps** or **sandals**?
您要找包鞋還是涼鞋呢？ pump 名 淺口高跟鞋 sandal 名 涼鞋

1430 Do you prefer round toe or **square** toe?
你喜歡圓頭的還是方頭的？ square 形 正方形的

1431 I want to **check out** both.
我兩種都想看一下。 check out 片 (口)看看；試試

1432 Are there any must-buys this **season**?
有沒有這一季必敗的鞋款？ season 名 季；季節

1433 **Peep** toe pumps are all the **rage** this summer.
今年夏天超流行魚口鞋的。 peep 動 使出現 rage 名 風靡一時之物

1434 The pointed toe shoes are **classic**, so you can always wear them.
這雙尖頭鞋是經典款，不會退流行。 classic 形 經典的

1435 I'm afraid that my feet are too **wide** to wear them.
我怕我的腳太寬，可能穿不了。 wide 形 寬的

1436 If you have wide feet, you should get a size larger.
如果你的腳掌比較寬，建議買大一號的尺寸。

1437 I am looking for a pair of pretty and elegant pointed toe high heels.
我想找一雙漂亮又優雅的尖頭高跟鞋。

1438 The pair of gold evening sandals goes with any dress perfectly.
這雙金色的晚宴涼鞋很百搭，配任何洋裝都好看。

1439 These will definitely make you **sparkle** all night long.
這雙鞋肯定會讓你整晚都美艷動人。 sparkle 動 使閃耀

1440 Mary Jane pumps are elegant and can go with any **outfit**.
瑪莉珍鞋很優雅，也很好搭配衣服。 outfit 名 全套服裝

1441 Classic Mary Jane round toe shoes have **instep straps**.
典型的瑪莉珍鞋是圓頭，腳背上有帶子的。
instep 名 腳背 strap 名 帶子

1442 How about this pair of shoes?
這雙鞋怎麼樣？

1443 I don't like its side **buckle**.
我不喜歡它旁邊的扣環。 buckle 名 扣環

1444 I love **boots**, but this pair of high heels also looks gorgeous. It's really a hard choice.
我喜歡靴子，但這雙高跟鞋看起來好美，實在很難取捨。

boot 名 靴子

1445 I am a bit **hesitant** because the shoes might be a bit **narrow**.
這雙鞋對我來說可能會有點窄，所以我還在考慮。
hesitant 形 躊躇的 narrow 形 窄的

1446 Why don't you try them on and walk around in them?
你怎麼不先試穿，走一走再決定？

1447 What size of shoes do you wear?
請問您都穿幾號的鞋呢？

1448 My shoe size is **typically** 7, but sometimes 6.5.
基本上穿七號，有時會穿到六號半。 typically 副 典型地

1449 The shoes are a bit loose.
這雙鞋有點大，穿起來鬆鬆的。

1450 Do you have anything smaller?
有小一點的尺寸嗎？

1451 OK. Let me get a bigger size for you.
沒問題，我去拿大一號的給你。

1452 This pair of shoes is just my size.
這雙鞋我穿起來剛剛好。

1453 I couldn't go any higher than that since I am not comfortable in heels.
我不愛穿有跟的鞋子，所以比那個還高跟的鞋我穿不了。

1454 The height is perfect and the bottoms of the shoes are not **slippery**.
這雙鞋的高度剛好，鞋底也不會滑。 slippery 形 容易滑的

1455 The height is great but the design is what I love the most.
高度剛好適合，不過我最愛的是它的設計。

1456 The price is **reasonable**, so that's a **plus**.
價錢公道這點更棒。reasonable 形 價錢公道的 plus 名 好處

1457 These gorgeous silver **flats** match many of my outfits.
這雙漂亮的銀色平底鞋搭配我大部分的服裝都很好看。
flat 名 平底鞋

1458 The sandals are great to wear with jeans.
這雙涼鞋配牛仔褲很好看。

1459 My sister loves **leopard** print high heels.
我姐姐很喜歡豹紋的高跟鞋。leopard 名 美洲豹

1460 I love its **man-made sole**.
我喜歡它手工製作的鞋底。
man-made 形 人工的 sole 名 鞋底；襪底

1461 I am looking for a pair of **loafers** for my husband.
我在幫我先生找一雙休閒鞋。loafer 名 平底休閒鞋

1462 Does he prefer loafers with straps or not?
他喜歡有鞋帶的，還是沒有鞋帶的休閒鞋？

1463 He prefers **plain** toe loafers.
他喜歡方頭休閒鞋。plain 形 樸素的；無花紋的

1464 If he is fashion-**conscious**, I recommend this pair. It is the latest.
如果他對流行趨勢很敏銳的話，我推薦這雙，這是我們最新的鞋款。conscious 形 意識到的

1465 OK. I want this pair. Can you **take off** the price **tag**?
那我要買這雙，你可以幫我拿掉價格標籤嗎？
take off 片 脫去 tag 名 標籤

1466 It's a good brand, and it's on sale at a reasonable price.
這個牌子很有名，而且現正特價中，很划算。

1467 How much are they? Is the price shown on the tag?
這雙多少錢？是標籤上的價格嗎？

1468 The **regular** price is NT$3,600, but now there is a 30% discount.
定價三千六，但現在有七折的優惠。 regular 形 正式的

1469 I'd like to use my **gift certificate**.
我要用禮券付帳。 gift certificate 片 禮券

1470 Do you want me to put them in a **box**?
請問您需要用鞋盒裝起來嗎？ box 名 盒子；箱子

1471 Do I need to wear **socks** with my flats?
我穿平底鞋的時候，要穿襪子嗎？ sock 名 襪子

1472 It depends on your taste. If you ask me, I would choose low cut socks.
其實都可以，如果是我的話，會穿短襪。

1473 I found the **quality** was not what I had hoped for.
我發現這品質跟我預期的有落差。 quality 名 品質

1474 The sole is slippery, and I did not find them **comfortable**.
鞋底會滑，而且穿起來又不舒服。 comfortable 形 舒適的

1475 I want to **return** this pair of shoes. There is a **hole** in the sole.
這雙鞋的鞋底破洞了，我要退貨。 return 動 退回 hole 名 洞

1476 Can I get a new pair?
我可以換雙新的嗎？

1477 We can **repair** the **entire** sole for you.
我們可以幫您換鞋底。 repair 動 修理 entire 形 全部的

1478 I need to change the heels. How long will it take?
我要換鞋跟，修這個需要多久時間呢？

日常雜貨哪裡逛

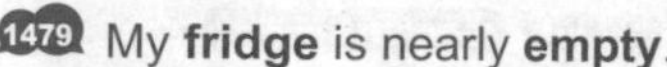

1479 My **fridge** is nearly **empty**.
我的冰箱幾乎空無一物了。fridge 名 (口)冰箱 empty 形 空的

1480 We need to go **grocery** shopping.
我們得去買菜了。grocery 名 食品雜貨

1481 Where are you going? I believe the market is closed today.
你要去哪裡買？超市今天不是沒開嗎？

1482 There's a new grocery store that has just **opened**.
有一家新開的雜貨店。open 動 使開張

1483 The supermarket is having a **grand** opening sale this weekend.
那間超市這個週末有舉辦開幕特賣。grand 形 盛大的

1484 How often do you go grocery shopping?
你多久去採買一次呢？

1485 My husband and I usually go shopping once a week.
我丈夫和我通常一週會去採買一次。

1486 My mother buys **produce** and meat at a **traditional** market.
我媽媽都在傳統市場買農產品和肉品。
produce 名 農產品 traditional 形 傳統的

1487 She says that the food in a traditional market is **fresh** and cheap.
她說傳統菜市場的菜既新鮮又便宜。fresh 形 新鮮的

1488 Also, the price is **negotiable**. That's my favorite part.
而且，還可以殺價，這是傳統市場最吸引我的地方。
negotiable 形 可協商的

1489 She usually gets free **green onions** or chili peppers when buying other items.
她採買時經常能拿到店家送的蔥或辣椒。green onion 片 蔥

1490 I don't like shopping at traditional markets because of the **crowds**.
我不喜歡上傳統市場，因為人擠人太可怕了。crowd 名 人群

1491 I like going to the **farmer's** market very much.
我很喜歡去逛農貿市場。farmer 名 農夫

1492 The one I usually go to is a **chain** grocery store.
我常去的那家是連鎖超市。chain 名 連鎖店

1493 It **offers** a wide variety of food and **household** items.
那裡有賣各式各樣的食物和日用品。
offer 動 提供　household 形 家用的；家庭的

1494 I collect grocery store **coupons**.
我會收集超市的折價券。coupon 名 折價券

1495 Using coupons is a great way to save money.
使用折價券是省錢的好方法。

1496 I like going shopping at a supermarket because **parking** is easy.
我喜歡去超市購物，因為停車很方便。park 動 停車

1497 I like the convenient shopping hours that **extend** far into the evening.
我喜歡超市，它營業到很晚，買東西很方便。extend 動 延長

1498 There's a small market just near my house.
我家附近有一間小型市場。

1499 The shopkeeper is nice and gives me free samples at times.
老闆人很好，常常給我免費的試用品。

1500 Do you have your shopping **list** with you?
你有帶購物清單嗎？ list 名 清單

1501 I don't need a shopping list because I always know what I need.
我不需要列清單，因為要買的東西都在我的腦海裡。

1502 Is a shopping **basket enough**?
一個購物籃夠裝嗎？ basket 名 籃子 enough 形 足夠的

1503 I think we'll buy a lot. Let me get a shopping **cart** first.
我們可能會買很多，我先去拿個購物推車。 cart 名 手推車

1504 There are several departments **inside** a supermarket.
超市裡分很多部門。 inside 介 在…的裡面

1505 They include the meat, fresh produce, **dairy**, and **canned** food departments.
裡面有肉品、生鮮、乳製品和罐頭食品區。
dairy 形 乳品的 canned 形 罐頭的

1506 The produce department offers a great variety of fruits and **vegetables**.
生鮮部門有各式各樣的蔬菜和水果。 vegetable 名 蔬菜

1507 Let's make some **mashed potatoes**!
我們來做馬鈴薯泥吧！ mash 動 把…搗成糊狀 potato 名 馬鈴薯

1508 Do you like **carrots** and **cucumbers** in your salad?
你的沙拉要放胡蘿蔔和小黃瓜嗎？
carrot 名 胡蘿蔔 cucumber 名 小黃瓜

1509 Cucumbers are OK for me, but not carrots.
小黃瓜可以，但不要加胡蘿蔔。

1510 Excuse me. Which **aisle** can I find the salad **dressing** in?
請問沙拉醬放在哪裡？aisle 名 走道 dressing 名 調料

1511 There is a salad **bar** right next to the produce department.
生鮮部門旁邊有一個沙拉吧。bar 名 酒吧；櫃台

1512 Let me put this head of cabbage into the shopping cart.
我先把這顆高麗菜放到購物車裡。

1513 These tomatoes and **beans** look beautiful.
這些蕃茄和豆子看起來很漂亮。bean 名 豆子

1514 How much are the **tomatoes**?
蕃茄怎麼賣？tomato 名 番茄

1515 Six for NT$60. They are really fresh and cheap.
很便宜，六顆六十元，而且它們都很新鮮。

1516 Tomatoes in that basket are much more **expensive**. Why?
那個籃子裡的番茄貴很多，為什麼？expensive 形 昂貴的

1517 Those are **organic**.
那些是有機的。organic 形 有機的

1518 The green **grapes** are on sale; should we get a **bunch**?
綠葡萄有特價，要買一串嗎？grape 名 葡萄 bunch 名 串；束

1519 I don't think so. The grapes don't look so good.
不要好了，那些葡萄的品質看起來不怎麼樣。

1520 The **skins** of the grapes look **wrinkly**.
葡萄皮看起來皺皺的。skin 名 水果皮 wrinkly 形 有皺紋的

1521 Why don't we buy a couple **slices** of **ham** for breakfast?

買幾片火腿當早餐吧！ slice 名 薄片 ham 名 火腿

1522 Ham is fine, but I prefer **bacon** or **sausage**.
火腿是不錯，但我更喜歡培根或香腸。
bacon 名 燻豬肉 sausage 名 香腸

1523 **Remind** me to get two **loaves** of bread before heading to the checkout.
提醒我結帳前要拿兩條麵包。 remind 動 提醒 loaf 名 一條麵包

1524 I also have to buy a **jar** of **pineapple** jam.
我還要買一瓶鳳梨果醬。 jar 名 寬口瓶 pineapple 名 鳳梨

1525 Let me show off my **secret** dish, Japanese pork and potato stew.
讓我秀一下我的私房菜—日式馬鈴薯燉肉。 secret 形 祕密的

1526 To make a pork **stew**, I need some **onions**.
要做燉肉的話，我還需要洋蔥。 stew 名 燉肉；燜菜 onion 名 洋蔥

1527 **Soy sauce** and **vinegar** are on my shopping list.
我的購物清單上有醬油和醋。 soy sauce 片 醬油 vinegar 名 醋

1528 I'll boil some broccoli and **cauliflower** as side dishes.
我會再燙一些青花菜和花椰菜當作配菜。 cauliflower 名 (白)花椰菜

1529 We can also stir-fry beef with **broccoli**.
我們也可以做青花菜炒牛肉。 broccoli 名 青花菜；綠花椰菜

1530 I want some steak and **veal cutlets**, please.
麻煩你，我想要買一些牛排和牛肉片。
veal 名 小牛肉 cutlet 名 肉片

1531 I also need three **pounds** of ground beef.
還有，再加三磅牛絞肉。 pound 名 (重量單位)磅

1532 We can buy some chicken **thighs**. They'll taste good if we roast them.
我們可以買一些雞腿，烤一烤會很好吃。 thigh 名 (鳥的)腿部

1533 The **salmon** steak looks very fresh, I will get some.
鮭魚排看起來很新鮮，我要買一些。 salmon 名 鮭魚

1534 Get some shrimp and **scallops**. I want to make seafood pasta.
買點蝦子和干貝吧，我想煮海鮮義大利麵。 scallop 名 扇貝

1535 Could you get the shrimp weighed?
可以幫我秤一下這些蝦子嗎？

1536 I need two jars of pasta sauce and some canned soup.
我需要兩罐義大利麵醬和一些罐裝湯。

1537 All the **pasta** sauces are sold out.
所有的義大利麵醬都缺貨。 pasta 名 義大利麵

1538 When are you going to buy **supplies** again?
什麼時候會補貨呢？ supply 名 庫存(貨)

1539 We've already **placed** an **emergency** order.
我們已經下了緊急訂單。
place 動 開出(訂單) emergency 名 緊急情況

1540 We believe we can fill the **shelves** with goods soon.
相信很快就能補貨了。 shelf 名 架子；擱板

1541 Should we get some **frozen** food?
我們要買冷凍食品嗎？ frozen 形 冰凍的

1542 We'd better **stock up** on some frozen foods in our freezer.
我們最好在冰庫備存一些冷凍食品。 stock up 片 儲備食物

1543 I heard that a **typhoon** is coming this **weekend**.
我聽說這個週末會有颱風。 typhoon 名 颱風 weekend 名 週末

1544 What do we need for **baking** a cake?

要做蛋糕的話，需要哪些東西呢？ bake 動 烘；烤

1545 The baking **section** is in aisle four.
烘培用品都放在第四走道。 section 名 區域

1546 You can find all the baking products there.
你可以在那邊找到所有烘培會用到的食材及工具。

1547 Do you want unsalted butter or salted butter?
你要無鹽奶油還是含鹽奶油？

1548 The low-fat milk is on sale! Do you want to get a **carton**?
低脂牛奶在特價耶！要不要買一瓶？ carton 名 紙盒

1549 Let me check the **expiration** date first.
我先看一下保存期限。 expiration 名 期滿；終結

1550 Wow! The milk will expire in two days. No wonder it's on sale.
哇！這牛奶再兩天就過期了，難怪要打折。

1551 Don't forget to get two cartons of **ice cream**.
別忘了買兩盒冰淇淋。 ice cream 名 冰淇淋

1552 I can't decide which flavor to buy.
我無法決定要買哪一種口味。

1553 There're some free samples. Let's try some.
那邊有試吃品，我們去嚐嚐吧。

1554 Let's get the safest flavors, **vanilla** and chocolate.
那我們買最萬無一失的口味—香草和巧克力。 vanilla 名 香草

1555 Look at the paper **towels**! Buy one get one free.
你看！紙巾有買一送一的優惠耶。 towel 名 毛巾；紙巾

1556 OK. Let's get four **rolls**.
好，那我們買四捲。 roll 名 (一)捲

1557 Where can I get **aluminum foil** and **plastic wrap**?
請問鋁箔紙和保鮮膜放在哪裡呢？
aluminum foil 片 鋁箔紙 plastic wrap 片 保鮮膜

1558 The aluminum foil is on the first shelf in aisle six.
鋁箔紙在六號走道的第一個架子上。

1559 What else do we need to buy?
我們還需要買些什麼嗎？

1560 I think we're done with shopping.
該買的應該都買齊了。

1561 Let's move to the **cashier's** desk.
我們去結帳吧。cashier 名 出納員

1562 I grabbed some chewing gum and **peppermint** when waiting in line.
在排隊等結帳時，我拿了幾條口香糖和薄荷糖。
peppermint 名 薄荷糖

1563 Look at the line!
天啊，大排長龍耶！

1564 Maybe we should go to the self-checkout counter.
我們也許應該去自動結帳櫃台結帳。

1565 I forgot to get a **tube** of **toothpaste**.
我忘了拿牙膏。tube 名 軟管 toothpaste 名 牙膏

1566 I'll wait in line and you can run to get the toothpaste.
我先排隊，你趕快去拿牙膏。

1567 How much did the **bill** come to?
這樣總共多少錢？bill 名 帳單

1568 It comes to NT$2,815 **in total**.
總共是新台幣二千八一十五元。in total 片 總共

1569 May I use the coupons?
我可以使用折價券嗎？

1570 You can use this coupon, but the other one is expired.
您可以使用這張折價券，但另一張已經過期了。

1571 Do you want to pay by cash or **credit card**?
請問您要付現還是刷卡呢？ credit card 片 信用卡

1572 Credit card, please.
我要刷卡。

1573 Here you go. Please **sign** here.
好了，請在這裡簽名。 sign 動 簽名

1574 Please keep your receipt, and all the items may be **refunded** within seven days.
請收好收據，所有商品在七天內都可以退款。 refund 動 退款

1575 Do you need a **shopping bag**? It costs NT$1.
需要購物袋嗎？一個一塊錢。 shopping bag 片 購物袋

1576 No, we've got our own bag.
不用了，我們有自備袋子。

1577 They're **heavy**. Why do we always buy so much stuff?
好重喔！為什麼我們每次都要買那麼多東西呢？ heavy 形 重的

1578 I enjoy **hanging around** in the bookstore and reading books.
我喜歡在書店閒晃、看書。 hang around 片 閒混

1579 The **bookstore** is my favorite hangout spot.
這家書店是我最喜歡用來打發時間的地方。 bookstore 名 書店

1580 My sister and I love reading. We can spend hours in a bookstore.
我妹妹和我喜愛閱讀，我們能在書店待上好幾個小時。

1581 I dropped by a very special bookstore yesterday.
我昨天順路去了一家很特別的書店。

1582 The bookstore is **roomy** and comfortable.
這家書店不但空間寬敞，又很舒適。 roomy 形 寬敞的

1583 It is **cozy** and full of the smell of coffee.
整間店的感覺很舒服，還飄散著咖啡香。 cozy 形 愜意的

1584 I enjoy jazz music playing in the background in a bookstore.
我喜歡書店播放輕柔的爵士樂，感覺很棒。

1585 Books are **arranged** by **genre**.
書籍依類別擺放。 arrange 動 整理 genre 名 種類

1586 There are **romance** novels, classic literature, **biographies**, and other books.
店裡有愛情小說、經典文學、傳記和其他類型的書籍。
romance 名 愛情小說 biography 名 傳記

1587 Magazines and new books are placed near the **entrance**.
雜誌和新書都放在靠近門口的地方。 entrance 名 入口

1588 I don't like that bookstore because many books are miscategorized.
我不喜歡那家書店，因為很多書都放錯類別了。

1589 The **layout** is **confusing** and changes **constantly**.
書擺得亂七八糟，還常常換位置。
layout 名 陳列 confusing 形 令人困惑的 constantly 副 時常地

1590 **Paperbacks** are usually cheaper than **hardcover** books.
平裝本通常比精裝本便宜。
paperback 名 平裝本 hardcover 形 精裝的

1591 I went to see if my favorite author has **published** anything new.

我去看我喜歡的作者有沒有新作品。 publish 動 出版

1592 Mark Twain is my favorite **author**.
馬克・吐溫是我最喜愛的作家。 author 名 作家

1593 I either go to the language learning section or the **fiction** section.
我不是去語言學習區，就是去小說區逛。 fiction 名 小說

1594 I went to the **bestseller shelf**, but there's nothing good there.
我去看暢銷書排行榜了，但沒看到什麼好書。
bestseller 名 暢銷書 shelf 名 書架

1595 Do you enjoy reading any particular genre?
你有特別喜歡讀的作品類型嗎？

1596 **Mystery** and **detective** novels are my favorite.
懸疑小說和偵探小說是我的最愛。
mystery 名 神祕 detective 名 偵探

1597 I enjoy reading everything except for non-fiction books.
除了非小說類的書籍我不怎麼看以外，其他類型的我都喜歡。

1598 I'm not very **artistic**, but I like to **dabble** sometimes.
我沒什麼藝術美感，但我有時會涉獵一下。
artistic 形 有藝術鑑賞力的 dabble 動 涉獵

1599 Have you read any good books these days?
你最近有讀到什麼不錯的書嗎？

1600 I am reading "Me Before You" now.
我最近正在看《遇見你之前》。

1601 It's the sweetest love story I've ever read.
那是我看過最甜美的愛情故事。

1602 I've read the book **cover to cover** twice.
這本書我從頭到尾讀了兩遍。 cover to cover 片 從頭到尾

1603 Have you read "The Help" written by Kathryn Stockett?
你看過凱瑟琳・史托基特寫的《姊妹》嗎？

1604 I read the Chinese **translation edition**.
我看的是中譯本。translation 名 翻譯 edition 名 版本

1605 I bought the Kindle edition.
我買了電子書的版本。

1606 No, I haven't. But I've seen the movie **adapted** from the novel.
我沒看過書，但我看過那本小說改編的電影。adapt 動 改編

1607 Is that book a great **read**?
那本書好看嗎？read 名 讀物

1608 This is the most wonderful book I've ever read
這是我讀過最棒的一本書了。

1609 The novel has a **complicated plot**.
這本小說的情節複雜。complicated 形 複雜的 plot 名 情節

1610 Several celebrities wrote **prefaces** for the book.
很多名人幫這本書寫序。preface 名 序言

1611 I was **extremely disappointed** after reading it.
我讀過之後，感到十分失望。
extremely 副 極度 disappointed 形 失望的

1612 The new book isn't selling very well.
這本新書賣得不怎麼樣。

1613 The **cover** of the book looks **weird**.
這本書的封面看起來好怪。cover 名 封面 weird 形 怪異的

1614 If you don't know where to spend your vacation, this is the book for you.
如果你不知道要去哪裡度假，這本書很適合你。

1615 The **photography** and printing in the travel book are beautiful.
這本旅遊書上的圖片和印刷都很精美。photography 名 攝影

1616 I enjoy shopping at used bookstores.
我喜歡去二手書店買書。

1617 These **secondhand** books are clean and have new covers.
這些二手書都很乾淨，封面也換新了。secondhand 形 第二手的

1618 I spent hours in a secondhand bookstore looking for **literary treasures**.
我花了好幾個小時在二手書店尋找文學典藏。
literary 形 文學的 treasure 名 貴重物品

1619 The **stationery** shop offers a variety of office supplies.
這家文具店有賣各式各樣的辦公用品。stationery 名 文具

1620 I need a **dozen pencils**.
我需要一打的鉛筆。dozen 名 一打 pencil 名 鉛筆

1621 How much is the tape **dispenser**?
這個膠帶台多少錢？dispenser 名 自動發放機

1622 Post-it notes are good for making **brief** notes.
便利貼很適合用來隨手記事。brief 形 簡略的

1623 I need thirty **staplers** for office use.
我需要三十個辦公室用的釘書機。stapler 名 釘書機

1624 I am looking for drawing tools. Where can I find them?
我想找製圖工具，請問放在哪裡呢？

1625 All the drawing tools and painting **materials** are in the fifth aisle.
所有的繪圖用品都放在第五走道。material 名 工具

1626 I've found lots of **bargain** stuff at the "Back to School" section.
我在開學用品區找到很多便宜的商品。bargain 名 特價商品

1627 The **bookends** are on sale. Buy two, get one free.
這些書擋有特價，買二送一。bookend 名 書擋

炫目的 3C 產品們
Hopping For Electronics

1628 My **laptop** is **broken**.
我的筆電壞了。laptop 名 筆記型電腦 broken 形 損壞的

1629 Do you want to have it **repaired**?
你要送修嗎？repair 動 修理

1630 I am facing the **dilemma** of buying a new PC or repairing my old one.
我不知道該直接買台新的，還是送修舊的。dilemma 名 困境

1631 The cost of repairing may be much more than buying a new one.
修理費用可能會比買台新電腦還貴。

1632 If I were you, I would definitely buy a new, fashionable and light laptop.
如果我是你，我會買台又新又時髦的輕薄筆電。

1633 A 3C store is **definitely** where you should go
你應該到 3C 賣場去。definitely 副 肯定地

1634 You can buy computers and **consumer electronics** there.

那裡有賣電腦以及消費性電子產品。

consumer 名 消費者 electronics 名 電子產品

1635 May I help you with anything?
請問您需要幫忙嗎？

1636 I am looking for a laptop.
我想找台筆記型電腦。

1637 Is there anything you can recommend?
你有特別推薦的機型嗎？

1638 What's your budget for a laptop?
您購買筆記型電腦的預算有多少呢？

1639 I hope the total cost can be **below** NT$25,000.
我希望金額在兩萬五千元以內。below 介 在…以下

1640 What size of laptop are you looking for?
您想找什麼尺寸的筆記型電腦呢？

1641 I want something small and light.
我想找小型又輕便的筆記型電腦。

1642 Is there something slimmer and lighter?
有沒有更薄、更輕的筆電？

1643 The **model** is the slimmest.
這個機型是最薄的了。model 名 型號；樣式

1644 The laptop is easy to **carry**.
這台筆電方便攜帶。carry 動 攜帶

1645 It's worth considering because of its **modern** design, great **portability**, and reasonable price.
這台很值得考慮喔！因為它的設計時尚、攜帶性佳、價錢也很合理。modern 形 時髦的 portability 名 可攜帶性

1646 The LCD **display** is 11 **inches**.
十一吋的液晶顯示器。display 名 顯示 inch 名 英吋

1647 The weight of the laptop is less than 1.5 **kilograms**.
這台筆電的重量不到一點五公斤。 kilogram 名 公斤

1648 The best part is that the battery lasts up to twelve hours.
最棒的是，電池的續航力長達十二個小時。

1649 This new laptop comes in five different colors to choose from.
這台新款的筆電推出了五種不同的顏色可供選擇。

1650 I prefer a larger size **screen**.
我比較喜歡大尺寸的螢幕。 screen 名 螢幕

1651 The big-sized screen creates a **stunning** entertainment experience.
大尺寸螢幕創造出絕佳的娛樂效果。 stunning 形 極漂亮的

1652 You can view documents side-by-side in the wide-screen instead of **scrolling** up and down.
在寬螢幕上，你可以直接並排文件觀看，不需要上上下下地滾動滑鼠滾輪。 scroll 動 捲起

1653 The biggest **drawback** is that it's too big to carry around.
最大的缺點就是尺寸太大，不便攜帶。 drawback 名 缺點

1654 Have you considered buying a **desktop**?
你有考慮買桌上型電腦嗎？ desktop 名 桌上型電腦

1655 What's the **capacity** of the hard **disc**?
這台硬碟的容量有多大？ capacity 名 容量 disc 名 電腦磁碟

1656 The hard drive surely has plenty of **available** space.
這個硬碟的空間絕對夠大。 available 形 有空的

1657 The **memory** is also important when purchasing a computer.

選購電腦時，記憶體容量也是很重要的考量點。
memory 名 記憶體

1658 The more memory in the computer, the more **efficiently** it will run.
記憶體愈大，電腦運作的速度就愈快。efficiently 副 效率高地

1659 The DRAM is **expandable**.
這個記憶體是可以再擴充的。expandable 形 可擴大的

1660 What's the sound card like?
那音效卡呢？是什麼規格？

1661 The **built-in** sound card is **sufficient** for almost all computer users.
電腦內建的音效卡對大部分的電腦使用者而言，綽綽有餘了。
built-in 形 內建的 sufficient 形 足夠的

1662 **Due to** my budget, I am considering building a desktop on my own.
因為預算的關係，我在考慮自己組裝電腦。due to 片 因為

1663 Are you sure? A computer consists of **numerous** components.
你確定嗎？一台電腦的零件很多耶。numerous 形 許多的

1664 I think I can do it if I get all the **components**.
如果買齊零件，應該沒有問題。component 名 零件

1665 I am looking for an **external** DVD writer.
我在找外接式的 DVD 燒錄機。external 形 外部的

1666 Does the **portable** DVD writer connect through a USB connection?
這台外接式 DVD 燒錄機是透過 USB 連接電腦的嗎？
portable 形 便於攜帶的

1667 You bet! Just **plug** the USB **cord** into your laptop.
沒錯！只要把 USB 接頭插到筆電上就行了。

plug 動 接通電源 cord 名 軟線

1668 Where can I buy **blank** DVDs?
哪裡可以買到空白的 DVD 燒錄片呢？ blank 形 無內容的

1669 I saw some last weekend at an electronics store on First Street.
我上週末在第一街的電器店有看到。

1670 Last time I checked, they were having a sale.
我上次看到的時候，正在特價呢。

1671 Should I buy a Mac or a PC computer running Microsoft Windows?
我該買蘋果電腦還是微軟作業系統的電腦呢？

1672 Is the software **compatible** with other operating systems?
這個軟體與其他的作業系統相容嗎？ compatiblo 形 相容的

1673 Does the **software** include Microsoft Office?
軟體有包含 Office 程式嗎？ software 名 軟體

1674 We offer a **trial version**, but it will expire after ninety days.
我們提供試用版，九十天後到期。 trial 形 試用的 version 名 版本

1675 After that, you have to purchase the regular version.
之後，您就要自行購買正式版的軟體。

1676 What type of service do you offer?
你們有提供什麼樣的服務呢？

1677 We offer **onsite** service, meaning a **technician** will come to your place to fix any computer problems.
我們提供到府服務。如果有任何電腦問題，我們會派技術人員到府處理。 onsite 形 現場的 technician 名 技術人員

1678 Does the computer **manufacturer** offer a **warranty**?

電腦廠商有提供保固嗎？
manufacturer 名 製造商 warranty 名 擔保

1679 Does the warranty cover both **hardware** and software?
保固有包含硬體和軟體嗎？ hardware 名 電腦硬體

1680 We provide repairs during the warranty **period**.
在保固期內，我們會提供維修服務。 period 名 期間

1681 How long is the warranty?
保固期有多長呢？

1682 It has a two-year warranty.
有兩年的保固期。

1683 Do you want **extended** warranty service?
您想要加購，以延長保固期嗎？ extended 形 延伸的

1684 After the warranty, you have to repair it at your own **expense**.
保固期過了之後，維修就得自費了。 expense 名 支出

1685 Can I return it for a full refund if I don't like it?
如果我不喜歡這個產品，可以全額退費嗎？

1686 Most store items can be exchanged or refunded with a receipt within thirty days of purchase.
大部分的店內商品在購買後三十天內，可憑收據退換貨。

1687 Not all products are **returnable** at the store.
不是所有的商品都可以退貨。 returnable 形 可返回的

1688 Things like movies, music and video games are not refundable.
像是電影光碟、唱片以及電動遊戲之類的商品，我們不退費。

1689 Computer hardware must be returned with any included software within fourteen days of receipt.
電腦硬體必須在購買後兩週內，連同內附的軟體憑收據辦理退貨。

1690 Computer software cannot be returned if it is **unsealed**.
電腦軟體如經拆封，就不能退貨。 unseal 動 去掉…的封條

1691 I need to buy a new **camera**.
我需要買一台新相機。 camera 名 相機

1692 I'll go with you. I want to **replace** my old digital camera.
我跟你一起去，我想淘汰我那台舊的數位相機。 replace 動 取代

1693 Do you have any **digital** cameras in mind to recommend?
你有沒有特別推薦的數位相機呢？ digital 形 數字的

1694 Sony just released a new **compact** digital camera.
索尼企業最近剛推出一部輕巧型數位相機。 compact 形 小巧的

1695 We can go to the store and try the real camera.
我們可以去店裡看實品。

1696 If you have the budget for it, you can consider a digital single-lens **reflex** camera.
如果你預算夠的話，可以考慮數位單眼相機。 reflex 名 映像

1697 What type of **features** are you looking for?
您想找什麼功能的相機呢？ feature 名 特徵；特色

1698 Is the size important to you?
大小呢？您很在意嗎？

1699 I want a camera with a large LCD display.
我希望找台大螢幕的相機。

1700 What are the features of this camera?
這台相機有什麼特色呢？

1701 How many **megapixels** does this digital camera have?

這台數位相機是幾百萬像素的？ megapixel 名 百萬像素

1702 Is it a wide **angle lens**?
這是廣角鏡頭的嗎？ angle 名 角度 lens 名 鏡頭

1703 How good is the **vibration reduction** function?
這台相機的防手震功能好不好？
vibration 名 振動 reduction 名 減少

1704 The digital camera focuses **automatically**.
這台數位相機是自動對焦的。 automatically 副 自動地

1705 It features an 8x **optical zoom** lens.
它以八倍光學變焦鏡頭為主要特色。
optical 形 光學的 zoom 名 變焦鏡頭

1706 The camera has a 3.5-inch touch screen LCD.
這台相機有三點五吋的觸控式液晶面板。

1707 The digital camera is **waterproof**.
這台數位相機是防水的。 waterproof 形 防水的

1708 The camera offers a soft skin **mode**.
這台相機有美膚模式可用。 mode 名 形式；模式

1709 That's cool! I need to buy one to **smooth out** my wrinkles.
真酷！我需要買一台來消除皺紋。 smooth out 片 消除；修正

1710 Face and smile **recognition function** is another fun feature.
臉部和笑容辨識的功能又是另一項有趣的特色。
recognition 名 認出 function 名 功能；作用

1711 The suggested **retail** price of the new camera is NT$9,900.
這台新相機的建議售價是九千九百元。 retail 形 零售的

1712 It sounds a bit expensive.
聽起來有點貴。

1713 It's a nice camera at that price.
以這麼高品質的相機而言，這個價錢不貴。

1714 You'll get a discount when buying extra memory cards and batteries.
若您加購記憶卡和電池，就能享有折扣。

1715 We offer you free **photographic** classes.
我們提供免費的攝影課程。photographic 形 攝影術的

1716 You can get a free camera case and a memory card.
相機包和記憶卡是附贈的。

1717 Is there any discount?
有折扣嗎？

1718 I am sorry, but it is sold at a **fixed** price.
不好意思，這是不二價。fixed 形 固定的

1719 It's the final price.
這已經是最低的價格，不可能更低了。

1720 Do you have an **installment** plan?
你們有分期付款的專案嗎？installment 名 分期付款

1721 Yes, you can pay in twelve easy monthly installments.
有，您可以分十二個月付款。

1722 I **struggled** between these two cameras.
這兩台相機我不知道要買哪一台才好。struggle 動 掙扎

1723 I just bought a new digital camera, and it works great!
我剛買了一台數位相機，超好用的！

1724 You can find a variety of cell phones and phone **accessories** in the store.
這家店有賣各式各樣的手機和手機配件。accessory 名 周邊產品

1725 I need to buy a screen **protector** to avoid **scratches**.
我得買個螢幕保護貼，以免刮傷螢幕。
protector 名 保護器 scratch 名 抓痕

1726 I don't think we should spend so much money on a **mobile** phone.
我覺得我們不應該花那麼多錢買手機。mobile 形 移動式的

1727 It's a smartphone. It has more functions than earlier models.
這是智慧型手機，功能比以前的手機更多。

1728 Smartphones **combine** mobile phone and PDA functions in one unit.
智慧型手機結合了手機和 PDA 的功能。combine 動 使結合

1729 You can email and **access to** your calendar **via** a smartphone.
你可以經由智慧型手機收發電子郵件、使用行事曆。
access to 片 進入 via 介 透過；憑藉

1730 The cell phone has lots of fun functions.
這款手機有很多好玩的功能。

1731 What's the **button** for?
這個按鍵是做什麼用的？button 名 按鍵

1732 Many cell phone features go **unused**.
很多的手機功能根本就用不到。unused 形 未使用的

Part 3

來到醫院掛號

SEEING A DOCTOR

UNIT 1 常見的感冒發燒
Catching A Cold

1733 Are you all right? You look **pale**.
你還好嗎？你的臉色好蒼白。 pale 形 蒼白的；灰白的

1734 I caught the **flu** from my colleague.
我被同事傳染感冒。 flu 名 流行性感冒

1735 Usually, I don't see a doctor for a cold.
我感冒的時候，大多不看醫生。

1736 But if my **symptoms** continue, I will go see a **doctor**.
不過，如果症狀一直沒有好轉，我就會去看醫生。
symptom 名 症狀 doctor 名 醫生

1737 My mother went to a **pharmacy**.
我母親去了藥局。 pharmacy 名 藥房

1738 She still feels sick after taking some **over-the-counter** medicine.
她吃了一些成藥，但還是不太舒服。
over-the-counter 形 不用處方箋的

1739 You'd better go see a doctor.
你最好還是去看一下醫生。

1740 Is there a **clinic nearby**?
這附近有診所嗎？ clinic 名 診所 nearby 形 附近的

1741 Hello. I'd like to make an **appointment**.
你好，我要掛號。 appointment 名 (正式的)約會

1742 Is this your first visit?
請問您是初診嗎？

1743 May I have your **medical** record number or ID number?
麻煩給我您的病歷號碼或身分證字號。 medical 形 醫療的

1744 Please **fill out** the first-visit record.
請填寫初診單。 fill out 片 填寫

1745 Which department do you want to visit?
您要掛哪一科？

1746 I have no idea. Could you make a **suggestion**?
我不知道，你可以給我建議嗎？ suggestion 名 建議

1747 What seems to be the **problem** with you?
請問您哪裡不舒服呢？ problem 名 問題

1748 I feel **chilly** and ache **all over**.
我全身發冷且酸痛。 chilly 形 冷颼颼的 all over 片 各處

1749 I suggest that you make an appointment with the Family Medicine Department.
我建議您看家醫科。

1750 I'd like to visit the **ENT** department.
我要掛耳鼻喉科。 ENT 縮 耳鼻喉科 (=ears, nose and throat)

1751 Do you have an **assigned** doctor?
您有指定的醫師嗎？ assign 動 指定

1752 May I have your health **insurance** card and two hundred dollars?
請給我您的健保卡和掛號費兩百元。 insurance 名 保險

1753 Your appointment **number** is fifty-eight.
您掛的是五十八號。 number 名 號碼

1754 Please go to clinic room 203.
請前往 203 號看診室。

1755 I might have a slight fever. / I might have a little **temperature**.

我可能有輕微發燒。 temperature 名 溫度

1756 Let me take your temperature. / Let me check your temperature.
我幫你量一下體溫。

1757 Don't worry. Your temperature is **normal**.
別擔心，你的體溫很正常。 normal 形 正常的

1758 Well, your temperature is 37.5 degrees. That's a **mild** fever.
你的體溫為 37.5 度，有一點點發燒。 mild 形 輕微的

1759 You have a high **fever**.
你發高燒了。 fever 名 發燒；熱度

1760 You have to **bring down** your fever first.
你必須先退燒才行。 bring down 片 降低

1761 Should I take a fever reducer?
我需要吃退燒藥嗎？

1762 Let me give you an **injection** of fever reducer.
我先幫你打退燒針。 injection 名 注射

1763 After the shot, please do not **rub** the area.
打完針以後，不要揉。 rub 動 摩擦

1764 It may hurt a little. Please be **patient**.
會有一點痛，要請你稍微忍耐一下。 patient 形 能容忍的

1765 I am not feeling well.
我覺得不太舒服。

1766 I have a terrible **headache**.
我的頭快要痛死了。 headache 名 頭痛

1767 I feel a little **dizzy**.
我有點頭暈。 dizzy 形 頭暈目眩的

1768 How long have you been feeling dizzy?

你頭暈的狀況是從什麼時候開始的？

1769 How long have you had these symptoms? / How long have you been **ill**?
你這個症狀多久了？ ill 形 生病的

1770 It's been **several** days.
已經好幾天了。 several 形 數個的

1771 Do you have a headache or any muscle aches?
你會頭痛或肌肉酸痛嗎？

1772 The back of my throat is **itchy** and **tickles**.
我覺得喉嚨癢癢的。 itchy 形 癢的 tickle 動 使發癢

1773 I **woke up** yesterday with a **sore throat** and a fever.
我昨天起床時，喉嚨很痛、又發燒。
wake up 片 起床 sore throat 片 喉嚨痛

1774 My throat feels **raw**.
我覺得喉嚨很痛。 raw 形 刺痛的

1775 I have an **irritated** throat.
我的喉嚨不舒服。 irritate 動 使難受；使疼痛

1776 My throat hurts when I **swallow**.
吞嚥的時候，我的喉痛會很痛。 swallow 動 嚥下

1777 I have a **burning** pain in my throat.
我的喉嚨像火燒般，痛得很厲害。 burning 形 強烈的

1778 It hurts, especially when I **cough** or swallow.
咳嗽或吞口水的時候，痛得更厲害。 cough 動 咳嗽

1779 Your **tonsils** are **swollen**.
你的扁桃腺發炎了。 tonsil 名 扁桃腺 swollen 形 浮腫的

1780 Mild coughing is a symptom of the common cold.
輕微的咳嗽是常見的感冒症狀。

1781 **Gargling** with warm salt water may help you **relieve** a sore throat.
用溫鹽水漱口可以減輕喉嚨痛的症狀。
gargle 動 漱口 relieve 動 減輕

1782 A cold usually begins with a sore throat followed by a running nose.
感冒初期會喉嚨痛，接著就開始流鼻水。

1783 I have a sore throat and a headache, but no nasal **drainage**.
我有喉嚨痛和頭痛的症狀，但沒有流鼻水。drainage 名 排水

1784 My daughter has a **running nose**.
我女兒的鼻水流個不停。running nose 片 流鼻水

1785 I can't stop coughing once it starts.
我只要一咳嗽，就會咳個不停。

1786 I have a coughing **spell**, and I get **short of** breath.
我一陣接著一陣地咳，簡直快喘不過氣來了。
spell 名 (疾病等的)一陣發作 short of 片 缺少；不足

1787 My father has a **dry** cough.
我爸爸有乾咳的毛病。dry 形 乾燥的；口渴的

1788 Do you have a **persistent** cough that brings up yellowish **mucus**?
你有持續性的咳嗽嗎？有沒有咳出黃痰？
persistent 形 持續的 mucus 名 黏液

1789 I cough up **phlegm**.
我咳嗽有痰。phlegm 名 痰；黏液

1790 I cough up **thick sputum**.
我咳出的痰很濃。thick 形 黏稠的 sputum 名 痰

1791 My phlegm is **bloody**. I am so worried about it.
我的痰有血絲，我好擔心喔！bloody 形 流血的

1792 I get phlegm in my throat and have difficulty in **breathing**.
我的喉嚨裡面有痰，而且覺得呼吸困難。 breathe 動 呼吸

1793 You should wear a **mask**.
你應該戴口罩。 mask 名 口罩

1794 Stop smoking, or you'll have a **violent** fit of **croupy** coughing.
不要再抽菸了，小心得到哮吼性咳嗽。
violent 形 猛烈的 croupy 形 哮吼性的

1795 You might be suffering from **bronchitis**.
你可能得了支氣管炎。 bronchitis 名 支氣管炎

1796 You need a **chest** X-ray.
你需要照張胸部 X 光。 chest 名 胸膛

1797 You might have **pneumonia**.
你可能得了肺炎。 pneumonia 名 肺炎

1798 Have you ever had any specific problems, such as **diabetes** or **asthma**?
以前有沒有得過什麼特殊疾病？例如糖尿病或氣喘。
diabetes 名 糖尿病 asthma 名 氣喘(病)

1799 What's the **medicine** for?
這個藥是做什麼用的？ medicine 名 藥；內服藥

1800 This is a **nasal decongestant**.
這是治鼻塞的藥。 nasal 形 鼻的 decongestant 名 解除充血藥

1801 Do I have to take vitamin **tablets**?
我需要吃維他命藥片嗎？ tablet 名 藥片

1802 Vitamin C can be found **naturally** in vegetables and fruits.
維他命 C 在很多蔬菜水果中都有。 naturally 副 自然地

1803 Vitamin C is a possible treatment for colds, or a possible way to **prevent** colds.

維他命 C 也可以用來治療或預防感冒。 prevent 動 預防

1804 Are you **allergic** to any medicine?
你有對任何藥物過敏嗎？ allergic 形 過敏的

1805 You should avoid taking these medicines because of your heart disease.
你有心臟病，應該盡量避免服用這些藥。

1806 This is your **prescription**. Please pick up your medicine at the pharmacy.
這是您的處方籤，請至藥局領藥。 prescription 名 處方

1807 You have to take this medicine after each meal.
這些藥請於三餐飯後服用。

1808 Take the pain reliever only when you need it.
止痛藥請於需要時服用。

1809 The **medication** will become less effective if you **overuse** it.
如果你濫用藥物，藥效就會降低。
medication 名 藥物 overuse 動 濫用

1810 Take these two kinds of medicines separately in two-hour **intervals**.
這兩種藥請分開服用，間隔時間為兩小時。 interval 名 間隔

1811 Please keep your medicine in the fridge.
藥物請置於冰箱保存。

1812 Get plenty of rest and drink lots of water.
多休息，多喝水。

1813 Please let me know if you have any **discomfort**.
若有任何不適，請一定要告訴我。 discomfort 名 不適

1814 If the symptoms **persist** or **worsen**, please contact your doctor.
若症狀未改善甚至惡化時，請與您的醫師聯絡。
persist 動 持續 worsen 動 惡化

1815 I prevent becoming infected by the flu by getting a flu shot every year.
為了預防感冒，我每年都打流感疫苗。

1816 Health should be your **priority**.
身體健康是最重要的。priority 名 優先

1817 You need a **health** check-up.
你應該去做健康檢查。health 名 健康

1818 I don't think it's a big problem. I am just **aging**.
我想不是什麼大問題，我只是年紀大了。age 動 變老

1819 I am going to have a **thorough** check-up.
我去做個徹底的檢查。thorough 形 徹底的

1820 How often do you get a check-up?
你多久做一次健康檢查？

1821 I have a regular physical **examination** every year.
我每年都會做一次健康檢查。examination 名 檢查

1822 My **company** offers us a physical examination every year.
我們公司每年都安排員工做體檢。company 名 公司

1823 Regular health exams help find problems that can be treated early.
定期做健康檢查能篩檢疾病，並及早治療。

1824 Early treatment can help prevent more serious problems.
及早治療可預防病情惡化。

1825 What **items** are **involved** in the health check-up?
健康檢查包含哪些項目呢？ item 名 項目 involve 動 包含

1826 There are two packages, **standard** and **superior** check-up plans.
我們有兩種健檢方案，標準健檢以及高階健檢。
standard 形 標準的 superior 形 較好的

1827 Please look at the **catalogue** for more details.
我們的目錄上有更詳細的說明。 catalogue 名 目錄

1828 It includes blood pressure and **pulse** checks, and height and weight measurement.
檢查項目包括血壓、脈搏數和身高體重。 pulse 名 脈搏

1829 Your vision, hearing, lungs, and **abdomen** will also be examined.
也會做視力、聽力、肺部及腹部的檢查。 abdomen 名 腹

1830 I'd like to have screening for **cancer**.
我想檢測一下我有沒有癌症。 cancer 名 癌症

1831 You can do PET scan, which is included in our superior check-up plan.
你可以做正子斷層掃描，高階健檢就包含這個項目。

1832 I encouraged my mother to get an examination for **breast cancer**.
我鼓勵母親去做乳房檢查。 breast cancer 片 乳癌

1833 **Mammograms** are important for women aged forty to forty-nine.
對四十幾歲的婦女而言，乳房 X 光檢查是很重要的。
mammogram 名 乳房 X 光攝影

1834 Do you have a history of **hypertension**, diabetes

or other diseases?
請問你有高血壓、糖尿病或其他疾病的病史嗎？
hypertension 名 高血壓

1835 Do you know your family medical history and **allergy** records?
請問你清楚你的家族病史和過敏紀錄嗎？ allergy 名 過敏症

1836 Have you ever been hospitalized or had an **operation** before?
你以前住過院或開過刀嗎？ operation 名 手術

1837 Do you regularly take any medicine?
你目前有沒有服用任何藥物？

1838 Have you lost or **gained** weight recently?
最近有體重減輕或增加的情形嗎？ gain 動 得到

1839 I will take your temperature and **blood pressure** first.
我先幫你量一下體溫和血壓。 blood pressure 片 血壓

1840 Your blood pressure is 126/87. It's normal.
你的血壓為一二六和八十七，很正常。

1841 You have hypertension. I'll prescribe some medicine for you.
你有高血壓，我會開一些藥給你。

1842 We will **draw** a blood sample, do an **EKG**, and take an X-ray.
我們等一下會替你抽血、做心電圖的檢查和照 X 光。
draw 動 汲取 EKG 縮 心電圖 (=electrocardiogram)

1843 Roll up your right sleeve and make a loose **fist**, please.
請捲起你右手的袖子，並輕輕握拳。 fist 名 拳頭

1844 Please do not eat anything or drink water before the examination.
在檢查之前，請不要吃任何東西，連水也不可以喝。

1845 I am going to take an X-ray of your chest.
我現在要幫您照胸部 X 光。

1846 Please **take off** your top and put on this gown.
請脫掉你的上衣，換上這件衣服。take off 片 脫去(衣物)

1847 Please **remove** all **metal** objects, like your watch and necklace.
身上若有像手錶或項鍊之類的金屬物品，都請拿掉。
remove 動 脫去 metal 名 金屬

1848 Remain **still**. You mustn't move **unless** I say OK.
在我說「可以」之前，請不要動。still 形 不動的 unless 連 除非

1849 Take a deep breath in and out, please.
請深吸一口氣，再吐氣。

1850 The EKG shows that you have an **irregular** pulse.
心電圖顯示你的心律不整。irregular 形 無規律的

1851 I am scheduled for an **EEG** next Monday.
我下週一要做腦波檢查。
EEG 縮 腦波圖(=electroencephalogram)

1852 If your family members have diabetes, your blood sugar level should be checked.
如果你們家族有糖尿病史，你就應該要做一下血糖指數的檢測。

1853 You have a **genetic predisposition** to diabetes.
因為遺傳的關係，你會比一般人容易得糖尿病。
genetic 形 遺傳的 predisposition 名 傾向

1854 Come back to draw blood for a blood sugar test two hours after a meal.
請於飯後兩小時回來抽血，做血糖檢測。

1855 Your blood sugar **index** is still a little high.
你的血糖指數還是有點高。index 名 指數

1856 Please stick to the diet prescribed by the

dietician.
請遵照營養師的指示進食。dietician 名 營養學家

1857 Please leave the samples in separate **containers.**
請將樣本放在不同的容器中。container 名 容器

1858 Your **uric acid** is too high.
你的尿酸太高了。uric 形 尿的 acid 名 酸

1859 You should start to change your **diet.**
你得改變飲食習慣才行。diet 名 飲食；食物

1860 I suggest that you eat something like **lean** meat, vegetables and tofu.
我建議你吃一些像瘦肉、蔬菜和豆腐類的食物。lean 形 無脂肪的

1861 Seafood, meat and animal **intestines** must be avoided.
不能吃海鮮、肉類和動物的內臟。intestine 名 腸

1862 All check-ups are done.
你的檢查都已經做完了。

1863 The examination report will take about half an hour. Take a rest first.
檢查報告大概要等半個小時左右，請先休息一下。

1864 The report will take fifteen days.
檢查報告十五天後才會出來。

1865 Be regular in exercising. It can **improve** your health.
請維持規律的運動習慣，那能增進健康。improve 動 增進

1866 Stay **calm** so that your blood pressure won't go up.
心情要放輕鬆，血壓才不會上升。calm 形 平靜的

1867 I have had some **stomach** problems since I was a kid.

我從小胃就不太好。stomach 名 胃

1868 Has anyone in your family also had the problem?
家裡還有其他人有這樣的毛病嗎？

1869 My grandmother and my father had stomach problems, too.
我奶奶和我爸爸也有胃痛的毛病。

1870 I am suffering from a terrible **stomachache**.
我的胃好痛。stomachache 名 胃痛

1871 I have an **upset** stomach.
我有點反胃。upset 形 攪亂的

1872 I feel that my stomach is **squeezed**.
我感覺到胃絞痛。squeeze 動 榨；擠

1873 I have vomiting and **watery diarrhea**.
我上吐下瀉。watery 形 稀薄的 diarrhea 名 腹瀉(=diarrhoea)

1874 Is your **stool** black?
有解黑便嗎？stool 名 糞便

1875 My father has **heartburn**.
父親有胃灼熱的問題。heartburn 名 胃灼熱

1876 I have a **duodenal ulcer**.
我有十二指腸潰瘍。duodenal 形 十二指腸的 ulcer 名 潰瘍

1877 Is it a **dull** pain or a **prickling** pain?
是隱隱作痛？還是刺痛？dull 形 隱約的 prickle 動 刺痛

1878 It's a **sharp** pain.
是刺痛。sharp 形 鋒利的；急劇的

1879 Does it hurt when I **press** here?
按這裡會痛嗎？press 動 按壓

1880 You have a slight **GI** infection.
你有輕微的腸胃炎。GI 縮 腸胃的(=gastrointestinal)

1881 You suffer from **gastritis**.
你患了胃炎。gastritis 名 胃炎

1882 You might have a case of stomach **cramps**.
你可能得了胃痙攣。cramp 名 痙攣

1883 I will arrange an **endoscopy** for you.
我會幫你安排內視鏡檢查。endoscopy 名 內視鏡檢查

1884 It **enables** the physician to look inside the stomach.
內視鏡檢查能讓醫師看見你胃部的情形。enable 動 使能夠

1885 What is it? A **gastroscopy**?
那是什麼？照胃鏡嗎？gastroscopy 名 胃鏡檢查

1886 Yes, a gastroscopy is an **upper** GI endoscopy.
對，胃鏡就是一種內視鏡檢查，那是專門照上部腸胃區的。
upper 形 上面的

1887 Does it hurt much?
會不會很痛啊？

1888 I heard that it might be very painful.
我聽說那可能會很痛。

1889 I'm so afraid of that. Is there any **alternative**?
我好害怕，能用其他的檢測替代嗎？alternative 名 替代品

1890 Gastroscopy is a safe and **painless** examination.
照胃鏡很安全，而且完全不會痛。painless 形 不痛的

1891 You might have some discomfort, but it is **tolerable**.
你可能會感到有點不舒服，但都在可忍受的範圍之內。
tolerable 形 能容忍的

1892 Take the **sedative** before the examination.
檢查之前，請先服用鎮靜劑。sedative 名 鎮靜劑

1893 It makes the **procedure** easily tolerable for you.

這會讓你在檢測的過程中，感覺舒服一點。procedure 名 程序

1894 Your exam is finished. This is your report.
檢查已經完成，這是你的報告。

1895 You have too much stomach acid.
你的胃酸過多。

1896 You've got a **peptic** ulcer, but it's not too serious.
你有消化性潰瘍，但情況還不算很嚴重。peptic 形 消化的

1897 Please come back to recheck at the **Outpatient Department** in two weeks.
兩個星期後請再回來門診複診。Outpatient Department 片 門診部

1898 Your next appointment with the doctor is next Friday morning; you are No.36.
您下次複診的時間為下週五上午，掛三十六號。

1899 When eating, you should **chew** your food thoroughly and swallow it slowly.
吃東西要細嚼慢嚥。chew 動 咀嚼

1900 We've found a **tumor** in your stomach.
我們在你的胃裡發現了腫瘤。tumor 名 腫瘤

1901 Luckily, we have an **early detection**.
幸好我們及早發現。early 形 早期的 detection 名 發覺

1902 Is the death rate for stomach cancer high?
胃癌的死亡率高不高？

1903 Is it a **terminal** cancer?
是癌症末期嗎？terminal 形 末期的；終點的

1904 Will the cancer **spread** to other **organs**?
癌細胞會不會擴散到其他器官？spread 動 使擴散 organ 名 器官

1905 You need **surgery** to remove the cancer cells.
你需要開刀切除癌細胞。surgery 名 手術

1906 After that, you need **chemotherapy**.
手術結束之後，你必須接受化療。 chemotherapy 名 化學療法

1907 I am undertaking **radiotherapy**.
我正在接受放射治療。 radiotherapy 名 放射療法

1908 I am worried that the cancer might **reoccur**.
我擔心癌症復發。 reoccur 動 復發

來外科門診掛號
When I Got Injured

1909 You are bleeding! Let me get you some **bandages**.
你在流血耶！我去拿繃帶過來。 bandage 名 繃帶

1910 Do you have a **first-aid kit** handy?
你手邊有急救箱嗎？ first-aid 形 急救(用)的 kit 名 工具箱

1911 I have some Band Aids and alcohol.
我有 OK 繃和酒精。

1912 What happened? The **cut** looks serious.
發生什麼事了？那道傷口看起來好嚴重。 cut 名 傷口

1913 What's wrong? How did you hurt yourself?
怎麼回事？你怎麼會傷到自己？

1914 I am going to **sterilize** the **wound** first.
我會先消毒傷口。 sterilize 動 消毒 wound 名 傷口

1915 It might be a bit painful when **hydrogen peroxide** is applied.
擦雙氧水時可能會有一點痛。

hydrogen 名 氫 peroxide 名 過氧化物

1916 After that, I will **suture** your wound.
之後，我再幫你縫合傷口。 suture 動 縫合(傷口)

1917 Try to keep the wound clean and dry.
傷口請保持乾淨，不要碰到水。

1918 How often should I change the **dressing**?
我多久要換一次藥？ dressing 名 敷藥

1919 You need to change the dressing once **daily**.
每天換一次藥。 daily 副 每日

1920 You can clean the wound with **aseptic cotton swabs** and **iodine**.
你可以用無菌棉花棒沾優碘清潔傷口。
aseptic 形 無菌的 cotton swab 片 棉花棒 iodine 名 碘酒

1921 Most patients will improve in one to two weeks.
大部分的病人會在一至二個星期內好轉。

1922 The wound is red, swollen, and painful.
我的傷口紅腫，又很痛。

1923 There is some **yellowish**, **foul**-smelling fluid coming from the wound.
有一些黃黃的、有味道的液體從傷口流出來。
yellowish 形 淡黃色的 foul 形 惡臭的

1924 Does the wound have **pus**?
傷口有流膿嗎？ pus 名 膿汁

1925 It's probably **infected**.
也許是傷口感染了。 infect 動 傳染；感染

1926 You need an injection. Please roll up your sleeve.
你需要打針，請捲起袖子。

1927 I feel much better. The shot has certainly **taken effect**.

我覺得好多了，真是一針見效。 take effect 片 生效

1928 You need a **CT** scan first.
您得先做電腦斷層掃描。
CT 縮 斷層掃描(=Computer Tomography)

1929 I'll also arrange an **MRI** for you.
我也會幫你安排核磁共振檢查。
MRI 縮 核磁共振檢測(=Magnetic Resonance Imaging)

1930 Will the operation **cure** my disease completely?
開刀可以根治我的病嗎？ cure 動 治癒

1931 Is there any possibility it will be **recurrent**?
有沒有復發的可能？ recurrent 形 一再發生的

1932 Is it a **major** operation?
那是大手術嗎？ major 形 重要的

1933 Will I have a local or general **anesthesia**?
我需要局部麻醉還是全身麻醉？ anesthesia 名 麻醉

1934 Should I have surgery now, or can I do it later?
我一定要現在開刀嗎？還是可以之後再開？

1935 Is the surgery **dangerous**?
這個手術會不會很危險？ dangerous 形 危險的；不安全的

1936 All surgery has **risks**. Don't **worry**; the risks for this operation are rather low.
只要是手術，都會有風險。但別擔心，這個手術的風險很低。
risk 名 危險；風險 worry 動 擔心；發愁

1937 Your **surgeon** will meet with you and explain the potential risks.
開刀醫師會來向你說明手術的潛在風險。 surgeon 名 外科醫生

1938 Understanding the possible **complications** can help you make a better decision.
清楚可能會有的併發症之後，你才能好好做決定。
complication 名 併發症

1939 You can **seek** a second opinion before having surgery.
在動手術之前，你可以徵詢其他醫師的意見。 seek 動 徵求

1940 Yours is **scheduled** to be the first operation tomorrow morning.
你被排在明早的第一場手術。 schedule 動 將…列入時間表

1941 Please do not eat or drink anything after **midnight**.
晚上十二點後需禁食。 midnight 名 午夜

1942 You can wipe your lips with a wet **swab** when you feel thirsty.
口渴的話，可以用海綿沾水，塗在嘴唇上。 swab 名 醫用海綿

1943 Please change into the operating gown.
請換上手術袍。

1944 You can ask the nurse if you have any **inquiries**.
若有任何問題，可以問護理人員。 inquiry 名 疑問；問題

1945 A surgical **drain** is used to remove pus and blood.
手術引流管是用來排膿和血水的。 drain 名 排水管

1946 Anthony **called** it **off** because he was hit by a motorcycle.
安東尼今天請假，因為他被機車撞到。 call off 片 取消

1947 Is he **conscious**?
他的意識還清醒嗎？ conscious 形 神智清醒的

1948 His right leg was **critically injured**.
他的右腳受重傷。 critically 副 嚴重地 injure 動 傷害

1949 He has a serious head **injury**.
他頭部的外傷很嚴重。 injury 名 損害；傷害

1950 The man needs first aid.
這名男子需要急救。

1951 Call an **ambulance**!
快叫救護車！ ambulance 名 救護車

1952 Lift him up and place him on a **stretcher**.
把他抬到擔架上。 stretcher 名 擔架

1953 He needs a blood **transfusion**.
他需要輸血。 transfusion 名 輸血；輸液

1954 The **supply** of the blood bank is getting low.
血庫裡面的庫存量愈來愈少了。 supply 名 供應量

1955 We need somebody to **donate** blood for him.
我們需要有人捐血給他。 donate 動 捐獻

1956 His Glasgow **Coma** Scale (GCS) score is six.
他的昏迷指數是六。 coma 名 昏迷

1957 He needs **brain** surgery immediately.
他需要立刻動腦部手術。 brain 名 腦部

1958 How was the operation?
手術的情形如何？

1959 Don't worry. Her operation went **smoothly**.
別擔心，她的手術很順利。 smoothly 副 順利地

1960 This patient just had an operation, and it was **uneventful**.
這個病人剛開完刀，一切都很順利。 uneventful 形 平靜無事的

1961 Be careful with your wound. Keep it dry for a week.
請小心傷口，一個星期內都不能碰到水。

1962 Keep the wound away from water until the skin **recovers** completely.
傷口完全復原之前，請不要碰到水。 recover 動 恢復

1963 Please come back to have your **stitches** removed next Saturday.

下週六請回門診拆線。 stitch 名 (縫合傷口的)針線

1964 See the doctor again as **indicated** on the outpatient pre-registration form to remove the **sutures**.
之後請依門診預約單的時間回院複診，再拆線就可以了。
indicate 動 指出 suture 名 縫合用的線

1965 I fell and **sprained** my **knee**.
我摔了一跤，結果扭到膝蓋。 sprain 動 扭傷 knee 名 膝蓋

1966 My right arm was **dislocated**.
我的右手臂脫臼了。 dislocate 動 使脫臼

1967 The first step is to get some X-rays done to see what the **fracture** pattern is.
首先要照 X 光，確定是哪一類的骨折。 fracture 名 骨折

1968 We'll see how **badly displaced** the fracture is.
我們再看骨頭移位的情況有多嚴重。
badly 副 嚴重地 displace 動 移開

1969 What is the treatment for an **ankle** fracture?
踝關節骨折要怎麼治療？ ankle 名 腳踝

1970 Treatment of an injured ankle may require a **cast** or even surgery.
踝關節受傷可能需要打石膏，甚至可能要開刀。 cast 名 石膏

1971 I am going to put on the cast now.
我現在要幫你上石膏了。

1972 You have to use a walking stick while your leg is in **plaster**.
在腳打上石膏的這段期間，你都要用拐杖。 plaster 名 熟石膏

1973 Start to walk slowly, and then increase your speed **gradually**.
剛開始不要走太快，慢慢增加速度。 gradually 副 逐步地

1974 Limit your **movement** so that your injury does

not worsen.
盡量不要做太大的動作，以免傷勢惡化。movement 名 動作

1975 Is there anything else I have to **watch out** for?
還有其他需要注意的事項嗎？watch out 片 當心

1976 You will need to apply an **ice pack** three times a day.
一天冰敷三次。ice pack 片 冰袋

1977 **Apply** hot water after twenty-four hours.
二十四小時之後才能熱敷。apply 動 塗；敷

1978 Any of these should not be kept on for more than twenty minutes.
每次敷的時間不要超過二十分鐘。

1979 Is there any food I should **avoid**?
有什麼食物是我不能吃的嗎？avoid 動 避免

1980 You have to start with **liquids**.
剛開始，你只能吃流質的食物。liquid 名 液體

1981 How about my daily activities?
那我的日常活動呢？會受影響嗎？

1982 You can do whatever you did before the surgery.
可以照常活動，沒有問題。

1983 Don't carry anything **heavy** for the next four months.
四個月內不要提重物。heavy 形 重的；沉的

1984 It will affect the wound's **agglutination**.
那會影響傷口癒合。agglutination 名 黏結

1985 My doctor just told me to stay in the **hospital** for a few weeks.
醫生剛剛告訴我必須住院幾個星期。hospital 名 醫院

1986 This is your room. It's a **semi-private** room.

這是您的病房，是間雙人房。 semi-private 形 半私人的

1987 If you have any problems, please press the button.
若有任何問題，請按這個按鈕通知護理人員。

1988 I'm your **day-care** nurse today.
我是今天負責照顧您的日班護士。 day-care 形 日間護理的

1989 The doctor will be here around two o'clock.
醫生兩點左右會來看您。

1990 If your wound hurts, the doctor can prescribe you some pain-reliever.
如果傷口會痛，醫生可以開止痛藥給您。

1991 Has Dr. Wang made the morning **ward rounds**?
王醫師早上巡過房了嗎？ ward 名 病房 round 名 巡視

1992 How do you feel today?
你今天覺得怎麼樣？

1993 To be honest, I feel **worse**.
老實說，我覺得更難受了。 worse 形 更差的

1994 I feel much better. Thank you.
我覺得好多了，謝謝你。

1995 You've made great **progress**.
你的情況進步很多喔。 progress 名 進步

1996 What is the patient's **condition**?
那位病人的情況怎麼樣了？ condition 名 情況

1997 Her condition became **critical** last night and she was sent to ICU.
她昨晚病情危急，被送到加護病房。 critical 形 危急的

1998 She is very **stable**. She can be transferred to a normal ward tomorrow.
她的情況很穩定，明天就能轉到普通病房了。 stable 形 穩定的

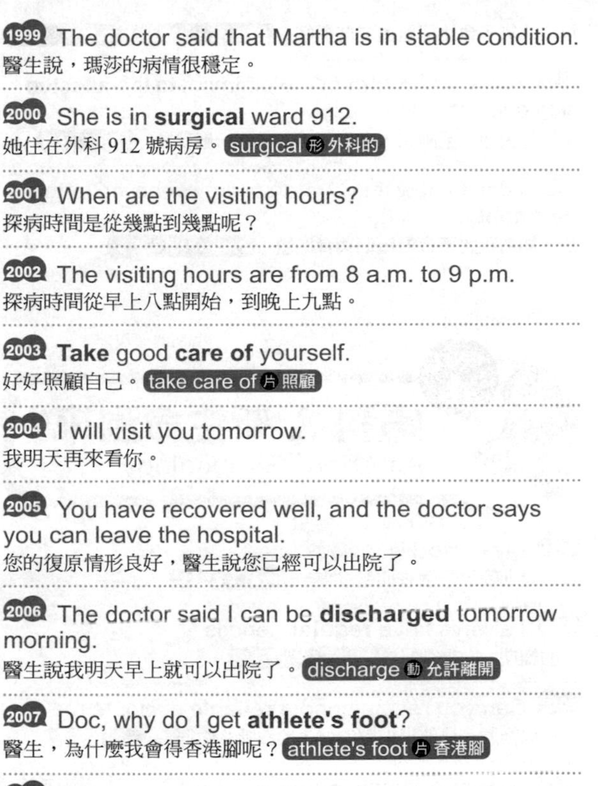

1999 The doctor said that Martha is in stable condition.
醫生說，瑪莎的病情很穩定。

2000 She is in **surgical** ward 912.
她住在外科 912 號病房。 surgical 形 外科的

2001 When are the visiting hours?
探病時間是從幾點到幾點呢？

2002 The visiting hours are from 8 a.m. to 9 p.m.
探病時間從早上八點開始，到晚上九點。

2003 **Take** good **care of** yourself.
好好照顧自己。 take care of 片 照顧

2004 I will visit you tomorrow.
我明天再來看你。

2005 You have recovered well, and the doctor says you can leave the hospital.
您的復原情形良好，醫生說您已經可以出院了。

2006 The doctor said I can be **discharged** tomorrow morning.
醫生說我明天早上就可以出院了。 discharge 動 允許離開

2007 Doc, why do I get **athlete's foot**?
醫生，為什麼我會得香港腳呢？ athlete's foot 片 香港腳

2008 **Fungus** grows easily in warm and **moist** places.
溫暖潮溼的地方最容易滋生黴菌。 fungus 名 真菌 moist 形 潮溼的

2009 Keep your feet clean and dry to prevent fungus from growing.
注意足部衛生，並保持乾燥才能防止黴菌滋生。

2010 Dry your feet and the **gaps** between toes thoroughly after a shower.
洗完澡之後，要把腳和指縫擦乾。 gap 名 缺口

2011 **Cotton** socks are better than **nylon** or silk ones.

棉質的襪子會比尼龍襪或絲襪好。cotton 形 棉製的 nylon 名 尼龍

2012 Apply a thin **film** of the ointment to the affected skin once or twice a day.
藥膏每天塗一至兩次，在患部擦薄薄的一層就好。film 名 薄層

2013 I don't know if I have an allergic reaction to this **ointment**.
我不知道我會不會對這個藥膏過敏。ointment 名 藥膏

婦科 & 新生命到來 All About Gynecology

2014 My **period** is a week late.
我的經期晚了一個星期還沒來。period 名 月經

2015 I always have **regular** periods.
我的經期一向很準。regular 形 有規律的

2016 Can you recommend a **reliable** doctor to me?
你可以推薦一位值得信賴的醫生給我嗎？reliable 形 可信賴的

2017 I prefer a female **gynecologist**.
我比較喜歡給女婦產科醫師看診。gynecologist 名 婦科醫生

2018 I agree. I don't feel comfortable with a male gynecologist.
我和你一樣，給男的婦產科醫師看診，我會感到不自在。

2019 I don't care about the **gender** as long as the doctor is professional.
只要醫生夠專業，是男是女我都不在意。gender 名 性別

2020 Please go to the **registration station** first.

請先至報到處。registration 名 掛號 station 名 所；局

2021 How long does your **menstrual** cycle last?
你月經的週期通常是幾天？menstrual 形 月經的

2022 **Typical** menstrual cycles last about twenty-eight days.
一般的月經週期是二十八天。typical 形 典型的

2023 I'd like to have a **pregnancy** test.
我想要驗孕。pregnancy 名 懷孕

2024 Please go to the **OPD** lab for a urine test.
請到門診檢驗室驗尿。OPD 縮 門診部(=outpatient department)

2025 Please use this cup to **collect** your urine.
請使用這個尿杯。collect 動 收集

2026 After collecting your urine, bring it to that counter.
結束之後，請把尿杯拿到那個櫃檯。

2027 There are tissues and **tampons** inside the cabinet. Feel free to use them.
櫃子裡有衛生紙和衛生棉條，有需要請自取。tampon 名 衛生棉條

2028 Please go to the **pelvic** examination room and prepare for a check-up.
請至內診的診療室準備檢查。pelvic 形 骨盆的

2029 Please lie down on the examination table. Loosen up you bra, and lift up your top.
請平躺在診療台上，解開內衣，並把上衣往上拉。

2030 Please take off your pants and **underwear** and then lie down.
請脫掉褲子和內衣褲，然後平躺。underwear 名 內衣

2031 Please cover yourself with the **blanket**.
請蓋上毯子。blanket 名 毛毯

2032 Please move **further** down.

請再躺下來一點。 further 副 進一步地

2033 We have done with the **examination** now.
我們已經檢查完畢了。 examination 名 檢查

2034 You may get down from the examination table.
你可以離開診療床了。

2035 After you get dressed, please wait outside, and the doctor will explain the results to you.
穿好衣服後，請在外面稍候，醫師會向你說明檢查結果。

2036 **Congratulations**! You are pregnant.
恭喜！你懷孕了。 congratulations 名 祝賀；恭喜

2037 It's the seventh week of your **pregnancy**.
你懷孕七週了。 pregnancy 名 懷孕

2038 Is this your first baby?
這是你的第一胎嗎？

2039 When is the **due date** of my wife's pregnancy?
請問，我太太的預產期是什麼時候？ due date 片 到期日

2040 Her due date will be at the end of September.
她的預產期會是九月底。

2041 Great! He or she will be a **Libran**.
太好了！他（她）會是個天秤座寶寶。 Libran 名 天秤座的人

2042 You might have some morning **sickness**.
你早上可能會有孕吐的現象。 sickness 名 噁心；嘔吐

2043 What should I **be aware of** during my pregnancy?
懷孕期間，我有什麼必須注意的事情嗎？ be aware of 片 意識到

2044 Don't **carry** anything heavy.
不要提重物。 carry 動 提；扛；搬

2045 Get eight hours of sleep every night and take

frequent rest during the day.
每天要睡滿八小時，白天要多休息。 frequent 形 頻繁的

2046 I don't know if I need an **amniocentesis**.
我不知道我需不需要做羊膜穿刺術。 amniocentesis 名 羊膜穿刺術

2047 Are there any risks in doing an amniocentesis?
做羊膜穿刺會不會有危險？

2048 It's a common and low-risk **prenatal** test for birth **defects**.
這是很普遍的產前檢測，風險很低，可以檢查出胎兒有沒有缺陷。
prenatal 形 產前的 defect 名 缺陷

2049 When should I get one done?
我應該在什麼時候做檢查呢？

2050 It is usually done between fifteen and twenty weeks of pregnancy.
通常在懷孕十五週到二十週時做檢查。

2051 Amniocentesis is recommended for women at advanced **maternal** ages.
我們會建議高齡產婦做羊膜穿刺術。 maternal 形 母親的

2052 The first three months of pregnancy is crucial for **fetal** development.
懷孕初期的三個月，是胎兒發育的關鍵階段。 fetal 形 胎兒的

2053 Please come back to my **clinic** for prenatal check-ups regularly.
請定期回來做產檢。 clinic 名 診所

2054 It's very important to make sure you **deliver** a healthy baby.
確保胎兒的健康很重要。 deliver 動 分娩

2055 You should not use over-the-counter medicines during pregnancy.
懷孕期間，請不要亂服成藥。

2056 You can wear loose cotton clothes during your pregnancy.
懷孕期間可穿著寬鬆的棉質服裝。

2057 You mustn't wear high heels.
禁止穿高跟鞋。

2058 Walking is a highly recommended **exercise** for pregnant women.
對孕婦而言，散步是我們十分推薦的運動。 exercise 名 運動

2059 Please lift up your clothes so the doctor can listen to baby's **heartbeat**.
請把衣服往上拉，醫生才能檢查胎兒的心音。 heartbeat 名 心跳

2060 It is normal to gain about twelve to fifteen kilos during pregnancy.
整個懷孕期間，體重增加十二到十五公斤很正常。

2061 Your baby is growing slower than **average**.
你的寶寶生長得比一般胎兒遲緩。 average 名 平均

2062 I go to the restroom very often. Is that normal?
我很頻尿，一直跑廁所，這正常嗎？

2063 That's because the **fetus** compresses your **bladder**.
那是因為體內胎兒壓迫到你的膀胱。
fetus 名 胎兒 bladder 名 膀胱

2064 Have you ever had a **premature** delivery or a **miscarriage**?
你有早產或流產過嗎？ premature 形 早產的 miscarriage 名 流產

2065 Are you going to have a natural childbirth or a **Caesarian section**?
你想要自然產還是剖腹產？ Caesarian section 片 剖腹生產

2066 A Caesarian section is not covered by National Health Insurance.
健保不負擔剖腹產的費用，需自費。

2067 I am having terrible **labor** pain.
我開始陣痛，痛死人了！ labor 名 分娩

2068 My labor has started.
陣痛開始了。

2069 Does it mean that I will deliver the baby soon?
是不是表示我快要生了？

2070 My water broke.
我的羊水破了。

2071 Rosa can try **artificial insemination**.
羅莎可以試試人工受孕。 artificial 形 人工的 insemination 名 懷孕

2072 Don't use **sanitary pads** too often.
平時少用護墊。 sanitary 形 衛生的 pad 名 襯墊；護墊

2073 Change pads often during the menstrual periods.
月經期間，必須勤換衛生棉。

2074 Take showers instead of baths.
盡量淋浴，不要泡澡。

2075 Please put one **suppository** into your **vagina** every day before sleep.
請於每天睡前塞一顆藥劑入陰道內。
suppository 名 栓劑 vagina 名 陰道

2076 The suppository will **melt** later so you should use a pad.
藥片會自行溶化，所以要墊護墊。 melt 動 融化

2077 Look at the **ultrasound** image. You have a **fibroid**.
請看一下超音波的影像，你有子宮肌瘤。
ultrasound 名 超音波 fibroid 名 子宮肌瘤

2078 That's the reason why you have abdomen pains.
這就是你肚子痛的原因。

2079 What are some common symptoms of **menopause**?
更年期婦女常見的症狀有哪些？ menopause 名 更年期

2080 Women might have hot flashes, night sweat, frequent **urination**, and so on.
女性們可能會有熱潮紅、盜汗、頻尿等症狀。
urination 名 撒尿

2081 Bone **loss** is also a common one.
骨質疏鬆也是常見的症狀。 loss 名 喪失；損失

UNIT 5 擺脫「面子」問題 About The Skincare

2082 I have something like a **rash** all over my back, shoulders, and upper arms.
我的背部、肩膀和手臂上都長了像是疹子的東西。 rash 名 疹子

2083 I have **rubella** and itchiness.
我全身起紅疹，很癢。 rubella 名 德國麻疹

2084 Jerry has red **specks** on his face.
傑瑞的臉上長紅斑。 speck 名 斑點

2085 Did you eat any food you may have been allergic to?
你是不是吃了一些會過敏的食物？

2086 I get severe **hives** whenever I eat **mango**.
一吃芒果，我身上就會冒出嚴重的蕁麻疹。
hives 名 蕁麻疹 mango 名 芒果

2087 I'm allergic to **seafood**.

我對海鮮過敏。 seafood 名 海鮮

2088 How to **identify** the main cause of my allergies?
要如何分辨導致我過敏的主因呢？ identify 動 確認

2089 A sample of your blood can be taken and then tested.
抽血檢查可以測得出來。

2090 The **itching** will **get worse** if you take a hot shower, because the pores of your skin will **dilate** from the heat.
盡量不要洗熱水澡，熱水會使毛細孔擴張，導致患部更癢。
itching 名 癢 get worse 片 惡化 dilate 動 擴大

2091 To avoid injury to your skin, don't **scratch** it when it itches.
發癢的部位，請盡量不要去抓它，以免抓傷皮膚。 scratch 動 抓

2092 Avoid spicy food and drinks with **caffeine** like tea, coffee, and Coke.
避免吃辛辣的食物或含咖啡因的飲料，像是茶、咖啡、可樂之類的。 caffeine 名 咖啡因

2093 It's a case of **herpes**.
這是皰疹的病例。 herpes 名 皰疹

2094 Herpes is caused by a **virus**.
皰疹是由病毒所引起的。 virus 名 病毒

2095 Patients should get as much rest as possible. They shouldn't push themselves.
患者需要多休息，不能過度勞累。

2096 Stop all the medicine that you are taking now.
不管你現在有服用什麼藥，請全面停止，都不能吃。

2097 To recover fully, you have to apply the prescribed ointment regularly.
醫生開給你的藥膏請按時塗抹，這樣才能完全復原。

2098 I am getting more and more **pimples** on my face.
我臉上的痘痘愈來愈多了。 pimple 名 粉刺；青春痘

2099 I have been so bothered by annoying **acne**.
長粉刺的情況已經困擾我很久了。 acne 名 粉刺

2100 It's really annoying. Can acne be **prevented**?
真的很煩耶！粉刺可以預防嗎？ prevent 動 預防；阻止

2101 There are many different causes of acne.
粉刺形成的原因有很多。

2102 **Overactive glands**, diet, **mood** and genetics are the main factors.
內分泌失調、飲食、情緒和遺傳等都是主要的因素。
overactive 形 過於活躍的 gland 名 腺 mood 名 心情

2103 It's important to get **sufficient** sleep.
有充足的睡眠很重要。 sufficient 形 足夠的；充分的

2104 Doctor, you're right. I have trouble sleeping.
醫師，你說的沒錯，我有失眠的困擾。

2105 Do you **stay up late** a lot?
你是不是經常熬夜？ stay up late 片 熬夜

2106 No, but I am working on a big **project** which gives me a lot of pressure.
沒有，但我手邊的這個案子讓我的壓力激增。 project 名 企劃

2107 Choose suitable **cosmetics**, skin care products and cleansers.
要選擇適合的化妝品、保養品和清潔用品。 cosmetics 名 化妝品

2108 Staying relaxed and balancing your diet can also **lessen** your symptoms.
放鬆心情和飲食均衡也能減緩症狀。 lessen 動 減輕

2109 I'd suggest you stop using makeup for a while.
我會建議你這陣子都不要上妝。

2110 I will prescribe you some ointment. Apply it after washing your face.
我會開一些藥膏給你，洗完臉後擦。

2111 Alpha **hydroxyl** acids (AHAs) can cure your pimples.
果酸可以用來治療青春痘。 hydroxyl 名 氫氧根

2112 It won't be **healed** in a few days. Please be patient.
不會在短短的幾天內就好，請您要有耐心。 heal 動 治癒

2113 I have **rough** skin.
我的皮膚很粗糙。 rough 形 粗糙的

2114 You can consider IPL (Intense Pulsed Light) treatment.
您可以考慮做脈衝光治療。

2115 IPL, a skin treatment, is commonly used to improve skin problems.
脈衝光是一種皮膚的治療方式，常用來改善皮膚問題。

2116 The IPL fee is not covered by NHI (National Health Insurance).
健保不給付脈衝光的治療費用。

2117 How much does it cost?
費用怎麼算？

2118 Is it **worth** it to get IPL treatment?
花那個錢打脈衝光值得嗎？ worth 形 有…的價值

2119 I don't think so. After the first treatment, I did not see any change at all.
我覺得不值得，我打過一次，根本看不出有什麼變化。

2120 I have done IPL five times. Most of my **freckles** have gone away.
我打過五次脈衝光，大部分的雀斑都不見了。 freckle 名 雀斑

2121 The results are immediately **visible**.
立即見效呢。 visible 形 可看見的

2122 I found it is **worthwhile** doing.
我覺得很值得。 worthwhile 形 值得做的

2123 Does it hurt much?
會不會很痛啊？

2124 It is a bit painful in **certain areas**, but tolerable.
某些部位會有點痛，但都在可忍受的範圍內。
certain 形 某；某些 area 名 範圍；區域

2125 I just had an IPL treatment today, and so far, there have been no **side effects**.
我打脈衝光到現在都沒有產生什麼副作用。 side effect 片 副作用

2126 After IPL treatment, you can use **therapy** lotion.
做完脈衝光治療後，你可以使用這瓶護理用的乳液。
therapy 名 治療；療法

2127 The lotion can increase **elasticity** and reduce **roughness** and dry **spots**.
這瓶乳液能增加皮膚彈性，並減少粗糙及乾燥斑點的產生。
elasticity 名 彈性 roughness 名 粗糙 spot 名 斑點

2128 **Cryotherapy** is commonly used for removing **warts** and moles.
冷凍療法常用來去除疣跟痣。 cryotherapy 名 冷凍療法 wart 名 疣

2129 Cryotherapy uses liquid **nitrogen** to freeze skin **lesions**.
冷凍療法使用液態氮，藉此凍起皮膚的病變細胞。
nitrogen 名 氮 lesion 名 損害

2130 The cold temperature kills the cells in the **superficial** layers of the skin.
極低的溫度能殺死皮膚表層的細胞。 superficial 形 表面的

2131 It may be mildly painful, particularly when it is applied to the face.

可能會感覺到輕微的疼痛，尤其是治療臉部時。

2132 Cryotherapy won't **leave** a wound.
冷凍治療不會留下傷口。 leave 動 留下；剩下

2133 You can take a bath or shower as usual.
你可以正常地洗澡。

2134 In a week or two, the **scab** will dry up and fall off without a scar on it.
大約一至兩週後，結痂就會脫落，不會留下疤痕。 scab 名 痂

2135 You need to avoid **exposure** to the sun during the treatment.
治療期間請避免照射到陽光。 exposure 名 暴露

2136 Could you tell me what to watch out for after the cosmetic **laser** surgery?
請問雷射治療後要注意些什麼呢？ laser 名 雷射

2137 Keep the wound away from water after the treatment.
治療結束後，傷口盡量不要碰水。

2138 You will feel **scorching** heat and some swelling after the treatment.
治療後會有灼熱感以及些微的腫脹。 scorching 形 灼熱的.

2139 You can use a towel with ice **tubed** inside on the wound to **ease** the pain.
可以用毛巾裹冰塊冰敷，以減輕疼痛感。
tube 動 弄成管狀 ease 動 減輕；緩和

2140 Use **sterile** cotton swabs with **normal saline** to clean the wound.
請以消毒棉花棒沾生理食鹽水清潔傷口。
sterile 形 消過毒的 normal saline 片 生理食鹽水

2141 If the wound does not heal, keep applying the ointment to avoid **infection**.
如果傷口尚未癒合，請持續抹藥膏，以免感染。 infection 名 傳染

2142 Wearing wide-**brimmed** hats and **long-sleeved** shirts is a good way to protect your skin.
戴寬帽緣的遮陽帽以及穿長袖襯衫是防曬的好方法。
brimmed 形 有邊的 long-sleeved 形 長袖的

2143 You need to reapply the **sunscreen** at least every three hours.
你至少每三個小時要補擦一次防曬乳。sunscreen 名 防曬乳

2144 Your case is **severe**, and I will prescribe you some **oral steroid** therapy.
你的症狀比較嚴重，我會開一些口服類固醇給你服用。
severe 形 嚴重的 oral 形 口服的 steroid 名 類固醇

2145 You may not be able to **concentrate** after taking the medicine.
服用藥物後，可能會造成注意力無法集中。concentrate 動 集中

2146 Do not drive or **operate** any dangerous machines.
請不要開車或操作危險性機械。operate 動 操作

2147 My hair is thin, and I am going **bald**.
我的頭髮好稀疏，快要禿頭了。bald 形 禿頭的

2148 Have you considered getting a hair **transplant**?
你有考慮過植髮嗎？transplant 名 移植

UNIT 6 照顧靈魂之窗 Problems With My Eyes

2149 I'd like to make an appointment to see someone in the **Ophthalmological** Department.
我想要掛眼科。ophthalmological 形 眼科的

2150 When is the visiting schedule for the Ophthalmology Department?
請問何時有眼科的門診？

2151 What's wrong with your eyes?
你的眼睛怎麼了嗎？

2152 My eyes are red and painful.
我的眼睛又紅又痛。

2153 Are your eyes **sensitive** to light?
眼睛會畏光嗎？ sensitive 形 敏感的

2154 Put your head here. I am going to examine your eyes.
請把頭放這裡，我現在要幫你檢查眼睛。

2155 Do your eyes **itch**?
眼睛會癢嗎？ itch 動 發癢

2156 Yes, they are **unbearably itchy**.
會啊，癢到受不了。 unbearably 副 無法忍受地 itchy 形 癢的

2157 It must be allergic **conjunctivitis**.
那一定是過敏性結膜炎。 conjunctivitis 名 結膜炎

2158 Typical symptoms include redness, itching, tearing and sensitivity to light.
典型的症狀包括眼睛紅、發癢、流淚和畏光。

2159 Is it **contagious**?
這種病會傳染嗎？ contagious 形 接觸傳染性的

2160 Do your eyes get tired easily?
你的眼睛很容易感到疲倦嗎？

2161 When I look at close things, my eyes get tired.
當我看近物的時候，眼睛就會感到疲倦。

2162 The main cause of eye **fatigue** is **spending** too many hours working on the computer.

眼睛疲勞主要是因為看電腦的時間過長所造成的。
fatigue 名 疲勞；勞累 spend 動 花費

2163 After working on the computer for thirty to forty minutes, remember to stand up and walk around to rest your eyes.
使用電腦三十到四十分鐘就要起來走動，讓眼睛休息。

2164 I've been staying up late and my eyes have been **bleary**.
我最近一直熬夜，結果搞得視線模糊不清。 bleary 形 朦朧的

2165 A few minutes' reading **tires** my eyes.
看書看不到幾分鐘，眼睛就疲倦了。 tire 動 使疲倦

2166 Use artificial tears when necessary. It can relieve symptoms.
有需要時，就滴人工淚液，它能緩解你的症狀。

2167 My **eyesight** seems to be gradually worsening.
我的視力好像愈來愈差了。 eyesight 名 視力

2168 My vision is **blurred**.
我的視線模糊不清。 blurred 形 模糊不清的

2169 In both eyes? You might need an **optometry** test.
兩隻眼睛都是嗎？你可能需要驗光。 optometry 名 驗光

2170 You might be **nearsighted** if you have no problems seeing things up close but have trouble seeing things that are **far away**.
如果你看近的物體沒問題，但東西一遠就看不清楚，那就應該是近視了。 nearsighted 形 近視的 far away 片 遠處

2171 I have been nearsighted since I was a kid.
我從小就近視了。

2172 Is laser eye surgery safe?
眼睛的雷射手術安全嗎？

2173 The treatment is pretty **safe** now.
這種治療現在很安全了。safe 形 安全的

2174 Laser eye surgery removes a small amount of eye **tissue** to **reshape** the **cornea**.
眼睛雷射手術會去除眼睛一部份的組織，再重新塑型角膜。
tissue 名 (動植物的)組織　reshape 動 再成形　cornea 名 角膜

2175 **Rigid** contact lenses can reshape the **curvature** of your cornea.
這種硬式隱形眼鏡可以矯正角膜的彎曲度。
rigid 形 硬式的　curvature 名 彎曲

2176 I am farsighted, so I have to hold things far from me to see them clearly.
我有遠視，所以我得把東西拿遠一點，才看得清楚。

2177 I can't do **fine** work.
比較精細的工作，我就做不來。fine 形 細微的

2178 Perhaps it's a matter of age that I have difficulty seeing the road map.
也許是老了，我現在看地圖都會感到很吃力。

2179 You need reading glasses.
你需要戴老花眼鏡了。

2180 I can't get my **contacts** out.
我的隱形眼鏡摘不下來。contact 名 隱形眼鏡

2181 How many hours do you wear contact lenses a day?
你的隱形眼鏡一天戴幾個小時？

2182 Don't wear contact lenses more than eight hours a day.
隱形眼鏡一天不可戴超過八小時。

2183 Contact lenses should be cleaned thoroughly after use.
隱形眼鏡在戴完之後，要徹底清潔。

2184 Stop wearing contact lenses for at least a week.
至少一個星期先不要戴隱形眼鏡。

2185 I get a headache when I wear my **glasses**.
我一戴眼鏡就頭痛。glasses 名 眼鏡

2186 You need a new prescription for your eyeglasses.
你需要重新配一副眼鏡了。

2187 Please go to the **opposite** desk for an eye examination.
請到對面的櫃台檢查視力。opposite 形 對面的

2188 Use this bottle of eye **drops** four times a day, but only one drop at a time.
這瓶眼藥水一天點四次，一次只需要點一滴。drop 名 滴劑

2189 The eye drops will dilate your **pupils**. When I put these eye drops in your eyes, they might **sting**. But don't worry, it's perfectly normal.
這瓶眼藥水有散瞳的作用，滴的時候可能會有刺痛感，是正常現象，別擔心。pupil 名 瞳孔 sting 動 刺痛

2190 The street lights far away have a ring around them like a **rainbow**.
遠方的街燈形成一層光圈，就像彩虹一樣。rainbow 名 彩虹

2191 I always see things **double**.
一個東西在我眼裡會變成兩個。double 形 雙的；成雙的

2192 My grandmother has serious **astigmatism**.
我外婆的散光很嚴重。astigmatism 名 散光

2193 While one of my eyeballs focuses on an object, the other drifts in another direction.
當我的一顆眼球注視某樣物品時，另一顆就會偏離目標。

2194 You can get surgery to cure your **squint**.
你可以做斜視的矯正手術。squint 名 斜視

2195 My eyes are **gummed** up and **watery**.

我的眼睛睜不開，而且會分泌淚液。 gum 動 發黏 watery 形 水的

2196 I often have **greenish discharge** in my eyes when I wake up.
我起床時，眼睛常常會分泌綠色的眼屎。
greenish 形 呈綠色的 discharge 名 排出物

2197 The tear **ducts** in your eyes are blocked, so you need an examination.
你的淚腺阻塞，需要做檢查。 duct 名 輸送管

2198 There are black **dots** in my vision.
我看到好多個黑點。 dot 名 點

2199 I see web-like **shadows** sometimes.
我有時候會看到網狀的影子。 shadow 名 影子；幻影

2200 Are these symptoms so-called **floaters**?
這些症狀是所謂的飛蚊症嗎？ floaters 名 飛蚊症

2201 How long have you noticed the black spots in your eyes?
像這樣「眼睛出現黑點」的症狀有多久了？

2202 Things look cloudy, and the light looks **dim**.
東西看起來很模糊，光線也暗淡不清。 dim 形 暗淡的

2203 What I am looking at seems dark.
眼前的東西，黑漆漆的一片，根本看不清楚。

2204 Is it a case of **glaucoma**?
這是青光眼嗎？ glaucoma 名 青光眼

2205 Glaucoma is a disease of the **optic nerve**.
青光眼是視神經出了問題。 optic 形 視覺的 nerve 名 神經

2206 Patients' vision may become **constricted**.
病人的視野會變狹窄。 constricted 形 狹隘的

2207 Without **proper** treatment, it may lead to complete **blindness**.

如果沒有適當的治療，甚至可能失明。

proper 形 適當的　blindness 名 失明

2208 Are there any symptoms in early **stage** glaucoma?

青光眼初期會有什麼症狀嗎？stage 名 階段

2209 Usually, there is no **obvious** symptom in the early stage.

初期通常不會有什麼明顯的症狀。obvious 形 明顯的

2210 My eyes feel like they have **sand** in them.

我的眼睛好像有沙子進去。sand 名 沙

2211 I am afraid you have **trachoma**.

你可能得砂眼了。trachoma 名 砂眼

2212 Trachoma is an **infectious** disease of the eye.

砂眼是一種會傳染的眼疾。infectious 形 傳染性的

2213 It is spread easily through contact with an infected person's hands.

如果接觸砂眼症病人的手，就容易被感染。

2214 I can't tell one color from another.

我沒有辦法區別顏色。

2215 I seem to be color-**blind**.

我大概是個色盲。blind 形 盲的

2216 The **intraocular** pressure may cause **nausea** or vomiting.

眼壓可能會引起噁心感或嘔吐。

intraocular 形 眼內的　nausea 名 噁心

2217 You need an **IV** injection to reduce the intraocular pressure immediately.

你需要做靜脈注射，以快速降低眼壓。

IV 縮 靜脈內的(=intravenous)

2218 I feel **nauseous** sometimes.

我有時候會想吐。 nauseous 形 令人作嘔的

2219 I'll arrange some tests to check your optic nerve.
我會幫你安排做視神經檢查。

2220 The doctor recommends that you do a **fluorescein angiography**.
醫師建議您做螢光血管攝影的檢查。
fluorescein 名 螢光黃 angiography 名 血管造影法

2221 Do I need an injection of a **contrast medium**?
需要打顯影劑嗎？ contrast 名 對比 medium 名 媒介物

2222 I have a prickling pain in my right eye.
我的右眼有刺痛的感覺。

2223 There's a **throbbing** pain in my left eye.
我的左眼有抽痛的感覺。 throbbing 形 抽痛的

2224 You probably have some kind of nerve problem.
你可能有神經方面的問題。

2225 I'd suggest you visit the **Neurology** Department.
我會建議你掛神經內科。 neurology 名 神經學

2226 Use these two kinds of eye drops separately with a five-minute interval.
這兩種眼藥水請分開使用，點完一種隔五分鐘，再點另外一種。

2227 This ointment is for **external** use only on the skin around your eyes.
這支是外用藥膏，只能塗在眼周。 external 形 外用的

2228 Don't let the ointment get in your eyes.
藥膏不要碰到眼睛。

2229 You need long-term treatment with eye **medications** and an **operation**.
你需要長期使用眼睛的藥物，還需要開刀治療。
medication 名 藥物 operation 名 手術

必須看牙醫了
Seeing A Dentist

2230 I have a **toothache**. / My tooth hurts. / I feel a pain in my teeth.
我牙痛。toothache 名 牙痛

2231 I need to go to a **dentist**.
我需要去看牙醫。dentist 名 牙醫

2232 Toothaches occur when the **pulp** inside your tooth gets inflamed.
牙痛通常是因為牙齒內的牙髓發炎。pulp 名 牙髓

2233 The dentist will carefully examine your teeth and may take X-rays.
牙醫會仔細地檢查你的牙齒，可能還會幫你照 X 光片。

2234 Which dentist do you usually see?
請問您平常給哪位醫生看診呢？

2235 Doctor Lin is **available** right now. I'll make an appointment for you.
目前林醫師有空，我馬上幫您安排。available 形 有空的

2236 I have an appointment with Dr. Zheng at 11:30.
我跟鄭醫師約好十一點半看診。

2237 May I have your treatment **schedule**?
您有帶約診單嗎？schedule 名 日程安排表

2238 May I have your NHI card, please?
請給我您的健保卡。

2239 Sure, here you are.
好的，這是我的健保卡。

2240 I'm **awfully** in pain.
我真的好痛。awfully 副 極度地；非常地

2241 How long do I need to wait?
我需要等多久呢？

2242 About fifteen minutes. You will be **next**.
大約十五分鐘，您是下一位。next 名 下一個人或物

2243 One of my teeth in the back hurts.
後排有顆牙很痛。

2244 One of my front teeth is **chipped**.
我其中一顆門牙有個缺口。chip 動 造成缺口

2245 Let me check. Open your mouth, please.
我幫你檢查一下，請張開嘴巴。

2246 A tooth that was treated five months ago has started to hurt.
五個月前治療過的那顆牙又痛了。

2247 The **filling** of this tooth **cavity** fell out.
蛀洞補的地方脫落了。filling 名 填補物 cavity 名 (牙的)蛀洞

2248 A **cap** has **fallen off**.
齒冠脫落了。cap 名 蓋；罩 fall off 片 脫離

2249 The tooth is **inflamed** and swollen.
那顆牙齒發炎，並腫了起來。inflame 動 使發炎

2250 How long has the toothache lasted?
你的牙齒痛多久了？

2251 I have problem chewing because of a toothache.
因為牙齒痛，所以我無法好好咀嚼。

2252 I have been suffering from eating problems for days.
我已經好幾天都沒辦法好好吃東西了。

2253 I have been chewing only on the right side for a long time.
我已經很久都只用右邊的牙齒咀嚼了。

2254 Don't eat too many **sweets**. They will **decay** your teeth.
不要吃太多甜食，那會害你蛀牙的。
sweet 名 甜點 decay 動 蛀壞

2255 **Tooth decay** is one of the most common dental **disorders**.
蛀牙是牙科疾病中最常見的一種。
tooth decay 片 蛀牙 disorder 名 小病

2256 A cavity can grow bigger and deeper over time if you **ignore** it.
如果你不理會蛀牙，蛀洞就會愈來愈大。ignore 動 不理會

2257 If you have a cavity, it's important to get it **filled**.
如果你有蛀牙，把蛀洞補起來是很重要的。fill 動 填補

2258 Remember to have a regular **dental** check-up every six months.
記得每半年做一次牙齒定期檢查。dental 形 牙齒的

2259 I have a throbbing toothache.
我的牙齒會陣陣抽痛。

2260 It is a steady **piercing** pain that is really unbearable!
刺痛的感覺一直沒消失，實在叫人受不了！piercing 形 銳利的

2261 Even a slight touch to the tooth is **intensely** painful.
只是輕輕碰到牙齒，也痛得要命。intensely 副 極度

2262 It's a throbbing pain that hurts as far as my ears and my neck.
連我的耳朵和脖子都跟著抽痛。

2263 How often do you **brush** your teeth?

你多久刷一次牙？ brush 動 刷

2264 I brush my teeth with **fluoride** toothpaste after every meal.
每餐飯後，我都會用含氟的牙膏刷牙。 fluoride 形 氟化物的

2265 You need to brush your teeth at least twice a day.
你一天至少要刷兩次牙。

2266 I **floss** my teeth every day.
我每天都用牙線清潔牙齒。 floss 動 用牙線清潔

2267 I gargle with **mouthwash** whenever I finish eating.
只要有吃東西，我就會用漱口水漱口。 mouthwash 名 漱口水

2268 Mouthwash **temporarily** kills the **bacteria** in your mouth.
漱口水可以暫時殺死口腔內的細菌。
temporarily 副 暫時 bacteria 名 細菌

2269 I'd like to have my teeth cleaned.
我想要洗牙。/ 我希望清潔一下牙齒。

2270 You have a lot of **tartar** on your back teeth.
你後排的牙齒有好多牙垢。 tartar 名 牙垢

2271 You need regular dental cleaning.
你需要定期洗牙。

2272 I have an appointment for teeth **whitening**.
我有預約做牙齒美白。 whitening 名 變白

2273 Teeth whitening can lighten the teeth and remove **discoloration**.
牙齒美白能讓牙齒變亮，還可以去除汙垢。 discoloration 名 汙點

2274 I'd like to make an appointment for a dental **implant**.
我想要預約植牙。 implant 名 植入物

2275 My grandmother had all her teeth **pulled out** and got a set of false teeth.
我奶奶拔掉所有牙齒，換了一口假牙。pull out 片 拔出

2276 I'd like to have my **dentures** checked.
可以檢查一下我的假牙嗎？denture 名 假牙

2277 The tooth **smarts** when I eat something cold.
我一吃冰冷的食物，牙就痛得受不了。smart 動 引起劇痛

2278 I have a piercing pain when I eat something **sour**.
我一吃酸的東西，牙就痛得像被什麼刺到一樣。sour 形 酸的

2279 You have sensitive teeth.
你有敏感性牙齒。

2280 The **gums** bleed whenever I brush my teeth.
我一刷牙，牙齦就出血。gum 名 齒齦；牙床

2281 I think you have some sort of gum disease.
我覺得你可能得了某種牙齦疾病。

2282 One of my **molars** is loose.
我有一顆臼齒搖搖欲墜。molar 名 臼齒

2283 My wisdom tooth aches. Do I need an **extraction**?
我的智齒好痛，需要拔掉嗎？extraction 名 拔出

2284 If possible, I'd rather not have the tooth extracted.
如果可以，我想保留這顆牙齒。

2285 You need to have this tooth pulled out.
你這顆牙必須拔掉。

2286 It won't take long.
不會花很久的時間。

2287 You may feel a bit **uncomfortable**.
你可能會有一點不舒服。uncomfortable 形 不舒服的

2288 I was given an injection of local anesthetic when **undergoing** treatment.

我在治療時有局部麻醉。undergo 動 接受(治療)

2289 You will feel a little **numb**.

你會感到有點麻。numb 形 麻木的

2290 OK. We've finished now.

好了，我們完成了。

2291 Don't eat anything until the **anesthetic** goes away.

麻藥退之前不要吃東西。anesthetic 名 麻醉劑

2292 After a tooth extraction, avoid eating anything too hot.

拔牙之後，別吃太燙的食物。

2293 Please take the anti-**inflammatory** drug regularly.

請按時服用消炎藥。inflammatory 形 炎症性的

2294 Take a pain reliever if the pain comes back.

如果又痛了，吃一顆止痛藥。

2295 If you don't feel better, please come back to the clinic.

如果你感覺沒有比較好，請再回來看診。

2296 I am kind of shy because my teeth just won't grow in **evenly**.

我有點害羞，因為我的牙齒不整齊。evenly 副 均勻地

2297 My teeth used to be **crooked**, but they look great now.

我的牙齒以前也歪七扭八的，但它們現在看起來很整齊。

crooked 形 歪的

2298 I wore **braces** for two years.

我戴過兩年的牙套。braces 名 矯正器

2299 You can get clear braces or braces that are the same color as your teeth.
你可以戴透明款，或是和你牙齒顏色一樣的牙套。

2300 How long do I need to wear them?
我需要戴多久？

2301 Most people usually wear braces for about one to two years.
大部分的人需要戴一到兩年的牙套。

2302 I won't see the dentist until I can't **stand** the pain any longer.
除非痛到受不了，否則我不會去看牙醫。 stand 動 忍受

2303 I am afraid of the sound of the dental **drill**.
我很怕牙鑽頭發出來的聲音。 drill 名 鑽頭

精神面也要照顧
More About Emotions

2304 I am very **pessimistic** about life.
我對人生感到悲觀。 pessimistic 形 悲觀的

2305 Everything seems **meaningless** to me.
對我而言，每件事都毫無意義。 meaningless 形 無意義的

2306 I don't want to go out at all.
我一點都不想出門。

2307 Am I **autistic**?
我會不會得了自閉症？ autistic 形 孤僻的

2308 I suggest you see a **psychiatrist**.

我建議你去看精神科醫師。psychiatrist 名 精神科醫師

2309 I am not saying that you are **psycho**.
我不是說你有精神病。psycho 形 精神病的

2310 Maybe you have too much pressure and need someone to encourage you.
你可能壓力過大，需要旁人來給你一點鼓勵。

2311 A **significant** number of people suffer from mental illness.
很多人都深受精神疾病所苦。significant 形 顯著的

2312 Most mental disorders can be treated by medicine and **psychotherapy**.
大部分的精神疾病都能用藥物或心理治療控制。
psychotherapy 名 心理療法

2313 Most mental disorders take time to cure.
大部分精神疾病的療程都很花時間。

2314 I feel **depressed** all the time.
我一直都感到沮喪。depressed 形 沮喪的；憂鬱的

2315 Most of the time, I feel **hopeless** about my life.
大部分的時間，我都覺得我的人生毫無希望。hopeless 形 無望的

2316 How long have you had these feelings?
你這種想法維持多久了？

2317 It has been six months since I got divorced.
從我離婚之後，就一直有這個念頭，已經有半年之久。

2318 It was a **traumatic experience**.
那是精神上的創傷。traumatic 形 創傷性的 experience 名 經歷

2319 How's your **appetite**?
你的胃口好嗎？appetite 名 食慾；胃口

2320 I don't **feel like** eating most of the time.
大部分的時間，我都沒有食慾。feel like 片 想要(+V-ing/N)

2321 I've become **short-tempered** and **moody**, especially to my family.
我變得暴躁易怒又情緒化，尤其在家人面前更是如此。
short-tempered 形 易怒的 moody 形 情緒化的

2322 I **suspect** that they don't love me anymore.
我懷疑他們都不愛我了。suspect 動 懷疑

2323 You might be **oversensitive**.
你可能太過敏感了。oversensitive 形 過於敏感的

2324 Do you feel **nervous** all the time?
你隨時都會感到緊張不安嗎？nervous 形 緊張不安的

2325 Yes, I am always **anxious** about my life.
會啊，我對人生總是感到焦慮不安。anxious 形 焦慮的

2326 I worry about everything, including **trivial** things.
就連雞毛蒜皮的小事，我都會擔心不已。trivial 形 瑣碎的

2327 I really don't think I have enough **courage** to move on.
我真的不知道自己有沒有勇氣走下去。courage 名 勇氣

2328 I even have thoughts of **suicide**.
我甚至有自殺的念頭。suicide 名 自殺

2329 To tell the truth, I have a feeling of **inferiority**.
老實說，我有自卑感。inferiority 名 自卑感

2330 I don't tell others about my illness because they might laugh at me.
我怕別人取笑我，所以沒有跟任何人提起我的病症。

2331 Is the quality of your sleep **poor**?
你的睡眠品質是不是很差？poor 形 缺乏的

2332 I can't sleep at all.
我完全無法入睡。

2333 It usually takes me hours to fall to sleep.

我通常得輾轉好幾個小時，才會睡著。

2334 I **wake up** several times during my sleep.
晚上睡覺的時候，我會醒來好幾次。wake up 片 醒來

2335 I feel like crying whenever I wake up.
每次醒來就會想哭。

2336 You are **suffering from insomnia**.
你得了失眠症。suffer from 片 受…困擾 insomnia 名 失眠症

2337 You definitely need a good night's sleep.
你確實需要好好睡一覺。

2338 The sleeping **pills** can help you sleep.
安眠藥可以幫助你入睡。pill 名 藥丸；藥片

2339 Is it **habit forming**?
會不會上癮啊？habit 名 習慣 form 動 形成

2340 Don't worry. The medicine is only prescribed in low **doses**.
別擔心，它們的劑量很低。dose 名 劑量

2341 I believe you have a **psychosomatic** disease.
你患有一種身心疾病。psychosomatic 形 身心相關的

2342 You have been **diagnosed** with **depression**.
你患有憂鬱症。diagnose 動 診斷 depression 名 憂鬱症

2343 Depression makes you feel hopeless and **helpless**.
憂鬱症會讓你感到絕望和無助。helpless 形 無助的

2344 Depression has no single cause.
憂鬱症不是單一因素所造成的。

2345 You may have no idea why depression has **struck** you.
你可能不知道為什麼憂鬱症會找上你。strike 動 打；擊

2346 Things like the breakup of a relationship, or the death of a loved one can bring on depression.
跟男女朋友分手或心愛的人過世，都有可能引發憂鬱症。

2347 Some people become depressed because of the changes in their lives, like starting a new job, or getting married.
有些人則會因為生活有了改變而憂鬱，例如換新工作或結婚。

2348 People who have low self-**esteem** and negative thinking are at higher risks of becoming depressed.
自卑和思想負面的人比較容易得到憂鬱症。 esteem 名 評價

2349 **Genetics** play an important part in depression and can run in families for **generations**.
憂鬱症的發生和基因有很大的關連，而且會在家族中遺傳好幾代。
genetics 名 遺傳學 generation 名 世代

2350 My grandmother killed herself several years ago.
我的外婆幾年前自殺了。

2351 She had been **hysterical**.
她以前很歇斯底里。 hysterical 形 歇斯底里的

2352 She was diagnosed with **schizophrenia**.
她被診斷出精神分裂症。 schizophrenia 名 精神分裂症

2353 I think David is **under** too much pressure.
我覺得大衛的壓力太大了。 under 介 處於…情況之下

2354 Psychiatrists should be very patient.
精神科醫師都必須非常有耐心。

2355 How can **mental** disorders be treated?
心理疾病要如何治療呢？ mental 形 心理的

2356 I will prescribe you some **antidepressants**.
我會開一些抗憂鬱的藥給你。 antidepressant 名 抗憂鬱劑

2357 You also need psychotherapy.
你也需要做一些心理治療。

2358 I can arrange a professional **psychotherapist** for you.
我會安排一位專業的心理治療師給你。
psychotherapist 名 心理治療師

2359 You can also try some **relaxation** activities.
也可以試試一些能讓你放鬆的活動。relaxation 名 放鬆；緩和

2360 Doing some deep breathing will help you relax.
深呼吸能幫助你放鬆。

2361 Why don't you go traveling? It usually helps a lot.
你何不去旅行？那通常會有很大的幫助。

2362 Traveling can bring you out of your depression.
旅行能一掃憂鬱。

2363 Don't think too much. You didn't do anything wrong.
不要想太多，你沒有做錯任何事。

2364 Tomorrow is another day!
明天又是嶄新的一天！

2365 If you smile to the world, the world smiles back to you.
如果你對世界微笑，世界也會對你微笑。

2366 I am glad you are more of a positive **thinker** now.
很高興你現在比較會正面思考了。thinker 名 思考者

NOTE

Part 4

推薦休閒活動

IN MY LEISURE TIME

UNIT 1 愈來愈夯的單車行
Cycling With Friends

2367 Let's go for a **bike ride**!
我們去騎腳踏車吧！ bike 名 腳踏車 ride 名 兜風

2368 Do you want to go **mountain** biking this weekend?
這個週末想騎腳踏車登山嗎？ mountain 名 山

2369 I just found a new cycling **trail**.
我剛發現一條新的自行車道。 trail 名 小道

2370 I want to share the **joy** of biking with you.
我想跟你分享騎自行車的樂趣。 joy 名 樂趣

2371 Cycling has become **hot** in recent years.
近幾年，騎自行車變得很夯。 hot 形 熱門的

2372 Taiwan's cycling population has increased **remarkably**.
台灣的騎單車人口明顯增加許多。 remarkably 副 明顯地

2373 Regular cycling is a great way to **stay** healthy.
規律地騎單車是維持身體健康的好方法。 stay 動 保持

2374 The government is **promoting** bicycling, too.
政府也極力推廣單車運動。 promote 動 發揚；促進

2375 The supply of bicycles is unable to **meet the demand**.
腳踏車供不應求。 meet the demand 片 滿足需求

2376 In recent years, many people have gone bicycling for **recreation**.
這幾年，許多人都將騎單車視為一種休閒活動。
recreation 名 消遣；娛樂

2377 **Recreational** cycling has become quite popular, especially on weekends.
休閒腳踏車變得十分熱門，尤其是週末。recreational 形 消遣的

2378 You can go biking with your kids there.
你可以帶小孩去騎腳踏車。

2379 The 17-kilometer bike path in Hsinchu is built along the **coastline**.
新竹的十七公里單車道是沿著海岸線興建的。coastline 名 海岸線

2380 You can enjoy the beautiful ocean view while cycling.
你可以邊騎腳踏車，邊享受海洋的美景。

2381 There are some newly built cycle paths in Taipei City.
台北市有很多新完成的自行車道。

2382 What are the **conditions** like over there?
那裡的路況如何？condition 名 狀態；環境

2383 The condition of the trail is not perfect, but it is **acceptable**.
車道的路況雖稱不上完美，但還在可以接受的範圍之內。
acceptable 形 可以接受的

2384 Several bike paths have been built, but only a few people use them regularly.
很多自行車道都建好了，但使用的人數卻很少。

2385 I can't stand cycling in such **sweltering** weather.
我受不了在這種悶熱的天氣裡騎腳踏車。sweltering 形 悶熱的

2386 Getting **sunburned** is not fun at all.
曬黑可是一點都不好玩。sunburned 形 曬黑的

2387 I don't like cycling on a busy road.
我不喜歡在車水馬龍的路上騎腳踏車。

2388 Let's **hit the road**!

我們出發吧！ hit the road 片 (口)上路；出發

2389 Check your bike's **tire** pressure before you hit the road.
上路前，記得檢查一下你輪胎的胎壓。 tire 名 輪胎

2390 I am a new biker. How do I start?
我是自行車新手，要怎麼開始騎呢？

2391 You'd better ride your bike for short journeys **at the beginning**.
剛開始騎車時，最好從短程的開始。 at the beginning 片 開始

2392 Then, you can gradually increase the **distance** and speed.
然後，再慢慢增加距離和速度。 distance 名 距離

2393 I'm afraid of biking.
我不敢騎腳踏車。

2394 Don't worry! I've **got your back**.
別擔心！我在你後面看著。 get one's back 片 照應某人

2395 You should keep your eyes on the road at all times when biking.
騎腳踏車的時候，要隨時注意路況。

2396 Bikers should follow traffic **signals**, too.
腳踏車騎士也必須遵守交通號誌。 signal 名 信號器

2397 My average riding speed is about 15-20 kph.
我騎車的平均時速大約是每小時十五到二十公里。

2398 Cycling too fast makes me feel **scared**.
騎太快會讓我感到害怕。 scared 形 恐懼的

2399 Cycling too fast could be very **dangerous**.
腳踏車騎太快可能會出意外。 dangerous 形 危險的

2400 Slow down, or you might hit somebody.
騎慢一點，不然你可能會撞到別人。

2401 I hate cars that **force** me off the road.
我討厭把我逼到路邊的車子。force 動 強迫

2402 Watch out for the slower **newbies**.
小心那些慢吞吞的新手。newbie 名 新手

2403 I almost **crashed last time** because I tried to avoid the slow riders.
上次為了要閃過那些騎得慢的人，我差點就摔車了。
crash 動 倒下 last time 片 上一次

2404 Sometimes you have to walk a bike when the **sidewalk** is crowded.
如果人行道很擠，你就要下來牽單車。sidewalk 名 人行道

2405 Do you have a **helmet** on?
你有戴安全帽嗎？helmet 名 安全帽

2406 Always wear a properly **fitting** helmet when riding a bike.
騎腳踏車時，一定要戴大小吻合的安全帽。fitting 形 合適的

2407 You should find a helmet that meets the **proper** standards.
你應該找頂有安全認證的安全帽。proper 形 合乎體統的

2408 Do you know how to wear a helmet correctly?
你知道安全帽的正確戴法嗎？

2409 Wearing a helmet is important because most bike accidents involve head injuries.
大部分的自行車意外都是頭部受傷，所以戴安全帽很重要。

2410 A **brightly** colored helmet is **visible** to drivers and other cyclists.
亮色系的安全帽能讓汽車駕駛和其他單車客看得清楚。
brightly 副 明亮地；閃亮地 visible 形 可看見的

2411 I just bought a **utility** bike.
我剛買了一輛多功能自行車。utility 形 有多種用途的

2412 I can ride the utility bike to work every day.
我可以每天騎這輛多功能自行車去上班了。

2413 Look at my new mountain bike!
看看我新買的登山自行車！

2414 This mountain bike is **identical** to the one that I saw in a magazine.
這部登山車和我在雜誌上看到的一模一樣。identical 形 完全相同的

2415 I decided to buy a new bike when I came across an ad.
我是因為剛好看到廣告，才決定要買新的腳踏車。

2416 It's the best bicycle **brand**.
這是自行車界的第一品牌。brand 名 商標；牌子

2417 The **folding bike** has twenty-one gears.
這台小摺有二十一段變速。folding bike 片 摺疊式自行車

2418 **Road bikes** are usually more expensive than mountain bikes.
公路車通常比登山車貴。road bike 片 公路車

2419 The new road bike just **rolled out**.
這是剛推出的最新款公路車。roll out 片 推出

2420 It comes with a water **bottle cage**.
還附贈一個水壺架。bottle cage 片 水壺架

2421 The **freewheel** gear **cluster** is the best part of the bicycle.
這個多片式飛輪組是這部車最棒的地方。
freewheel 名 飛輪 cluster 名 組

2422 The leather **handcrafted saddle** is gorgeous.
這款真皮手工坐墊真是美呆了。
handcrafted 形 手工製的 saddle 名 車座

2423 I like the pink **handlebars** and **pedals**.
我喜歡粉紅色的手把和腳踏板。

handlebar 名 (腳踏車的)手把 pedal 名 腳踏板

2424 The color is perfect for female bikers.
這個顏色很適合女性車友。

2425 You really know a lot about the parts of a bicycle.
你真了解腳踏車的零件。

2426 You can find all the bike **gear** in a bike shop.
你可以在腳踏車店裡找到所有的裝備。 gear 名 設備

2427 I also bought new cycling clothing and **gloves**.
我也買了新的自行車衣和手套。 glove 名 手套

2428 Bike **jerseys** are designed specifically for the needs of cyclists.
自行車衣是依騎車者的需求設計的。 jersey 名 賽車上衣

2429 I plan to go biking around Taiwan with my friends.
我計劃和朋友一起騎單車環島。

2430 You guys are really **adventurous**.
你們幾個還真有冒險精神。 adventurous 形 愛冒險的

2431 Are you crazy? You guys really want to ride a bike around the island?
你們真是瘋了！你們幾個真的要騎單車環島嗎？

2432 Long-distance rides are certainly a big challenge for me.
騎長途的路程對我來說實在是很大的挑戰。

2433 This bike **event** is held every year.
這項單車賽事每年都會舉辦。 event 名 事件

2434 I have **taken part in** this bike event for the past three years.
我前三年都有參加這項單車賽事。 take part in 片 參加

2435 This event **attracts** thousands of people every year.

這項活動每年都吸引數千名的民眾參加。 attract 動 吸引

2436 The Tour de France is the biggest cycling event in the world.
「環法自行車賽」是世界上最盛大的自行車賽事。

2437 Bicycle **rentals** are available **throughout** the city.
這個城市到處都可以租到腳踏車。
rental 名 租賃　throughout 介 遍布

2438 You can rent a public bicycle at an **automated kiosk**.
你可以在自動租賃站租公共腳踏車。
automated 形 機械化的；自動化的　kiosk 名 小亭

2439 There are several automated kiosks in Taipei and Kaohsiung.
台北和高雄都設有很多自動租賃站。

2440 The rental shop offers a wide range of bikes to rent.
這家出租店裡的單車類型很多，可以任選。

2441 How much is the bicycle rental **rate**?
腳踏車的租金怎麼算？ rate 名 費用

2442 **Rents** are shown on the board.
租金都寫在板子上了。 rent 名 租金

2443 **Daily** rental rates are cheaper than hourly ones.
租整天的費用會比以小時計費的便宜。 daily 形 每日的

2444 The price **includes** a helmet.
這個價錢還包含一頂安全帽。 include 動 包含

2445 I want to **return** my rental bike.
我想要還腳踏車。 return 動 歸還

2446 Most rental bikes are in poor condition.
供租用的腳踏車，大部分的車況都不好。

2447 May I **borrow** your bike?
我可以向你借腳踏車嗎？ borrow 動 借；借入

2448 If you don't ride a bike for months, you need to check the tires.
如果你的單車幾個月沒騎了，就得檢查輪胎還有沒有氣。

2449 Bike tires lose air when the bike is not being used. Why?
腳踏車如果很久沒騎，輪胎就會沒氣，這是為什麼啊？

2450 I need to get my tires **pumped up**.
我必須幫我的輪胎充氣。 pump up 片 給(輪胎等)充氣

2451 Where can I get an **air pump**?
哪裡有打氣筒呢？ air pump 片 氣泵；打氣筒

2452 You can use my **portable** air pump.
你可以用我的攜帶式打氣筒。 portable 形 便於攜帶的

2453 My bike **chain** might have fallen off.
我的腳踏車鏈條可能脫落了。 chain 名 鍊子

2454 Yes, the chain on your bike has come loose.
沒錯，你腳踏車的鏈條鬆了。

2455 It seems that something is wrong with my **brakes**.
我的煞車好像有點問題。 brake 名 煞車

2456 I can replace my bike tires and **inner tubes** on my own.
我會自己換腳踏車的輪胎和內胎。 inner tube 片 內胎

2457 Fixing a bike sounds very **complicated**.
修理腳踏車聽起來很複雜。 complicated 形 複雜的

2458 The shop provides basic support services for cyclists.
這家店提供車友基本的自行車服務。

2459 My bike was **stolen**.
我的腳踏車被偷了。 steal 動 偷；竊取

2460 Where did you **park** your bike?
你把腳踏車停在哪裡？ park 動 停放(車輛等)

2461 I parked it outside and went into a **convenience** store.
我進去超商時，把車停在店家外面。 convenience 名 便利設施

2462 Didn't you **lock up** your bike?
你的腳踏車沒上鎖嗎？ lock up 片 鎖起來

2463 I did, but the **thief** broke the bike lock.
我有上鎖，但小偷把鎖撬開了。 thief 名 小偷

2464 I lost the key to my bike lock.
我車鎖的鑰匙不見了。

2465 Don't you have **spare** keys?
你沒有備用鑰匙嗎？ spare 形 備用的

2466 I got a **road rash** while riding my bike.
我騎腳踏車時跌倒擦傷了。 road rash 片 高速騎車造成的擦傷

2467 I am too tired to ride any faster.
我實在太累，騎不動了。

2468 If you're too tired to ride the bike, just **walk** it.
如果你真的騎不動，就用牽的吧。 walk 動 陪…走

2469 Let's **take a break** at the bike rest stop.
我們在單車休息站休息一下吧。 take a break 片 休息

2470 Riding a bike really **tires** me **out**.
騎腳踏車真的把我累壞了。 tire out 片 使疲憊不堪

2471 It took about four hours to finish the bike ride.
全程大概騎了四個小時左右。

2472 A two-hour ride **along** a bike path is enough for

me.
對我來說，沿著自行車道騎兩個小時就很夠了。along 介 沿著

2473 My brother cycled for 36 **kilometers** yesterday.
我弟弟昨天騎了三十六公里的自行車。kilometer 名 公里

UNIT 2 到戶外露營吧 Let's Go Camping!

2474 I love nature, and that's why I always **go camping** in my free time.
我喜愛大自然，所以我一有空就會去露營。go camping 片 露營

2475 Camping gives people an opportunity to **get away from** the city life.
露營能讓人遠離都市生活。get away from 片 遠離

2476 Camping brings me closer to nature.
露營讓我更接近大自然。

2477 You can do a lot of activities in the **wilderness**.
你能在野外從事很多活動。wilderness 名 荒野

2478 When going camping, we rely on our skills to survive in the wild.
去露營時，我們得依靠野外求生技能才行。

2479 Which do you prefer: **backpacking** or car camping?
你比較喜歡當背包客，還是開車去露營？backpacking 名 背包旅行

2480 Camping is the most **fun** outdoor recreational activity.
露營是最有趣的戶外休閒活動。fun 形 有趣的

2481 I don't like camping because I hate **mosquito** bites.
我不喜歡露營，因為我討厭被蚊子咬。mosquito 名 蚊子

2482 I just heard that there's a nice **campsite** near here.
我聽說這附近有個很棒的露營區。campsite 名 露營地

2483 The campsite is located near a beach with mountains behind them.
那個營地靠近海邊，背後還有山環繞。

2484 It is better for you to know some **basics** about camping.
你最好先了解一些露營的基本常識。basic 名 基本原則

2485 I found several useful camping **tips** on a website.
我在網站上找到一些實用的露營訣竅。tip 名 訣竅

2486 Going camping sounds like we have to **prepare** a lot of stuff.
露營聽起來要準備好多東西。prepare 動 準備

2487 If you want comfortable camping, an **R.V.** is necessary.
如果你想要有一趟舒適的露營之旅，那就必須準備好露營車。
R.V. 縮 休旅車(=Recreation Vehicle)

2488 Camping without **tents** is not real camping.
少了帳篷的話，根本就算不上露營了。tent 名 帳篷

2489 I have all my camping equipment in my **garage**.
所有的露營裝備都放在我的車庫裡。garage 名 車庫

2490 **Folding** tables and chairs are **essential**.
摺疊式桌椅是必備的。folding 形 摺疊式的 essential 形 必要的

2491 You'll take a couple of wool **blankets**, won't you?
你會帶幾條毛毯吧？blanket 名 毛毯

2492 How many **sleeping bags** do we need?

我們需要幾個睡袋？ sleeping bag 片 睡袋

2493 I want to get **a** new **pair of** hiking boots.
我想買雙新的登山靴。 a pair of 片 一雙

2494 I am not good at using camp **stoves**.
我不太會用露營用的爐子。 stove 名 火爐

2495 A gas stove is worth buying.
瓦斯爐很值得買。

2496 Where can I buy gas **containers**?
哪裡買得到瓦斯罐呢？ container 名 容器

2497 It's important to plan what food we will bring for camping.
計劃露營時要帶什麼食物是很重要的。

2498 Bringing too much food could be a **waste**.
帶太多食物會造成浪費。 waste 名 浪費

2499 A good **Swiss** Army Knife is a must-bring when going camping.
去露營時，一定要帶瑞士刀。 Swiss 形 瑞士的

2500 You might **encounter** some **insects** or **snakes** around your camping area.
露營場附近，可能會有一些昆蟲或蛇。
encounter 動 遇到 insect 名 昆蟲 snake 名 蛇

2501 Should we bring some **foam** to sleep on?
我們需要帶充氣式睡墊嗎？ foam 名 充氣式睡墊

2502 Don't forget to apply insect **repellent**.
別忘了擦防蚊液。 repellent 名 驅蟲劑

2503 I also brought a first-aid kit, hat and sunscreen
我也帶了急救箱、帽子和防曬乳。

2504 The **scenery** around the new campground is **breathtaking**.

這個新開發的營區風景真是令人嘆為觀止。
scenery 名 風景 breathtaking 形 驚人的

2505 Is camping **allowed** here?
這裡可以露營嗎？allow 動 允許

2506 Camping is **prohibited** by the **river**.
河邊禁止露營。prohibit 動 禁止 river 名 河

2507 The campground was crowded and **cramped**.
露營區被擠得水洩不通。cramped 形 狹窄的

2508 Does the campground offer shower **facilities**?
這個營區有提供淋浴設備嗎？facility 名 設施

2509 It does, but the showers **lack privacy**.
有提供，不過淋浴的場所不夠隱密。lack 動 缺乏 privacy 名 隱私

2510 We can **unpack** and start to set up camp.
我們可以卸下裝備，準備露營了。unpack 動 卸下

2511 Could you help me **pitch** the tent?
你能幫我搭帳篷嗎？pitch 動 搭(帳篷)

2512 We are going to **build** a **campfire**.
我們要生營火了。build 動 生(火) campfire 名 篝火

2513 **Awesome**! A campfire has long been a symbol of camping.
太棒了！營火一直都是露營的象徵。awesome 形 令人驚嘆的

2514 Starting a campfire can be a bit **challenging**.
生營火頗具挑戰性。challenging 形 具挑戰性的

2515 Cooking food is one of the most **enjoyable** camping traditions.
露營必備的活動中，烹煮食物的樂趣可是數一數二的。
enjoyable 形 有樂趣的

2516 We have some **ready-to-eat** camp food, such as cheese and **crackers**.

我們有準備一些即食品，像起司和蘇打餅乾之類的。
ready-to-eat 形 即食的 cracker 名 餅乾

2517 The fire needs **tending**.
要有人看著火才行。tend 動 照料；注意

2518 There you go! This hot dog is ready to eat.
好了！熱狗已經熟了。

2519 I've brought some **beer** to go with hot dogs.
我帶了一些啤酒來配熱狗。beer 名 啤酒

2520 The beer is in the **cooler**.
啤酒放在冰桶裡。cooler 名 冷藏箱

2521 I saw a snake **crawling** into your sleeping bag.
我看到有蛇鑽進你的睡袋。crawl 動 爬行

2522 I didn't know that you were so afraid of snakes.
我不知道你原來很怕蛇。

2523 I went camping at Sun Moon Lake with my relatives last weekend.
我上週末和親戚一起到日月潭露營。

2524 We loved the scenery **surrounding** the campsite.
我們很喜歡露營區四周的風景。surround 動 圍繞

2525 The beautiful weather made our camping awesome.
好天氣讓我們的露營很成功。

2526 I've gone camping with my family since I was a kid.
我從小就常跟著家人去露營。

2527 Camping is a **pleasant** way for family members to connect with each other.
露營是聯繫家人感情的好方法。pleasant 形 令人愉快的

2528 My last camping trip with friends left me with **unforgettable memories.**
上次和朋友去露營的經驗，是我心中難忘的回憶。
unforgettable 形 難忘的　memory 名 回憶

2529 The weather will be beautiful tomorrow. Let's go fishing.
明天會是個好天氣，我們去釣魚吧！

2530 I am going fishing this Saturday; wanna **come along**?
我這週六要去釣魚，你要一起來嗎？ come along 片 一起來

2531 I'll go with you. I want to **try out** my new fishing **rod**.
我和你一起去，我想試試我的新釣竿。 try out 片 試用　rod 名 竿

2532 Fishing is gaining more and more **popularity** nowadays.
現在釣魚的人愈來愈多了。 popularity 名 普及；流行

2533 I can catch fish with a **worm** and a **hook**.
我只需要一條蟲餌和一個魚鉤，就能釣到魚。
worm 名 蟲　hook 名 鉤

2534 I like to fish in the **ocean** while my brother likes to fish in a pond.
我喜歡海釣，我弟弟則喜歡在池塘釣魚。 ocean 名 海洋

2535 Fishing is my new **hobby**.
釣魚是我的新嗜好。 hobby 名 嗜好

2536 I prefer to go fishing early in the morning.
我喜歡一大清早去釣魚。

2537 I almost forget all about my work and personal problems when fishing.
釣魚時，我能將大部分的公事和日常瑣事拋在腦後。

2538 I usually **think** things **over** when fishing.

我通常在釣魚時思考事情。 think over 片 仔細考慮

2539 I have had some **unpleasant** fishing experiences.
我有一些不愉快的釣魚經驗。 unpleasant 形 不愉快的

2540 How come? Fishing is a fun activity that helps you **relax**.
怎麼會？釣魚是能讓人放鬆的一大樂事。 relax 動 放鬆

2541 You can **turn** fishing **into** something easy and fun.
釣魚可以變得簡單又有趣。 turn into 片 變成

2542 Just grab a rod, a **reel** and some **bait**. You can do it, too.
只要有釣竿、捲線軸和魚餌就行了，你也辦得到。
reel 名 繞線輪 bait 名 餌

2543 Having the proper fishing gear is important even if you are not a **pro**.
就算不是專業釣手，還是要帶合適的釣魚裝備。 pro 名 專業人員

2544 Make sure that everything you need is inside your **tackle** box.
要確定你所需的物品都有放進釣具箱中。 tackle 名 裝備

2545 I always prepare an extra line and hook in case I need them when fishing.
我去釣魚時都會多準備一個釣魚線和釣鉤，以備不時之需。

2546 It is a good idea to bring extra fishing lines and hooks.
你有多準備釣魚線跟釣鉤，真是明智之舉。

2547 My fishing line **snapped**.
我的釣魚線斷了。 snap 動 突然折斷；拉斷

2548 This is the hook and these are the **weights**.
這是釣鉤，這些是鉛錘。 weight 名 重物

2549 They make the hook **sink**.
鉛錘的功能是讓釣鉤沉下去。 sink 動 下沉

2550 Did you remember to bring the bait?
你有記得帶魚餌嗎？

2551 I brought some **squid** and **prawns**.
我帶了一些烏賊和蝦子。 squid 名 烏賊 prawn 名 蝦

2552 See! These are my new **waders**.
你看！這是我的新防水褲。 wader 名 (與靴相連的)防水褲

2553 The maximum breaking **strain** is fifteen kilograms.
它能承受的最大重量是十五公斤。 strain 名 負擔

2554 The water looks good today. We might catch some big fish.
今天的海面狀況看起來不錯，我們也許能抓到大魚。

2555 It's nice that the water is **quiet**.
真好！水面很平靜。 quiet 形 平靜的

2556 Maybe we can catch some fish for dinner.
我們搞不好能抓到魚當晚餐吃喔。

2557 Where can I catch **tuna**?
哪裡可以捕到鮪魚呢？ tuna 名 鮪魚

2558 You may need to go **deep-sea** fishing.
那你可能要去深海捕囉！ deep-sea 形 深海的

2559 The water is a bit **choppy** out here.
這裡的風浪有點大。 choppy 形 波浪起伏的

2560 The wind is getting stronger.
風變大了。

2561 I am getting a little **seasick**.
我有點暈船。 seasick 形 暈船的

2562 I don't know how to **cast**.
我不知道要怎麼拋竿。 cast 動 扔；擲

2563 Don't worry! I'll teach you. It's not that hard.
別擔心！我會教你，其實沒那麼難。

2564 This is a **closed** reel. It's easy.
這是密閉式的捲線輪，很容易使用的。 closed 形 封閉的

2565 You just hold the rod here and push this button down with your **thumb**.
你只要握住竿子這裡，用大拇指按下這個按鈕。 thumb 名 大拇指

2566 Then, **release** it at the end of your cast. Like this.
竿子甩出去之後，就把按鈕放開，像這樣。 release 動 鬆開

2567 Where did you learn how to fish?
你在哪裡學會這些釣魚方法的啊？

2568 My father **taught** me how to fish when I was a kid.
小時候，我爸爸教過我怎麼釣魚。 teach 動 教導

2569 My grandfather taught me these tips.
這些是我爺爺教我的祕訣。

2570 Maybe you can teach me a few **tricks**.
也許你可以教我幾招。 trick 名 竅門；手法

2571 We can try out the **lures**.
我們可以試試魚餌。 lure 名 誘餌；魚餌

2572 There are some lures in the tackle box.
釣具箱裡有一些魚餌。

2573 When you feel a bite, **jerk** the **pole** to hook the fish.
感覺有魚上鉤時，就要迅速拉竿，把魚釣起來。
jerk 動 猛地一拉 pole 名 竿

2574 I've got a **bite**! / The fish are **biting**.

有魚上鉤了！ bite 名 咬；一口之量 動 咬

2575 Give it some time to take the bait!
給魚一些時間咬餌。

2576 I've got it! It feels like a big one.
我抓到牠了！好像是條大魚。

2577 Be careful! Don't lose it.
小心一點！不要讓牠跑掉了。

2578 I've got my first one for the day.
我釣到今天的第一條魚了。

2579 It's a **mackerel**. They're good for steaming.
是鯖魚，清蒸很好吃喔。 mackerel 名 鯖魚；青花魚

2580 **Hand** me the **pliers**, please.
請把鉗子拿給我。 hand 動 傳遞 pliers 名 鉗子

2581 You are quite a **fisherman**.
你真是位專業的漁夫。 fisherman 名 漁夫

2582 We are lucky that we caught a lot of fish!
今天釣到好多魚，真是太幸運了！

2583 You can bring some home by storing them inside an ice **bucket**.
你可以把一些魚放在冰桶裡帶回家。 bucket 名 水桶

2584 Don't forget to put some ice inside to keep the fish from **spoiling**.
不要忘了放冰塊進去，魚才不會腐壞。 spoil 動 腐敗

聊聊各種球類運動
Playing Ball Games

2585 Basketball season is right **around the corner**.
籃球季快開打了。around the corner 片 即將來臨

2586 I am a basketball **nut**.
我是超級籃球迷。nut 名 狂熱者；…迷

2587 Michael Jordon is my favorite **athlete**.
麥可．喬丹是我最喜愛的運動員。athlete 名 運動員

2588 He broke lots of records during his **career** with the Bulls.
在公牛隊的期間，他打破了許多紀錄。career 名 生涯

2589 You can find basketball **courts** everywhere.
到處都可以看到籃球場。court 名 場地

2590 Do you want to shoot some **hoops**?
要不要去打籃球啊？hoop 名 籃框

2591 That big guy kept **waving** his arms in my face.
那個大塊頭老是在我面前揮手阻擋。wave 動 揮手；搖動

2592 He **fouled** several times during the second half.
下半場他犯了好幾次規。foul 動 (比賽中)犯規

2593 Each **foul shot** is worth one point.
罰球進了能得一分。foul shot 片 罰球

2594 That player shot seven **baskets** during the game.
那名選手在比賽中投進了七球。basket 名 籃網

2595 He is going to shoot from the **free throw line**.
他要從罰球線投籃了。free throw line 片 罰球線

2596 This game is a **tug of war** between the players.
這場球賽是兩隊間的拉鋸戰。tug of war 片 拉鋸戰；拔河

2597 It was a **close** game.
比賽雙方的實力很接近。close 形 勢均力敵的

2598 They have a 50/50 chance of **grabbing** the ball.
他們有均等的搶球機會。grab 動 抓取；奪取

2599 The outcome of the game can still be changed in the last **second**.
就算到了最後一秒，仍有機會扭轉比賽結果。second 名 秒

2600 For me, it is very **nerve-racking** in the final minutes.
球賽的最後幾分鐘，我超緊張的。nerve-racking 形 使人極不安的

2601 Our school team will compete in the basketball **tournament**.
我們學校的校隊打入了籃球錦標賽。tournament 名 錦標賽

2602 Do you watch baseball games?
你有看棒球比賽嗎？

2603 I don't follow baseball, but my boyfriend does.
我不看棒球，但我男朋友有在看。

2604 There are usually nine **innings** in a baseball game.
一般而言，每一場棒球賽會有九局。inning 名 (棒球的)一局

2605 The Americans are crazy about Major **League** Baseball.
美國人很熱衷於大聯盟。league 名 聯盟

2606 I am a **huge** MLB **fan**, too.
我也是大聯盟的狂熱球迷。huge 形 巨大的 fan 名 迷

2607 I am a big fan of the Boston Red Sox.
我是波士頓紅襪隊的死忠球迷。

2608 The Yankees are my favorite baseball team.
洋基隊是我最喜愛的球隊。

2609 Yankee fans would never **root for** the Red Sox.
洋基隊的粉絲絕不會幫紅襪隊加油。root for 片(口)為…打氣

2610 They have been long-time **enemies**.
長久以來，他們都是勢不兩立的。enemy 名 敵人

2611 Have you ever gone to a **ballpark** to see a game?
你有到棒球場看過比賽嗎？ballpark 名 棒球場

2612 I watch Major League Baseball games **online** or on ESPN.
我都透過網路或 ESPN 體育台看大聯盟的賽事。online 副 連線地

2613 Do you want to go to a baseball game with me?
想不想和我一起去看棒球比賽呢？

2614 Let's meet at the front gate of the baseball **stadium**.
我們約在棒球場的大門口見面吧。stadium 名 體育場

2615 Fenway Park, **established** in 1912, is a historical baseball park.
芬威球場建於 1912 年，是個歷史悠久的球場。establish 動 建立

2616 I can see the action very clearly when watching a game at a stadium.
在體育場內，球員的動作都能一覽無遺。

2617 I feel excited when fans are **yelling** and **shouting** together.
當所有的球迷一起大喊時，我會感到很興奮。
yell 動 喊叫　shout 動 叫嚷

2618 I prefer seats close to the center field so that I can see the whole **diamond**.
我比較喜歡靠近中央的座位，因為這樣可以看到整個棒球場。

diamond 名 棒球場

2619 I bought three **infield** reserved tickets behind the home plate.
我買了三張本壘板後方的內野保留票。 infield 名 內野

2620 Infield reserved tickets behind second base are all sold out.
二壘後方的內野保留票全都賣光了。

2621 Do you have any **outfield** unreserved tickets near left field?
左外野的自由座位還有票嗎？ outfield 名 外野

2622 Did you see the **starter** on that team?
你看到那隊的先發投手了沒？ starter 名 先發投手

2623 The **pitcher** on the **mound** is the ace of the team.
投手丘上的那名投手是隊上的王牌。
pitcher 名 投手 mound 名 投手踏板

2624 Strike out!
三振出局！

2625 It's a wild pitch, and the ball hit the **backstop**.
那是個暴投，球打到了捕手。 backstop 名 捕手

2626 It's a foul ball. It was hit outside the **baseline**.
是個界外球，球滾出底線了。 baseline 名 底線

2627 The **batter** hit it too high!
打者這一球打得太高了！ batter 名 打擊手

2628 It's a **fly ball**. / It was a **can of corn**!
是個高飛球。 fly ball / can of corn 片 高飛球

2629 It was an easily caught fly ball.
是個很容易接的高飛球。

2630 It was an outstanding catch by the **outfielder**.

外野手這球接得漂亮。outfielder 名 外野手

2631 It's a **moon shot**! / It's a very long, high home run.
是個又深又遠的全壘打！moon shot 片 又高又遠的全壘打

2632 And It's a **grand slam**. / And it's a home run with the bases loaded.
而且是個滿貫全壘打。grand slam 片 滿壘全壘打

2633 He has hit forty-six home runs in his baseball career.
在他的棒球生涯中，已經擊出了四十六支全壘打。

2634 That was a **daring steal**.
那是個大膽的盜壘。daring 形 大膽的 steal 名 盜壘

2635 They've got three **left on bases**.
他們留下三人的殘壘。left on base 片 殘壘

2636 The crowd is **booing**. / They are giving a **Bronx cheer**.
觀眾噓聲四起。boo 動 發出噓聲 Bronx cheer 片 譏刺的噓聲

2637 Why do people stand up during the 7th inning?
比賽到第七局的時候，為什麼大家都要站起來呢？

2638 "7th-inning **stretch**" is a **long-standing** tradition in America.
第七局的伸展活動是美國棒球比賽的傳統。
stretch 名 伸展；伸懶腰 long-standing 形 存在已久的

2639 People sing "God Bless America" during the 7th-inning stretch.
第七局的伸展活動中，大家會齊唱《天佑美國》。

2640 Isn't the World Cup coming soon?
世界杯足球賽快開打了吧？

2641 The 2018 FIFA World Cup will **kick off** in Russia.
二〇一八年的世足賽將於俄羅斯登場。kick off 片 開球

2642 FIFA **takes place** every four years.
世足賽每四年舉辦一次。take place 片 舉行；發生

2643 When the World Cup comes, I even don't sleep or eat.
世界盃一開打，我甚至不吃不睡呢！

2644 **Soccer** is not a popular sport in Taiwan.
足球運動在台灣不怎麼流行。soccer 名 足球

2645 Still, a lot of Taiwanese follow the FIFA World Cup.
但還是有很多台灣球迷瘋世界盃足球賽。

2646 I have no idea about the rules of soccer.
我對足球的規則完全不了解。

2647 What does "double-header" mean?
什麼是「連賽兩場」？

2648 That's when two teams play two games **in a row**.
那是指兩隊連續交鋒兩次。in a row 片 接連不斷地

2649 Which teams are playing?
現在是哪兩隊在比賽？

2650 It's Italy versus New Zealand.
現在是義大利對抗紐西蘭。

2651 Which soccer team do you **support**?
你支持哪一隊啊？support 動 支持

2652 I'll just wait to see if my team can make it to the semi-finals.
我會等著，看我支持的球隊能不能挺進準決賽。

2653 The next game is England versus Brazil.
下一場比賽是英國對抗巴西。

2654 I bet it will be really exciting.
我敢打賭這場比賽一定會超級精采。

2655 I can't wait to watch it!
我好期待！

2656 The game will decide if Germany reaches the Round of 8.
這場比賽將決定德國是否能進入八強。

2657 Argentina won their **opening match** 1-0 over Nigeria.
開幕賽中，阿根廷以一比零的成績擊敗奈及利亞。
opening 名 開始　match 名 比賽；競賽

2658 Everyone has their eyes on Lionel Messi of Argentina.
所有人的目光焦點都放在阿根廷隊的梅西身上。

2659 The Dutch can create a **goal** from any situation.
荷蘭隊在任何情況下都能進攻。goal 名 得分數

2660 The **referee** gave David a **penalty**.
裁判判大衛犯規。referee 名 裁判　penalty 名 處罰

2661 He received a penalty because of a **handball**.
他因為打手球被判犯規。handball 名 手球

2662 It was a **legitimate tackle**!
那是合理的阻截耶！legitimate 形 正當的　tackle 名 阻截鏟球

2663 It's **out of play**.
球出界了。out of play 片 出界

2664 The **midfield** defender took a corner kick.
那位中場防守球員踢了一個角球。midfield 名 中場

2665 Only one minute of play left.
離比賽結束只剩一分鐘了。

2666 Goal!
射門得分！

2667 Do you want to play tennis?
要不要打一場網球呢？

2668 Think you can beat me? Just **bring it on**!
想要打贏我嗎？儘管放馬過來！ bring it on 片 放馬過來

2669 All eyes were on Yen-Hsun Lu at the 2010 Wimbledon Open.
盧彥勳是二〇一〇年溫布頓網球公開賽中的焦點。

2670 Yesterday's match was a heartstopper.
昨天的比賽真是緊張刺激。

2671 Can I borrow your **racket**? Jessica and I are going to play **badminton** this afternoon.
可以跟你借球拍嗎？我下午要和潔西卡打羽毛球。
racket 名 球拍 badminton 名 羽毛球

2672 Badminton is similar to tennis.
羽毛球和網球很類似。

2673 Both tennis and badminton are played on a court with a net across it.
網球和羽毛球都需要在有網子的球場上進行。

熱愛健身房訓練
Going To The Gym

2674 Working out at the gym has gained **incredible** popularity over the last decade.
這十年來，上健身房運動的人數遽增。 incredible 形 驚人的

2675 Don't **underestimate** the importance of exercise.
不要低估了運動的重要性。 underestimate 動 低估

2676 Doing exercise has been proven to **benefit** all populations.
運動被證實對所有年齡層的人都有益處。benefit 動 有益於

2677 Not only **adolescents** but also seniors need regular exercise.
不只是青少年，老人家也需要定期運動。adolescent 名 青少年

2678 Doing exercise regularly can help you stay **fit**.
規律的運動能維持健康。fit 形 健康的；強健的

2679 Do you **work out** a lot?
你常去健身嗎？work out 片 運動鍛鍊

2680 It depends. I try to go to the gym three to four times a week.
看情況，我一星期會盡量抽三到四天的時間去健身房。

2681 But, you know, sometimes I am just too busy to work out.
但是，我有時候忙到根本沒時間去健身。

2682 I am a fitness **freak**, and I work out at the gym every day.
我是個健身狂，每天都上健身房。freak 名 怪胎

2683 I **jog** four kilometers on the **treadmill** every morning.
我每天早上都在跑步機上慢跑四公里。
jog 動 慢跑 treadmill 名 跑步機

2684 Working out makes me feel more **confident**.
健身能讓我更有自信。confident 形 自信的

2685 Do you prefer working out at a gym or jogging on a **track**?
你喜歡上健身房，還是去運動場慢跑？track 名 跑道

2686 Don't you think that working out at a gym is **boring**?

你不覺得待在健身房運動很無聊嗎？ boring 形 乏味的

2687 Working out at a gym helps you avoid sunburn.
在健身房運動可以避免曬傷。

2688 What's the rate for a gym **membership**?
健身俱樂部的會費是多少呢？ membership 名 會員身分

2689 You can ask the **receptionist**.
你可以問一下接待員。 receptionist 名 櫃台接待員

2690 We have annual, semi-annual and **monthly** memberships. Which would you like to apply for?
我們的會員分為年度、半年度和以月份計這幾種，請問您想加入哪一種呢？ monthly 形 每月的

2691 I would like to pay month-to-month.
我想要月付費用。

2692 How much should I pay on a month-to-month **basis**?
如果是月繳的話，我一個月要付多少錢呢？ basis 名 基礎

2693 You can **take advantage of** the pre-paid bonus plan for extra savings.
你可以利用預付方案，會有更多額外的優惠。
take advantage of 片 利用

2694 This is the best package rate for a membership.
想要入會的話，這個方案是最划算的了。

2695 He signed up for a **lifetime** membership at the gym.
他加入了健身房的終身會員。 lifetime 形 終身的

2696 I decided to buy a two-year membership.
我決定購買兩年的會員資格。

2697 I just re-joined a **fitness** center after two years of not working out.
停止健身兩年後，我又重新加入健身俱樂部。 fitness 名 健康

2698 All the members can use the **steam** room.
所有的會員都可以使用蒸氣室。steam 名 蒸氣

2699 I love enjoying a **sauna** after a gym workout.
在健身房運動完之後，我喜歡去洗個三溫暖。sauna 名 桑拿浴

2700 I really enjoy **sweating**.
我真的很喜歡流汗的感覺。sweat 動 使出汗

2701 I can show you more about our facilities.
我會帶你參觀更多的設備。

2702 Look at your orange peel **syndrome**.
看看你的橘皮組織。syndrome 名 併發症狀

2703 Getting thinner in the **belly** has been my dream.
讓小腹平坦一直是我的夢想。belly 名 腹部

2704 I hope I can have a **flat abs**.
我真希望能有平坦的小腹。flat 形 平坦的 abs 名 腹部肌肉

2705 By doing so, you can burn off your belly fat easily.
這麼做就能輕鬆消除小腹的肥油。

2706 Many middle-aged men have **beer bellies**.
很多中年男子都有啤酒肚。beer belly 片 啤酒肚

2707 Try doing some **sit-ups**.
試著做幾個仰臥起坐。sit-up 名 仰臥起坐

2708 Flabby arms are embarrassing, especially when I wear a sleeveless top.
蝴蝶袖真的很令人尷尬，尤其是穿無袖上衣的時候。

2709 How can I get rid of **flabby** arms?
怎麼做才能跟蝴蝶袖說掰掰呢？flabby 形 不結實的

2710 Look at that **spare tire** around that middle-aged woman's waist.

看看那位中年婦女腰部的贅肉。spare tire 片 腹部贅肉

2711 Debby's **wimpy biceps** bother her a lot.
鬆弛的二頭肌對黛比造成很大的困擾。
wimpy 形 無用的 biceps 名 二頭肌

2712 Pear-shaped women have small waists but big **hips**.
西洋梨身材的女人腰圍細，但臀圍大。hip 名 臀部

2713 Can I just work on the worst parts of my body?
我可以只鍛鍊身體最胖的部位嗎？

2714 I need to burn some calories **in no time**.
我必須要快速消耗一些卡路里。in no time 片 很快；立即

2715 I want to maintain my body and increase **muscle tone**.
我想要維持身材，增加肌肉張力的強度。muscle tone 片 肌肉張力

2716 I work out in order to lose weight and get into good shape.
我是為了減肥和維持身材才健身的。

2717 Are you trying to reduce **body fat**?
你想要減低體脂肪嗎？body fat 片 體脂肪

2718 I try to do **cardiovascular** activity with a low-calorie diet to maintain my physical **appearance**.
為了維持體態，我有試著做心肺運動，再加上低卡飲食的控制。
cardiovascular 形 心血管的 appearance 名 外觀

2719 I am going to **develop** my chest muscles.
我要鍛鍊胸肌。develop 動 使發達

2720 Doing weight training can build chest muscles.
重量訓練可以鍛鍊胸肌。

2721 If you continue to exercise, you will lose weight and be fit.
如果你持續運動，就能減肥，還能擁有完美的體態。

2722 Warm up first so you don't pull any muscles or **cramp up**.
先做暖身運動，才不會拉傷肌肉或抽筋。 cramp up 片 抽筋

2723 There are a variety of classes in the gym, such as **yoga** and **aerobics**.
健身房提供多元化課程，像是瑜珈和有氧運動都有。
yoga 名 瑜珈 aerobics 名 有氧運動

2724 The fitness center also offers many group classes.
這家健身俱樂部還提供許多團體課程。

2725 My mother does yoga three times a week.
我的母親一週做三次瑜珈。

2726 I do **Pilates** regularly.
我習慣做皮拉提斯運動。 Pilates 名 皮拉提斯

2727 It's the most effective exercise for **tightening**.
想讓身材緊實，那是最有效的運動。 tightening 名 繃緊；緊縮

2728 There are some tips to make your body **firm**.
有一些能讓你變得更結實的技巧。 firm 形 結實的；牢固的

2729 Look **straight ahead**.
直視前方。 straight 形 筆直的 ahead 副 向前

2730 Stand and **balance** on one leg.
用單腳站立，並保持平衡。 balance 動 保持平衡

2731 Kick the other leg out **slightly** behind you.
另一隻腳輕輕地向後踢。 slightly 副 輕微地

2732 Hold the **pose** for at least fifteen seconds.
維持這個姿勢至少十五秒。 pose 名 姿勢

2733 You need to **concentrate** on your balance and breathing
必須專注在平衡以及你的呼吸上。 concentrate 動 專注於

2734 Doing this exercise can **tone up** your muscles.
這個運動能強化你的肌肉。 tone up 片 強化

2735 **Spinning** class can help you develop a firm **butt**.
飛輪有氧能幫助你鍛鍊出緊實的臀部。
spinning 名 飛輪運動 butt 名 臀部

2736 I've been taking spinning classes for about six months.
我已經上了六個月的飛輪有氧課。

2737 This is the best exercise for a sexy, firm butt.
這是造就性感、緊實臀部的最佳運動。

2738 I enjoy cycling on a **stationary** bike.
我很喜歡騎健身腳踏車。 stationary 形 不動的

2739 How often do you do aerobics every week?
你每週做幾次有氧運動？

2740 I take aerobics classes twice a week.
我一週上兩次有氧課。

2741 My sister likes taking aerobic boxing classes.
我姐姐喜歡去上拳擊有氧的課程。

2742 I am not good at aerobics because I can never follow the **instructor**.
我不太會跳有氧舞蹈，因為我都跟不上老師的動作。
instructor 名 教練

2743 If you watch others doing it a few times, you can pick up the basic **moves** easily.
看別人做幾次，你很快就能學會基本動作了。 move 名 移動

2744 Try the leg press.
試試蹬腿訓練機吧！

2745 I work out three times a week, and I can leg-press up to 200 kilograms.
我一週健身三次，現在我的大腿最重可以舉到兩百公斤了。

2746 I don't want to create large, **unattractive** muscles.
我不想要練出難看的大肌肉。 unattractive 形 無吸引力的

2747 I am afraid of **strength** training.
我很怕做重量訓練。 strength 名 力氣；強度

2748 After training, I could **hardly** walk for two days.
訓練結束之後的兩天，我幾乎無法走路。 hardly 副 幾乎不

2749 You should always start from low and slowly work up to heavier weights.
至於舉重，你應該從輕的開始，然後才逐漸增加重量。

2750 If you're really interested, you should look into getting a **personal** trainer.
如果你真的有興趣，應該找個私人教練。 personal 形 私人的

2751 Even if you don't plan on being a serious body builder, it's a good idea.
即使你的目標不是成為健美先生或健美小姐，這依然是個好主意。

2752 Trainers teach you a lot about the best and safest way to use weights.
教練會教你最好、最安全的舉重方法。

UNIT 5 夏日必備水上活動 The Water Activities

2753 The weather has been scorching hot over the past few days here.
過去幾天，這裡的天氣熱到都快能把人烤焦了。

2754 Do you feel like going to the swimming pool?

你想要去游泳池嗎？

2755 We can go swimming to **cool off**.
我們可以去游泳，消消暑。cool off 片 使感到涼快

2756 Cindy swam twenty **laps** this morning.
辛蒂今天早上游了二十趟。lap 名 (游泳池的)一個來回

2757 I've done my ten laps for the day.
我已經游完今天的十趟來回了。

2758 I like to go to the indoor pool at the **gymnasium**.
我喜歡去體育館的室內游泳池。gymnasium 名 體育館；健身房

2759 It's a solar-heated swimming pool.
那是座利用太陽能加熱的溫水游泳池。

2760 Swimming in a **heated** pool in winter is great.
冬天在溫水游泳池裡游泳的感覺很棒。heated 形 熱的

2761 I don't like to get water in my eyes.
我不喜歡眼睛進水的感覺。

2762 The swimming pool water contains **chlorine**.
游泳池的水含氯。chlorine 名 氯

2763 The pool water irritates our eyes and skin.
池水對我們的眼睛和皮膚有害。

2764 Do you use **earplugs**?
你用耳塞嗎？earplug 名 耳塞

2765 Earplugs keep the water out.
耳塞能防止耳朵進水。

2766 I'll just get my **trunks** and **goggles**.
我去拿一下我的泳褲和蛙鏡。
trunk 名 男用運動褲 goggle 名 護目鏡

2767 Sam forgot his swimming trunks.
山姆忘了帶泳褲。

2768 Don't forget your swimming cap.
不要忘記你的泳帽。

2769 You are not allowed to go into the pool without a cap.
沒有戴泳帽，不能進游泳池。

2770 My new swimming cap matches my **polka dot** bathing suit.
我的新泳帽和我的圓點泳裝配成一套。 polka dot 片 圓點花樣

2771 You can put your personal stuff in the **locker**.
你可以把私人物品放到置物櫃裡。 locker 名 衣物櫃

2772 Read the pool rules before you go in.
下水前，記得看一下游泳池的規則。

2773 Swimmers should **adhere to** the pool rules.
游泳者要遵守泳池規則。 adhere to 片 忠於

2774 I love swimming! It's lots of fun, and it's a great exercise.
我喜歡游泳，很好玩，是個很棒的運動。

2775 Swimming is my **major pastime** in summer.
游泳是我夏天的主要消遣。 major 形 主要的 pastime 名 消遣

2776 Swimming is the best exercise for the heart and **lungs**.
游泳是對心肺功能最有益的運動。 lung 名 肺

2777 I don't really like swimming.
我不太喜歡游泳。

2778 I can't control my breathing while swimming.
我游泳時不會換氣。

2779 I can't swim.
我是個旱鴨子。

2780 My friend and I joined a swim camp last summer.
我和朋友去年參加了游泳夏令營。

2781 Swimming is **scary** for me.
我非常害怕游泳。scary 形 引起驚慌的

2782 Getting into the pool is a big **challenge** for me.
踏入游泳池對我而言真是一大挑戰。challenge 名 挑戰

2783 How big is this pool?
這座游泳池有多大？

2784 This is a **competitive** pool.
這是比賽用的游泳池。competitive 形 競爭性的

2785 It's an **Olympic** size pool, and it is fifty meters long.
這座游泳池是奧運標準池，有五十公尺長。Olympic 形 奧林匹克的

2786 It's quite deep at the deep **end**.
深水區的水位很深。end 名 末端；盡頭

2787 Let's go into the swimming pool.
我們快下水吧！

2788 The water is **chilly**! I'd rather stay in the spa pool.
水好冰喔！我待在溫水池就好了。chilly 形 冷到讓人不適的

2789 You'll **warm up** as soon as you start swimming.
一旦開始游，就會暖和起來了。warm up 片 變暖

2790 Adam jumped into the water and made a big **splash**.
亞當跳下泳池，濺起好大的水花。splash 名 濺；潑

2791 Do you see an empty **lane**?
你有看到空的水道嗎？lane 名 泳道；跑道

2792 Great! Let's jump on in!
太棒了！我們跳下水吧！

2793 Once you're used to it, try to **speed up**.
習慣之後，就試著加快速度吧。 speed up 片 加速

2794 I can swim if I have a **kickboard**.
只要有浮板，我就能游泳。 kickboard 名 浮板

2795 You can use the life **preserver**.
你可以使用救生圈。 preserver 名 救生用具

2796 Can you teach me how to swim?
你能教我怎麼游泳嗎？

2797 I just want to learn the basics of swimming.
我只想學會基本的游泳招數而已。

2798 Show me what you know about swimming first.
你先游給我看看吧。

2799 Beginning swimmers had better stand in the **shallow** end of the pool.
游泳的初學者最好待在淺水區。 shallow 形 淺的

2800 Hold onto the **edge** of the pool.
手扶著泳池的邊緣。 edge 名 邊緣

2801 Hold your nose and sink yourself in the water.
憋氣，然後把頭埋到水裡。

2802 **Extend** your legs out behind you.
雙腳向後伸直。 extend 動 伸出；擴展

2803 Then, start to kick and splash in the water.
然後，開始打水。

2804 Kicking can keep you **afloat**.
打水能讓你浮起來。 afloat 形 漂浮著的

2805 **Controlling** breathing is the most difficult part for a beginner.
對初學者而言，換氣是最難的。 control 動 控制

2806 I just learned how to breathe in and out properly while swimming.
我才剛學會吸氣和吐氣。

2807 The water irritates my **throat** all the time.
我總是被水嗆到。 throat 名 喉嚨

2808 Don't **panic**. Just grab my hand. I'll lead you to the other side.
別害怕，抓好我的手，我會帶你到另一邊。 panic 動 十分驚慌

2809 Don't worry. Every swimmer swallows some water at the beginning.
別擔心，每個游泳的初學者都喝過水。

2810 I finally learned how to control my breath while swimming **freestyle**.
我終於學會自由式的換氣方法了。 freestyle 名 自由式

2811 **Rotate** your head and take a breath.
先轉頭，再吸氣。 rotate 動 轉動

2812 When did you learn to swim?
你什麼時候學會游泳的？

2813 I learned to swim when I was in **kindergarten**.
我上幼稚園時就學游泳了。 kindergarten 名 幼稚園

2814 Now I can **swim like a fish**.
我現在的泳技很好喔。 swim like a fish 片 游得像魚般流暢無阻

2815 Now you can do the freestyle really well.
你的自由式現在已經游得很好了。

2816 Could you do **the crawl**?
你會游自由式嗎？ the crawl 名 自由式

2817 The **breaststroke** is the only way I know how to swim.
蛙式是我唯一會的游法。 breaststroke 名 蛙式

2818 I can do the dog **paddle**.
我會狗爬式。paddle 名 划

2819 I also learned the **backstroke** recently.
我最近也學了仰式。backstroke 名 仰式

2820 I can swim freestyle and backstroke very well.
我的自由式和仰式都游得很好。

2821 Doing the backstroke is very relaxing.
游仰式是很放鬆的。

2822 The **butterfly** looks so cool, but it's difficult for me to do.
游蝶式看起來真酷，但對我來說太難了。butterfly 名 蝶式

2823 The **advanced** class will **start with** the butterfly. It's just too difficult for others.
進階班將從蝶式開始教起，但這對其他人來說太難了。
advanced 形 高等的 start with 片 以…開始

2824 Throw your arms **forward**.
手臂向前伸。forward 副 向前

2825 Pull the water and kick harder.
划水，然後再踢用力一點。

2826 Am I too old to learn swimming?
我這個年紀學游泳會不會太晚了？

2827 I hate my swimming coach's **tough** training.
我的游泳教練太嚴格了，我討厭他的魔鬼訓練。tough 形 嚴格的

2828 He is a **qualified** swimming instructor.
他是一名合格的游泳教練。qualified 形 合格的

2829 Can you **dive**?
你會跳水嗎？dive 動 跳水

2830 Have you ever dived from a three-meter board?
你曾從三公尺高的跳板跳過水嗎？

2831 Diving from the five- and ten-meter boards is scary.
從五公尺和十公尺高的跳板跳下來真恐怖。

2832 Bill can do a **cannonball** off the board.
比爾會抱膝跳水。cannonball 名 抱膝跳水

2833 My brother is a **lifeguard**.
我的哥哥是一名救生員。lifeguard 名 救生員

2834 He is an **expert** swimmer.
他是一名游泳高手。expert 形 熟練的

2835 A lifeguard's job is to watch everybody at the pool.
救生員的工作是要留意每一個在游泳池的人。

2836 The lifeguard is **on duty** today.
這位救生員今天值班。on duty 片 當值；上班

2837 He saved a **drowning** boy yesterday.
他昨天救了一個溺水的男孩。drowning 形 溺水的

2838 I got a **cramp** in the pool.
我剛剛在游泳池裡抽筋了。cramp 名 抽筋

2839 Didn't you warm up before going into the pool?
你下水前沒先做暖身運動嗎？

2840 Going to the beach is the funnest thing about summer.
夏天最好玩的活動莫過於去海邊了。

2841 The beach is always **crowded** at this time of the year.
每年的這個時候，海邊都人山人海。crowded 形 擁擠的

2842 Hawaii is a **paradise** for water lovers.
夏威夷是愛好水上活動者的天堂。paradise 名 天堂

2843 I hope I can take a beach **break** in Hawaii.
我希望能到夏威夷享受沙灘假期。 break 名 休息

2844 I want to wear my new **bathing suit**.
我想穿我新買的泳裝。 bathing suit 片 泳裝

2845 The swimming suit you just bought looks so fashionable.
你新買的泳裝看起來好時髦喔。

2846 I wear a **one-piece** swimming suit.
我都穿連身式的泳裝。 one-piece 形 整件的

2847 I don't wear bikinis because I don't feel comfortable.
我不穿比基尼，因為我會感到不自在。

2848 I don't wear bikinis because my boyfriend won't let me.
我不穿比基尼，因為我男朋友不准我穿。

2849 I wear **flip-flops** to the beach.
我穿夾腳拖鞋去海邊。 flip-flops 名 夾腳拖鞋

2850 Wearing flip-flops at the beach is very comfortable.
在沙灘上穿夾腳拖很舒服。

2851 Look at the **crystal** clear sea!
看！海水真清澈。 crystal 形 清澈的

2852 I just want to lie on the sand.
我只想要躺在沙灘上。

2853 Lying on a beach chair is a **delight**.
躺在海灘椅上真是享受。 delight 名 樂事

2854 I am a sun lover.
我很愛曬太陽。

2855 I love taking a **sunbath** on the sand.
我很喜歡躺在沙灘上做日光浴。sunbath 名 日光浴

2856 Let's start **tanning**.
我們來曬出古銅色的肌膚吧！tan 動 使曬成棕褐色

2857 A **suntan** makes you look healthier.
古銅色的肌膚看起來更健康。suntan 名 曬黑；棕色

2858 Don't forget to **put on** some sunscreen.
別忘記擦防曬乳。put on 片 在皮膚上塗某物

2859 Could you help me apply some sunscreen?
你可以幫我擦防曬乳嗎？

2860 Wearing **sunglasses** in the boiling heat is a **must**.
在這樣的烈日下，一定得戴太陽眼鏡。
sunglasses 名 太陽眼鏡 must 名 必須做的事

2861 They are **grilling** in the sun.
他們正被烈日炙烤著。grill 動 被炙烤

2862 I don't want to get a **sunburn**.
我可不想被曬傷。sunburn 名 曬傷

2863 To avoid sunburn, you should not stay in the sun for too long.
要避免被曬傷，就不要在太陽底下待太久。

2864 You may bring some **waterproof** sunscreen.
你也可以帶防水的防曬乳去。waterproof 形 防水的

2865 Sitting in **the shade** is also a great idea.
坐在陰涼處也是個不錯的方法。the shade 名 陰涼處

2866 Why don't we rent a beach **umbrella**?
我們去租個沙灘遮陽傘吧！umbrella 名 傘

2867 Do you have any beach **towels**?

你有帶海灘毛巾嗎？ towel 名 毛巾

2868 Let's **go for a walk** on the beach.
我們去海灘上散步吧。 go for a walk 片 散步

2869 Maybe we can find some pretty **shells** or rocks to bring home.
我們也許能夠找到漂亮的貝殼或石頭帶回家。 shell 名 貝殼

2870 I'm going down to the beach for a jog.
我要去海邊慢跑。

2871 I just want to put myself in a chair on the beach and do nothing.
我只想窩在海灘椅上，什麼事都不做。

2872 The **hammock** looks very comfortable.
這個吊床看起來很舒適。 hammock 名 吊床

2873 What other things can we do at the beach?
我們在海邊還能從事哪些活動呢？

2874 Building **sandcastles** on the beach is free and fun.
在沙灘上堆沙堡既不用錢又好玩。 sandcastle 名 沙堡

2875 I will take **shovels** and buckets to the beach.
我會帶鏟子和水桶去海邊。 shovel 名 鏟子

2876 You can play beach volleyball or go Jet-skiing.
你可以玩沙灘排球，也可以騎水上摩托車。

2877 Going **Jet-skiing** is just too much for me.
騎水上摩托車對我來說太刺激了。 Jet-skiing 名 水上摩托車

2878 I'm not crazy about **parasailing**, either.
我對水上拖曳傘也沒什麼興趣。 parasailing 名 帆傘運動

2879 How about going **snorkeling**? It's safe and fun.
還是去浮潛呢？既安全又好玩。 snorkeling 名 浮潛

2880 What if I can't swim?
如果我不會游泳怎麼辦？

2881 You have to wear a life jacket when snorkeling.
浮潛時，你必須穿上救生衣。

2882 I hope we can see lots of fish when we go snorkeling. That's the whole point!
希望我們能看到很多魚，因為那是浮潛的重頭戲！

2883 I saw beautiful **coral reefs** while snorkeling.
我浮潛時看到美麗的珊瑚礁。 coral reef 片 珊瑚礁

2884 Diving in the warm Caribbean Sea must be a great pleasure.
能在溫暖的加勒比海潛水肯定是一大樂事。

2885 I don't think I want to wear a **wet suit** and carry a **tank**.
我不太想穿潛水衣和背著氧氣筒。 wet suit 片 潛水服 tank 名 罐

2886 We're not going **scuba diving**. We're going snorkeling!
我們不是要去深潛，而是浮潛。 scuba diving 片 水肺潛水

2887 We'll each need a **mask**, a **snorkel**, and some **flippers**.
我們每人需要一個面罩、一支呼吸管，還有蛙鞋。
mask 名 防護面具 snorkel 名 呼吸管 flipper 名 蛙鞋

2888 I don't know how to use a snorkel.
我不知道潛水呼吸管要怎麼使用。

2889 Put this end of the snorkel in your mouth when you're in the water.
下水之後，把管子的這端放進嘴巴裡。

2890 The other end **sticks** out of the water.
管子的另一端伸出水面。 stick 動 伸出

2891 We can wear flippers.

我們可以穿上蛙鞋。

2892 Maldives is a diving paradise.
馬爾地夫是潛水天堂。

2893 The reefs are terrific in Maldives.
馬爾地夫的珊瑚礁美極了！

2894 I saw many **schools** of **tropical** fish when diving.
我潛水時看到好幾群熱帶魚游來游去。
school 名 魚群 tropical 形 熱帶的

2895 What a waste to stay in the shade! Let's go **surfing**!
一直呆坐太可惜了吧！我們去衝浪吧。surfing 名 衝浪

2896 No one can **hang ten** better than him.
論衝浪技術，沒有人比得過他。hang ten 片 衝浪

2897 You really know how to have fun on the beach.
你真的對在海邊玩樂很有一套耶。

偶爾來場影視饗宴
About TV And Movies

2898 Have you got **cable** TV?
你有裝有線電視嗎？cable 名 有線電視

2899 I only have **satellite** television.
我只有裝衛星電視。satellite 名 衛星

2900 You need to pay a monthly **subscription** fee if you have cable TV.
如果裝第四台，你每個月就必須付費。subscription 名 訂閱

2901 Ordering a pay-per-view program **incurs** an extra charge.
如果你要看付費節目，就得另外繳費。incur 動 招致

2902 You can check the TV schedule online.
你可以上網看一下電視節目表。

2903 Here is the TV **listings** for this week.
這是本週的電視節目表。listing 名 列表

2904 Where's the **remote** control?
遙控器在哪裡？remote 形 遙控的

2905 Hurry! Turn to **channel** 26.
快點！轉到二十六台。channel 名 頻道

2906 I don't want to miss my favorite Korean drama.
我不想錯過我最愛的韓劇。

2907 The **lead** actress is not only beautiful, but her acting is fantastic.
女主角不僅長得漂亮，演技也是一流的。lead 形 最重要的

2908 I like Japanese dramas better than Korean dramas.
比起韓劇，我比較喜歡日劇。

2909 Locally made **soap operas** have high ratings.
本土連續劇的收視率都很高。soap opera 片 肥皂劇

2910 My mother watches soap operas every day.
我媽媽每天都看連續劇。

2911 Soap operas are usually shown during **prime** time.
連續劇通常會在黃金時段播出。prime 形 主要的；最好的

2912 Is there anything worth watching on the TV tonight?
今天晚上有什麼值得看的節目嗎？

2913 No, it's all **repeats** again.
沒有，都是重播。 repeat 名 重演；重播

2914 There's a **program** on that I really want to watch.
有一個我很想看的節目會上演。 program 名 節目

2915 A game show is on right now.
現在正在播一個遊戲節目。

2916 Could you please **turn up** the TV? I can't hear it.
可以麻煩你把電視的音量調大一點嗎？我聽不到。 turn up 片 開大

2917 I need to prepare for tomorrow's test. Could you **turn off** the TV?
我必須準備明天的考試，你可以關掉電視嗎？ turn off 片 關掉

2918 What TV programs do you like?
你喜歡看什麼電視節目？

2919 I watch whatever's on.
電視在播什麼，我就看什麼。

2920 I like watching sports and news.
我喜歡看體育節目和新聞。

2921 I love Oprah's **talk show**.
我喜歡看歐普拉的脫口秀。 talk show 片 脫口秀

2922 Talk shows are becoming more and more popular in Taiwan.
談話性節目在台灣愈來愈受歡迎了。

2923 I've been in the show's audience.
我有當過那個節目的現場觀眾。

2924 Who is following "The Voice"?
誰有看《美國之聲》這個節目？

2925 I started watching **halfway** through the second season and **got hooked**.
我從第二季的中途開始看，之後就著迷了。

halfway 副 在中途　get hooked 片 迷上

2926 Do you like **variety** shows?
你喜歡看綜藝節目嗎？ variety 名 綜藝節目

2927 I don't watch variety shows because most of them are low budget.
我不常看綜藝節目，因為絕大部分都是低預算製作，很粗糙。

2928 I hate celebrity gossip.
我討厭演藝圈的八卦新聞。

2929 Some gossip is **spread** to promote celebrities.
有些八卦是為了提高藝人的曝光而故意放出來的。 spread 動 傳播

2930 I like variety shows because I can see **comedians** and funny **contests**.
我喜歡綜藝節目，因為可以看諧星和有趣的競賽。
comedian 名 諧星　contest 名 競賽

2931 Who is your favorite variety show host or **hostess**?
你最喜歡的綜藝節目主持人是誰？ hostess 名 女主持人

2932 I think Kevin Tsai is a hard-working host, and he's very humorous.
我覺得蔡康永是個很認真的主持人，也很幽默。

2933 Did you watch the **documentary** about **healthcare** last night?
你有看昨天播的醫療紀錄片嗎？
documentary 名 紀錄片　healthcare 名 醫療保健

2934 Yes, the documentary was worth watching, wasn't it?
有啊，這部紀錄片很值得看，對吧？

2935 Most documentaries are **educational**.
大部分的紀錄片富有教育意義。 educational 形 有教育意義的

2936 Do you like **reality shows**?

你喜歡看實境秀嗎？ reality show 片 真人實境秀

2937 Not much. I think some reality shows are arranged, not real.
不怎麼喜歡，我覺得有些實境秀是安排好的，並不真實。

2938 Do you have a favorite TV actor or actress?
你有喜歡的電視演員嗎？

2939 I can't remember the actors' names very well.
我不太記得演員的名字。

2940 Do you watch any **TV series**?
你有在看電視影集嗎？ TV series 片 電視影集

2941 This summer's most popular TV series will be on tonight.
今年夏天最受歡迎的電視影集今晚就要開播了。

2942 I just watch some **clips** of the TV program on the Internet.
我只在網路上看過這個節目的某些片段。 clip 名 剪輯片段

2943 I enjoy watching old comedy series, like "The Cosby Show".
我喜歡看老式的喜劇影集，例如《天才老爹》。

2944 CSI is my favorite American **crime** drama television series.
CSI 是我最喜歡的美國犯罪影集。 crime 名 犯罪

2945 I wouldn't miss an **episode** for anything.
打死我都不會錯過任何一集。 episode 名 (電視劇的)一集

2946 I am **looking forward to** the next season of CSI.
我在等 CSI 下一季的播出。 look forward to 片 期待

2947 You can watch a **rerun**.
你可以看重播。 rerun 名 重播

2948 Why do you want to watch the program?

你為什麼想看這個節目？

2949 I love it because the **pace** is very fast.
因為劇情的步調很快，所以我喜歡。pace 名 步調

2950 The **plot** is very exciting.
劇情很刺激。plot 名 情節

2951 My favorite American **sitcom** is "Friends".
《六人行》是我最愛的美國情境喜劇。sitcom 名 情境喜劇

2952 It is not on now.
現在已經沒播了。

2953 I used to watch it every week.
我以前每個星期都要看。

2954 Which **character** do you like the most?
你最喜歡哪一個角色？character 名 角色

2955 I think it's truly a television **masterpiece**.
我覺得這真是電視界的經典之作。masterpiece 名 傑作

2956 How long do you spend watching TV every day?
你每天都看多久的電視？

2957 It depends. Sometimes, I even don't have time to watch TV.
不一定，有時候我根本沒時間看電視。

2958 I spend a huge amount of time watching TV.
我花很多時間看電視。

2959 I can hardly **imagine** a life without TV.
我很難想像生命中沒有電視，會變成什麼樣子。imagine 動 想像

2960 I only watch TV on the weekends.
我只有週末的時候會看電視。

2961 I watch TV for more than three hours every day.
我每天都看超過三小時的電視。

2962 We are not allowed to watch TV on school days.
我們除了寒暑假以外，都不准看電視。

2963 Do you like to sit in front of the TV **after work**?
你下班後喜歡看電視嗎？ after work 片 下班後

2964 My grandmother watches weather reports on TV every night.
我奶奶每天晚上都看氣象預報。

2965 To tell the truth, I think TV programs are getting worse.
老實說，我覺得電視節目的水準愈來愈差了。

2966 Some TV stations only want to make money.
有些電視台只是為了賺取利潤。

2967 Many TV programs have a **negative** influence on kids.
很多電視節目對小孩都有負面的影響。 negative 形 負面的

2968 Sometimes, turning off the TV is good for your health.
有時候，關掉電視有益健康。

2969 Turning off the television will gain many people at least two hours per day.
只要關掉電視，很多人每天至少能多出兩個小時的時間。

2970 I don't want to watch the news. What else is on?
我不想看新聞，有其他的節目嗎？

2971 I found that the news on TV is full of blood and **violence**.
我發現電視新聞充斥著血腥暴力的畫面。 violence 名 暴力

2972 I'd rather watch something that can bring me peace and **relaxation**.
我寧願看些能讓我感到平靜與放鬆的節目。 relaxation 名 放鬆

2973 My brother changes the channel **frequently** while watching TV.
我弟弟看電視的時候會一直轉台。 frequently 副 頻繁地

2974 Stop **flipping** through the channels.
不要再一直轉台了。 flip 動 翻閱

2975 There are too many annoying **commercials**.
有太多煩人的電視廣告。 commercial 名 廣告

2976 I change the channel whenever a commercial comes on.
一進廣告我就會轉台。

2977 You've been watching TV for more than three hours.
你已經看了三個多小時的電視了。

2978 Take a break from TV!
把電視關了，休息一下吧！

2979 I watch TV whenever I have nothing to do.
只要沒事做，我就會看電視。

2980 You're a real couch potato.
你真的是個標準的沙發馬鈴薯。

2981 Watching TV and eating snacks at the same time make you **gain weight**.
邊看電視邊吃零食會讓你變胖。 gain weight 片 發胖

2982 Staying in is boring; why don't we go to a movie?
待在家好無聊，我們去看電影吧！

2983 I go to the movies once or twice a month.
我一個月會去看一到兩次電影。

2984 I never go to the **cinema**. I watch films on TV.
我從來不去電影院，我都看電視播的影片。 cinema 名 電影院

2985 The sound and **visual effects** are better in the **theater**.
電影院的音效和視覺效果都比較好。
visual 形 視覺的 effect 名 效果 theater 名 劇院

2986 It's expensive to see movies in the theater.
去電影院看電影很貴。

2987 I usually wait until the movie comes out on DVD.
我通常會等到 DVD 出來才看。

2988 This movie theater shows **double features**.
這家電影院可連看兩片。double features 片 一次看兩部電影

2989 I used to watch second-run movies when I was a student.
我學生時代都看二輪片。

2990 Most of the second-run movie theaters are small and **dirty**.
大部分的二輪戲院都很小，場地又髒亂。dirty 形 髒的

2991 **Matinee** showings are a little cheaper but not much.
下午場會便宜一點，但是差不了多少。matinee 名 下午場

2992 A matinee is an afternoon showing of a movie.
「matinee」這個字是指電影的下午場。

2993 How can I get tickets cheaper than those at the **box office**?
如何買到比售票口賣得便宜的票呢？box office 名 售票處

2994 Is there a discount for students?
學生有折扣嗎？

2995 The first show of the day is usually much cheaper.
早場的電影通常會便宜很多。

2996 Matinee shows are sometimes only half the price of evening ones.
下午場的票價有時候只有晚場的一半呢！

2997 The advanced booking for the coming attraction begins today.
即將上映的電影票從今天開始預售。

2998 When will the movie be released?
這部電影什麼時候上映呢？

2999 You can check out the release date on the website.
你可以上他們的網站，上面有寫上映日期。

3000 It's not in Taiwan yet. / It's not on yet in Taiwan.
這部片還沒有在台灣上映。

3001 They made a **racy trailer**.
他們製作了簡短有力的預告片。 racy 形 生動的 trailer 名 預告片

3002 I like to see the trailers before the actual movie.
我喜歡看正片開始前的預告片。

3003 Movies in Taiwan are **rated** into four groups.
台灣的電影分為四個等級。 rate 動 列入等級

3004 The movie is rated "R".
這部電影是 R 級的。

3005 Those under eighteen years old are **restricted** from watching R-rated movies.
十八歲以下的觀眾不能觀看 R 級電影。 restrict 動 限制

3006 Do you eat **popcorn** or other snacks while watching a film?
你看電影時會吃爆米花或其他零食嗎？ popcorn 名 爆米花

3007 Popcorn is the best **choice**.
爆米花是最佳選擇。 choice 名 選擇

3008 Watching a movie is not complete without popcorn.
少了爆米花，就不像在看電影了。

3009 You can bring food that doesn't have a strong smell into a theater in Taiwan.
在台灣，你可以攜帶味道不重的食物進電影院。

3010 Bringing in food is not allowed in many American movie theaters.
美國很多電影院都禁帶外食。

3011 I don't eat popcorn when watching a movie because it **distracts** me.
邊看電影邊吃爆米花會害我分心，所以我不吃。 distract 動 使分心

3012 Turn off your cell phone during a movie.
看電影時，請關掉手機。

3013 It is **extremely rude** to talk on the phone while watching movies.
在電影播放的中途講電話是很不禮貌的。
extremely 副 極其；非常　rude 形 無禮的；粗魯的

3014 In American theaters, you can sit wherever you want.
在美國的電影院，你可以自由入座。

3015 I'm afraid that my listening **comprehension** is not good enough to understand everything.
我怕我聽力不好，無法了解電影的內容。
comprehension 名 理解力

3016 The movie has Chinese **subtitles**.
這部電影有中文字幕。 subtitle 名 字幕

3017 I have a date this Saturday. What movie would you suggest?
我這週六要去約會，你有沒有什麼推薦的電影啊？

3018 I **happen to** know how to pick a good date movie.
我剛好知道怎麼挑選適合約會的電影。 happen to 片 碰巧

3019 First, check the movie listings to see what **options** are available.
首先要確認電影時刻表，看有哪些選擇。 option 名 選擇

3020 It should absolutely be a romantic comedy or some other **chick flick**.
浪漫喜劇片當然是首選，或是其他女生愛看的電影也可以。
chick flick 片 年輕女生愛看的電影

3021 Most girls love **romantic** comedies more than **action movies**.
比起動作片，大部分的女生都比較喜歡浪漫喜劇片。
romantic 形 羅曼蒂克的 action movie 片 動作片

3022 A **horror** movie might be a nice choice.
恐怖片或許是個不錯的選擇。 horror 名 恐怖；震驚

3023 Maybe she would feel scared and sit closer to you.
搞不好她會覺得害怕，就會靠你近一點。

3024 I went to a late show with my girlfriend last night.
我昨晚跟我的女朋友去看了午夜場電影。

3025 We saw a movie **entitled** "Star Wars". / We saw a movie called "Star Wars".
我們看了《星際大戰》。 entitle 動 給…稱號

3026 Have you watched the latest film just released last Friday?
你去看了上週五剛上映的那部電影了嗎？

3027 I don't like it because it's too **commercial**.
那部片的商業氣息太重了，我不喜歡。 commercial 形 商業性的

3028 I love the movie because it has so many **twists**

and turns.
我喜歡這部電影，因為劇情曲折離奇。 twists and turns 片 曲折

3029 The **setting** of the film is Los Angeles.
這部電影是在洛杉磯取景的。 setting 名 背景；布景

3030 Not all movies that make money are good.
並非所有賣座的電影都是好電影。

3031 The **screenplay** is **awful**. What a waste of time!
這部片的劇本爛透了，真是浪費我的時間！
screenplay 名 電影劇本 awful 形 極壞的；極糟的

3032 What kinds of movies do you like?
你喜歡看哪種類型的電影？

3033 I like action movies and **comedies**.
我喜歡動作片和喜劇片。 comedy 名 喜劇

3034 I like dramas. They usually **express** something **deep**.
我喜歡劇情片，這種片子通常會有較深的內涵。
express 動 表達 deep 形 深刻的

3035 I like all kinds of movies except for **tragedies**.
悲劇以外的電影我都喜歡。 tragedy 名 悲劇

3036 I love movies with happy **endings**.
我喜歡看有美好結局的電影。 ending 名 結局

3037 I don't like foreign films **dubbed** in Chinese.
我不喜歡外國電影用中文配音。 dub 動 (為外國影片)配音

3038 "Sleepless in Seattle" is one of my favorite movies.
《西雅圖夜未眠》是我最喜歡的電影之一。

3039 It **featured** Tom Hanks and Meg Ryan.
這部片是由湯姆漢克和梅格萊恩主演的。 feature 動 由…主演

3040 I can't forget the last **scene** when they met at the **Empire** State Building.
男女主角最後在帝國大廈相遇，那一幕我無法忘懷。
scene 名 一個鏡頭 empire 名 帝國

3041 I cried when I saw that **touching** scene.
一看到這感人的一幕，我就哭了。 touching 形 令人感動的

3042 "Pay It Forward" is my favorite movie, and it has a positive message.
《讓愛傳出去》是我最喜愛的電影，這部片所傳達的訊息很正面。

3043 Who played the teacher in the film? Kevin Spacey?
飾演劇中教師一角的人是誰？凱文．史貝西嗎？

3044 The importance of **education came home to me** after seeing this movie.
看完這部電影之後，我深深了解到教育的重要性。
education 名 教育 come home to sb. 片 某人理解…

3045 The movie "The Bucket List" was really **thought-provoking**.
《一路玩到掛》這部電影真的很發人省思。
thought-provoking 形 發人深省的

3046 “Avatar” was the year's top **grossing** movie in 2009.
《阿凡達》是二〇〇九年的票房冠軍。 gross 動 獲得總收入

3047 It's the first 3D movie I've ever seen.
這是我看的第一部 3D 電影。

3048 I absolutely loved this film because it was a breathtaking piece of work.
這部電影有很多令人嘆為觀止的畫面，所以我很喜歡。

3049 I don't like it, although the **majority** of people think it's great.
雖然這部片廣受好評，但我就是不喜歡。 majority 名 多數

3050 Actually, I like "2012" better than "Avatar".
事實上，比起《阿凡達》，我比較喜歡《2012》。

3051 "2012" is a **disaster** movie about the end of the world.
《2012》是一部在講世界末日的災難片。disaster 名 災難

3052 There were lots of breathtaking scenes in the movie.
這部電影裡有許多驚險的場面。

3053 I was **overwhelmed**.
我深深地被征服了。overwhelm 動 征服；壓倒

3054 There is no better film than this one.
沒有比這部電影更出色的作品了。

3055 Did you watch the movie "The A-Team"?
你有看過《天龍特攻隊》這部電影嗎？

3056 I know that it's based on a popular TV series of the 80s.
我知道這部片改編自八〇年代的熱門影集。

3057 Who's the **director**?
這部片的導演是誰？director 名 導演

3058 Joe Carnahan is the director.
導演是喬・卡納翰。

3059 This is a critically **acclaimed** film. / This is a popular movie.
這是一部有口碑的好電影。acclaimed 形 受到讚揚的

3060 The movie is really a classic piece of **cinematography**.
這部電影真是一部經典藝術之作。cinematography 名 電影藝術

3061 It's an Oscar-winning film.
這是部奧斯卡得獎影片。

3062 The box office returns from the film hit over $100 million.
這部電影的票房成績達到一億美元以上。

3063 It **shattered** all **previous** box office records.
它打破了票房紀錄。shatter 動 粉碎 previous 形 先前的

3064 That movie was **hilarious**!
那部電影超爆笑的！hilarious 形 極可笑的

3065 From beginning to end, the film made everyone laugh.
電影從開始到結束，整場觀眾都笑聲不斷。

3066 I love the **witty dialogue** in the movie.
我喜歡電影中詼諧的對白。witty 形 詼諧的 dialogue 名 對白

3067 Two thumbs up!
棒極了！

3068 Brad Pitt looked super sexy in the **close-ups**.
布萊德彼特的特寫鏡頭超性感的。close-up 名 特寫鏡頭

3069 It's a **splatter movie**.
這是一部很噁心的虐殺片。splatter movie 片 血腥電影

3070 You'll feel a sense of **suspense**!
你會感到膽顫心驚喔！suspense 名 掛慮；擔心

3071 The dubbing of the film is not good.
這部電影的配音配得不好。

3072 It wasn't as exciting as I had **expected**.
這部電影沒有我想像中刺激。expect 動 期待

3073 That movie did nothing for me.
那部電影無法引起我的共鳴。

3074 I didn't get the movie at all.
我完全看不懂那部電影。

3075 There was no point to that movie.
那部電影完全沒有重點。

3076 That movie sucked! I can't believe my brother recommended it to me.
那部電影爛透了！我弟弟竟然推薦我來看，真不敢相信。

3077 I read a movie **review** about the film.
我看了那部電影的影評。 review 名 評論

3078 The critic's **admiration** for the movie was **lukewarm**.
評論家對這部電影的評價很普通。
admiration 名 讚美 lukewarm 形 冷淡的

3079 Several celebrities appear as guest stars in the movie.
這部電影有很多大咖演員客串演出。

3080 The action **flick** has a star-studded cast.
這部動作片的卡司很堅強。 flick 名 (俚)電影

3081 Jet Li is the greatest action star.
李連杰是最棒的動作片演員。

3082 Denzel Washington is an African American, and he is my favorite actor.
丹佐・華盛頓是非裔美國人，他是我最喜愛的演員。

3083 I also like his performances in "Inside Man" and "Deja Vu".
我也喜歡他在《臥底》和《時空線索》這兩部片裡的表現。

3084 I am a member of the Denzel Washington Fan Club; are you?
我有加入丹佐・華盛頓的粉絲團，你有嗎？

3085 That previously unknown actress **burst onto the scene** in a recent movie.
那個沒名氣的女演員在最近一部電影中迅速竄紅。

burst onto the scene 片 突然竄紅

3086 You're right! She **suddenly** became **ridiculously** famous.
沒錯！她突然變得很有名。
suddenly 副 突然 ridiculously 副 不可思議地

3087 She was **nominated** for best supporting actress.
她被提名最佳女配角獎。nominate 動 提名

3088 The actress's performance was **poignant**.
那名女演員的表現令人印象深刻。poignant 形 強烈的；深刻的

3089 He finally won an Oscar after being nominated several times.
在被多次提名之後，他終於贏得一座奧斯卡獎座。

UNIT 7 音樂薰陶之旅

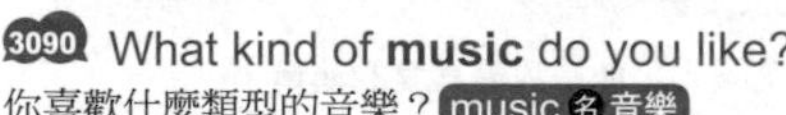

Preference For Music

3090 What kind of **music** do you like?
你喜歡什麼類型的音樂？music 名 音樂

3091 What kind of music do you **listen to** these days?
你最近都聽什麼音樂？listen to 片 聽

3092 Do you listen to R&B?
你聽藍調音樂嗎？

3093 I used to listen to **pop music**, but I love **jazz** more now.
我以前聽流行音樂，但我現在比較喜歡爵士樂。
pop music 片 流行音樂 jazz 名 爵士樂

3094 Listening to jazz at night helps me relax.
晚上聽爵士樂能幫助我放鬆心情。

3095 I usually listen to **soft music**.
我常聽輕音樂。 soft music 片 輕音樂

3096 I love New Age music because it brings me **peace**.
我喜歡新世紀音樂，因為聽了會感到平靜。 peace 名 (心的)平靜

3097 I like all kinds of music.
所有類型的音樂我都喜歡。

3098 I **rarely** listen to music.
我很少聽音樂。 rarely 副 很少

3099 Do you buy CDs? Many people buy MP3s online now.
你還會買 CD 嗎？現在很多人都是上網購買 MP3。

3100 This **album** is one of those **diamonds in the rough**, but few have noticed it.
這張唱片真的很棒，可惜沒什麼人知道。
album 名 專輯 a diamond in the rough 片 璞玉

3101 The whole album is worth listening to.
這張專輯的每一首歌都很值得聽。

3102 We've got some new **stereo** equipment.
我們添購了新的音響設備。 stereo 形 立體音響的

3103 I love your home **entertainment** system.
我很喜歡你的家庭娛樂系統。 entertainment 名 娛樂

3104 The best part is the surround-sound **speakers**.
最棒的是這套環繞音響。 speaker 名 揚聲器

3105 The **amplifier** cost me a lot.
這台擴音器花了我一大筆錢。 amplifier 名 擴音器

3106 I often listen to love songs by Celine Dion.
我常聽席琳・狄翁的情歌。

3107 She has a **fascinating** voice.
她的歌聲十分動人。 fascinating 形 迷人的

3108 She's a **talented** singer.
她是位天賦異稟的歌手。 talented 形 才華橫溢的

3109 I believe she was born with a **brilliant** voice.
我相信她的好歌喉是與生俱來的。 brilliant 形 出色的

3110 A-mei is a famous Taiwanese **aboriginal** singer.
張惠妹是著名的台灣原住民歌手。 aboriginal 形 原住民的

3111 Many aboriginal singers are very good at singing and dancing.
很多原住民歌手都能歌擅舞。

3112 She won the Best **Mandarin** Female Singer **award** at the Taiwan Golden Melody Awards.
她獲得金曲獎最佳女歌手。 Mandarin 名 華語 award 名 獎

3113 Her full voice established her as a major **presence** on the pop music scene.
她渾厚的嗓音讓她得以在流行歌壇佔一席之地。 presence 名 存在

3114 She is releasing a new album this month.
她這個月發行新專輯。

3115 Did you buy her newest album? I've already got it.
你買了她的最新專輯嗎？我已經買了。

3116 I love the sixth **track** the best.
我最喜歡第六首歌。 track 名 音軌；軌道

3117 I am a super fan of Jay Chou.
我是周杰倫的超級粉絲。

3118 The **rhythm** and **lyrics** of his songs are fantastic.
他的歌無論詞曲都很棒。 rhythm 名 韻律 lyric 名 歌詞

3119 The lyrics **reminded me of** my ex-girlfriend.
歌詞讓我想到我的前女友。 remind sb. of 片 使某人回想起

3120 The single he just released went straight to number one on the **charts**.
他最新發行的單曲直衝排行榜第一名。 chart 名 進入排行榜

3121 The song is **topping** the charts.
這首歌登上排行榜冠軍。 top 動 達到…的頂部

3122 Wu-Bai is a well-known Taiwanese rock singer.
伍佰是知名的台灣搖滾歌手。

3123 May Day's songs are mostly written by the **vocalist**, Ashin.
五月天的歌曲大部分是主唱阿信寫的。 vocalist 名 歌手；主唱

3124 I wouldn't miss a single May Day **concert**.
我絕不會錯過五月天的任何一場演唱會。 concert 名 演唱會

3125 Their concerts are always **fully** booked.
他們演唱會的票總是銷售一空。 fully 副 完全地

3126 Jolin showed up as a special guest at the end of the concert.
演唱會即將進入尾聲的時候，蔡依林以特別嘉賓的身分登台。

3127 I love to go to concerts, but I can't **afford** the tickets.
我喜歡聽演唱會，但票價太貴，我負擔不起。 afford 動 負擔得起

3128 It has been a decade since the rock band last went on **tour**.
這個搖滾樂團距上次巡迴演唱已經十年了。 tour 名 巡迴演出

0129 Have you got the **tickets**?
你票買好了嗎？ ticket 名 票；入場券

3130 Why do you like that **rocker**?
你為什麼喜歡那位搖滾歌手？ rocker 名 搖滾歌手

3131 He's got a **unique**, smoky voice.
他有獨特的的煙嗓子。 unique 形 獨特的

3132 That makes his voice sound very sexy.
那讓他的聲音聽起來很性感。

3133 My father collects **vinyl** records.
我的爸爸收集黑膠唱片。 vinyl 名 乙烯基

3134 My mother loves **folk** music very much.
我的媽媽很喜歡民俗音樂。 folk 形 民間的

3135 Folk songs and campus songs were popular in the 80s.
民謠和校園民歌在八〇年代很風行。

3136 I keep my radio on **all day long**.
我整天都開著收音機。 all day long 片 一整天

3137 What's the name of the song?
這首歌的歌名是什麼？

3138 It's "Need You Now", sung by Lady Antebellum.
是由懷舊女郎唱的《想念你》。

3139 Who's your favorite D.J. on ICRT?
你在 ICRT 最喜歡的 DJ 是誰？

3140 I joined a **rock band** in college.
我大學時期曾加入一個搖滾樂團。 rock band 片 搖滾樂團

3141 I was the **drummer** of a rock band.
我是搖滾樂團的鼓手。 drummer 名 鼓手

3142 My sister is the vocalist in a band.
我姐姐是樂團的主唱。

3143 She was a backing singer before becoming a

lead singer.
她在成為主唱之前，擔任合音的角色。

3144 The **guitarist** and the bass player are her friends from college.
吉他手和貝斯手都是她的大學同學。 guitarist 名 吉他手

3145 I sometimes go to nightclubs to listen to **live** music with friends.
我有時會和朋友去夜店聽現場演唱。 live 形 現場表演的

3146 Do you go to **concerts** often?
你常去聽音樂會嗎？ concert 名 音樂會；演奏會

3147 Have you ever been to a concert at The National Music Hall?
你有沒有去國家音樂廳觀賞音樂會的經驗呢？

3148 I have the program listings; **wanna** check it out?
我有節目表，要看看嗎？ wanna 縮 (口)想要(= want to)

3149 My husband and I love going to classical music concerts and the **opera**.
我和我先生都很喜歡去聽古典音樂會與歌劇。 opera 名 歌劇

3150 My boyfriend is not **into** classical music.
我男友不怎麼喜歡古典樂。 into 介 (口)對…有興趣

3151 **In my opinion**, most classical music lovers are **elderly** people.
我覺得大部分的古典音樂愛好者都是上了年紀的人。
in one's opinion 片 在某人看來 elderly 形 上了年紀的

3152 Young people usually enjoy listening to pop music.
年輕人通常喜歡聽流行音樂。

3153 I've reserved two tickets for tonight's **piano** concert.
我已經訂了兩張今晚鋼琴演奏會的票。 piano 名 鋼琴

3154 What time does the concert **start**?
音樂會幾點開始呢？ start 動 發生；開始

3155 It'll end **around** 10:30 p.m.
晚上十點半左右會結束。 around 介 大約；將近

3156 Should I wear an **evening dress**?
我應該穿晚禮服嗎？ evening dress 片 晚禮服

3157 There is a famous **orchestra** coming to Taiwan next month.
下個月有個知名的管弦樂團要來台灣。 orchestra 名 管弦樂團

3158 Who is the **conductor** of the orchestra?
管弦樂團的指揮是誰？ conductor 名 指揮

3159 I am going to play the **clarinet** at an orchestra performance tonight.
我將在今晚的管絃樂團演奏單簧管。 clarinet 名 單簧管；黑管

3160 Do you play any musical **instrument**?
你會彈奏樂器嗎？ instrument 名 器具

3161 I can't play any musical instruments, but I **appreciate** good music.
我不會彈奏任何樂器，但我懂得欣賞音樂。 appreciate 動 欣賞

3162 How long have you been learning the piano?
你的鋼琴學多久了？

3163 I used to **play the piano** in elementary school.
我小學的時候有在彈鋼琴。 play the piano 片 彈鋼琴

3164 I have wanted to be a great pianist since I was a child.
我從小就夢想成為一名偉大的鋼琴家。

3165 Beethoven is my favorite **composer**.
貝多芬是我最愛的音樂家。 composer 名 作曲家

3166 Mozart is a great classical music composer.
莫札特是一位偉大的古典樂作曲家。

3167 I started to read **sheet music** when I was five.
我五歲開始學認樂譜。 sheet music 片 散頁的樂譜

3168 Learning to read sheet music helped me improve my **knowledge** of music **theory**.
學認樂譜幫助我理解樂理。 knowledge 名 知識 theory 名 學理

3169 I hardly need to read sheet music when playing the piano.
我彈鋼琴時幾乎不用看譜。

3170 I can **play** most popular music **by ear**.
我不用看譜，憑記憶就能彈奏大部分的流行樂曲。
play...by ear 片 不看譜，憑記憶或聽力演奏

3171 Yo-yo Ma is a great **cellist**.
馬友友是一名很棒的大提琴家。 cellist 名 大提琴演奏者

3172 I've been learning the **cello** for years.
我學了好幾年的大提琴。 cello 名 大提琴

3173 Playing **percussion** is fun, like **xylophone**.
彈奏木琴之類的打擊樂器很有趣。
percussion 名 打擊樂器 xylophone 名 木琴

3174 I can play the **harmonica** and the **accordion** very well.
我的口琴和手風琴都很拿手。
harmonica 名 口琴 accordion 名 手風琴

3175 I love the sound of the **saxophone**.
我喜歡薩克斯風的聲音。 saxophone 名 薩克斯風

UNIT 8 來吧！舞動身體 Dancing With Others

3176 I really need to relax. Let's go dancing!
我需要好好放鬆一下，我們去跳舞吧！

3177 Dancing's great **fun** and keeps you fit.
跳舞既好玩又能維持身材。fun 名 樂趣；有趣的人(或事物)

3178 I don't know how to dance.
我對舞蹈一竅不通。

3179 I bet you'll be into dancing once you start to dance.
相信我，一旦你開始跳舞，就會愛上它了。

3180 Dancing can **firm up** hip muscles.
跳舞能讓臀部的肌肉緊實。firm up 片 使(身體部位)結實

3181 Almost everyone of all ages can dance.
幾乎所有年紀的人都能跳舞。

3182 Dancing is my favorite way to **unwind**.
跳舞是我最愛的放鬆法。unwind 動 使心情輕鬆

3183 I enjoy dancing to the **beat** of the music.
我喜歡隨著音樂的節奏起舞。beat 名 拍子；節奏

3184 I enjoy dancing like there's no one watching.
我很喜歡不在意他人眼光，盡情舞動的感覺。

3185 I have danced in competitions for years.
我已經參加好幾年的舞蹈比賽。

3186 I want to improve my dance **skills**.
我想要提升舞技。skill 名 技術；技能

3187 Can you move more slowly? I am **new to** dancing.
你的動作可不可以慢一點？我是舞蹈的初學者。
new to 片 對…沒經驗

3188 I found that I have bad balance while dancing.
我發現我跳舞時的平衡感很差。

3189 I don't have balance problems, but I feel dizzy when **making turns**.
我沒有平衡的問題，但轉圈時會頭暈。 make turns 片 轉圈

3190 My cousin wants to **get into shape** by dancing.
我堂姊想藉由跳舞來雕塑身材。 get into shape 片 塑身

3191 I decided to learn how to dance after seeing the movie "Shall We Dance?".
我是因為看了電影《來跳舞吧！》而決定要學跳舞的。

3192 Do you know where I can find a **reliable** dance class?
你知道要上哪兒找值得信賴的舞蹈教室嗎？ reliable 形 可靠的

3193 You might need to spend some time **surfing** the Internet.
你可能需要花點時間上網找一找。 surf 動 在電腦上瀏覽

3194 You can find dance classes at dance **studios** and fitness centers.
舞蹈工作坊和健身中心都有舞蹈課程。 studio 名 工作室

3195 The teacher offers **free trial** classes for newcomers.
針對初學者，老師有提供免費的試上課程。 free trial 片 免費試用

3196 There are a lot of different kinds of dance classes, such as aerobics, Latin dance, and modern dance.
舞蹈課的種類也很多，像是有氧舞蹈、拉丁舞和現代舞。

3197 **Ballroom dancing** is a wonderful social activity.
國標舞是個很棒的社交活動。ballroom dancing 片 國標舞

3198 Can I learn how to dance from DVDs?
我能看 DVD 學跳舞嗎？

3199 How do you know which dance style is **suitable** for you?
你怎麼知道哪一種舞蹈適合你？suitable 形 適合的

3200 Trying a couple of classes may help you **make a decision**.
多試試幾種舞蹈，也許更容易做決定。make a decision 片 做決定

3201 My son loves dancing **hip-hop**.
我兒子熱愛跳街舞。hip-hop 名 嘻哈音樂

3202 The hand **movements** and steps seem complicated.
手的動作和舞步看起來很複雜。movement 名 動作

3203 Lisa **enrolled in** a belly dancing class.
麗莎報名了肚皮舞的課程。enroll in 片 報名；註冊

3204 I heard that belly dancing can keep you in shape.
我聽說跳肚皮舞能維持身材的曲線。

3205 I agree. Belly dancing is a great exercise.
我同意，肚皮舞是一項很好的運動。

3206 I need to buy a traditional belly dancing **costume**.
我需要買套傳統的肚皮舞服裝。costume 名 服裝

3207 Belly dancing is one of the traditional Middle Eastern dances.
肚皮舞是中東舞蹈的一種。

3208 The instructor showed us how to **shake** our hips.
老師教我們如何搖動臀部。shake 動 搖動；抖動

3209 Women who belly dance look **graceful** and charming.
跳肚皮舞的女生看起來既優雅又迷人。 graceful 形 優雅的

3210 The popularity of belly dancing is growing throughout the world.
肚皮舞在全世界愈來愈盛行了。

3211 I can teach you how to dance **for free**.
我可以免費教你跳舞。 for free 片 免費

3212 Jason taught me how to do basic dance steps.
傑森教了我一些基本的舞步。

3213 Let me show you how to dance the **waltz**.
我教你怎麼跳華爾滋。 waltz 名 華爾滋

3214 You need a **partner** for dancing the waltz.
跳華爾滋需要舞伴。 partner 名 夥伴

3215 The man's right arm should go hang onto the lady's left **shoulder blade**.
男士的右手臂要放在女士的左肩胛骨上。
shoulder blade 片 肩胛骨

3216 The lady's left hand should hang onto the man's right shoulder.
女士的左手放在男士的右肩上。

3217 My feet get **tangled up** all the time when dancing.
我的雙腳總是交纏在一起，不聽使喚。 tangle up 片 纏成一團

3218 Let me show you some simple steps.
我做一些簡單的舞步給你看。

3219 Follow my **lead**.
跟著我的腳步。 lead 名 指導

3220 I'll lead you.
我來帶著你跳。

3221 Move your feet to the beat.
跟著節奏移動你的腳步。

3222 Then, start to **sway** with your hips and feet.
接著搖動你的臀部與雙腳。 sway 動 搖動；搖擺

3223 In the U.S., prom night is one of the most important nights for all high school kids.
在美國，高中畢業舞會是青少年最重要的舞會之一。

3224 Susan needs a **prom** dress.
蘇珊需要一件舞會穿的洋裝。 prom 名 (口)學校舞會

3225 Are you going to the school dance?
你要去參加學校舞會嗎？

3226 Do you want to come to the prom with me?
要不要跟我去參加畢業舞會呢？

3227 May I have this dance? / Shall we dance?
我有這個榮幸邀你共舞嗎？

3228 Would you like to dance with me? / Would you care to join the dance?
跟我共舞，好嗎？

3229 Could we have another dance?
我們可以再跳一支舞嗎？

3230 I feel **nervous** when going on the dance floor.
踏上舞池的時候，我好緊張。 nervous 形 緊張不安的

3231 You can ask your partner to lead.
你可以請舞伴帶著你跳。

3232 Don't **hug** your partner too **tight**.
不要把你的舞伴抱得太緊。 hug 動 擁抱 tight 形 緊的

3233 Keep the hug loose if you don't have a relationship.
如果他不是你正在交往的對象，就得保持一定的距離。

Part 5

來場國外的壯遊

TRAVELING AROUND

UNIT 1 啟程前的準備

UNIT 2 介紹觀光景點

UNIT 3 出發！出境的重點句

UNIT 4 乘坐飛機 & 入境

UNIT 5 不可不顧的食與住

UNIT 6 迷路 & 乘車二三事

UNIT 7 租一輛車趴趴走

UNIT 8 交通規則 & 意外

UNIT 9 處理旅遊麻煩事

▸145

啟程前的準備
Before The Departure

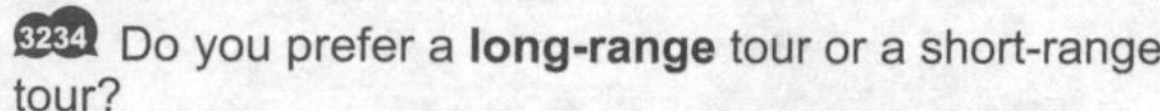

3234 Do you prefer a **long-range** tour or a short-range tour?
你比較喜歡長程旅行還是短程旅行？ long-range 形 遠程的

3235 I prefer a one-stop tour rather than a multi-country tour.
我比較喜歡停留在一個國家的定點旅行，不喜歡走馬看花。

3236 Do you have any **plans** for summer vacation?
你暑假有什麼計畫嗎？ plan 名 計畫

3237 I'm **going on a vacation** to Thailand.
我要去泰國旅行。 go on a vacation 片 去度假

3238 I'm **backpacking** across Japan this summer vacation.
我今年暑假要到日本自助旅行。 backpack 動 帶輕便行李去旅行

3239 I plan to go on a long **journey**.
我打算來一趟長途旅行。 journey 名 旅行；旅程

3240 I have always wanted to go backpacking through **Europe**.
我一直想到歐洲自助旅行。 Europe 名 歐洲

3241 I am doing some **budget traveling** to Nepal next month. Do you want to go with me?
我下個月要到尼泊爾自助旅行，走低預算省錢路線，要不要一起去？ budget traveling 片 精打細算的旅行

3242 No way. I like to stay at five-star **hotels**.
才不要，我喜歡住五星級飯店。 hotel 名 飯店；旅館

3243 Do you prefer a backpacking trip or a group

inclusive package?
你喜歡自助旅行還是跟團？ inclusive 形 包含的

3244 I hate **package tours**.
我討厭跟團。 package tour 片 套裝旅遊

3245 Many of the package tours are shopping tours.
很多套裝行程都是購物旅遊團。

3246 They always wake you up before 8 a.m., and you have to stay with the group all day.
他們會在早上八點前叫你起床，而且一整天都得跟著行程跑。

3247 There's no **adventure**!
一點冒險的感覺都沒有！ adventure 名 冒險活動

3248 I like **independent travel**.
我喜歡自由行。 independent travel 片 自由行

3249 Independent vacation packages typically **consist of** air travel and hotel.
自由行的套裝行程通常包含機票和飯店的費用。
consist of 片 由…組成

3250 Some of them include **transfers** to and from the airport.
有些還包含機場接送的服務。 transfer 名 轉運

3251 Have you gone on a **cruise**?
你有搭過郵輪嗎？ cruise 名 (坐船)旅行

3252 A trip across either the Pacific Ocean or the Atlantic Ocean is fine with me.
不管是橫渡太平洋或大西洋，我都覺得很好。

3253 I'm going on a cruise to Alaska.
我要搭郵輪去阿拉斯加。

3254 What is your favorite travel **destination** in the whole world?
你最喜歡的旅遊景點是哪裡？ destination 名 目的地

3255 I went to Quebec several years ago, and I think it was my favorite trip.
我幾年前去過魁北克，那應該是我最愛的一次旅遊了。

3256 How often do you go traveling?
你多久旅行一次？

3257 It depends. I usually travel abroad once or twice a year.
不一定，通常每年會出國一到二次。

3258 You are lucky. I've never gone **abroad**.
你真幸運，我從來沒有出過國。 abroad 副 到國外

3259 I can only afford **domestic** travel.
我只負擔得起國內旅遊。 domestic 形 國內的

3260 I hope I can travel **overseas** someday.
真希望有一天能出國玩。 overseas 副 在國外

3261 I don't know how to plan my trip.
我不知道要如何規劃旅程。

3262 The first step is **deciding** when and where you are going.
首先，你得決定時間以及想去的地點。 decide 動 決定

3263 It is best to plan at least six months **prior to** leaving.
最好是在出發前六個月就開始規劃。 prior to 片 在…之前

3264 You can **search** travel information **online**.
你可以上網搜尋旅遊資訊。 search 動 搜尋 online 副 連線地

3265 I often go to websites to **browse** travel information shared by travelers.
我常會上網，瀏覽旅遊達人分享的旅遊資訊。 browse 動 瀏覽

3266 I am **stuck** between Samui and Iceland.
我不知道要去蘇美島還是冰島。 stick 動 (口)被…難住

3267 I would choose Iceland if I were you.
如果是我的話，會選冰島。

3268 I would choose to go somewhere that is very different from where I live.
我會選擇和我居住的城市很不一樣的地方。

3269 Go to any place that is away from the **harsh** realities of life.
只要能讓你遠離嚴酷的現實，任何地方都可以啊。 harsh 形 嚴酷的

3270 I had a great time when touring New Zealand last summer.
我去年夏天的紐西蘭之旅很愉快。

3271 What's your **dream** holiday destination?
你夢想中的旅遊景點是哪裡？ dream 形 理想的；如夢的

3272 My dream place is the most beautiful country in the world, Switzerland.
我最想去瑞士，那是全世界最美的國家。

3273 I **am dying to** go to Switzerland, too.
我也超想去瑞士的。 be dying to 片 極想；渴望

3274 Have you ever been to Switzerland?
你有去過瑞士嗎？

3275 I've never been to Switzerland, but my brother lives there.
我沒去過，但我哥哥住在那裡。

3276 What is Switzerland like?
瑞士是什麼樣的地方啊？

3277 Switzerland is best **known** for its beautiful mountains and chocolate.
瑞士最有名的就是山脈的美景和巧克力。 known 形 知名的

3278 Its **railway** system is also very **famous**.
瑞士的鐵路系統也很有名。 railway 名 鐵路 famous 形 有名的

3279 Paris is definitely the **fashion center** of the world.
不容置疑地，巴黎是世界的時尚中心。
fashion 名 時尚 center 名 核心

3280 That's it! Let's go to Paris!
決定了，我們去巴黎吧！

3281 Do I need a **visa** to go to **France**?
去法國需要簽證嗎？ visa 名 簽證 France 名 法國

3282 You need to **apply for** the European Schengen Visa.
你必須申請申根簽證。 apply for 片 申請

3283 You can apply for single **entry** or **multiple** entry visas.
你可以申請單次入境或多次入境。
entry 名 進入 multiple 形 多樣的

3284 If you go to the U.S., you have to apply for a visa.
如果你要去美國，就必須辦美簽。

3285 Don't forget to check the **expiration** date of your passport.
別忘了看一下護照有沒有過期。 expiration 名 期滿

3286 The expiration date of your passport should be longer than six months from the date of your trip.
護照的有效期限，必須比你的出國日還多出六個月才行。

3287 If it is **expired**, you won't be able to go abroad.
如果過期，你就出不了國。 expire 動 滿期；屆期

3288 I've got my passport **renewed**.
我的護照已經重新換發了。 renew 動 使更新

3289 Are you a **budget** traveler?
你是精打細算型的背包客嗎？ budget 形 低廉的

3290 If you reserve airline tickets and hotels early, they may be cheaper.
如果你提早訂機票和旅館，也許會比較便宜。

3291 You can find cheaper tickets during the **low season**.
淡季的機票比較便宜。low season 片 淡季

3292 Have you **reserved** a seat?
你有沒有預先訂機位？reserve 動 預訂

3293 No, I don't know how to make a **reservation**.
沒有，我不知道要怎麼訂位。reservation 名 預訂

3294 Reservations can be made directly with **airlines** on their website.
你可以直接上航空公司的網站訂位。airline 名 航空公司

3295 You can also make a reservation via a travel **agency**.
你也可以透過旅行社訂位。agency 名 代理機構

3296 Making a reservation with a travel agent is simple and convenient.
透過旅行社訂位既簡單又方便。

3297 The price depends on what **class** you are flying on.
票價會因搭乘的艙等而有所不同。class 名 級別

3298 Business class seats are way too expensive.
商務艙的座位太貴了。

3299 I can only afford an economy class ticket.
我只付得起經濟艙的機票。

3300 I'd like to **book** a ticket, please.
我想要訂機票。book 動 預訂

3301 What's your destination, please?
請問您的目的地是哪裡？

3302 I plan to **fly** to Paris.
我要去巴黎。 fly 動 乘飛機旅行

3303 Are you flying on a domestic flight or an international flight?
請問您是搭國內線還是國際線？

3304 When will your **departure** date be?
請問您的出發日期是哪一天？ departure 名 出發；啟程

3305 I'd like to leave on the 1st of July.
我七月一日出發。

3306 How many direct flights are there to Paris every week?
每週有幾班直飛巴黎的飛機呢？

3307 Three. The direct flights are on every Monday, Wednesday and Friday.
有三班直航班機，星期一、三、五各一班。

3308 A **one-way** ticket or a round-trip ticket?
請問要訂單程票還是來回票？ one-way 形 單程的

3309 I would like a **round-trip** ticket, please.
我要訂來回票。 round-trip 形 來回的

3310 I would like to buy a one-way ticket to Bangkok.
我要買一張到曼谷的單程機票。

3311 I'd like a round-trip ticket to Seattle.
我要買一張到西雅圖的來回機票。

3312 And when is your **return** date?
您的回程日期是？ return 名 歸；返回

3313 I am not sure. Can I buy an open return ticket?
不確定耶，我可以買不限回程時間的機票嗎？

3314 Do you have any seat preference?
您有比較喜歡哪裡的座位嗎？

3315 I am flying with my sister. We'd like two seats together.
我跟我妹妹一起，所以我們要兩個在一起的位子。

3316 I don't want a **middle** seat, if possible.
可以的話，我不想要夾在中間的位子。 middle 形 中間的

3317 I would like a **window seat**.
我想要坐靠窗的位置。 window seat 片 靠窗的座位

3318 Could I get a seat away from the **lavatory**?
我可不可以要離廁所遠一點的位子？ lavatory 名 盥洗室

3319 If you have any special **dietary** requirements, please let us know in advance.
如果您有特殊的飲食需求，請事先告知。 dietary 形 飲食的

3320 We will **provide** you with a suitable meal.
我們會提供適合的餐點給您。 provide 動 提供

3321 A **minimum** of 24-hour notice is required for all special meal **requests**.
若有特殊的餐點需求，請至少於起飛前二十四小時通知我們。
minimum 名 最低限度 request 名 要求

3322 My mother and I are **vegetarians**.
我的母親和我都吃素。 vegetarian 名 素食者

3323 No problem, madam. We've prepared you a vegetarian meal.
沒問題，女士，我們已經替您準備好素食餐點了。

3324 Is it a **direct** flight?
這是直飛的班機嗎？ direct 形 直接的

3325 There is a flight stopping at Bangkok only for a short **while**.
有一架班機，只會在曼谷稍停片刻。 while 名 一段時間

3326 Do you have any flights in the morning?
有早上的班機嗎？

3327 A moment, please. Let me check the **timetable** for you.
請稍等，我查一下時刻表。 timetable 名 時刻表

3328 It's a night flight, and the departure time is 10:25 p.m.
那是晚上的班機，晚上十點二十五分起飛。

3329 We've also got a morning flight, but you need to **transfer** in Hong Kong.
另外有一班早上的班機，不過需要在香港轉機。 transfer 動 轉乘

3330 When is the **arrival** time?
抵達時間是幾點呢？ arrival 名 到達

3331 The flight will depart from Taipei at 9 a.m.
這班飛機上午九點從台北起飛。

3332 It will arrive in Charles de Gaulle Airport at about six the next evening.
第二天下午六點左右抵達戴高樂機場。

3333 I prefer the direct flight. Are there any seats available?
我比較喜歡直飛的班機，請問還有座位嗎？

3334 There are some seats available. Would you like to book now?
還有空位，請問您現在要訂位嗎？

3335 May I have your **full name** and passport number, please?
請給我您的全名和護照號碼。 full name 片 全名

3336 Sir, your ticket has been booked.
先生，您的機票已訂位完成。

3337 Your seats on Flight CI-939, departing at 10:25 p.m. on May 1, have been confirmed.
你的班機已經確定為 CI-939 次班機，五月一日晚上十點二十五分起飛。

3338 You have to pay the **fare** seven days before departure.
出發前七日需完成付款。fare 名 票價

3339 I am sorry, but the seats are completely booked at this **moment**.
很抱歉，目前機位全滿。moment 名 指定時刻

3340 I can put you on the waiting list.
我可以替您安排後補。

3341 I'm done with all **advance** bookings.
我事先已經全部預約好了。advance 形 預先的；事先的

3342 You'd better **reconfirm** your reservation.
你最好再確認一次你的預約。reconfirm 動 再確認

3343 I'd like to **confirm** my reservation to Boston on June 8.
我想要確認我六月八日到波士頓的訂位。confirm 動 證實

3344 Your name, flight number, and the date, please?
請給我您的名字、班機號碼和日期。

3345 I'd like to **change** my reservation.
我想要更改預約的機票。change 動 改變

3346 I'd like to fly on June 15 on the same flight.
我想要改到六月十五日的同一班次。

3347 I'd like to **cancel** my reservation.
我想取消我預訂的機票。cancel 動 取消

3348 Your reservation for flight TY-836 on September 28 from Chicago to Boston has been canceled.
已經替您取消九月二十八日從芝加哥飛往波士頓 TY-836 班機的訂位了。

3349 It's a **nonrefundable** ticket.
這張機票不接受退票。nonrefundable 形 不可退費的

3350 I'd like to change my flight due to some personal reasons.
由於一些個人因素，我想要改搭別的班機。

3351 Let me check your reservation. Your name, please?
我查一下您的訂位紀錄，請給我您的大名。

3352 Which flight are you going to change to?
您要改搭的班機為何呢？

3353 May I change to any flight two days later?
我可以改搭兩天後的班機嗎？任何一班都可以。

3354 I am afraid that all flights are fully booked on that day.
那天所有的班機都客滿了。

3355 Do you want me to put you on the waiting list?
您要等待候補嗎？

3356 Please do so. When will you inform me if I've got a seat?
好，請幫我候補。如果我候補上了，你們何時會通知我呢？

3357 My **itinerary** is finally set.
我的行程終於確定了。 itinerary 名 路線

3358 I will **leave for** Heidelberg tomorrow.
我明天就要前往海德堡了。 leave for 片 到某地去

3359 I **packed** my **luggage** yesterday.
我的行李都打包好了。 pack 動 裝箱 luggage 名 行李

3360 Do you need any help in packing?
需要我幫你打包嗎？

3361 Did you pack your **transformer**? You can't forget it.
你有帶變壓器嗎？這個千萬不能忘。 transformer 名 變壓器

3362 Could you collect my mail and newspapers while I am **away**?
我不在家時，可以幫我收信件和報紙嗎？ away 副 不在；外出

3363 Please **water** the flowers in my front **yard**.
請幫我澆水，照顧前院的花。 water 動 澆水 yard 名 庭院

3364 How will you get to the **airport**?
你要怎麼去機場？ airport 名 機場

3365 I am **taking a taxi**. It is more convenient **considering** all my luggage.
我要搭計程車去。考慮到我的行李數量，還是搭計程車最方便。
take a taxi 片 搭計程車 consider 動 考慮到

3366 I can **drive** you to the airport.
我可以載你去機場。 drive 動 用車送(人)

3367 Let's **load** the luggage into the **trunk**.
我們把行李放進行李箱吧。 load 動 裝載 trunk 名 汽車的行李箱

3368 Which **terminal** is your plane taking off from?
你的班機是從哪個機場航廈起飛？ terminal 名 航空站

3369 Terminal one, if I remember it right.
如果我沒記錯的話，應該是第一航廈。

3370 Which airline do you take?
你搭哪一家航空公司的飛機？

3371 Enjoy your trip!
祝你玩得愉快！

3372 Bon **voyage**! / Have a safe trip!
一路順風！ voyage 名 航海；航行

3373 I'm going to miss you.
我會想你的。

3374 Bring me some **souvenirs**!
記得帶紀念品回來給我喔！ souvenir 名 紀念品

介紹觀光景點
Let's Go Sightseeing!

3375 Are there any **must-see** places in the city?
這個城市有什麼非看不可的景點嗎？ must-see 形 必看的

3376 Could you recommend some **tourist attractions** to us?
你可以推薦一些觀光景點嗎？ tourist attraction 片 觀光勝地

3377 Are you interested in visiting **theme parks**?
你對主題樂園有沒有興趣？ theme park 片 主題樂園

3378 I don't feel like going to any **amusement** parks.
我不太想去遊樂園。 amusement 名 娛樂

3379 I'd like to spend one day in Boston.
我想要花一天的時間造訪波士頓。

3380 There are many **historic** buildings in Boston.
波士頓有很多歷史建築。 historic 形 具歷史意義的

3381 A visit to Boston must include a walk along the **historical Freedom** Trail.
到波士頓旅遊，一定要造訪深具歷史意義的「自由之路」。
historical 形 歷史的 freedom 名 自由

3382 The Freedom Trail is a red **brick** path through **downtown** Boston.
「自由之路」是一條貫穿波士頓市區的紅磚步道。
brick 名 磚塊 downtown 形 城市商業區的

3383 It starts from Boston Common and ends at Bunker Hill **Monument** in Charlestown.
「自由之路」的起點是波士頓公園，終點是查爾斯鎮的邦克山紀念碑。 monument 名 紀念碑

3384 Then you can have lunch at Quincy Market.
之後，你可以去昆西市場吃午餐。

3385 Quincy Market is the most-visited tourist destination in Boston.
昆西市場在波士頓是最多人造訪的旅遊景點。

3386 You can't miss New England **clam** chowder.
你絕對不能錯過新英格蘭風味的蛤蜊濃湯。 clam 名 蛤蜊

3387 Are there any tour services at this hotel?
你們旅館有安排觀光旅遊的服務嗎？

3388 We offer **a variety of** tours.
我們有提供各式各樣的旅遊行程。 a variety of 片 各式各樣的

3389 We have half-day and full-day tours.
我們有半日遊和一日遊的團。

3390 We'd like to join a full-day tour.
我們想要參加一日遊的團。

3391 I'd like to join a Chinese-speaking tour.
我想要參加用中文導覽的團。

3392 Do you have any tours **at a discount**?
你們有正在優惠特價的旅遊團嗎？ at a discount 片 打折扣

3393 Is this a **guided tour**?
這是有導遊同行解說的旅遊團嗎？ guided tour 片 有導遊的團

3394 Does this tour cover **major** tourist attractions?
這個團會參觀主要的觀光景點嗎？ major 形 主要的；重要的

3395 Would you like a **brochure** with prices and details?
請問您要一份有價格和詳細說明的簡介嗎？ brochure 名 小冊子

3396 Do you have a brochure in Chinese?
你們有中文版的簡介嗎？

3397 I am sorry. We only have an English version.
抱歉，我們的簡介只有英文版。

3398 Can I book a **city tour** here?
我可以在這裡報名參加市區觀光嗎？ city tour 片 市區觀光

3399 Where can I reserve a boat tour?
在什麼地方可以預約遊船觀光呢？

3400 How long does the tour spend at each **spot**?
每一個景點會停留多久呢？ spot 名 地點

3401 Will we have free time when we go to Piazza di Spagna?
到了西班牙廣場之後，我們會有自由活動的時間嗎？

3402 Will there be time to buy souvenirs?
會給我們買紀念品的時間嗎？

3403 I am really dying to **go shopping**.
我真的好想去逛街。 go shopping 片 逛街

3404 Is there a tour to Disneyland?
會有到迪士尼樂園的團嗎？

3405 Absolutely. We also have a tour to Universal Studio.
有啊！我們還有去環球影城的團。

3406 What's the difference between tour A and tour B?
行程 A 與行程 B 有什麼不同呢？

3407 Tour A is a sightseeing tour while tour B is a shopping tour.
行程 A 是以觀光為主的旅遊團，而行程 B 則以購物為主。

3408 What kind of tour do you feel like joining?
您比較想參加哪一種旅遊團呢？

3409 Which tour would you recommend?
你會推薦哪一種旅遊團？

3410 Those brochures are free.
旅遊簡介可免費索取。

3411 Can I have a city **map**?
我可以拿一份市區地圖嗎？ map 名 地圖

3412 I **highly** recommend the night-time tour.
我十分推薦夜間觀光。 highly 副 非常；很

3413 The night-time view of Paris is **fantastic**!
巴黎的夜景真的是太迷人了！ fantastic 形 驚人的

3414 The Eiffel Tower is lit up at night, and it's amazing.
艾菲爾鐵塔晚上會被照亮，真的很美。

3415 This **tour package** sounds great! How much is it?
這個團的行程聽起來很棒，費用多少呢？
tour package 片 套裝的旅遊行程

3416 A one-day tour is $110 for one person and a half-day tour is $65.
一日遊每位一百一十元，半日遊每位六十五元。

3417 Does your one-day tour include **lunch**?
一日遊有提供午餐嗎？ lunch 名 午餐

3418 Yes, the **fee** includes a lunch and a **soft drink** coupon.
是的，費用包含午餐和一張飲料折價券。
fee 名 費用 soft drink 名 不含酒精的飲料

3419 How many people are there in the tour?
一團有多少人呢？

3420 What time does the tour **depart**?
幾點鐘出發呢？ depart 動 出發

3421 Our tours depart at eight every morning.
每天早上八點出團。

3422 Will we take a **tour bus**?
我們會搭遊覽車嗎？ tour bus 片 觀光巴士

3423 Where should we wait for the tour bus?
我們應該在哪裡等遊覽車呢？

3424 Please give me your name and **room** number.
請給我您的大名和房間號碼。 room 名 房間

3425 Let's meet at 7:30 a.m. at the **lobby** of your hotel.
我們早上七點半在您下榻的飯店大廳等您。 lobby 名 大廳

3426 When does the tour **finish**?
這個團的行程幾點會結束？ finish 動 結束

3427 We will get back to your hotel before 6 p.m.
我們下午六點前會回到您的飯店。

3428 Should I tip the **tour guides**?
需要付導遊小費嗎？ tour guide 片 導遊

3429 I don't know how much I should tip the tour guide.
我不知道要付給導遊多少小費。

3430 We usually tip the tour guides 10% of the tour price.
我們通常會付團費的百分之十給導遊，當作小費。

3431 Good morning, I am your tour guide. Please just call me Jeff.
早安，我是你們的導遊，叫我傑夫就可以了。

3432 Our first **stop** is downtown Toronto.
我們的第一站會到多倫多市區。 stop 名 停車站

3433 Did you see the **tower**? It's just gorgeous!
你有看到那座塔嗎？真的太美了！ tower 名 塔；塔樓

3434 Is it one of the **landmarks** of Toronto?

那是多倫多的地標之一嗎？ landmark 名 地標

3435 It's CN Tower, and it was **completed** in 1976.
那是加拿大國家電視塔，建於一九七六年。 complete 動 完成

3436 Toronto's CN Tower was once the world's tallest tower.
多倫多的加拿大國家電視塔曾是世界上最高的塔。

3437 What a place! **No wonder** my friend suggested I visit it.
真是太美了！難怪我朋友推薦我來這裡。 no wonder 片 難怪

3438 The next attraction is Niagara Falls.
下一個景點是尼加拉大瀑布。

3439 We are going to see one of the biggest **waterfalls** in the world.
我們要去參觀全世界最大的瀑布。 waterfall 名 瀑布

3440 Will we see it from the Canadian side or the U.S. side?
我們會從加拿大那一邊看瀑布？還是從美國這一邊？

3441 Seeing from the **Canadian** side is more breathtaking.
從加拿大那一邊看過去會比較震撼。 Canadian 形 加拿大的

3442 Get your **camera** ready!
把相機準備好！ camera 名 照相機

3443 This is my first time here.
這是我第一次來這裡。

3444 Wow! I've never seen a waterfall like this. Let's **take a photo**!
哇！我從來沒看過這麼壯觀的瀑布，來照相吧！
take a photo 片 照相

3445 I have a **tripod** with me.
我有帶腳架。 tripod 名 三腳架

3446 I found a **scenic** place. Let's go there.
我發現一個風景很美的地方，我們去那裡吧。scenic 形 風景秀麗的

3447 Excuse me, could you take a picture of us, please?
不好意思，可以請你幫我們拍張照嗎？

3448 It's **automatic**. Just **press** here.
這是傻瓜相機，只要按這裡就可以了。
automatic 形 自動的　press 動 按

3449 Could you take a picture of us with the waterfalls?
可以幫我們拍張照嗎？後面的瀑布也要一起入鏡。

3450 The waterfalls are really worth seeing.
這瀑布確實值得一看！

3451 It's very **impressive**, too. I guess I'll never forget this.
也很令人印象深刻，我想我一輩子都不會忘掉這個景色。
impressive 形 令人印象深刻的

3452 Let's take a photo in front of the fountain.
我們在噴水池前照張相吧。

3453 Is your camera waterproof?
你的相機防水嗎？

3454 What time does the amusement park open?
遊樂園幾點開門啊？

3455 Let's get an all-day **pass**.
我們買一日票吧。pass 名 入場證

3456 I have student ID. Let's get student tickets at the ticket **booth**.
我有學生證，我們去售票亭買學生票吧。booth 名 貨攤

3457 I'd like two adult and two student tickets, please.
我要買兩張全票，兩張學生票。

3458 Here are your passes. Have fun.
這是您的門票，祝您玩得愉快。

3459 I want to go on all the rides.
我要玩遍所有的遊樂設施。

3460 Look! A **roller coaster**! Let's take a ride!
看！是雲霄飛車耶！我們去玩吧！ roller coaster 片 雲霄飛車

3461 The roller coaster ride is too much for me.
雲霄飛車對我來說太可怕了。

3462 I'd just like to go on something **mild**, like the **merry-go-round**.
我只敢玩一些比較溫和的，例如旋轉木馬。
mild 形 溫和的　merry-go-round 名 旋轉木馬

3463 The merry-go-round? Come on! That's for little kids.
旋轉木馬？拜託，那是小朋友玩的吧。

3464 How about the **bumper cars**?
那碰碰車呢？ bumper car 片 碰碰車

3465 Excuse me. Is this the **line** for the Freefall ride?
請問這裡是在排自由落體嗎？ line 名 行列

3466 We should have come earlier to **beat the rush**.
我們應該提早來的，這樣才能避開人潮。
beat the rush 片 避開人潮

3467 How can we get to the **pirate** ship?
海盜船在哪裡？我們要怎麼去呢？ pirate 名 海盜

3468 It's in **section** B. We can take a **trolley**.
它在 B 區，我們可以搭小火車去。
section 名 區域　trolley 名 有軌電車

3469 Do you know when the **parade** will start?
遊行什麼時候開始呢？ parade 名 遊行

3470 The parade will start at 6 p.m., followed by a **fireworks** show.
遊行將於晚上六點開始，接下來還有煙火秀。 firework 名 煙火

3471 Hey! There's Mickey Mouse! I'm going to take a photo with him.
米老鼠在那裡！我要去跟他合照。

3472 Where can I find a **gift shop**? I didn't see one anywhere.
哪裡有禮品店呢？我到處都找不到。 gift shop 片 禮品店

3473 I want to get some souvenirs for my friends.
我想去買一些紀念品送朋友。

3474 We'd better buy souvenirs as gifts for those who did not make the trip.
我們最好買些紀念品送給那些無法來旅遊的人。

3475 It's **difficult** to shop for my brother.
要挑送我哥哥的禮物還真難。 difficult 形 困難的

3476 I know a **perfect** gift for him.
我知道有件禮物很適合他。 perfect 形 理想的

3477 The **tie-clip** with a panda on it is just so cute.
有貓熊圖案的領帶夾真的好可愛。 tie-clip 名 領帶夾

3478 I'd like to buy the teddy bear for our teacher. What do you think?
我想買這隻泰迪熊給老師，你覺得怎麼樣？

3479 You always give our teachers gifts. No wonder you are a **teacher's pet**.
你總會送老師禮物，難怪你這麼得老師的歡心。
teacher's pet 片 受老師寵愛的學生

3480 These **magnets** look good. I'll get some.
這些磁鐵看起來很不錯，我要買幾個。 magnet 名 磁鐵

3481 The souvenirs are so expensive! I didn't expect

this.
這裡的紀念品都好貴！我沒想到價格會高成這樣。

3482 Change of plans! I will only get some **postcards** for my friends.
計畫改變了！我就買些明信片送朋友吧。 postcard 名 明信片

3483 The gift shop is a **tourist trap**.
這間禮品店專門敲觀光客竹槓。 tourist trap 片 敲詐旅客的店家

3484 I got ripped-off at that tourist trap.
我被那家觀光黑店敲詐了。

3485 I'm looking for something with a local **flavor**.
我在找有本地特色的東西。 flavor 名 風味

3486 Maple **syrup** is considered a classic Canadian souvenir.
楓糖漿被認為是典型的加拿大紀念品。 syrup 名 糖漿

3487 What is the most popular souvenir in Japan?
在日本，什麼是最受歡迎的紀念品啊？

3488 You can buy this Japanese lucky cat cell phone **strap**.
你可以買這個日本招財貓的手機吊飾。 strap 名 皮帶

3489 The **mug** with a Tokyo map on it is very special.
上面印有東京地圖的馬克杯很特別。 mug 名 馬克杯

3490 OK, I'll get it. Could you wrap it in **bubble wrap** for me?
好，我要買這個。你可以幫我用氣泡紙包起來嗎？
bubble wrap 片 氣泡紙

3491 I'd like it to be **wrapped** as a gift.
請幫我包成禮物。 wrap 動 包；裹

3492 Do you want to pay the **bill** now?
您要結帳了嗎？ bill 名 帳單

3493 Yes. Do you accept **traveler's checks**?
是的，你們收旅行支票嗎？ traveler's check 片 旅行支票

3494 I went to lots of attractions and had a great time.
我去看了很多景點，玩得很愉快。

3495 I think I'm **exhausted**. Can we go back to the hotel?
我覺得我已經精疲力竭了，我們可以回飯店了嗎？
exhausted 形 精疲力盡的

UNIT 3 出發！出境的重點句 About The Departure

3496 **Passengers** should **check in** at least two hours before their flight time.
在飛機起飛前兩個小時，旅客就要到機場的櫃台報到。
passenger 名 乘客 check in 片 到達並登記

3497 Which terminal should we go to?
我們應該去哪個航廈？

3498 We should go to the departure terminal for sure.
我們要到出境的航廈。

3499 I almost missed the plane.
我差點錯過這班飛機。

3500 If you don't get on this plane, there's another one that leaves in an hour.
如果您沒趕上這班飛機，再一個小時就有另一班起飛。

3501 What time does the next flight leave?
下一班飛機幾點起飛呢？

3502 Where is the Evergreen Airlines check-in counter?
請問長榮航空公司的報到櫃檯在哪裡？

3503 When you check in with an e-ticket, you only have to show your passport to get your boarding pass.
如果你是持電子機票報到，只需出示護照，就能拿到登機證。

3504 I'd like to check in.
我要辦理報到手續。

3505 May I have your passport, please?
麻煩出示您的護照。

3506 I don't see your reservation on our **computer**.
我們的電腦裡沒有您的訂位紀錄耶。 computer 名 電腦

3507 It's **impossible**. I made a reservation, and here is my ticket.
不可能吧！我有訂位，這是我的機票。 impossible 形 不可能的

3508 Sir, I am afraid you are at the wrong counter.
先生，您恐怕走錯櫃檯了。

3509 We are China Airlines, not EVA Airlines.
這裡是華航的櫃檯，不是長榮。

3510 How many **pieces** of luggage can I take?
我可以帶幾件行李呢？ piece 名 一件

3511 Each person is allowed to carry two pieces of luggage.
每位旅客可以攜帶兩件行李。

3512 I have two check-in bags and one **carry-on** bag.
我有兩件託運行李及一件登機行李。 carry-on 形 可隨身攜帶的

3513 May I see your carry-on bag, please?
我可以看一下您的登機行李嗎？

3514 Airlines have special **restrictions** on carry-on **baggage**.
針對登機行李，航空公司通常都有特別的限制。
restriction 名 限制規定 baggage 名 行李

3515 A carry-on bag can weigh up to 7 kg.
隨身行李最重不能超過七公斤。

3516 What is the free baggage **allowance**?
免費的行李限制重量是多少？allowance 名 允許額

3517 Each passenger is allowed a total of twenty kilos on economy, thirty kilos on business, and forty kilos on First class.
每位經濟艙的旅客能託運二十公斤的行李，商務艙三十公斤，頭等艙四十公斤。

3518 Please put your luggage on the **scale**.
請您將行李放到磅秤上。scale 名 磅秤

3519 Is my luggage **overweight**?
我的行李有超重嗎？overweight 形 超重的

3520 I'm sorry, but you have to pay an **excess** baggage **charge**.
很抱歉，您必須付行李超重的費用。
excess 形 過量的 charge 名 費用

3521 There will be an overweight-luggage charge of $600.
要跟您收行李超重費六百元。

3522 Here are some **tags** for your check-in luggage.
這些是託運行李的標籤。tag 名 標籤

3523 Will the baggage be checked through to my destination?
行李會直接運送到目的地嗎？

3524 I think that I've earned enough **mileage** for an **upgrade**.

我想我累積的里程數足以升等了。
mileage 名 行駛哩數　upgrade 名 升級

3525 Can I upgrade to business class?
我可以升等到商務艙嗎？

3526 Yes sir, you are qualified to upgrade.
可以的，先生，您符合升等的資格。

3527 I can upgrade to business class because I have an upgrade coupon.
我有一張升等券，所以能升等到商務艙。

3528 Sir, we are going to upgrade you to business class.
先生，我們可以將您升等到商務艙。

3529 You sometimes can get an upgrade when you are traveling alone.
你一個人搭飛機時，有時會得到升等的機會。

3530 Will the mileage be credited to my account?
這些里程有累積了嗎？

3531 Yes, sir. You can also **redeem** credits within six months of your flight.
有的，先生，六個月之內的里程您都可以補登。redeem 動 彌補

3532 Here is your boarding pass and passport.
這是您的登機證和護照。

3533 These are your **baggage claim** tags.
這是您的行李貼條。baggage claim 片 認領行李

3534 One goes on your suitcase and the other is the baggage claim tag.
一張貼在您的行李上，另一張是認領行李用的。

3535 The flight will begin boarding around 9:15 a.m., at Gate A7.
登機時間為上午九點十五分左右，於 A7 門登機。

3536 Your seat is 32C.
您的座位在 32C。

3537 Am I **through** here?
我的手續都辦完了嗎？ through 形 完成的

3538 They are all **in order**.
一切都辦妥了。 in order 片 情況良好

3539 What is the **gate** number, again?
請問，你剛剛說登機門是幾號？ gate 名 出入口

3540 You board at Gate A7. You can follow the **signs**.
A7 號登機門，您可以跟著指示牌走。 sign 名 標誌

3541 Is Japan Airlines flight 509 departing **on time**?
日本航空 509 次班機會準時起飛嗎？ on time 片 準時

3542 The flight has not yet taken off in Hong Kong due to the heavy **fog**.
這架班機受到濃霧影響，所以尚未從香港起飛。 fog 名 霧；霧氣

3543 Your flight will be **delayed** for fifty minutes.
您的班機會延遲五十分鐘。 delayed 形 延遲的

3544 Is the plane **on schedule**?
飛機會準時起飛嗎？ on schedule 片 準時

3545 Due to **weather conditions**, all flights to Japan will be delayed.
因為天候不佳，所有飛往日本的班機都將延後起飛。
weather condition 片 天氣狀況；氣候條件

3546 Our flight was delayed for four hours due to some **engine** problems.
我們的飛機因為引擎故障，延遲了四個小時。 engine 名 引擎

3547 It hasn't been decided yet when the plane will **take off**.
飛機起飛的時間尚未確定。 take off 片 起飛

3548 We will inform all passengers of the new departure times ASAP.
我們會盡快通知各位旅客新的起飛時間。

3549 The details will be shown on the flight information **board**.
詳細情況將顯示於班機訊息板上。 board 名 布告牌

3550 We truly **regret** the **inconvenience**.
造成您的不便，我們深表歉意。
regret 動 為…感到抱歉 inconvenience 名 不便

3551 Thank you for your **cooperation** and **patience**.
感謝各位的合作及耐心等候。
cooperation 名 合作 patience 名 耐心

3552 Let's **proceed** to the passport **inspection** area.
我們去護照查驗櫃台吧。 proceed 動 繼續進行 inspection 名 檢驗

3553 Let's walk through the **metal detector**.
我們要通過金屬檢測器。 metal 名 金屬 detector 名 檢驗器

3554 Please **empty out** your **pockets** and put all metal objects in this **tray**.
請把口袋裡的東西拿出來，並將所有金屬物品放在這個盤子上。
empty out 片 清空 pocket 名 口袋 tray 名 盤子；托盤

3555 Please take off your shoes as well.
也請你把鞋子脫掉。

3556 The metal detector **beeps** as I walk through.
我通過時，金屬檢測器嗶嗶作響。 beep 動 發出嗶嗶聲

3557 Please **step back**, sir. Are you wearing any metal **accessories**?
先生，請退後一步。請問您有配戴任何金屬飾品嗎？
step back 片 後退 accessory 名 飾品

3558 The metal **buckle** on your belt may have **set** it **off**.

可能是皮帶的金屬扣環引起的。 buckle 名 扣子 set off 片 引發

3559 Please step through the detector again, sir.
先生，請再走過檢測器一次。

3560 Step **aside**, please. We'll have to do a special check of your clothes.
請靠邊站，我們得對你的衣物做特別檢查。 aside 副 到旁邊

3561 Sorry, sir, I have to check your bag as a **security precaution**.
抱歉，先生，基於安全考量，我們必須檢查您的袋子。
security 名 安全 precaution 名 預防措施

3562 They **frisked** me and went through everything in my bag.
他們搜我的身，並翻遍我的袋子檢查。 frisk 動 搜身

3563 When are we boarding?
我們什麼時候要登機？

3564 It's still early. Do you want to buy anything?
還早呢，你想買點什麼嗎？

3565 Good. We still have time for shopping at duty-free shops.
太好了，我們還有時間逛免稅店。

3566 I prefer to take a rest at the airport **lounge**.
我寧願到機場的貴賓室休息。 lounge 名 休息室；候機室

3567 Lounges also provide beverages like coffee, tea, juice, beer and other alcoholic beverages.
貴賓室還提供飲料，如咖啡、茶、果汁、啤酒和其他酒類。

3568 OK. You stay here and I am going shopping.
好！那你留在這裡，我去逛街。

3569 What's my duty-free wine and **cigarettes** allowance?
請問帶免稅菸酒的限額是多少？ cigarette 名 香菸

3570 You can ask the **salesperson** there.
你可以問一下店員。 salesperson 名 店員

3571 Only ticketed passengers can **purchase** duty-free items.
只有登機旅客才可以購買免稅商品。 purchase 動 購買

3572 There's a café just across from the lounge area. Want a cup of coffee?
候機室對面有間咖啡館，你想喝咖啡嗎？

3573 I'm catching a **connecting flight** to Taipei. Where do I go?
我要轉機去台北，要去哪裡轉機呢？ connecting flight 片 轉接班機

3574 Where do I go to catch my connecting flight?
我要到哪裡轉機呢？

3575 I'm transferring to flight YY-006 to Tokyo.
我要轉搭 YY-006 次班機去東京。

3576 Is this the **transit** counter?
這裡是過境櫃檯嗎？ transit 名 過境，中轉

3577 I'm a transit passenger for this flight.
我是這班飛機的過境旅客。

3578 Where shall we wait?
我們要在哪裡候機呢？

3579 You'll have to wait at the transit lounge.
您必須在過境室裡等候。

3580 We can board half an hour before our plane takes off.
起飛前半小時開始登機。

3581 We can't get on the plane until they make the boarding call.
在聽到登機廣播前，我們不能登機。

3582 Excuse me; is this the line for flight DT-123 to San Francisco?
不好意思，請問這裡排的是前往舊金山的 DT-123 次班機嗎？

3583 Attention, please. The boarding gate for flight TY-836 to Tokyo has changed to A10.
各位乘客請注意，前往東京的 TY-836 次班機，其登機門已改至 A 10。

3584 Passengers of flight TY-836 please proceed to gate A10 for boarding.
搭乘 TY-836 次班機的旅客，請前往 A10 登機門準備登機。

3585 Thank you for your patience. Flight TY-836 is now boarding.
謝謝您的耐心等候，TY-836 次班機現在可以登機了。

3586 Please have your boarding pass **handy**.
請將登記證拿在手上。 handy 形 手邊的

3587 We now invite all first class and business class passengers to board.
我們現在請所有頭等艙及商務艙的旅客登機。

3588 We invite those passengers with small children or those **requiring** special **assistance** to come to the boarding counter.
我們現在請有小孩子和需要特別幫助的旅客來登機櫃台。
require 動 需要 assistance 名 幫助

3589 All passengers seated in **rows** 56 to 70 may now board.
現在請座位在五十六排到七十排的乘客登機。 row 名 (一)排

3590 We will now be accepting all **remaining** passengers to board.
我們現在請其餘所有的乘客登機。 remaining 形 剩下的

UNIT 4 乘坐飛機 & 入境
On the Plane & Arrival

3591 I can't find my seat. Where is 34B?
我找不到座位，請問 34B 在哪裡？

3592 May I see your boarding pass? I can help you find your seat.
可以看一下您的登機證嗎？我來幫您找座位。

3593 This way, please.
這邊請。

3594 Your seat is in the **rear** of the **cabin** on the right.
您的座位在機艙的右後方。 rear 名 後面 cabin 名 客艙

3595 There's someone sitting on the seat.
有人坐在這個位子上。

3596 Excuse me, madam. I am afraid you are in the wrong seat.
女士，不好意思，我想你坐錯位子了。

3597 I think this is my seat.
這應該是我的位子。

3598 Oh, sorry. My **fault**. So...12A is a window seat?
抱歉，是我的錯，所以 12A 應該是靠窗的位子嗎？ fault 名 錯誤

3599 Could we exchange seats?
我們可以交換位子嗎？

3600 I prefer an **aisle** seat.
我比較喜歡走道旁的座位。 aisle 名 走道

3601 Could you put this bag in the **overhead compartment** for me?

可以請你幫我把袋子放到上方的置物櫃裡嗎？
overhead 形 在頭頂上的 compartment 名 隔間

3602 The compartment seems to be full.
置物櫃好像滿了。

3603 I'll put my **purse** under the seat in front of me.
那我把皮包放在我前面的位子底下。purse 名 (女用)手提包

3604 This is my first time taking an airplane.
這是我第一次搭飛機。

3605 How do you feel? I was really nervous **during** my first flight.
感覺如何？我第一次搭飛機的時候很緊張呢。during 介 在…期間

3606 I'm **a little** excited and **a little** nervous.
有點興奮，也有點緊張。a little 片 一點

3607 Looking out of the window sometimes **scares** me.
從窗戶看出去有時會讓我害怕。scare 動 使恐懼

3608 Just **take it easy**. It's fun.
放輕鬆就好了，很好玩的。take it easy 片 放輕鬆

3609 I **swear** that I will never fly **economy class** again.
我發誓我再也不要坐經濟艙了。
swear 動 發誓 economy class 片 經濟艙

3610 These seats are so small!
這些位子太小了！

3611 I feel like a **sardine**.
我感覺自己像在擠沙丁魚。sardine 名 沙丁魚

3612 Please **fasten** your **seat belt**.
請繫好安全帶。fasten 動 繫緊 seat belt 片 安全帶

3613 Sir, please keep your seat in the **upright**

position.
先生，麻煩您把座椅豎起來。 upright 形 豎的；直立的

3614 May I use my laptop now?
我現在可以使用筆電了嗎？

3615 No, you may not use electronic **devices** until the seat belt sign has been **turned off**.
不行，在安全帶指示燈熄滅前，您不能使用電子產品。
device 名 裝置 turn off 片 關掉

3616 Ladies and **gentlemen**, this is World Airlines flight TY-836 **bound for** Seattle.
各位女士先生，這是全球航空即將飛往西雅圖的 TY-836 次班機。
gentleman 名 先生；男士 bound for 片 準備前往

3617 This is head **flight attendant**, Eva Huang.
我是座艙長，黃伊娃。 flight attendant 片 空服員

3618 **On behalf of** World Airlines, we welcome you aboard flight TY-836 from Taipei to Seattle.
謹代表全球航空，歡迎各位搭乘從台北飛往西雅圖的 TY-836 次班機。 on behalf of 片 代表

3619 The flying time today is about eleven hours and forty minutes.
今天的飛行時間大約為十一個小時又四十分鐘。

3620 Our expected time of arrival is 3:45 p.m. local time, August 9.
我們預計於當地時間八月九日，下午三點四十五分抵達。

3621 If you need any assistance, please **contact** the flight attendant.
如果您需要協助，請與空服人員聯絡。 contact 動 聯繫

3622 In a few minutes, we'll be **serving soft drinks**, followed by lunch.
我們稍後將提供冷飲服務，隨後即將提供午餐。
serve 動 供應(飯菜) soft drink 片 不含酒精的飲料

3623 Duty-free sales will follow the meal service.
用餐後，我們會進行免稅商品的販售。

3624 For further details on service, please **refer to** the in-flight magazine.
關於其他服務細節，請參閱機上雜誌。 refer to 片 參考

3625 We wish you a **pleasant** flight. Thank you.
希望您有個愉快的旅程，謝謝。 pleasant 形 令人愉快的

3626 This is your **captain** speaking.
這是機長廣播。 captain 名 機長

3627 We've reached **cruising altitude**, and I've turned off the seat belt sign.
我們現在已達到巡航高度，安全帶指示燈也已關閉。
cruise 動 巡航 altitude 名 高度；海拔

3628 Still, for your safety, please keep your seat belt fastened when you are in your seat.
不過，為了您的安全，坐在座位上時仍請繫好安全帶。

3629 Our seats have **personal** video screens.
我們的座椅有個人螢幕。 personal 形 個人的

3630 And it shows where we are over the ocean, our speed, and altitude.
螢幕上會顯示我們在海洋上方的位置、飛行速度及高度。

3631 The airplane is flying at an altitude of 25,000 **feet**.
飛機目前的飛行高度為兩萬五千英尺。 foot 名 英尺

3632 What's the **actual** flying time from here to Seattle?
從這裡到西雅圖的實際飛行時間是多久？ actual 形 實際的

3633 How long is the flying time?
飛行時間是多久呢？

3634 How much longer until we **land**?

離降落還有多久？ land 動 使降落

3635 What time will we **arrive**?
我們什麼時候會抵達呢？ arrive 動 到達

3636 We've **crossed** the International Date Line.
我們越過了國際換日線。 cross 動 越過

3637 What's the **time difference** between Taipei and Seattle?
台北和西雅圖的時差是多少？ time difference 片 時差

3638 Please set your watch **back** an hour.
請把錶撥慢一個小時。 back 副 向後

3639 I am afraid that I will have **jet lag** when I get there.
好擔心我到了那邊會有時差。 jet lag 片 時差(指飛行後的生理疲倦感)

3640 I'm still on Taipei time!
我還在過台北的時間！

3641 When do you start to serve dinner?
請問什麼時候會開始供應晚餐呢？

3642 We're just getting it ready now. It shouldn't be too long.
我們現在正在準備，應該不會太久。

3643 Ladies and gentlemen, we'll be serving dinner in a few **minutes**.
各位女士先生，我們稍後即將供應晚餐。 minute 名 分鐘

3644 Today's dinner choices are fried **noodles** with beef and **rice** with chicken.
今日的晚餐有牛肉炒麵和雞肉飯兩種選擇。
noodle 名 麵條 rice 名 米

3645 You can see the menu in the pocket in front of you.
您可以參考座位前方置物袋中的菜單。

3646 Madam, we have fried noodles with beef and rice with chicken. Which one do you **prefer**?
女士，我們有牛肉炒麵和雞肉飯，請問您要哪一種？
prefer 動 更喜歡

3647 I'd like rice with chicken, please.
我要雞肉飯，謝謝。

3648 Do you have any **instant** noodles?
請問你們有泡麵嗎？ instant 形 速食的；即溶的

3649 I am sorry, but we don't offer any instant noodles now.
很抱歉，我們現在不提供泡麵了。

3650 Anything to drink?
要喝點什麼嗎？

3651 What kind of **drinks** do you have?
有什麼飲料呢？ drink 名 飲料

3652 We have **mineral** water, juice, soda, beer, and wine.
我們有礦泉水、果汁、汽水、啤酒和葡萄酒。 mineral 形 礦質的

3653 Apple juice, please.
我要蘋果汁，謝謝。

3654 Have you prepared any food for **vegetarians**?
機上有準備素食嗎？ vegetarian 名 素食者

3655 You have to **request** the vegetarian food when making reservations.
在訂機位的同時，您就必須預訂素食。 request 動 要求

3656 I reserved a vegetarian meal when I checked in.
我在機場櫃台報到時有預訂素食餐。

3657 Yes, madam. It will be served **soon**.
有的，女士，您的餐點很快就會送來。 soon 副 很快地

3658 Are you **finished**?
請問您用完餐了嗎？ finish 動 吃完；用完

3659 Yes, please **take away** the tray.
是的，餐盤可以收走了。 take away 片 拿走

3660 Would you like some coffee or tea?
您要喝咖啡或茶嗎？

3661 Can I ask you to **lower** your **window blind**, please?
可以請你將遮陽板放下來嗎？
lower 動 降下 window blind 片 百葉窗

3662 Look! We're way above the **clouds** now.
看！我們現在已經在雲的上方了。 cloud 名 雲

3663 You may not use the lavatory now.
你現在不能上洗手間。

3664 Look at the light at the top of the **entrance**.
看入口處上方的燈。 entrance 名 入口

3665 All the lavatories are **occupied**.
洗手間目前都有人在使用。 occupied 形 在使用的

3666 But I can't wait. Are there any other **washrooms** around?
但是我憋不住了，還有其他廁所嗎？ washroom 名 洗手間

3667 There are more lavatories in the back.
後面還有廁所。

3668 The lavatories in the rear of the plane are **vacant**.
機艙後面的洗手間是空的。 vacant 形 空著的

3669 Passengers are not allowed to **smoke** in any area of the cabin.
乘客在機艙內的任何地方都不能抽菸。 smoke 動 抽菸

3670 Could I get a **toy** for my daughter, please?
我可以幫我的女兒要個玩具嗎？ toy 名 玩具

3671 Let's see what the **in-flight** entertainment is.
來看看飛機上有什麼娛樂設備。 in-flight 形 飛行中的

3672 Could you show me how to use the remote control?
可以教我怎麼使用遙控器嗎？

3673 Can you help me with this **earphone**? Something's wrong with it.
你能幫我看看這副耳機嗎？好像有點問題。 earphone 名 耳機

3674 The **headphones** don't work. Can I get another pair?
這副耳機壞了，可以換一副新的給我嗎？
headphone 名 頭戴式耳機

3675 The in-flight movie starts in about ten minutes.
機上電影大約再十分鐘開始播放。

3676 Why is the plane **bouncing** so much?
飛機為什麼顛得這麼厲害？ bounce 動 彈回；彈起

3677 It's just a little **turbulence**.
只不過是輕微的亂流而已。 turbulence 名 (氣體等的)紊流

3678 My ears are all **blocked up**.
我耳鳴。 block up 片 堵塞

3679 My ears are **popping**.
我的耳朵塞住了。 pop 動 突然出現；突然發生

3680 Try chewing this piece of gum or try **yawning** or swallowing.
試試嚼口香糖，或打個哈欠、吞口水看看。 yawn 動 打呵欠

3681 It'll be fine **as soon as** the plane gets out of the turbulence.
只要脫離亂流，就沒事了。 as soon as 片 一…就…

3682 Do you have medicine for **airsickness**?
你們有暈機藥嗎？ airsickness 名 暈機

3683 I'd better get the **airsick** bag ready.
我最好還是先準備好嘔吐袋。 airsick 形 暈機的

3684 The airsickness bag is in the seat pocket.
椅背的置物袋裡有嘔吐袋。

3685 We have a **head wind**.
我們遇到了逆風。 head wind 片 逆風

3686 We are now experiencing turbulence.
我們正飛過亂流圈。

3687 For your own safety, please return to your seat and fasten your seat belt.
為了各位的安全，請回到座位上，並繫好安全帶。

3688 **Kindly remain** seated until the "FASTEN SEAT BELT" sign has been turned off.
在「扣安全帶」的指示燈熄滅之前，請各位坐在座位上。
kindly 副 勞駕，請 remain 動 保持

3689 We'll be landing soon.
我們即將準備降落。

3690 Please make sure that your **seatback** is in the upright position.
請確定您的椅背已經扶正。 seatback 名 椅背

3691 Do you need a **Disembarkation** Card and Customs **Declaration** Form?
請問您需要入境卡和海關申報單嗎？
disembarkation 名 登陸 declaration 名 聲明

3692 Can you tell me how to **fill out** this disembarkation card?
請教我怎麼填寫這張入境卡好嗎？ fill out 片 填寫

3693 You can find **instructions** on the back.

卡片的背面有填寫說明。instruction 名 用法說明

3694 We are now **approaching** Seattle Airport.
我們即將抵達西雅圖機場。approach 動 接近

3695 The local time is 3:40 p.m., and the ground temperature is 20 degrees **Centigrade**, or 73 degrees **Fahrenheit**.
當地時間為下午三點四十分，地面溫度為攝氏二十度 / 華氏七十三度。Centigrade 名 攝氏度 Fahrenheit 名 華氏溫標

3696 Don't forget to take your personal **belongings** when leaving the **aircraft**.
下機時請記得您的隨身物品。
belongings 名 隨身物品 aircraft 名 飛機

3697 Thank you for flying with us.
感謝您搭乘本次的班機。

3698 We hope you enjoyed your flight and that we have the chance to serve you again.
希望您滿意本次飛行，並期待能有機會再次為各位服務。

3699 I am getting a connecting flight to Boston at the Seattle Airport.
我要在西雅圖機場轉機到波士頓。

3700 May I **stay** on the plane?
我可以待在飛機上嗎？stay 動 停留；留下

3701 All passengers are required to **disembark** and wait in the airport.
所有乘客都必須下機，在機場等候轉機。disembark 動 登陸

3702 Please bring all of your bags with you.
請把所有的行李都帶著。

3703 How long of a **layover** do we have?
我們中途會停留多久？layover 名 臨時滯留

3704 Do we have to pick up our check-in bags?

我們得拿出託運行李嗎？

3705 How long will we stop at this airport?
我們會在這個機場停留多久呢？

3706 Let's go through **customs**.
我們去辦理通關手續吧！ customs 名 海關

3707 Here is the **immigration** area. Get your passport out.
入境檢查區到了，快把護照準備好。 immigration 名 移居

3708 Which way should I go for immigration?
我要在哪裡辦入境手續呢？

3709 Please go to a "Non-**Citizen**" window.
請到「非本國人」的窗口辦理。 citizen 名 公民

3710 There are long lines of arriving passengers.
剛抵達的乘客都在排隊，排得可真長。

3711 All the non-citizen **travelers** have to fill out an arrival card and give it to the immigration **officers**.
所有非本國的旅客都要填寫入境卡，再交給移民官。
traveler 名 旅客；遊客 officer 名 官員

3712 May I see your ticket and passport, please?
請將您的機票和護照給我，謝謝。

3713 I am sorry; my English is not good enough.
抱歉，我的英文不怎麼好。

3714 Could you get a Chinese speaker?
這裡有會說中文的人嗎？

3715 Would you show me your disembarkation card, please?
麻煩給我您的入境卡。

3716 Is this your first time in the U.S.?
這是您第一次來美國嗎？

3717 Have you ever been in the United States before?
您以前來過美國嗎？

3718 I've been here twice.
我來過兩次。

3719 What is the **purpose** of your **visit**?
您來這裡的目的是什麼呢？ purpose 名 目的 visit 名 參觀

3720 I am taking an English **course**.
我是來上英文課程的。 course 名 課程

3721 I'm with a **tourist** group.
我是跟著旅行團來的。 tourist 名 觀光者

3722 We are doing some sightseeing.
我們是來觀光的。

3723 I am here for a vacation.
我是來度假的。

3724 I am here **on business**.
我是來出差的。 on business 片 出差

3725 What **line** of business are you in?
請問您從事的行業是什麼？ line 名 行業；擅長

3726 I am a **college** teacher.
我是大學講師。 college 名 大學

3727 How long do you plan to stay? / How long will you be staying?
您計劃要停留多久呢？

3728 I'll be here for three weeks.
我將停留三個星期。

3729 Where are you going to stay?
您會住在哪裡呢？

3730 I will be staying at a local hotel.

我會住在當地的旅館。

3731 I'll stay with my brother.
我會住在我的哥哥家。

3732 I will stay in a school **dormitory**.
我會住在學校宿舍。dormitory 名 宿舍

3733 Are you going to visit any other **countries**?
您也會去其他國家嗎？country 名 國家

3734 Go through the passport control and security check, and then go straight on.
驗完護照和安全檢查之後，往前直走。

3735 Do you have any plants or meat products? Any fruits or vegetables?
你們有帶植物或肉品嗎？有攜帶水果或蔬菜嗎？

3736 **Agricultural** products are not allowed to be brought into the U.S.
美國禁止攜帶任何農產品入境。agricultural 形 農業的

3737 You might be **fined** or **jailed**.
你有可能會被罰款或坐牢。fine 動 罰款 jail 動 拘留

3738 Please put your bags on the counter.
請將行李放在櫃台上。

3739 Please **open** your bag.
請打開袋子。open 動 打開；展開

3740 Have you got any **foreign currency** with you?
您身上有攜帶任何外匯嗎？foreign 形 外國的 currency 名 貨幣

3741 Excuse me, where is the **quarantine** section?
請問檢疫處在哪裡？quarantine 名 檢疫

3742 May I see your health **certificates**?
我可以看一下你們的健康證明嗎？certificate 名 證明書

3743 You are **clear**. You may go now.
檢查已經完成，你們可以離開了。clear 形 清除了的；清白的

3744 Where can I claim my checked luggage?
我要到哪裡提領我的託運行李呢？

3745 Just **follow** the baggage claim sign.
跟著「領取行李」的指示牌走就可以了。follow 動 跟隨

3746 I need a luggage cart. Can you go get one?
我需要行李推車，你可以幫我推一台過來嗎。

3747 Which **carrousel** is for flight TY-836?
請問 TY-836 次班機的行李在哪個轉盤？carrousel 名 轉盤

3748 Does the luggage come out here?
行李會從這裡出來嗎？

3749 I need a hand with my luggage, please.
我需要人幫忙搬行李，謝謝。

3750 Let me help you with that. Show me which luggage is yours.
我來幫你，哪一個是你的行李？

3751 Look! There comes my luggage.
那是我的行李！

3752 Excuse me. I believe you took the wrong luggage. That's mine.
不好意思，你似乎拿錯行李了，那是我的。

3753 My luggage hasn't arrived yet.
我的行李還沒到。

3754 Where is the **lost** luggage counter?
行李遺失櫃檯在哪裡呢？lost 形 遺失的

3755 Excuse me, but my bag didn't come out.
不好意思，我的行李沒出來。

3756 Please fill out the form, and **hand** it to the woman there.
請填寫這張表格，填完之後交給那邊的女士。hand 動 給；傳遞

3757 Show me your baggage claim ticket, and I'll try to find it for you.
請給我看一下您的行李條，我會試著幫您找到它的。

3758 The airline will pay you **compensation** if we don't find it.
如果我們沒有找到，航空公司會理賠的。compensation 名 賠償金

3759 Please **deliver** the baggage to my hotel as soon as you've **located** it.
找到行李的話，請盡快送到我的旅館來。
deliver 動 運送　locate 動 找出

3760 What's in your **suitcase**?
您的行李箱裡有什麼？suitcase 名 小型旅行箱

3761 There are just some clothes and personal belongings.
只有一些衣服和個人用品。

3762 Please open your suitcase.
請打開您的行李箱。

3763 I regret the **inconvenience**, but there's nothing I can do about it.
造成您的不便很抱歉，但我一定得這樣做。inconvenience 名 不便

3764 It's the **regulation**.
這是規定。regulation 名 規定；規章

3765 You may **close** your suitcase.
您可以關上行李了。close 動 關閉；蓋上

3766 I'm afraid you have to leave them with us **for the moment**.
恐怕得請您把這些東西暫時留在我們這裡。

for the moment 片 暫時

3767 We'll have to get them **examined**.
我們必須要做一些檢查。 examine 動 檢查

3768 Do you have anything to **declare**?
您有沒有要申報的東西？ declare 動 申報(納稅品等)

3769 I don't have anything to declare.
我沒有需要申報的東西。

3770 I have a camera I want to give as a gift to my family.
我帶了照相機，是要送給家人的。

3771 Let me look at the receipt, then.
請讓我看一下收據。

3772 According to the law, you can only bring one **carton** of **cigarettes**.
依法律規定，你只能帶一條香菸喔！
carton 名 一紙盒 cigarette 名 香菸

3773 You have to pay the **tax**.
你必須繳稅。 tax 名 稅；稅金

3774 Customs officers have the right to **confiscate** it if you don't pay the tax.
如果你不付稅金的話，海關有權利沒收物品。 confiscate 動 沒收

3775 Did you have any trouble with customs?
你過海關時有麻煩嗎？

UNIT 5

不可不顧的食與住
Eating And Housing

3776 When you travel to popular destinations during **peak seasons**, you'd better reserve **accommodations** before the trip.
當你選擇在旺季去熱門的旅遊景點時，最好事先預訂好房間。
peak season 片 旺季　accommodation 名 住處

3777 I am looking for a hotel under NT$2,000.
我在找新台幣兩千元以下的旅館。

3778 Good morning, the One Hotel. How may I help you?
早安，第一飯店您好，我能為您服務嗎？

3779 Hello, I'd like to make a reservation.
你好，我想要訂房。

3780 Hold on, please. I'll put you **through** to the reservation center.
請稍後，我替您轉接至訂房中心。 through 副 電話接通(+to)

3781 When will that be for?
請問您哪一天要入住呢？

3782 I'd like to **book** a room for next weekend. What are your rates?
我下個週末想訂一個房間，請問房價是多少？ book 動 預定

3783 Do you have any rooms **available**?
你們還有空房嗎？ available 形 可得到的

3784 I'm sorry, but we are fully booked. / We have no **vacancies** now.
抱歉，所有的房間都已客滿。 vacancy 名 空房

3785 How many nights will you be staying?
請問您要住幾個晚上呢？

3786 I'll be staying for four nights.
我要住四個晚上。

3787 May I have your name, please?
請問客人的名字是？

3788 How many persons will be staying in the room?
請問有幾位要入住呢？

3789 What kind of room would you like to book?
請問您想要訂什麼樣的房型呢？

3790 I'd like to reserve a double room.
我要訂一間雙人房。

3791 What kind of room do you need? A smoking or non-smoking room?
請問您要什麼樣的房間呢？吸煙還是非吸煙的房間？

3792 I prefer a room with an **ocean view**.
我想要一間看得到海景的房間。 ocean 名 海洋 view 名 景色

3793 We'd like to have a quiet, non-smoking room with a mountain view.
我們想訂安靜、看得到山景的非吸煙房間。

3794 What kind of room would you prefer?
請問您比較喜歡什麼樣的房型呢？

3795 Would you like a king-size bed or a twin-bedded room?
您想要一張大床還是兩張單人床呢？

3796 We would like a double room with a king-size bed.
我們要訂附大床的雙人房。

3797 Please give us a room with two double beds.

請給我們有兩張雙人床的房間。

3798 How much is it for a **standard** room?
標準房型的價格是多少呢？ standard 形 標準的

3799 Our rates for single rooms are NT$2,000, and doubles are NT$2,500.
單人房的房價是一晚兩千元，雙人房則為兩千五百元。

3800 I need an extra bed. How much should I pay?
我需要加一張床，這樣要付多少錢呢？

3801 You have to pay NT$800 for an extra bed.
加一張床的費用為八百元。

3802 How about a **suite**?
那套房要多少錢？ suite 名 套房

3803 Suites are NT$3,600 per night.
套房是一晚三千六百元。

3804 Does the **price** include tax?
請問這個價錢含稅嗎？ price 名 價格

3805 The **service charge** and tax are included.
服務費和稅金已包含在內。 service charge 片 服務費

3806 Do you have any discount if we stay longer?
如果多住幾天，會有折扣嗎？

3807 Yes, we offer a 15% discount if you stay for six days and over.
有的，住六晚以上房價打八五折。

3808 Does the charge include breakfast?
有附早餐嗎？

3809 A **complimentary** breakfast **buffet** is offered every morning.
每天早上都有附自助式早餐。
complimentary 形 贈送的 buffet 名 自助餐

3810 Would you like the **continental** breakfast or the American breakfast?
您想要歐式早餐還是美式早餐？ continental 形 大陸的

3811 Is there anything else I can **assist** you **with**?
還有什麼需要協助的嗎？ assist with 片 協助

3812 To **guarantee** your hotel reservation, it is necessary to pay for the first night as a **deposit**.
為了確保訂房，您必須先支付一個晚上的費用，當作押金。
guarantee 動 擔保 deposit 名 押金

3813 Is the deposit refundable?
押金是可以退還的嗎？

3814 How much notice do you require for a reservation **cancellation**?
取消訂房要多久前通知呢？ cancellation 名 取消

3815 We require a 48-hour notice.
我們需要四十八小時前通知。

3816 How **far** are you from the airport?
你們那裡距離機場多遠？ far 形 遠的；遙遠的

3817 Do you **provide** transportation to and from the airport?
你們有機場接 / 送機的服務嗎？ provide 動 提供

3818 Yes. We have a free **shuttle bus** service.
有的，我們免費提供機場接駁公車的服務。 shuttle bus 片 接駁公車

3819 I'd like to check in, please.
我想要登記住房。

3820 Do you have a reservation?
請問您有訂房嗎？

3821 I've made a reservation, but I forgot my hotel **confirmation** number.
我有訂房，但我忘了我的旅館確認碼是幾號。

confirmation 名 確定

3822 May I have your ID or passport, please?
麻煩給我您的身分證或護照。

3823 A moment, please. I'll look for your reservation **details**.
請稍候，我確認一下您的訂房資料。 detail 名 細節

3824 Yes, Mr. Lee. Your room is ready.
有的，李先生，您的房間已經準備好了。

3825 Your room is 3605. Here are the key cards.
您的房間為 3605 號房，這是您的房卡。

3826 You may leave your luggage here, and a **porter** will bring it to your room later.
您可以把行李放在這裡，等一下服務員會將行李送到您的房間。
porter 名 服務員

3827 I can **take care of** my baggage myself.
行李我自己拿就可以了。 take care of 片 處理

3828 Can I leave the room key at the counter when I go out?
我外出的時候，可以把房間鑰匙留在櫃台嗎？

3829 We can **keep** the key so you won't lose it.
為防遺失，我們可以替您保管鑰匙。 keep 動 保留

3830 Can we get a **wake-up call** at six tomorrow?
明天早上六點能不能叫我們起床？ wake-up call 片 電話叫醒服務

3831 Excuse me, where can I send out some faxes and go on the Internet?
請問哪裡可以傳真和上網？

3832 You can access the Internet and send faxes in our business center.
您可以在商務中心上網及發送傳真。

3833 You can use your laptop to access the Internet in your room.
你可以用筆電在房間上網。

3834 We reserved a room with a view.
我們預訂了一間看得到風景的房間。

3835 Hello? This is room 1815. The **shower** doesn't work.
喂？這裡是 1815 號房，我們房間的蓮蓬頭壞了，不能用。
shower 名 淋浴器

3836 I can't believe that there isn't any hot water!
竟然沒有熱水，令人不敢相信！

3837 The toilet is **clogged**.
馬桶堵住了。clog 動 堵塞；塞滿

3838 The **sink** isn't **draining** properly.
洗臉台的水流不下去。sink 名 水槽 drain 動 使流出

3839 The air conditioner seems broken.
空調好像壞了。

3840 The **lamp** is not working.
燈壞掉了。lamp 名 燈

3841 Could you send someone to fix it, please?
你能派人來修理一下嗎？

3842 May I have my **bed sheet** changed?
可以幫我換床單嗎？bed sheet 片 床單

3843 I need one more **towel** and some **soap**.
我還需要一條毛巾和香皂。towel 名 毛巾 soap 名 肥皂

3844 I need an **electrical adapter**.
我需要一個插座轉接器。electrical 形 電的 adapter 名 轉接器

3845 A **maid** will send them up in a minute.
服務人員稍後將幫您送去。maid 名 女僕

3846 Do you want to change to another room?
您想要換一間房嗎？

3847 I'll find you another room immediately.
我馬上幫您找另外一間房間。

3848 If you don't want to be **disturbed**, just hang the "Do not disturb" sign on your door **knob**.
如果你不想被打擾，把「請勿打擾」的牌子掛在門上就可以了。
disturb 動 打擾　knob 名 (門上的)把手

3849 What facilities are provided in the hotel?
你們飯店還有提供什麼設施？

3850 We have a gym, a sauna, and an indoor swimming pool.
我們有健身房、三溫暖，以及室內游泳池。

3851 How late is the sauna open?
三溫暖開到多晚？

3852 It's **open** twenty-four hours.
二十四小時都有開。open 形 營業的

3853 We also have **laundry** services.
我們還有提供洗衣服務。laundry 名 洗衣店

3854 Just leave your clothes in the laundry bag.
把要洗的衣服放在洗衣袋中就可以了。

3855 Could you tell me how to use the personal **safe** in the closet?
你可以教我使用衣櫃裡的保險箱嗎？safe 名 保險櫃

3856 I'm hungry. Could we order **room service**?
我好餓，我們叫客房服務，好嗎？room service 片 客房服務

3857 This is room 2160. I'd like to order some **sandwiches**.
這是 2160 號房，我們想要點三明治。sandwich 名 三明治

3858 Of course; we'll send it up to your room in fifteen minutes.
沒問題，我們十五分鐘後會送去您的房間。

3859 I'll be checking out today.
我今天要退房。

3860 What is your **checkout** time?
你們的退房時間是幾點？checkout 名 結帳離開的時間

3861 Could you please have my bill ready?
可以先把我的帳單準備好嗎？

3862 I'd like to check out, please. This is my key.
麻煩你，我要退房，這是我的鑰匙。

3863 Did you take anything from the **mini-bar** today?
您今天有沒有用過冰箱裡的東西呢？mini-bar 名 (客房的)小冰箱

3864 Yes, we had two **bottles** of apple juice.
有的，我們喝了兩瓶蘋果汁。bottle 名 瓶子

3865 There seems to be a problem with my bill.
我的帳單好像有問題。

3866 There are some **extra** charges on my bill.
我的帳單上有加收額外的費用。extra 形 額外的

3867 I didn't make any long **distance** phone calls.
我沒有用房內分機打過任何長途電話。distance 名 距離

3868 We didn't drink anything from the mini-bar except for mineral water.
除了礦泉水以外，我們沒有從房間的冰箱取用任何飲料。

3869 Aren't the **snacks** in the room free?
房間裡放的點心不是免費的嗎？snack 名 點心；小吃

3870 You also charged me for a movie, but I didn't order any movies.
你們還扣了電影的費用，但我沒有看電影。

3871 Please wait a moment. I'll check it for you.
請稍等，我幫您查一下。

3872 I am sorry. We have given you the wrong bill.
很抱歉，我們給錯帳單了。

3873 How would you like to **pay**?
請問您要怎麼付款？ pay 動 支付

3874 I'd like to pay **via** credit card, please.
我要刷卡，謝謝。 via 介 經由

3875 Please sign on the **dotted** line.
請在虛線上簽名。 dotted 形 有點的

3876 Do you want me to call a **taxi** for you?
需要幫您叫計程車嗎？ taxi 名 計程車

3877 No, thanks. I am taking the airport shuttle.
不用了，謝謝，我會搭機場接駁車。

3878 My flight is leaving late tomorrow. Can I arrange for a late checkout?
我的班機明天很晚才飛，我可以晚一點退房嗎？

3879 We can **postpone** your checkout time to 3 p.m. Will that be OK?
我們將您的退房時間延至下午三點，這樣可以嗎？
postpone 動 延遲

3880 Thank you for staying. We hope to serve you again in the near future.
感謝您選擇本飯店住宿，希望很快能有機會再為您服務。

3881 I am **starving**! Let's get something to eat.
我快要餓死了！我們去找點東西吃吧。 starving 形 挨餓的

3882 Good idea! But I don't know where to go.
好主意！但我不知道要吃什麼。

3883 What do you feel like eating?

你想吃什麼？

3884 I want to eat something really yummy.
我想吃一些真的很美味的食物。

3885 I prefer something **light**.
我想吃點清淡的東西。 light 形 清淡的

3886 Could you recommend a good **restaurant** for us?
你有什麼好餐廳可以推薦給我們嗎？ restaurant 名 餐廳

3887 Do you know any good restaurants around here?
你知道附近有什麼不錯的餐廳嗎？

3888 Maybe you can find one in the **guidebook**.
你也許能在旅遊書裡找到。 guidebook 名 旅行指南

3889 Let's ask the **concierge** in the hotel.
我們去旅館的服務台問一下。 concierge 名 旅館的服務台職員

3890 I know just the place to go.
我正好知道一間好餐廳。

3891 The restaurant is usually busy. You'd better make a reservation first.
這家餐廳總是高朋滿座，你最好先訂位。

3892 Hello, may I make a reservation for Saturday night?
你好，我想預定星期六晚上的位子。

3893 Sorry, we don't accept reservations on the phone on weekends.
抱歉，我們週末不接受電話訂位。

3894 I would like to make a reservation for four at 6 o'clock.
我想預定六點鐘的位子，共有四個人。

3895 How many people in your **party**, please?

請問你們有多少人呢？ party 名 聚會

3896 There are eight of us.
我們有八個人。

3897 Do you have a table for six?
你們有六人桌嗎？

3898 Sorry. All the tables are reserved.
抱歉，所有的位子都滿了。

3899 When will a table be available?
幾點才會有位子呢？

3900 We won't have a table **open** until 8 p.m.
八點以後才會有空位喔。 open 形 空缺的

3901 OK. Then, we want a **booth** at 8:30 p.m.
好，那就預定八點半的位子。 booth 名 餐廳的雅座

3902 Sure, please tell me your name and phone number.
好的，請給我您的大名和電話號碼。

3903 The table will be held for ten minutes after your reservation time.
位子將替您保留十分鐘。

3904 I'd like to cancel my reservation for tomorrow.
我想要取消明天的訂位。

3905 This is our **breakfast** menu.
這是我們早餐的菜單。 breakfast 名 早餐

3906 I'll **take your order** in a few minutes.
我等一下再過來幫您點餐。 take one's order 片 替某人點餐

3907 What's the difference between these two?
這兩種有什麼不同？

3908 The first one is continental breakfast.

第一種是歐式早餐。

3909 We serve **cereal** and **pastries**, with a selection of juices.
有麥片、糕點，還有幾種果汁可以選擇。
cereal 名 麥片 pastry 名 糕點

3910 Besides orange juice and apple juice, we also have **pineapple** juice.
除了柳橙汁和蘋果汁，我們還有鳳梨汁。 pineapple 名 鳳梨

3911 Of course, you may have either coffee or tea.
當然，您也可以選擇咖啡或茶。

3912 The other one is American breakfast.
另一種是美式早餐。

3913 It comes with two eggs and **ham**.
它有附兩個蛋和火腿。 ham 名 火腿

3914 You will also have toast and **hash browns**.
還有吐司和薯餅。 hash 名 剁碎的食物 brown 名 褐色

3915 We serve two kinds of **jam**.
我們提供兩種果醬。 jam 名 果醬

3916 **Blueberry** and strawberry. Which do you prefer?
藍莓醬和草莓醬，您要哪一種？ blueberry 名 藍莓

3917 Do you want some **maple** syrup to go with the **pancakes**?
您要不要楓糖搭配鬆餅？ maple 名 楓樹 pancake 名 薄煎餅

3918 Sure, maple syrup goes perfectly with pancakes.
當然要，楓糖和鬆餅真是絕配。

3919 How do you like your eggs? **Scrambled** or **boiled**?
您的蛋要怎麼煮？要炒蛋還是水煮蛋？
scramble 動 炒蛋 boil 動 煮熟

3920 Soft-boiled, please.
半熟蛋，謝謝。

3921 Don't **overdo** it.
不要煮得太熟。overdo 動 把…做得過分

3922 I'd like my eggs sunny-side-up.
我要太陽蛋。

3923 I want my eggs over hard.
蛋的兩面都要煎熟。

3924 I'd like my coffee without cream.
我的咖啡不要加奶精。

3925 Could I have some more coffee, please?
請再幫我加一些咖啡好嗎？

3926 We'd like a table for two, please.
請給我們兩人座，謝謝。

3927 Would you prefer a smoking or non-smoking area?
請問要吸煙區還是非吸煙區的位子呢？

3928 Can we push these three tables together?
我們可以把這三張桌子併在一起嗎？

3929 We'd like a table by the window, if possible.
可以的話，請給我們靠窗的位子。

3930 Yes, we do have a table available right now. Follow me, please.
目前正好有空位，請跟我來。

3931 Here is your table. And here are your menus.
這是你們的位子，菜單在這裡。

3932 Do you have a **vegetarian** menu?
有沒有素食的菜單？vegetarian 形 素菜的

3933 May I **bring** you something to drink?
你們要不要先喝點什麼飲料？ bring 動 帶來

3934 I'll just have water, thank you.
我只要水就好，謝謝。

3935 Would you like some **cocktails** before dinner?
晚餐前要不要先來點雞尾酒呢？ cocktail 名 雞尾酒

3936 We'd like some red wine before dinner.
我們想在晚餐前喝點紅酒。

3937 May I have a look at the wine list?
我可以看一下酒單嗎？

3938 The wine list is on the back of the menu.
菜單最後幾頁就是酒單。

3939 I am not good at ordering.
我不太會點菜。

3940 Could you help me with ordering?
你可以幫我點菜嗎？

3941 You guys can share Buffalo wings as an **appetizer**.
開胃菜的部分，你們可以點一份水牛城雞翅分著吃。
appetizer 名 開胃菜

3942 We also want cheese **sticks**.
我們還要點一份起司條。 stick 名 棒狀物

3943 How large are the **portions**?
這個的份量很多嗎？ portion 名 一份；一客

3944 It's for four to six people.
一份可供四到六個人食用。

3945 We'd like one Margherita **pizza** to share.
我們要一份瑪格麗特披薩，大家一起吃。 pizza 名 披薩

3946 What is the **soup** of the day?
今天的「本日推薦湯品」是什麼呢？ soup 名 湯

3947 We have onion soup and **borsch**.
我們有洋蔥湯和羅宋湯。 borsch 名 羅宋湯

3948 I'll have the clam chowder.
我要點蛤蠣海鮮濃湯。

3949 What's today's **special**?
今天的特餐是什麼？ special 名 特色菜

3950 The Alaska salmon is today's special.
今日特餐是阿拉斯加鮭魚。

3951 What's the **specialty** of your restaurant?
你們餐廳的招牌菜是什麼？ specialty 名 特產；名產

3952 Our **salami spaghetti** is very good.
我們的臘腸義大利麵很美味。
salami 名 臘腸 spaghetti 名 義大利麵

3953 This is my first time here. Could you recommend something special?
這是我第一次來，你可以推薦一些特別的菜嗎？

3954 Our **roast** beef is a bestseller.
我們的烤牛肉是最暢銷的。 roast 形 烘烤的

3955 May I suggest our specialty - **shish kebabs**?
請嚐嚐我們的招牌肉串。 shish kebab 片 烤肉串

3956 Many guests like our **smoked** salmon.
很多客人喜歡我們的煙燻鮭魚。 smoked 形 燻製的

3957 Our **cod** is very fresh.
我們的鱈魚很新鮮。 cod 名 鱈魚

3958 You can try our pigs' **knuckles** with **sauerkraut**, or sausage.
你可以試試我們的德國豬腳加酸菜，或來份香腸。

knuckle 名 (指)關節 sauerkraut 名 德國泡菜

3959 Good idea. I'd like some German beer to go with that.
好主意，我還要點德國啤酒來搭配。

3960 Is there any **particular** brand of beer you like?
對於啤酒的牌子，您有特別的喜好嗎？ particular 形 特定的

3961 Another glass of **draft beer**, please.
請再來一杯生啤酒。 draft beer 片 生啤酒

3962 For **side order**, would you like **onion rings** or **French fries**?
配菜的部分，您要點洋蔥圈還是薯條呢？
side order 片 配菜 onion ring 片 洋蔥圈
French fries 片 薯條(=French fried potatoes)

3963 Would you like to order now? / Are you ready to order?
您準備要點餐了嗎？

3964 What would you like to order? / What can I get for you?
您要點什麼呢？

3965 I'd like to start with an appetizer.
我想先點個開胃菜。

3966 I'll have a **mixed** salad with Italian dressing.
我要綜合沙拉佐義大利沙拉醬。 mixed 形 摻雜的

3967 Would you like any dressing on your salad?
您的沙拉要不要加沙拉醬？

3968 I'd like Thousand Island dressing, please.
請幫我加千島醬，謝謝。

3969 I'd like a Caesar salad.
請給我一份凱薩沙拉。

3970 Have you decided on your **entrée**?
您的主菜決定要點什麼了嗎？ entrée 名 主菜

3971 It's really hard to **make up my mind**.
很難決定要點什麼耶。 make up one's mind 片 決定

3972 What's **in season** right now?
現在當季的食材有什麼呢？ in season 片 當令的

3973 Does the **rib** eye come with mashed potatoes?
肋眼牛排有附馬鈴薯泥嗎？ rib 名 肋；肋骨

3974 The **filet mignon** is **charcoal**-broiled and very tasty.
這菲力牛排是用碳烤的，非常好吃。
filet mignon 片 菲力牛排 charcoal 名 木炭

3975 How would you like your **steak** done?
您的牛排要幾分熟呢？ steak 名 牛排

3976 I want it **medium-well**, please.
七分熟，謝謝。 medium-well 形 七分熟的

3977 Steak tastes the best when it is cooked **medium**.
五分熟的牛排是最美味的。 medium 形 中等熟度的

3978 I'd like the New York steak, medium, please.
我要紐約牛排，五分熟，謝謝。

3979 I'll try the **lobster**.
我想點龍蝦來試試看。 lobster 名 龍蝦

3980 Good **choice**! It's our most popular dish!
您真會選！這可是我們最有人氣的招牌菜呢！ choice 名 選擇

3981 What kind of **sauce** do you like?
您喜歡什麼樣的醬汁呢？ sauce 名 醬汁

3982 I don't want any sauce on it, please.
我不要淋醬汁，謝謝。

3983 I don't want it too **spicy**.
不要太辣。spicy 形 辛辣的

3984 I'll have the same dish as that gentleman.
我要點和那位男士一樣的菜。

3985 Would you like your coffee with your dinner or later?
請問您的咖啡是跟晚餐一起上，還是稍後再上呢？

3986 With my dinner, please. And can you take my order for **dessert later**?
跟晚餐一起上好了。另外，甜點我可以等一下再點嗎？
dessert 名 甜點 later 副 較晚地；更晚地

3987 Would you like to order anything else, sir?
先生，還需要什麼其他的嗎？

3988 No, that will be all, thanks.
不用，這些就可以了。

3989 Let me **repeat** your order.
我重複一下您剛剛點的菜。repeat 動 重複

3990 Your order will be ready soon.
餐點等一下就會為您送上來。

3991 Your **lasagna**, sir.
先生，您點的千層麵來了。lasagna 名 千層麵

3992 Thanks. It looks great.
謝謝，看起來很好吃。

3993 How are your pork **chops**?
你的豬排好吃嗎？chop 名 排骨

3994 They are very fresh and **flavorful**.
很新鮮，也很美味。flavorful 形 有風味的

3995 The steak is very **tender** and **juicy**. I love it.
牛排很嫩、又多汁，我很喜歡。tender 形 嫩的 juicy 形 多汁的

3996 I've been waiting for twenty minutes for my order.
我已經等了二十分鐘，但餐點都還沒上來。

3997 I'm sorry, but Saturday night is our busiest night of the week.
很抱歉，星期六晚上是我們一週最忙的時候。

3998 I'm sorry, but I didn't order this.
抱歉，我沒有點這個。

3999 These noodles are cold. Can you bring me another dish?
這麵都已經冷掉了，可以幫我換一盤嗎？

4000 The **chicken** is **tasteless**.
雞肉沒有味道。 chicken 名 雞肉 tasteless 形 沒味道的

4001 The fried rice is too **salty** and too **greasy**.
炒飯太鹹也太油了。 salty 形 鹹的 greasy 形 油膩的

4002 But this steak is **undercooked**! It's almost **raw**!
但這塊牛排根本沒熟！我還看得到血呢！
undercooked 形 未熟的 raw 形 生的

4003 May I ask what you ordered again?
可以再向您確認一次您點了什麼嗎？

4004 Didn't you order your steak **rare**?
您不是點三分熟的牛排嗎？ rare 形 半熟的

4005 No, I ordered it **well-done**.
不是，我點的是全熟。 well-done 形 全熟的

4006 I'm sorry about the mistake.
很抱歉，我們弄錯了。

4007 I'll take it back to the kitchen and bring you another one.
我拿回廚房，再換一份給您。

4008 My steak is too **tough**.

我的牛排太老了。tough 形 老的；咬不動的

4009 I think it was **overcooked**.
我覺得煮得太熟了。overcook 動 煮過頭

4010 I want to speak with your **manager**.
我要和你們的經理談談。manager 名 經理

4011 I'm sorry that my son **spilled** the juice all over the table.
不好意思，我兒子打翻果汁，弄得整張桌子都是。spill 動 使溢出

4012 I'll clean up your table **right away**.
我馬上幫您清理桌子。right away 片 立刻

4013 What a delicious meal! I'm so **full**.
真是美味的一餐！我吃得好飽。full 形 吃飽的

4014 You can take the rest of your chicken home in a **doggie bag**.
你可以把剩下的雞肉打包回家。doggie bag 片 (打包用的)食物袋

4015 Please **wrap** this **up** for me.
這個請幫我打包。wrap up 片 包裹

4016 May I order take-out here?
這裡可以點外帶的食物嗎？

4017 We only have **spring rolls** today for take-out.
今天的外帶食物只有春捲。spring roll 片 春捲

4018 Could I have the bill, please? / Check, please.
請幫我們結帳，好嗎？/ 我要結帳，謝謝。

4019 Does the price include the service charge?
服務費有包含在這個價格裡嗎？

4020 How much tip should we leave?
我們該給多少小費呢？

4021 It's on me. / I'll pay the bill. / It's my **treat**.

這餐算我的。treat 名 請客

4022 Let's **go Dutch**. / Let's **split** it.
我們各付各的吧。go Dutch 片 各自付帳 split 動 分擔

4023 There's a fast-food restaurant over there. We could get a **burger**!
那裡有一家速食店，我們可以去吃漢堡！burger 名 漢堡

4024 I'd like a large seafood pizza with extra cheese.
我要一份大的海鮮披薩，起司要加多一點。

4025 Is that for here or for take-out?
內用還是外帶？

4026 I'd like to order a chicken sandwich and a large order of French fries.
我要點一份雞肉三明治和大薯。

4027 One cheeseburger and an orange juice, please.
我要點起司漢堡和柳橙汁，謝謝。

4028 What do you want on your cheeseburger?
您的起司漢堡想加什麼佐料呢？

4029 I'll have **ketchup** and onion.
我要加番茄醬和洋蔥。ketchup 名 番茄醬

4030 Is the Coke large or small?
可樂要大杯還是小杯的呢？

4031 Where can I get a **straw** and **napkins**?
請問哪裡有吸管和餐巾紙呢？
straw 名 吸管 napkin 名 餐巾紙

4032 Two hamburgers and two coffees to go, please.
我要外帶兩份漢堡和兩杯咖啡。

迷路 & 乘車二三事
Finding My Way

4033 I believe we are **lost**.
我覺得我們迷路了。lost 形 迷路的

4034 I need to ask for **directions**.
我得去問個路。direction 名 方向

4035 I have no idea where I am on this map.
我完全搞不清楚現在我是在地圖上的哪裡。

4036 Where are you trying to go?
你想要去哪裡？

4037 I want to go back to my hotel.
我想要回我住的飯店。

4038 Which hotel are you staying in?
你住在哪個飯店呢？

4039 The Hyatt Hotel. I **marked** it on the map, but I lost the directions.
我住在君悅酒店，我有在地圖上做記號，但現在完全搞不清楚方向了。mark 動 做記號於

4040 You are on First **Avenue**.
你現在位於第一大道。avenue 名 大街；大道

4041 The Hyatt Hotel is just three blocks from here.
君悅酒店離這裡只有三條街的距離。

4042 I'm trying to go to **Union Station**.
我想去聯合車站。union 名 結合 station 名 車站

4043 Oh, you are **headed** in the wrong direction.
喔，你走錯方向了。head 動 朝向某處出發

4044 Excuse me. Where is the train station?
不好意思，請問要怎麼去火車站？

4045 Walk along Riverside Rd. to **Oak** St. and turn right.
沿著河濱路走，到橡樹街再右轉。oak 名 橡樹

4046 Go down Oak St. for two blocks.
沿著橡樹街走兩個街區。

4047 You will see the train station on your left.
火車站會在你的左手邊。

4048 It's pretty far from here.
那裡離這裡很遠。

4049 You'd better take a bus. Going **on foot** will take you over an hour.
你最好搭公車去，步行要一個小時以上才會到。on foot 片 步行

4050 Do you know where the nearest **bus stop** is?
請問最近的公車站牌在哪裡？bus stop 片 公車站

4051 It's pretty near. Just go straight, and it's down the street.
很近，這條街直走到底就是了。

4052 You'll see a **post office** first.
你會先看到一家郵局。post office 片 郵局

4053 The bus stop is around the **corner** from the post office.
公車站在郵局的轉角處。corner 名 街角

4054 It's **in front of** a beauty salon.
是在一家美容院的前面。in front of 片 在…的前面

4055 Is it **next to** the pharmacy?
是不是在藥局隔壁？next to 片 在…旁邊

4056 No, it's across from the pharmacy.

不是，是在藥局對面。

4057 The **barbershop** is between a **bakery** and a bookstore.
理髮廳位於麵包店和書局之間。
barbershop 名 理髮廳 bakery 名 麵包店

4058 I am looking for a **gas station**.
我正在找加油站。gas station 片 加油站

4059 Just drive east on 123 Road to Sunset **Boulevard** and turn right.
沿著 123 路往東開，到日落大道再右轉。boulevard 名 林蔭大道

4060 Then drive along Sunset Boulevard until you see the second **traffic light**.
沿著日落大道開，直到你看見第二個紅綠燈。traffic light 片 紅綠燈

4061 You'll find a gas station on your right.
你的右手邊會有一家加油站。

4062 Excuse me. Can you tell me how to get to Taiwan Bank?
請問一下，台灣銀行怎麼走？

4063 Walk along Kwang-ming 6th Road and cross Sheng-cheng 9th Road and you'll see it on your left.
走光明六路，穿過縣政九路，銀行會在你的左手邊。

4064 The Taiwan bank is across from a big **parking lot**.
台灣銀行的對面是一個很大的停車場。parking lot 片 停車場

4065 Is it located **kitty-corner** from the McDonald's?
是在麥當勞的斜對角嗎？kitty-corner 副 成對角線地

4066 Excuse me. I am looking for Red Apple Chinese Restaurant.
不好意思，我在找紅蘋果中國餐廳。

4067 Could you give me directions?

你可以告訴我怎麼走嗎？

4068 Do you have the address? It would make it clearer for me.
你有地址嗎？有的話會比較清楚。

4069 Yes, I have their **business card** with me.
有，我有名片。 business card 片 名片

4070 The restaurant is at No.10, Gold Coast Street.
餐廳在黃金海岸街十號。

4071 Is it far from here? Do I need to take the MRT or a taxi?
離這裡會很遠嗎？我需不需要搭地鐵或計程車呢？

4072 No, it's just a few blocks away.
不會，離這裡只有幾個街區而已。

4073 It's only a three-minute drive.
開車只要三分鐘就到了。

4074 Go west for three blocks and turn right on Gold Coast Street.
往西走三個街區，然後右轉黃金海岸街。

4075 You will see the sign of a big apple and that's it.
你會看到一個大大的蘋果招牌，就是那裡了。

4076 Could you tell me where Macy's is?
你可以告訴我梅西百貨在哪裡嗎？

4077 If I remember it correctly, it is right next to the **Sunlight Fitness** Center.
如果我沒記錯，應該是在陽光健身中心的隔壁。
sunlight 名 日光 fitness 名 健康

4078 I am sorry. I am a tourist here.
不好意思，我只是個遊客。

4079 Sorry, I am new here, too.

抱歉，我對這裡也不熟。

4080 You'd better ask one of the **locals**.
你最好問問當地人。 local 名 本地人

4081 Excuse me, could you show me the way to the nearest **supermarket**?
不好意思，你可以告訴我最近的超市要怎麼去嗎？
supermarket 名 超市

4082 There are two supermarkets **nearby**.
這附近有兩家超市。 nearby 副 在附近

4083 The nearest one is smaller.
距離最近的一家比較小。

4084 Go down Al Street for three blocks.
順著艾爾街走三個街區。

4085 You'll see a hospital on your right.
你會看到右手邊有一家醫院。

4086 There is a supermarket to the right of the hospital.
在醫院的右邊就有一家超市。

4087 There is another supermarket right in the **basement** of the **mall**.
另一家超市位於購物中心的地下室。
basement 名 地下室 mall 名 購物中心

4088 If you don't mind driving for ten minutes, you will find a bigger one.
如果你不介意開車開十分鐘的話，還可以找到一家更大的。

4089 If you drive along this road and go over a **bridge**, you will find it.
沿著這條路開，過了一座橋之後，就會看到了。 bridge 名 橋梁

4090 Excuse me, is this the way to Hsinchu Girls' Senior High School?

不好意思，請問這條路是往新竹女中的嗎？

4091 Yes, it is. Just go down Chung Hwa Road.
沒錯，只要沿著中華路走就可以了。

4092 It's near an **overpass**.
它就在天橋附近。 overpass 名 天橋

4093 Should I **go over** the **underpass**?
要過地下道嗎？ go over 片 穿過去 underpass 名 地下道

4094 I'm not sure. You can ask someone else when you get there.
我也不確定，你到那邊再問人吧。

4095 How long does it take to walk to the church from here?
從這裡走到教堂要多久？

4096 It's not far, only about a five-minute **walk**.
不會很遠，只要走五分鐘左右就到了。 walk 名 步行距離

4097 Should I **cut across** the tennis court?
需要穿越網球場嗎？ cut across 片 徑直穿過

4098 You can do that. That's a **shortcut**.
可以啊，那是條捷徑。 shortcut 名 捷徑

4099 Is there any place I can get a cup of coffee?
附近有沒有賣咖啡的店家？

4100 Of course. You can find one just around the corner.
當然有，轉角就有一家。

4101 My cell phone **battery** is dead. I need to find a **public** phone.
我的手機沒電了，我要找公共電話。
battery 名 電池 public 形 公共的

4102 Are there any public phones nearby?

這附近有公共電話嗎？

4103 There are several **pay phones** in front of the office building.
辦公大樓前面有好幾座公共電話。 pay phone 片 收費公共電話

4104 Don't worry. You can't miss it.
別擔心，你不可能看漏的。

4105 How can I get to city **hall**?
要怎麼去市政廳呢？ hall 名 會堂；大廳

4106 I am heading for city hall, too.
我正好也要去市政廳。

4107 I'll give you a **ride** if you'd like.
乾脆我載你去好了。 ride 名 兜風

4108 Excuse me, how can I get to the National **Museum**?
請問一下，要怎麼去國家博物館呢？ museum 名 博物館

4109 You can take a bus. It's more convenient.
你可以搭公車去，那樣更方便。

4110 Which bus should I take to get there?
請問要搭哪一線的公車呢？

4111 You can take bus No.18.
可以搭十八路公車去。.

4112 Is this bus bound for the **zoo**?
這輛公車是往動物園的嗎？ zoo 名 動物園

4113 No, this goes only **as far as** Children's Hospital.
沒有，這輛公車只到兒童醫院。 as far as 片 遠到…

4114 Do I need to **transfer**?
需要轉車嗎？ transfer 動 使換車

4115 Where should I change buses?

我要到哪一站轉車呢？

4116 You can change buses for the zoo at Park Station.
你可以到公園站換車到動物園。

4117 Then take bus No.5.
然後轉乘五號公車。

4118 **Get off** at the final stop.
搭到最後一站下車。 get off 片 下車

4119 How much is the bus **fare** to the zoo?
搭公車到動物園要多少錢？ fare 名 票價

4120 It costs NT$40 for one way and NT$35 for a return ticket.
單程票是四十元台幣，來回票是三十五元台幣。

4121 Should I buy a **ticket**?
我需要買車票嗎？ ticket 名 車票

4122 There's no need to buy a ticket. Just put the bus fare in the **box** on the bus.
不用買票，投錢到公車上的收費箱內就可以了。 box 名 箱子

4123 I only have **banknotes**. Can I get **change** back?
我只有鈔票，會找零嗎？ banknote 名 鈔票 change 名 零錢

4124 I'm afraid we don't give change on buses.
很抱歉，公車上不找零。

4125 May I use a **monthly pass**?
我可以使用月票嗎？ monthly 形 每月的 pass 名 通行證

4126 Could you tell me the bus number to downtown?
請問到市區的巴士是幾號車呢？

4127 You should take bus No.36.
你應該搭三十六路公車。

4128 I don't know where to get off the bus.
我不知道要在一站下車。

4129 Please let me know when we get to National **United** University, OK?
到國立聯合大學的時候，可以叫我一下嗎？ united 形 聯合的

4130 No worries. I'll tell you when.
別擔心，到的時候我會叫你。

4131 Excuse me, is next stop Freedom **Square**?
請問下一站是自由廣場嗎？ square 名 廣場

4132 How often does the bus run?
這路公車多久會來一班？

4133 Every ten minutes on weekdays and every twenty minutes on weekends.
平日是每十分鐘一班車，週末每二十分鐘一班。

4134 Buses are always crowded during peak hours.
公車在尖峰時間都很擁擠。

4135 The **train** leaves every thirty minutes.
每隔三十分鐘會有一班火車。 train 名 火車

4136 Where is the **ticket office**?
售票處在哪裡呢？ ticket office 片 售票處

4137 Are there any seats available for Manchester?
到曼徹斯特的車還有座位嗎？

4138 Do you want to catch an **express** or a local train?
您要搭特快車還是普通車呢？ express 名 特快車

4139 All tickets for local trains have been sold out.
普通車的位子都賣完了。

4140 Tickets for express trains are available.
特快車還有位子。

4141 Is there a **nonstop** train to Concord?
有沒有往康科特的直達車？ nonstop 形 直達的

4142 How much is the ticket for Concord?
到康科特的車票要多少錢？

4143 I'd like two tickets to Boston, please.
我要買兩張往波士頓的車票。

4144 I've booked a ticket for Boston online. Where can I get it?
我有在網路上預訂一張到波士頓的車票，請問要到哪裡領取？

4145 Please go to the ticket counter.
請至售票處。

4146 Could we get a group rate?
我們可以買團體票嗎？

4147 You won't get a group rate unless you have ten in your party.
要滿十個人，才能以團體票的價格購票喔。

4148 You can have a discount if you have a **student ID**.
如果你有學生證的話，可以打折。 student ID 片 學生證

4149 The children's fare is cheaper.
兒童票比較便宜。

4150 When is the next train to New York?
下一班往紐約的火車幾點開呢？

4151 When does the last train to New York depart?
前往紐約的末班火車幾點開呢？

4152 It departs at 8 p.m., so you've got to **hurry**.
晚上八點發車，所以你得快一點。 hurry 動 使趕快

4153 May I have a timetable?
可以給我一張時刻表嗎？

4154 Which **platform** does the train to San Diego leave from?
去聖地牙哥的火車要在哪個月台等？ platform 名 月台

4155 Let me check it first. Well, we need to wait on Platform 3A.
我看一下，嗯…我們要在 3A 月台候車。

4156 Will the train arrive on time?
這班火車會準時嗎？

4157 The train for Seattle is delayed.
往西雅圖的列車會誤點。

4158 The train will be arriving in ten minutes.
火車再過十分鐘就會到了。

4159 Hurry up! The train is leaving soon!
快點！火車要開了！

4160 What time are we **expecting** to arrive at San Francisco?
我們預計幾點會抵達舊金山呢？ expect 動 預計

4161 Why don't you ask the **conductor** when he comes by?
待會兒列車長過來的時候，你可以問他。 conductor 名 車掌

4162 Excuse me. Is this seat taken?
這個座位有人了嗎？

4163 May I **sit** here?
我可以坐這裡嗎？ sit 動 坐；就座

4164 I'm afraid this seat is taken.
抱歉，這個位子有人坐了。

4165 Is this the train to Seattle?
這是前往西雅圖的火車嗎？

4166 Please tell me when we get to Seattle.

到西雅圖的時候，請告訴我。

4167 It seems that you have taken the wrong train.
你好像搭錯火車了。

4168 Oh, you're on the wrong train.
喔！你搭錯車了。

4169 Where do I pay the fare?
我要去哪裡付費呢？

4170 On the train. The conductor will **collect** the fare.
在火車上繳費即可，車掌會和你們收費。collect 動 收帳

4171 May I see your ticket, please?
我可以看一下您的車票嗎？

4172 You can transfer with this ticket.
您可以憑這張車票轉車。

4173 It will arrive in a few minutes. Let's get our bags from the **rack**.
再過一下就會到了，我們把行李從行李架上拿下來吧。
rack 名 行李網架

4174 Gosh! I **fell asleep** and missed my station.
天啊！因為我睡著，所以坐過站了啦。fall asleep 片 睡著

4175 What should I do? I lost the ticket.
我的車票不見了，怎麼辦？

4176 Is this the shuttle into **town**?
這是進城的接駁公車嗎？town 名 市區

4177 Yes. But this one is full. You need to wait for the next one.
是的，但這台車已經客滿了，請等下一班車。

4178 What time does the next shuttle leave?
下一班接駁車幾點開？

4179 **According to** the timetable, it leaves every twenty minutes.
時刻表上說每二十分鐘就有一班車。 according to 片 根據

4180 Where is the nearest **subway** station?
最近的地鐵站在哪裡呢？ subway 名 地下鐵

4181 Where can I get a subway map?
哪裡可以拿到地鐵圖呢？

4182 You can get a free map at the **information** center.
服務中心有免費的地圖。 information 名 資訊

4183 How do I get to Times Square?
時代廣場要怎麼去呢？

4184 Where can I get a ticket for the subway?
要到哪裡買地鐵票呢？

4185 Go to the ticket **machine**. It's next to the counter.
售票機有賣，櫃台旁邊就找得到。 machine 名 機器

4186 I don't have any change. Where can I get some change?
我身上沒有零錢，哪裡可以換零錢呢？

4187 There's a change machine next to the ticket machine.
售票機旁邊有一台兌幣機。

4188 You can also get a store-valued ticket there.
你也可以在那裡購買儲值票。

4189 You can buy a one-day or three-day pass. It will be cheaper.
你可以買一日券或三日券，會比較便宜。

4190 How much is it for a three-day pass?
三日券要多少錢呢？

4191 Can I get an all-day pass from the machine, too?
售票機有賣一日遊的票嗎？

4192 No. You need to go to the **ticket window** for that.
不行，一日遊的票要到售票窗口買。ticket window 片 售票窗口

4193 Does this subway stop at the **Metropolitan** Museum?
地鐵在大都會博物館有站嗎？metropolitan 形 大都市的

4194 Take the Green Line to Central Park and get off there.
搭綠線到「中央公園」下車。

4195 How many stops before Central Park?
到中央公園前有幾站？

4196 Take the Red Line to First Street and then **switch** to the Blue Line going toward Times Square.
搭紅線到「第一街」，然後再轉乘往「時代廣場」的藍線。
switch 動 使轉換

4197 It is the next stop after Chinatown.
它就在「中國城」的下一站。

4198 The next train will arrive in three minutes.
下一班車會在三分鐘後到站。

4199 Is this bound for **Civil** Center?
這是前往「公民中心」的車嗎？civil 形 市民的

4200 I am afraid that you've **got on** the wrong line.
你搭錯線了喔。get on 片 上車

4201 Get off at the next stop and switch to the Red Line to get to Union Station.
下一站下車，再換紅線到「聯合廣場站」。

4202 Then you can take either the Yellow Line or Blue Line to Civil Center.
接著搭黃線或藍線，這兩線都會到「公民中心」。

4203 You're going the wrong way.
你走錯方向了。

4204 You need to catch a train going in the **opposite** direction.
你要搭的是反方向的車。 opposite 形 相反的

4205 I can't wait for the next train. I'm **in a hurry**.
我不能等下一班，我在趕時間。 in a hurry 片 急切；趕時間

4206 If you are in a hurry, take a taxi to the hotel.
若你趕時間的話，就搭計程車到旅館吧。

4207 Will you call a taxi for me?
你能替我叫輛計程車嗎？

4208 The taxi will arrive in five minutes. The number is 2780.
計程車五分鐘後會到，車號為 2780。

4209 Where can I catch a taxi?
我可以去哪裡搭計程車？

4210 You are not allowed to **hail** a taxi on the street.
你不能在路邊攔計程車。 hail 動 招呼

4211 The taxi **stand** is over there.
那裡有計程車招呼站。 stand 名 停車處；候車站

4212 Where are you going to, sir?
先生，請問您要到哪裡？

4213 The **intersection** of Loudon Rd. and Fifth Street.
我要到勞登路和第五街的路口。 intersection 名 十字路口

4214 Please take me to the nearest train station.
請載我到最近的火車站。

4215 Can you open the trunk for me, please?
可以幫我開後車廂嗎？

4216 How much do you charge for putting luggage in the trunk?
如果我放行李在後車廂，要收多少錢呢？

4217 How much does it cost to go to the airport?
到機場要多少錢？

4218 How much is the taxi fare?
計程車費用怎麼算？

4219 All taxis here charge according to the taxi **meter**, so please don't worry.
這裡所有的計程車都是按錶收費，請不用擔心。 meter 名 計量器

4220 The **initial** charge is NT$80.
從八十元開始起跳。 initial 形 開始的

4221 Then, it's NT$5 for every **additional** 300 **meters**.
之後，每三百公尺加收五元。 additional 形 額外的 meter 名 公尺

4222 How long will it take to get to the airport?
到機場要多久時間呢？

4223 How long will it take? I'm in a hurry.
多久能抵達呢？我趕時間。

4224 I can't drive too fast, or the police will give me a **ticket**.
我不能開得太快，否則會被警察開單。 ticket 名 罰單

4225 Take it easy. You'll be there **in time** for your flight.
放心吧，會趕上你的班機的。 in time 片 及時

4226 We can make it if there's no **traffic jam**.
只要沒有塞車，我們就能趕上。 traffic jam 片 塞車

4227 Could you please **slow down** a bit?
請開慢一點好嗎？ slow down 片 減低速度

4228 We'll have to make a **U-turn** here.
我們只得在這裡迴轉了。 U-turn 名 (車輛等的)迴轉

4229 Let me see if we can **back** out of here.
讓我看看能不能從這裡倒車出去。back 動 倒退

4230 The driver in the car **ahead** is too slow. Let's **overtake** him.
前面那輛車的司機開得太慢了，我們來超他車。
ahead 副 在前 overtake 動 超過

4231 Just stop here. I'll walk there myself.
請在這裡停車，我自己走過去就可以了。

4232 Just stop in front of the **flower** shop.
請在花店門口停車。flower 名 花卉

4233 Could you stop **somewhere** here for a minute?
你能就近停一下嗎？somewhere 副 在某處

4234 Stop on the corner after you go through the traffic light.
過了紅綠燈，在路口停就可以了。

4235 How much is the **total**?
總共多少錢？total 名 總數

4236 Thank you. Keep the change.
謝謝，零錢你留著就好，不用找了。

租一輛車趴趴走
Renting A Car

4237 Hertz Car Rental. May I help you?
赫茲租車中心，我能為您服務嗎？

4238 I would like to rent a car for five days.

我要租五天的車。

4239 What kind of car would you like?
您想要租什麼樣的車呢？

4240 What kind of cars do you have?
你們有哪些車款呢？

4241 Here is a list of our cars and prices.
這是我們有的車款和價格清單。

4242 We have **compacts**, plus mid-size and full-size cars.
我們有小型車、中型車和大型車。 compact 名 小型轎車

4243 How much is it if I **rent** a mid-size car for a week?
中型車租一個星期要多少錢呢？ rent 動 租用

4244 The **rental** is $55 per day.
租金是一天五十五美元。 rental 名 租金

4245 Do I have to pay a deposit?
我需要付押金嗎？

4246 You have to pay a deposit, but it is refundable if the car is not damaged.
您必須先付押金，只要歸還車子時沒有損壞，就能取回。

4247 Do you have any special **deals** this week?
這個禮拜有什麼特別的優惠方案嗎？ deal 名 交易

4248 Yes, we are now offering a weekly rate of $300 with **unlimited miles**.
有的，我們現在提供一星期三百元的價格，不限里程數。
unlimited 形 無限制的 mile 名 哩

4249 That sounds good. I'll take that one. What kind of car is it?
聽起來很棒，我就選那個方案吧。提供的車款是哪一型呢？

4250 Our mid-size car is a Toyota Rav4.
我們的中型車是豐田的 Rav4。

4251 Fine. I'd like to take it. Where can I pick up my car?
好，我就租這部車，那我可以在哪裡取車呢？

4252 May I have your international **driver's license** number?
可以給我您的國際駕照號碼嗎？ driver's license 片 駕照

4253 I need to take a **copy** of your driver's license.
我需要影印一下您的駕照。 copy 名 複製品

4254 Where are you picking up and returning the car?
請問您要在哪裡取車及還車呢？

4255 I'll pick it up at the airport and return it at your downtown **branch**.
我要在機場取車，之後在你們市區的分店還車。 branch 名 分公司

4256 What kind of insurance coverage would you like?
您要保哪些保險項目呢？

4257 Full coverage, please.
我要保全險。

4258 That's an extra thirty dollars per day.
那一天要額外加收三十元。

4259 The car will be ready for you to pick up then. Your confirmation number is Y2132.
我們會替您準備好車子，您的確認碼為 Y2132。

4260 Just go to our counter at the airport and they'll set you up.
只要去我們在機場的櫃台即可，他們會為您準備好的。

4261 Here's the **rental agreement**.
這是租車合約。 rental 形 供出租的 agreement 名 協議

4262 If you don't find any problem, please **sign** here.
如果沒有問題的話，請在這裡簽名。sign 動 簽名

4263 I'm here to pick up my car.
我是來取車的。

4264 Do you have a confirmation number?
您有確認碼嗎？

4265 You can check the instrument **panel** here. The **tank** is full now.
請確認一下儀表盤，油箱現在是滿的。
panel 名 儀表盤 tank 名 油箱

4266 You need to **refill** it before returning the car.
還車時，油箱必須加滿。refill 動 再裝滿

4267 What's the charge if I don't return it with a full tank?
如果我還車時沒加滿油箱，要收多少錢？

4268 There is a two-dollar-per-**gallon** charge.
一加侖二元。gallon 名 加侖

4269 Can I return the car in San Diego?
我可以在聖地牙哥還車嗎？

4270 Sure, you can return it at any of our branches in California.
沒有問題，在我們加州的任何一間分店都能還車。

4271 But you have to pay **extra** if you want to return it in another **state**.
不過，如果您要在別州還車的話，就要支付額外的費用。
extra 副 額外地；另外 state 名 州

4272 You'd better check the water and gas.
你最好先檢查一下水和油。

4273 Here is our **toll-free** number. Call us **whenever** you have questions.

這是我們的免付費電話，有任何問題都可以打來。
toll-free 形 免電話費的　whenever 連 無論什麼時候

4274 You can get maps and a free guidebook at the information desk.
到詢問台可以拿到免費的地圖和旅遊指南。

4275 Thank you for renting our car. Enjoy your trip!
謝謝您租用我們的車，好好享受旅程吧！

交通規則 & 意外
Driving Safely

4276 Pease **abide by** the traffic **signals**.
請遵守交通號誌。abide by 片 遵守　signal 名 信號

4277 Never **shift lanes** without putting on your turning signal.
變換車道時一定要打方向燈。shift 動 改變　lane 名 車道

4278 Don't **race** through yellow lights.
不要搶越黃燈。race 動 使全速前進

4279 **Running red lights** is very dangerous.
闖紅燈是很危險的。run a red light 片 闖紅燈

4280 People are not allowed to drive in a **zigzag**.
開車時禁止蛇行。zigzag 名 Z 字形

4281 It's **illegal** to pass on the **shoulder**.
利用路肩超車是違法的。illegal 形 不合法的　shoulder 名 路肩

4282 His license was **revoked** because of driving under the influence of alcohol or **drugs** (DUI).

他因酒後及吸毒後駕駛而被吊銷駕照。

revoke 動 撤銷　drug 名 毒品

4283 **Obey** the speed limit posted on signs along the roads.

請遵守路旁標示的最高速限行駛。obey 動 遵守

4284 Don't drive too fast, or you will get a **speeding** ticket.

不要開太快，否則你會收到超速的罰單。speeding 名 超速駕駛

4285 It's dangerous to follow too **closely**.

跟車跟得太近是很危險的。closely 副 接近地

4286 No **tailgating**! Always maintain a safe distance.

不要緊跟著前車！要保持安全距離。tailgate 動 緊跟著前車行駛

4287 People who race their cars cause a public **disturbance**, **risking** their own and others' lives.

飆車族會造成社會動亂，不僅是拿自己的命在開玩笑，還危及他人。disturbance 名 混亂　risk 動 以…作為賭注

4288 Never **back up** your car too fast.

倒車時的速度不要太快。back up 片 倒車

4289 Shift into the **reverse gear** and use the rearview mirror.

換打倒車檔，並用後視鏡確認。

reverse 形 顛倒的　gear 名 汽車排檔

4290 You are not supposed to park here. It's dangerous.

你的車不能停在這裡，很危險。

4291 You'll be fined for double-parking.

並排停車會被罰錢。

4292 Cars that are illegally parked on the red line will be **towed** away.

停在紅線的違規車輛會被拖吊。tow 動 拖；拉

4293 It's getting dark. Turn on the **headlights**.
天色變暗了，開頭燈吧。 headlight 名 車前大燈

4294 Don't turn on the **high-beam** headlights in heavy fog.
起濃霧時，不要開遠光燈。 high-beam 形 遠光的

4295 You can turn on your fog lights.
你可以開霧燈。

4296 A traffic jam, again. I guess we should call Jack to tell him we'll be late.
又塞車了，我們應該先打電話給傑克，和他說我們會遲到。

4297 Be patient when you are in **stop-and-go** traffic.
在車陣中走走停停時，要保持耐心。 stop-and-go 形 走走停停的

4298 Some road **construction** is **tying up** the traffic.
道路施工造成交通阻塞。 construction 名 建設 tie up 片 使受阻

4299 Let's drive around to **escape** the traffic jam.
我們繞個路，避開塞車路段吧。 escape 動 逃脫

4300 I know a shortcut. Please take a right turn at the next intersection.
我知道一條捷徑，請在下一個十字路口右轉。

4301 I can't get my car started.
我的車子無法發動。

4302 My car's engine won't start.
我的車子引擎無法發動。

4303 My car **broke down** on the freeway.
我的車在高速公路上拋錨了。 break down 片 停止運轉

4304 There seems to be something wrong with my car.
我的車好像出了一點問題。

4305 Can you hear a cracking noise under my engine?
你有聽到引擎發出的怪聲嗎？

4306 You should **pull over** as soon as you can.
你應該盡快靠邊停車。pull over 片 把車開到路邊

4307 I was pulled over to the **roadside** by a policeman.
我的車被警察攔下來停在路邊。roadside 名 路邊

4308 You have an emergency road **triangle** in your trunk, don't you?
你的後車箱裡有三角警告標誌吧？triangle 名 三角形之物

4309 Put the brakes on! There's a dog ahead.
快煞車！前面有一隻狗。

4310 My goodness! The brakes don't work.
天啊！煞車失靈了。

4311 Shift to a lower gear and try to slow down your car.
轉到低速檔，試著降低車速。

4312 My car got stuck in the **flood**.
我的車被困在洪水當中。flood 名 洪水

4313 I have a **flat tire**.
我的車子爆胎了。flat tire 片 爆胎

4314 Do you check the air pressure with a **tire gauge**?
你有用胎壓計量胎壓嗎？tire 名 輪胎 gauge 名 測量儀器

4315 Do you have a **spare tire** in your trunk?
你的後車箱裡有備胎嗎？spare tire 片 備胎

4316 I think we need a **jack** to **lift** the car.
我想我們需要千斤頂把車子抬起來。jack 名 千斤頂 lift 動 抬起

4317 Your battery is dead.
你的電池沒電了。

4318 I need to replace the **windshield wipers**. They have been used for more than two years.

我需要換雨刷，這雨刷已經超過兩年沒換了。
windshield 名 擋風玻璃 wiper 名 雨刷

4319 If you **file** a **claim** for a broken windshield, your insurance rates will go up.
如果你破掉的擋風玻璃有申請理賠，保險費率就會提高。
file 動 提出申請 claim 名 (根據權利而提出的)要求

4320 After a **vehicle** has been used for a while, some parts become loose or damaged, so it needs regular **tune-ups**.
車子使用一段時間後，有些零件會鬆掉或壞掉，所以必須定期做保養。vehicle 名 車輛 tune-up 名 調整

4321 Most cars require a tune-up about every 5,000 kilometers.
大部分的車子每五千公里就要保養一次。

4322 A regular tune-up usually includes oil and oil **filter** changes.
定期保養通常包括更換機油和燃油過濾器。filter 名 濾器

4323 A **mechanic** also checks the brakes and shock **absorbers**.
維修技師也會檢查煞車和避震器。
mechanic 名 技工 absorber 名 吸收器

4324 There's a **car accident** ahead.
前方有一起車禍。car accident 片 車禍

4325 Two cars **collided head-on** here.
兩部車正面對撞。collide 動 碰撞 head-on 副 迎頭

4326 The traffic has come to a dead stop.
交通完全癱瘓了。

4327 We have no idea how the accident **happened**.
我們不清楚這個事故是怎麼發生的。happen 動 發生

4328 My car was rear-ended by a **truck**.
我的車被一輛卡車追撞。truck 名 卡車

4329 A taxi broadsided my car.
我的車被一部計程車從側邊撞上。

4330 The rear **bumper** fell off, and the **chassis** is **crooked**.
後保險桿掉了，而且車子底盤都扭曲了。
bumper 名 保險桿 chassis 名 底盤 crook 動 使彎曲

4331 A **distracted** driver caused the serious accident.
心不在焉的駕駛是造成這場嚴重意外的主因。
distracted 形 思想不集中的

4332 The driver **denied** that it was his fault.
這名駕駛否認這是他的錯。deny 動 否認

4333 The man is a **witness** to the car crash.
那名男性是這起車禍的目擊證人。witness 名 目擊證人

4334 Did you get the **plate** number?
你有記下車牌號碼嗎？plate 名 車牌

4335 Before I realized it, the driver had fled. I only knew that it was a red Mazda.
在我回過神以前，駕駛就跑了。我只知道是一輛紅色的馬自達。

4336 The **runaway** driver may be put into jail.
肇事逃逸的司機可能會被判刑。runaway 形 逃跑的

4337 There was a **chain-reaction** accident on the highway.
高速公路上發生一起連環車禍。chain-reaction 形 連鎖的

4338 One car turned **upside-down**.
有一輛車翻覆了。upside-down 副 顛倒地

4339 Several cars were badly damaged in the **collision**.
好幾部車都嚴重受損。collision 名 碰撞

4340 There are five dead and three **injured** in the traffic accident.

這場車禍造成五死三傷。 injure 動 傷害

4341 One of the victims **passed out**. Call an **ambulance**!
有一名傷者昏倒了，快叫救護車！
pass out 片 失去知覺 ambulance 名 救護車

4342 All the injured people were carried to the local hospital.
所有的傷者都被送到當地的醫院了。

4343 The 12-year-old boy is the only **survivor**.
這名十二歲的男孩是唯一的生還者。 survivor 名 倖存者

4344 **Fortunately**, most people survived the accident **unharmed**.
幸運的是，大部分的人都毫髮無傷。
fortunately 副 幸運地 unharmed 形 無恙的

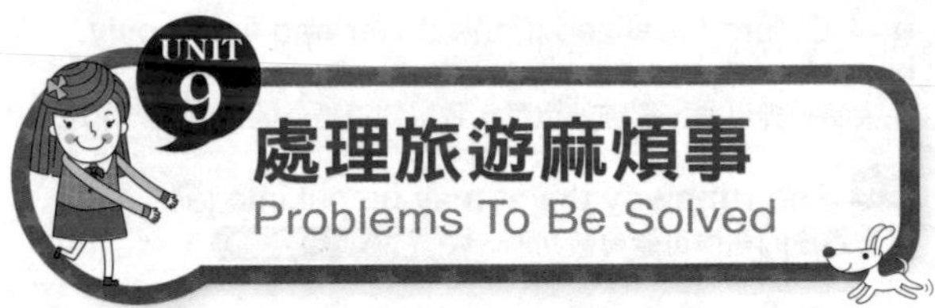

處理旅遊麻煩事 Problems To Be Solved

4345 I lost my passport. What should I do?
我的護照掉了，該怎麼辦才好？

4346 First, you should fill out a Report of Loss at a local **police station**.
首先，到當地的警察局取得失竊證明。 police station 片 警察局

4347 Then, you should get a new one as soon as possible.
然後，盡快辦理新護照。

4348 Where can I get a new one?

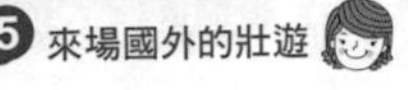

我要到哪裡申辦新護照呢？

4349 You'd better go to the Taipei **Representative** Office and get more details.
你最好到台北駐外代表處去確認細節。representative 形 代理的

4350 How long will it take to get my passport **reissued**?
補發護照要多久時間呢？reissue 動 使再發出

4351 Do you have a passport photo with you?
你有沒有帶護照用的相片？

4352 Yes, I always prepare two passport photos in case of any problems.
有，我都會準備兩張護照用的相片，以防突發狀況。

4353 You have to fill out the form and pay the fee.
你必須填寫這張表格，並支付相關費用。

4354 I forgot my camera in the **cab**.
我把照相機忘在計程車裡了。cab 名 計程車

4355 Do you **remember** the car number?
你還記得車號嗎？remember 動 記得

4356 I don't know, but the taxi driver is **bald**.
我不知道車號，只記得計程車司機是禿頭。bald 形 禿頭的

4357 Please give me your name, address, and telephone number.
請告訴我您的名字、住址和電話號碼。

4358 We'll call you if your camera is found.
若是找到照相機，會通知您的。

4359 My traveler's **checks** have been stolen.
我的旅行支票被偷了。check 名 支票

4360 I am here to report the loss of my traveler's checks.

我來掛失旅行支票。

4361 Where should I apply for reissue?
我要到哪理申請補發呢？

4362 May I see your receipts?
我需要看一下您的存根聯。

4363 I didn't sign those lost traveler's checks.
我沒有在遺失的旅行支票上簽名。

4364 We don't **replace** any unsigned checks.
我們不補發未簽字的支票。 replace 動 以…代替

4365 You should have signed them first when you bought them.
在購買旅行支票時，您就應該先簽名。

4366 I am looking for the lost-and-found counter.
我要找失物招領櫃台。

4367 The lost-and-found counter is on the first floor.
失物招領櫃台在一樓。

4368 I am **in trouble**.
我有麻煩了！ in trouble 片 在危險的處境中

4369 What's the matter?
發生什麼事了？

4370 I've lost my handbag.
我的包包不見了。

4371 Where did you lose it?
你的東西是 在哪裡遺失的？

4372 Well, I don't know **exactly**.
我不是很確定。 exactly 副 精確地

4373 Then, you should have a look in the hotel room first.

那你應該先回飯店的房間找找看。

4374 I left it in the restaurant.
我把它留在餐廳裡了。

4375 I couldn't find it when I went back.
我回去之後，就找不到了。

4376 Are there any **valuable** things in your bag?
包包裡有什麼貴重物品嗎？ valuable 形 值錢的

4377 Yes. I put everything in it. My wallet, passport, camera, and cell phone.
有，我所有的東西都在裡面，包括皮夾、護照、相機和手機。

4378 When I went to pay for our meal, I realized that my wallet was **missing**!
當我去付餐費時，才發現我的皮夾不見了。 missing 形 找不到的

4379 I have no idea where I left it.
我不知道是掉在哪裡了。

4380 What was in your **wallet**?
你的皮夾裡有什麼東西？ wallet 名 皮夾

4381 My credit cards and 300 U.S. dollars in cash were **inside** it.
裡面有我的信用卡以及三百美元的現金。 inside 介 在…的裡面

4382 Should I help you file a report with the police?
要不要我協助你向警方報案？

4383 Where is the nearest police station?
最近的警察局在哪裡呢？

4384 There is a police station around the corner.
轉角就有一間警察局。

4385 What are the police going to ask?
警察會問我什麼？

4386 They'll probably ask you to **describe** what happened.
他們應該會請你描述發生的過程。describe 動 描述

4387 What else can I do?
我還有什麼能做的嗎？

4388 Call the bank and cancel your credit cards.
打電話到銀行掛失你的信用卡。

4389 You should also ask the bank to stop any **payments**.
你也必須要求銀行止付所有費用。payment 名 付款

4390 I'd like to report a missing credit card, please.
麻煩你，我要掛失信用卡。

4391 You can cancel your card **temporarily** and wait to see if it **turns up**.
您可以暫時取消信用卡，看看之後會不會又找到了。
temporarily 副 暫時　turn up 片 (失去後)又被找到

4392 You can also cancel it **permanently**, and we'll send you a new card.
你也可以永久取消信用卡，我們會寄新卡給您。
permanently 副 永久地

4393 I want to report a **robbery**.
我想要申報一件搶案。robbery 名 搶劫案

4394 I was **mugged**.
我被搶了！mug 動 襲擊搶劫

4395 A man **grabbed** my purse in front of the train station and ran away.
有個人在火車站前搶了我的包包，並跑掉了。grab 動 奪取

4396 What does the man look like?
那個人長什麼樣子？

4397 I didn't see him clearly, but he wore a black top

with blue jeans.
我沒有看得很清楚，不過他穿著黑色上衣和牛仔褲。

4398 He's around **middle age**, not tall.
大概四、五十歲的中年男子，長得不高。 middle age 片 中年

4399 Did you get hurt?
您有受傷嗎？

4400 Luckily, I escaped **injury**.
還好，我沒受傷。 injury 名 傷害

4401 Were there any witnesses?
有沒有目擊者呢？

4402 I need you to fill out the form.
我需要您填寫這張表格。

4403 When can I hear from you?
什麼時候會有消息呢？

4404 We'll **contact** you as soon as we have **further** information.
若有進一步的消息，我們會盡快通知您。
contact 動 聯繫 further 形 進一步的

4405 Thank you very much! Please call me at this number.
非常謝謝你！請撥這個電話號碼給我。

4406 Don't walk alone in the **dark**.
夜晚不要獨自行走。 dark 名 暗處；黑夜

4407 Many people have been **attacked** on this street.
很多人在這條街上被襲擊。 attack 動 襲擊

4408 I had my pocket picked.
我被扒了。

4409 Is it possible to find the **pickpocket**?
有沒有辦法找到扒手呢？ pickpocket 名 扒手

4410 Somebody stole my **backpack**.
有人偷了我的背包。backpack 名 後背包

4411 What color is your backpack?
您的背包是什麼顏色的呢？

4412 My backpack is dark blue.
我的背包是深藍色的。

4413 What's inside your backpack?
背包裡面有什麼東西？

4414 A red wallet, a guidebook, a laptop and a pink **toiletries** bag.
有一個紅色皮夾、一本旅遊書、一台筆記型電腦和一個粉紅色化妝包。toiletry 名 化妝品

4415 Is this your bag?
這是你的包包嗎？

4416 Is anything missing?
有沒有什麼東西不見了呢？

4417 Everything is there, **except for** some cash.
除了一些現金之外，東西都在。except for 片 除了…以外

4418 You are my **savior**! Thank you very much.
你真是我的救星！非常謝謝你。savior 名 救星

4419 I didn't know what to do when the fire alarm **went off** in the hotel.
當飯店的火災警報響起時，我完全慌了手腳。go off 片 響起

4420 There was a **fire** this morning.
今天早上發生了火災。fire 名 火災

4421 Luckily, the fire was **put out** quickly.
還好，火很快就被撲滅了。put out 片 撲滅

Part 6

職場的老鳥與新手

AT THE OFFICE

UNIT 1 社會新鮮人找工作

UNIT 2 新人初來乍到

UNIT 3 聊聊工作 & 同事

UNIT 4 電話響起的應對

UNIT 5 通知！準備開會囉

UNIT 6 準備簡報 & 臨場表現

UNIT 7 商務往來 & 收單

UNIT 8 人事異動面面觀

UNIT 9 轉換跑道 & 退休

社會新鮮人找工作 Looking For A Job

4422 I recently received my **master's** degree in accounting and am currently seeking a position as an **accountant**.
我剛取得會計學的碩士學位，正在找會計人員的職缺。
master 名 碩士　accountant 名 會計師

4423 I am **looking for** something in marketing.
我想找行銷方面的工作。 look for 片 尋找

4424 I saw your Internet ad for a **salesperson**.
我看到你們網路上的廣告有在徵業務員。 salesperson 名 業務

4425 I'd be interested in applying for any **opening** you have for an **engineer**.
我有興趣申請貴公司提供的工程師職缺。
opening 名 職缺　engineer 名 工程師

4426 I notice that there are some job vacancies in your company.
我發現貴公司有職位空缺。

4427 I read your ad in Taipei **Daily** for the **position** of general manager.
我在《台北日報》看到你們徵總經理一職的廣告。
daily 名 日報　position 名 職位

4428 I am here about the **advertisement** for a salesperson.
我是看了你們招聘業務員的廣告而來應徵的。
advertisement 名 廣告

4429 I saw a job vacancy sign outside. Do you still have a vacancy?
我看見門外的告示牌上寫著要招募新血，請問你們還缺人嗎？

4430 I'm looking for a job. Do you have any vacancies?
我正在找工作，請問你們有缺人嗎？

4431 We do have a vacancy for a **plumber**.
我們確實在招水電工。plumber 名 水電工

4432 I'm looking for a **part-time** job. Are there any available here?
我正在找兼職工作，請問有職缺嗎？part-time 形 兼職的

4433 I'm sorry. The vacancy has been filled **already**.
抱歉，已經找到人了。already 副 已經

4434 Is there any other job for me here?
那還有什麼其他我能做的工作嗎？

4435 What are the **requirements** for the job?
這個工作需要具備哪些條件？requirement 名 必要條件

4436 They require one year of work experience or more.
他們需要一年以上的工作經驗。

4437 I am afraid that I am not **qualified**.
我擔心我不符合資格。qualified 形 合格的；勝任的

4438 I am a fresh **graduate** with no work experience.
我才剛從大學畢業，沒有任何工作經驗。graduate 名 大學畢業生

4439 I heard that fresh graduates will also be considered.
我聽說這家公司也會考慮錄用剛畢業的大學生。

4440 Having relevant experience is **preferable** but not **essential**.
有相關的經驗會比較好，但這並非必要條件。
preferable 形 更好的 essential 形 必要的

4441 Fresh graduates with good **communication** skills are encouraged to apply for the position.

歡迎有良好溝通技巧的社會新鮮人應徵這個職位。
communication 名 溝通

4442 I don't have any **legal background**.
我沒有任何法律背景。 legal 形 法律上的 background 名 背景

4443 Don't worry. Just **give it a try**.
別擔心，給你自己一個嘗試的機會吧。 give it a try 片 試試看

4444 You won't get that job if you don't **give it a shot**.
如果你連試都不試，根本就不可能得到那份工作的。
give it a shot 片 盡量去試

4445 I know a friend who works for that company.
我有個朋友在那家公司上班。

4446 I can recommend you to him.
我可以向他推薦你。

4447 Applying to the company requires an **aptitude** test.
到這家公司應徵需要做性向測驗。 aptitude 名 傾向

4448 I'm going to **complete** an application form and send it in as soon as possible.
我要把申請表填好，盡快寄出去。 complete 動 完成

4449 I would be willing to fly at my own expense to Seattle should you want a personal interview.
如果您願意安排個人面試的話，我很樂意自費飛往西雅圖面試。

4450 I am going to a job **interview** tomorrow.
我明天要去面試。 interview 名 面試

4451 It will be my first interview. I am **kind of** nervous.
這是我第一次參加面試，我有一點緊張。 kind of 片 有一點

4452 Do you have any **tips** for a **successful** interview?
你有什麼能成功通過面試的祕訣嗎？
tip 名 祕訣 successful 形 成功的

4453 It is important to be confident and **cool** in the interview.
面試時，表現出自信、冷靜的一面非常重要。 cool 形 冷靜的

4454 Offer a **handshake** before the interviewer **reaches out** for you.
在面試官伸出手前，你就得主動與對方握手。
handshake 名 握手 reach out 片 伸手

4455 A **firm** handshake and eye contact demonstrate confidence.
堅定的握手和眼神交流都能展現自信心。 firm 形 堅定的

4456 Remember to show **enthusiasm** and **demonstrate** confidence.
記得展現你的熱情和自信。
enthusiasm 名 熱情 demonstrate 動 顯示

4457 Speak **distinctly** in a confident voice, even though you may feel **shaky**.
即使你很緊張，講話時也要清楚、有自信。
distinctly 副 清晰地 shaky 形 緊張不安的

4458 Speak clearly and **enthusiastically** about your experience and skills.
談及自己的經驗和技能時，口齒要清晰、態度要熱忱。
enthusiastically 副 熱心地

4459 You'd better give examples that **highlight** your skills and **strengths**.
最好舉一些能突顯你技能與強項的例子。
highlight 動 強調 strength 名 長處

4460 Be prepared to **market** your skills and experience.
事前要準備好，把你的技能和經驗介紹給對方。 market 動 銷售

4461 The more you know about the company, the better chance you have of selling yourself.
對公司愈了解，推銷自己的機會就愈多。

4462 **Focus on** what you've learned from the experience.
把重點放在「你從過去的經驗中學到什麼」。 focus on 片 集中

4463 Don't speak **negatively** about your **past** employers.
不要說以前老闆的壞話。 negatively 副 否定地 past 形 以前的

4464 Answer questions fully and **get to the point**.
要完整地回答問題，並切中要點。 get to the point 片 談到要點

4465 Good morning, Miss Lee. I'm Nick, **director** of the marketing department.
早安，李小姐，我是尼克，行銷部門的主管。 director 名 主管

4466 Have a seat, please. And let's begin.
請坐，我們開始吧。

4467 Miss Lee, could you please introduce yourself?
李小姐，你可以做個自我介紹嗎？

4468 Could you talk about your **educational** background?
可以談談你的教育背景嗎？ educational 形 教育的

4469 I received a **bachelor's** degree in management from NTU this year.
我今年剛從台灣大學畢業，拿到管理學士學位。 bachelor 名 學士

4470 To do this job, you must have a degree related to English.
你必須具備英語相關科系的文憑，才能勝任這份工作。

4471 I just graduated from university with a **major** in English.
我剛從大學的英文系畢業。 major 名 主修科目

4472 What language do you speak **other than** Chinese?
除了中文之外，你還會講什麼語言？ other than 片 除了⋯

4473 Besides Chinese, my **mother tongue**, I can also speak English and French.
除了我的母語中文之外，我還會講英語和法語。
mother tongue 片 母語

4474 I've received a good education, and I am **fluent** in English and **Spanish**.
我曾接受良好的教育，英語和西班牙語都講得很流利。
fluent 形 流利的　Spanish 名 西班牙語

4475 Have you received any **honors** or **awards**?
你得過什麼勳章或獎品嗎？ honor 名 勳章　award 名 獎品

4476 I won a **scholarship** and **the first prize** in a speech contest while in college.
大學時期，我曾獲得獎學金及演講比賽的冠軍。
scholarship 名 獎學金　the first prize 片 冠軍

4477 Do you speak English well enough to communicate with **foreigners**?
你的英文能與外國人溝通交流嗎？ foreigner 名 外國人

4478 I think so. I used to be an **interpreter**.
應該沒問題，我以前做過口譯。 interpreter 名 口譯員

4479 I **majored in** English at college and earned a high score on NEW TOEIC.
我大學主修的是英語，新多益的成績也很高。 major in 片 主修⋯

4480 I believe the amount of English I know is **sufficient** to work in an American **firm**.
我的英語程度絕對足以勝任在美商公司的工作。
sufficient 形 足夠的　firm 名 公司

4481 Why do you consider yourself qualified for this job?
你為什麼認為自己符合我們對這個職位的要求呢？

4482 My past work experience is **closely** related to this job.

我過去的經驗與這份工作十分相關。 closely 副 接近地

4483 My educational background and **professional** experience make me qualified for the job.
我的教育背景和工作經驗使我能夠勝任這份工作。
professional 形 職業的

4484 Because I have three years of experience working with customers in a very **similar** environment, I feel I am the right person for the job.
我具備三年與客戶溝通合作的經驗，之前的工作環境也很類似，所以我覺得我能勝任這份工作。 similar 形 相似的

4485 I have experience and **expertise** in the area of customer support.
我具備客服方面的經驗和技能。 expertise 名 專門技術

4486 What do you think you would bring to the job?
你認為自己能為這份工作帶來什麼呢？

4487 Why should we **hire** you?
我們為什麼要雇用你呢？ hire 動 雇用

4488 I would say that I am enthusiastic, **responsible** and **organized**.
我很有熱忱、做事負責又有條理。
responsible 形 認真負責的　organized 形 有系統的

4489 I have good communication skills and problem-**solving abilities**.
我的溝通技巧很好，也具備解決問題的能力。
solve 動 解決　ability 名 能力

4490 I have the ability to stay focused in **stressful** situations.
即便是在高壓的環境下，我也能保持專注力。 stressful 形 壓力重的

4491 I can be **counted on** when the **going** gets tough.
面臨棘手的狀況時，我是值得依賴的對象。
count on 片 依靠　going 名 進展

4492 I believe I am ready and experienced enough to meet the challenge.
我已經準備好，也具備足以接受這份挑戰的經驗。

4493 I am a good team player and have the **desire** to create **excellent** work.
我是很好的團隊工作者，並有把工作做到最好的信念。
desire 名 渴望　excellent 形 傑出的；出色的

4494 I am not only **hard-working**, but also **easy-going**.
我不僅工作認真，個性也很隨和。
hard-working 形 勤勉的　easy-going 形 隨和的

4495 I know I would be a great **addition** to your team.
我一定能成為團隊的助力。addition 名 增加的人或物

4496 What **interest** you most about this job?
你對這份工作最感興趣的是什麼？interest 動 使發生興趣

4497 I like to work in a team and enjoy solving problems together.
我喜歡團隊合作，並與人共同解決問題的感覺。

4498 Why did you choose our company?
你為什麼選擇我們公司呢？

4499 How much do you know about our company?
你對於我們公司了解多少？

4500 Your company has **earned** a good **reputation** because of your high-quality products and your well-constructed management system.
貴公司一直享有盛名，不僅因為你們產品的品質很好，而且管理也極其完善。earn 動 贏得　reputation 名 聲譽

4501 I want to be a **senior administrative** assistant in a large foreign firm.
我想擔任大型國外企業的高階行政助理。
senior 形 高級的　administrative 形 行政的

4502 Do you have any **practical** experience as a **secretary**?
你有祕書工作的實務經驗嗎？
practical 形 實際的　secretary 名 祕書

4503 Do you have any **relevant** experience?
你有相關經驗嗎？ relevant 形 有關的

4504 Have you done this kind of job before?
你以前有做過類似的工作嗎？

4505 I am sorry to say that I have no experience in this **field**.
很抱歉，我沒有這方面的經驗。 field 名 領域

4506 Although I have no experience in this field, I'm willing to **learn**.
雖然我從未涉足這塊領域，但我很願意學習。 learn 動 學習

4507 I worked in a **fashion** shop last winter as a part-time salesperson.
我去年冬天在一家服飾店擔任兼職店員。 fashion 名 時裝

4508 I have been a secretary for six years.
我從事祕書的工作已經有六年了。

4509 I **am** well **acquainted with** office work and can handle business **correspondence** independently.
我很熟悉辦公室的工作，並能獨立處理對外的商務文書。
be acquainted with 片 了解　correspondence 名 通信

4510 I have been working in the **IT industry** over a decade.
我已經在資訊產業工作超過十年了。
IT 縮 資訊科技(= information technology)　industry 名 產業

4511 This is where I've spent most of my career, so I've **chalked up** fifteen years of experience exactly in this area.
我多數時間都投注在這個領域，就這個行業而言，我有十五年的

工作經驗。chalk up 片 取得

4512 I have been in the business for the last ten years and worked as the **superintendent** in the personnel department.
我過去十年在業界擔任人事部主任至今。superintendent 名 主管

4513 What have you learned from your **former** jobs?
你從以往的工作中學到什麼？former 形 從前的

4514 Could you tell me about some of your **accomplishments** from your **previous** jobs?
你可以談一下你之前的工作表現嗎？
accomplishment 名 成就 previous 形 以前的

4515 Would you talk about your **merits**?
能談談你的工作業績嗎？merit 名 功績

4516 When I was the sales manager for Taiwan Friendship Store, I succeeded in **raising** yearly sales **volume** by 25%.
在擔任台灣友誼商店的經理期間，我成功地把年銷售量提高了25%。raise 動 增加 volume 名 交易量

4517 I used to be a team leader and with our team's hard work, we were able to reduce **production costs** by 20%.
我以前是團隊的領導者，因為我們的努力，生產成本降低了百分之二十。production 名 生產 cost 名 費用

4518 As you can see from my **resume**, I have **extensive** experience in teaching.
從我的履歷上可以看到，我的教學經驗相當豐富。
resume 名 履歷 extensive 形 廣泛的

4519 What is important to you in a job?
對你來說，什麼是工作中最重要的事？

4520 I can learn and **grow** in my field.
我能在工作中學到東西，並不斷成長。grow 動 成長

4521 I hope to have a job which offers me an opportunity for **advancement**.
我希望能從事一個有升遷機會的工作。 advancement 名 晉升

4522 What certificates or technical **qualifications** have you **obtained**?
你有何種技術資格證照？ qualification 名 執照 obtain 動 得到

4523 I've got an **Associate** Professor's Qualification Certificate.
我獲得副教授的資格證書。 associate 形 副的

4524 I completed a computer-training **program**, and I am familiar with many different kinds of software.
我上過電腦培訓班，對許多電腦軟體都很了解。 program 名 課程

4525 What's your career **objective**?
你的事業目標是什麼？ objective 名 目標

4526 I hope I could be a leader of an **energetic** and **productive** sales team.
我希望自己擔任主管時，所負責的團隊是積極且多產的。
energetic 形 積極的 productive 形 多產的

4527 What do you want to be doing in this company in five years?
五年後，你打算在這間公司做什麼工作呢？

4528 I'm very interested in the European market. Hopefully, I would like to work in Brussels.
我對歐洲市場非常感興趣，可能的話，我想在布魯塞爾工作。

4529 Do you **mind** traveling? This job will require a lot of travel.
你介意出差嗎？這份工作經常需要出差。 mind 動 介意

4530 No, I don't mind at all. I enjoy traveling.
一點也不介意，我很喜歡出差。

4531 Do I need to **work shifts**?

我需要輪班嗎？ work shifts 片 做要輪班的工作

4532 Do you mind working on the night **shift**?
你介意上夜班嗎？ shift 名 輪班工作的時間

4533 Do you like **routine** work?
你喜歡一成不變的工作嗎？ routine 形 例行的

4534 You are a **job-hopper**.
你經常換工作。 job-hopper 名 經常換工作的人

4535 Why have you changed your jobs so **frequently**?
你換工作的次數為何這麼頻繁？ frequently 副 頻繁地

4536 What kind of **salary** are you expecting?
你的希望待遇是多少？ salary 名 薪水

4537 If possible, I am hoping for NT$30,000.
可能的話，我希望有三萬元台幣。

4538 What is the salary **range** for a similar position in the company?
請問貴公司類似的職位大概領多少薪水？ range 名 幅度

4539 What's the starting salary in the company?
請問貴公司的起薪是多少？

4540 That's all for the interview. Thank you for your interest in our company.
面試到此結束，謝謝你來參加本公司的面試。

4541 When will I know your decision?
我何時能知道你們的決定呢？

4542 You will be **hearing from** us soon. Send the next **candidate** in on your way out, please.
你很快就會收到我們的消息。出去的時候，麻煩你請下一位應徵者進來。 hear from 片 從⋯得到消息 candidate 名 應試者

4543 Will I be called back for a **second** interview?
會有第二次的面試嗎？ second 形 第二次的

4544 Thank you for taking time out of your busy schedule to interview me.
非常感謝您於百忙之中，抽出時間來面試我。

4545 I am calling **in regard to** our interview last Wednesday.
我打電話來是想詢問一下我上週三的面試情況。
in regard to 片 關於

4546 We're still **reviewing** your resume.
我們還在審核你的履歷。review 動 複審

4547 We haven't made our final decision yet.
我們尚未做出最終決定。

4548 When can I know whether I will be hired or not?
我何時才能知道是否被錄用了呢？

4549 We should know by next Friday whom we will hire.
下週五之前，我們就會決定聘用誰了。

4550 If your application is successful, we will **notify** you by mail.
如果你有被錄取，我們會寄信通知。notify 動 通知

4551 We're sorry that we can't offer you the job.
很抱歉，我們無法錄用你。

4552 Mr. Chang, I am calling to inform you that you're hired.
張先生，我打電話來是要通知你被錄取了。

4553 Considering your qualifications, we believe you'd be a good flight attendant.
考量你的能力後，我們相信你會成為一名好空服員。

4554 Will you take it?
你願意接受這份工作嗎？

4555 Thank you for hiring me. I'm very **proud** to be

employed by your firm.
謝謝您願意錄用我，能被貴公司錄用，實在榮幸之至。
proud 形 自豪的 employ 動 雇用

4556 I want to express my **appreciation** for giving me this chance.
謝謝您願意給我這個機會。appreciation 名 感謝

4557 I can **assure** you that you will not be **disappointed**.
我保證不會讓您失望。assure 動 擔保 disappointed 形 失望的

4558 You are hired. When can you start to work?
你被錄用了，什麼時候可以開始上班呢？

4559 When could you start working? / When can you start the job?
你什麼時候能開始上班？

4560 I can start tomorrow if you like.
需要的話，我明天就能上班。

4561 I can start as soon as I receive my **diploma** next month.
我下個月一拿到畢業證書，就能開始上班了。diploma 名 畢業證書

4562 I can start to work in a month.
我一個月後可以開始上班。

4563 You are hired. Please report to the personnel office on April first at eight o'clock in the morning.
你被錄用了，請於四月一日上午八點鐘到人事室報到。

4564 I will **report for duty** on the date **indicated**.
我會於指定的日期到公司報到。
report for duty 片 報到 indicate 動 指示；指出

4565 That's **settled** then. I'm glad to be able to offer the job.
那就這樣決定了，我很高興能提供你這份工作。settle 動 確定

4566 We'll expect you here next month; see you then.
我們期待下個月你的到任，再見。

4567 You have a three-month **probation period**.
你有三個月的試用期。 probation 名 試用 period 名 期間

4568 I really appreciate your offer, but I must **decline** it.
非常感謝貴公司的錄用，但我不得不拒絕這份工作。
decline 動 婉拒；謝絕

4569 **Frankly** speaking, I have been thinking that the position is not right for me since the interview.
坦白說，面試後我一直認為這個職位不適合我。 frankly 副 坦白地

4570 I am sorry, but I've just accepted another offer that I feel is more suitable.
很抱歉，我剛接受了另一份更適合我的工作。

4571 I phoned to check on my application, but they said they'd already hired someone.
我打電話去確認應徵的結果，但他們說已經找到人了。

4572 I have turned down the job.
我已經拒絕了這份工作。

新人初來乍到
About The Orientation

4573 Are you new here?
你是新來的嗎？

4574 I am a new employee. / I am a **newcomer**. / I am the new kid on the **block**.
我是新進員工。 newcomer 名 新來的人 block 名 團體

4575 It's my first day here.
今天是我第一天上班。

4576 My first day on the job has been **nerve-racking**.
第一天上班讓我神經緊繃。 nerve-racking 形 使人不安的

4577 I am the new assistant to the public relations manager.
我是新來的員工，擔任公關部經理的助理。

4578 I am a technician **on probation**.
我是來見習的技術人員。 on probation 片 在試用期中

4579 Welcome **aboard**! / Welcome to our team.
歡迎加入我們！ aboard 副 上(船、飛機…等)

4580 I hope you'll enjoy working with us.
希望我們會共事愉快。

4581 I look forward to working with you.
我很期待和你一起工作。

4582 If you have any questions, just feel free to ask.
若有任何問題，不用客氣，儘管發問。

4583 Everyone would be glad to **pitch in** when you are **struggling**.
當你遇到困難時，大家都會樂意助你一臂之力的。
pitch in 片 協力 struggle 動 艱難地進行

4584 Where should I **punch in**?
我應該在哪裡打卡？ punch in 片 打卡(記錄上班時間)

4585 You can find the time clock by the main **entrance**.
大門旁設有打卡鐘。 entrance 名 大門

4586 Please get to work on time and don't leave too early.
請不要遲到或早退。

4587 Don't forget to clock in and clock out.
上下班別忘了打卡。

4588 Our office hours are from 9 a.m. to 6 p.m.
我們公司是九點開始上班，六點下班。

4589 In our company, even managers have to clock in and clock out.
在我們公司，就算是經理也要打卡。

4590 We don't need to punch in and **punch out** here.
我們這裡不需要打卡。 punch out 片 打卡(記錄下班時間)

4591 I work a **flexible** schedule.
我的上下班時間很彈性。 flexible 形 有彈性的

4592 Could you tell me something about the **corporate** culture in this company?
你可以跟我說一下這間公司的企業文化嗎？ corporate 形 公司的

4593 Most engineers here work on **flextime**.
在我們公司，大部分工程師的上班時間都很彈性。
flextime 名 彈性的工作時間

4594 This **is** very **different from** other companies.
這一點和其他公司非常不同。 be different from 片 與…不同

4595 Does our company have a dress code?
我們公司有特別的服裝規定嗎？

4596 The dress code at our company requires men to wear ties and women to wear skirts.
我們公司對服裝的規定是：男性必須打領帶，女性則必須穿裙子。

4597 We all wear **casual** clothing on Fridays.
我們星期五都會穿休閒服裝。 casual 形 非正式的

4598 We can wear comfortable clothing like jeans to work on Fridays.
如果是星期五，就能穿得舒適一點，像是牛仔褲之類的。

4599 Could you please tell me something about the company?
你可以告訴我關於公司的事嗎？

4600 The company is a large **multinational** with several **branches** in many countries.
這家公司是一間大型跨國企業，在很多國家都設有分公司。
multinational 名 跨國公司 branch 名 分公司

4601 This is a government-owned company.
這家公司是國營企業。

4602 There are six main **departments** in our company.
我們公司有六大部門。department 名 部門

4603 The sales and marketing departments are on the first floor.
業務部和行銷部在一樓。

4604 The **financial** and accounting departments are on the second floor.
財務部和會計部在二樓。financial 形 財政的

4605 We also have a personnel department and a general **affairs** department.
我們還有人事部和總務部。affair 名 事務

4606 I'll take you down to your department and introduce you to the man you'll be taking orders from for the next few days.
我會帶你到你的部門，介紹指導人給你認識。接下來的幾天，他會負責指導你。

4607 I am going to introduce the colleagues and the new environment to you.
我來帶你認識新同事與新環境。

4608 Let me introduce you to all of the people in this department.
我來介紹這個部門的所有同仁給你認識。

4609 I'll show you around the office.
我來帶你認識辦公室的環境。

4610 Let me take you to your **cubicle**.
我帶你到你的座位吧。 cubicle 名 小隔間

4611 All the management staff have their own offices.
管理階層都會有屬於他們自己的辦公室。

4612 In our company, most employees work in **open-plan** offices.
在我們公司，大部分的員工都在開放式的辦公區上班。
open-plan 形 敞開的

4613 You will be working in an open-plan office.
你的位子在開放式辦公區裡。

4614 You can use these **filing cabinets** next to your desk.
你可以使用桌子旁邊的檔案櫃。 filing 名 文件歸檔 cabinet 名 櫃

4615 What office **supplies** do you need?
你需要哪些辦公文具呢？ supply 名 生活用品

4616 You can find the supplies in the **cupboard**.
文具用品都放在這個櫃子裡。 cupboard 名 壁櫥

4617 Let me introduce you to our **boss**.
我來幫你介紹一下我們的上司。 boss 名 上司

4618 Miss Wang is our leader. Just call her Jessica.
王小姐是我們的主管，叫她潔西卡就可以了。

4619 She has excellent **leadership** skills.
她很有領導能力。 leadership 名 領導

4620 All of her staff like her.
所有的同仁都很喜歡她。

4621 **By the way**, when is lunch break?
對了，午休時間是什麼時候？ by the way 片 順便提起

4622 Lunch break is from 12 to 1:30 p.m. and coffee break is from 3 to 3:30 p.m.
午休時間是從十二點到一點半，下午茶時間是從三點到三點半。

4623 What are my **duties**?
我該負責什麼工作呢？ duty 名 職責；職務

4624 You need to answer the phone and send out group email **announcements** to all the staff.
你得負責接聽電話，需要通知什麼消息時，發送群組電子郵件給所有員工。 announcement 名 通知

4625 You also have to help **organize** the manager's schedule.
你還必須幫忙安排經理的行程表。 organize 動 安排

4626 It's pretty much like what a secretary does.
跟祕書做的工作差不多。

4627 Excuse me. Where can I find a fax **machine**?
請問一下，傳真機在哪裡？ machine 名 機器

4628 It's on the second floor, right next to the coffee room.
在二樓，放在茶水間的隔壁。

4629 Could you please show me how to use the fax machine?
你可以教我怎麼使用傳真機嗎？

4630 Do you know how to deal with **paper jams**?
你知道要怎麼處理卡紙的問題嗎？ paper jam 片 卡紙

4631 I have **considerable** experience dealing with these problems.
我對於處理這些問題相當有經驗。 considerable 形 相當多的

4632 Judy can assist you with **photocopier issues**.
茱蒂可以幫助你處理影印機的問題。
photocopier 名 影印機 issue 名 問題

4633 If you have any problem with the copy machine, do not **attempt** to fix it yourself.
如果影印機出了問題，請不要擅自修理。 attempt 動 試圖

4634 Excuse me. How can I apply for my new business cards?
請問我要怎麼申請新名片？

4635 Fill out the application form and you can get your new business cards within two weeks.
填寫申請表之後，兩週內就可以拿到新名片了。

4636 Where can I find the Human Resources Department?
請問人力資源部在哪裡？

4637 It's **upstairs**. You have to fill out some forms on your first day.
在樓上，你第一天上班需要填寫一些表格。 upstairs 副 在樓上

4638 There will be an orientation for new employees at 1:00 p.m.
下午一點會有新進員工的訓練課程。

4639 All new employees are required to take a staff **training** course.
所有的新進員工都必須上員工訓練課程。 training 名 訓練

4640 I should **write** all these **down**.
我應該把這些都寫下來。 write down 片 寫下來

4641 The new job will be a bit tough in the beginning.
這份工作一開始的時候會有點辛苦。

4642 It takes a while to get a feel for the new job.
需要一點時間適應這份工作。

4643 Can you **handle** it?
你應付得了嗎？ handle 動 對待；處理

4644 I will **strive** for **excellence**.

我會盡力做到最好的。strive 動 努力 excellence 名 傑出

4645 Don't worry; you'll **master** everything soon.
別擔心，你很快就會上手了。master 動 掌握；精通

4646 You'll be fine once you get the **knack** of it.
一旦你抓到訣竅，就能做得很好。knack 名 訣竅

4647 I think my **benefits** package is very good.
我覺得我們公司的福利很好。benefit 名 好處

4648 The benefits that my company offers are not the best, but they're acceptable.
我公司的福利雖然不是最好的，但還可以接受。

4649 What kind of benefits do you offer?
公司提供哪些福利呢？

4650 I get free insurance and a two-week **annual leave** per year.
我享有免費的保險，一年還有兩週的年假可請。
annual leave 片 年假

4651 We have labor insurance, health insurance, and complimentary group insurance.
我們享有勞健保以及公司團保。

4652 We get **gift coupons** on our birthday and during three major annual **festivals**.
生日和三節時，公司會發放禮券給我們。
gift coupon 片 禮券 festival 名 節日

4653 We get cash **allowances** for the birth of a child, weddings and **funerals** of family members.
公司會發婚喪喜慶津貼。allowance 名 津貼 funeral 名 喪禮

4654 My company makes payment for my **pension**.
我的公司有提撥退休金。pension 名 退休金

4655 We get a **generous** pension after twenty years of service.

服務滿二十年以上，可得到豐厚的退休金。 generous 形 大量的

4656 We get **lifelong medical coverage** for ourselves and our families.
我們和家人都能得到終生的醫療給付。
lifelong 形 終身的 medical 形 醫療的 coverage 名 保險項目

4657 My company offers **private** health insurance.
我的公司有提供個人醫療保險。 private 形 私人的

4658 My benefit package includes private healthcare.
我們的公司福利還包括個人健康檢查。

4659 We have a company **excursion** every spring.
每年的春天，公司會舉辦員工旅遊。 excursion 名 遊覽團

4660 Will I get any **bonus** this year?
我今年會有分紅嗎？ bonus 名 紅利

4661 The best part is that my bonus is usually better than my salary.
最棒的是，我的分紅經常領得比月薪還高。

4662 He gets the **equivalent** of more than thirty months of salary every year, including bonuses.
包含分紅的話，他每年大約可以領到三十個月的薪水。
equivalent 形 等量的

4663 **Senior** supervisors can get **stock** options.
資深主管有股票選擇權。 senior 形 年資較深的 stock 名 股票

4664 Our company offers all employees stock options.
所有的公司員工都享有股票選擇權。

4665 We have the right to buy the company's **shares** at low prices.
我們有權以低價認購公司的股份。 share 名 股份；股票

4666 **Full-time** employees are **eligible** for annual leave based on their years of service.
正職員工可依年資休年假。

full-time 形 專職的　eligible 形 有資格的

4667 Anna is going to take **maternity leave** for one month.
安娜要請一個月的產假。maternity leave 片 產假

4668 She is going to take **parental leave**.
她要請育嬰假。parental leave 片 育嬰假

4669 She'll also get **parental subsidy**.
她還會得到育嬰津貼。parental 形 父母親的　subsidy 名 補貼

4670 We can use parental leave to take care of our children.
我們可以利用育嬰假來照顧小孩。

4671 The parental subsidy covers sixty percent of my salary.
育嬰津貼可領到薪資的六成。

4672 He is going to apply for **unpaid** leave for one year.
他要申請留職停薪一年。unpaid 形 無報酬的

4673 We have annual company **outings**.
公司每年會舉辦員工旅遊。outing 名 短途旅遊

4674 The **welfare** committee is planning a **year-end party** next month.
福委會正在籌辦下個月的公司尾牙。
welfare 名 福利　year-end party 片 尾牙

4675 Do you offer a dormitory to stay at?
請問公司有提供宿舍嗎？

4676 **Married** staff can apply to live in a family dormitory.
已婚員工可以申請家庭宿舍。married 形 已婚的

4677 Does the company offer any training courses?
公司有沒有提供訓練課程呢？

4678 We provide both classroom training and on-line courses.
我們提供實境訓練課程及網路課程。

4679 I also get a company car.
我還能用公司車。

4680 I drive the company car to visit clients.
我開公司車去拜訪客戶。

4681 Only staff on the payroll get free parking.
只有正職員工才能免費停車。

4682 My company has a little garden next to the parking lot as a smoking area for employees.
我的公司在停車場旁邊設了一座小花園，專門做為吸菸區使用。

4683 All the employees can use the gym and swimming pool.
所有員工都能使用健身房和游泳池。

4684 We get discounts when buying company products.
我們買公司產品可以打折。

4685 We get four free movies tickets every two months.
我們每兩個月就能拿到四張免費的電影票。

聊聊工作 & 同事
It's Chatting Time!

4686 I work for a trading company. / I am an office worker in a trading company.

我在一家貿易公司上班。

4687 Our **headquarters** are located in Seattle.
我們的總公司設於西雅圖。headquarters 名 總公司

4688 I am **in charge of** the trading department.
我是貿易部門的主管。in charge of 片 負責

4689 What department do you work in?
你在哪個部門上班？

4690 I work in the sales department.
我在業務部工作。

4691 I work for a hospital, and I am a **surgeon**.
我在醫院上班，是一名外科醫師。surgeon 名 外科醫生

4692 I am a bank **teller** working for a large bank.
我在一間大型銀行上班，是一名銀行出納員。teller 名 出納員

4693 I am a senior engineer of a **technology** company.
我是一家科技公司的資深工程師。technology 名 技術

4694 Our company **aims** for the highest in technology and the best in quality.
我們公司致力於生產最先進的科技與最高品質的產品。
aim 動 致力；意欲；旨在

4695 I work in a large, traditional **manufacturing** company.
我在一家大規模的傳統製造公司上班。manufacturing 名 製造業

4696 I manage a team of **designers**.
我管理一個設計師團隊。designer 名 設計師

4697 There are thirty people working under me.
我底下有三十位員工。

4698 I've just **started** my **own** company.
我剛成立自己的公司。start 動 著手　own 形 自己的

4699 My wife and I **run** a coffee shop.
我和太太經營一家咖啡廳。run 動 經營

4700 I am a **florist**, and I own a shop.
我是一位花商，擁有自己的花店。florist 名 花商

4701 I am on the company's payroll.
我是這家公司的正式員工。

4702 I am a **contract** teacher.
我是約聘教師。contract 名 合約書

4703 I am **undertaking** my **internship** in a bank.
我正在銀行實習。undertake 動 進行 internship 名 實習地位

4704 Todd works part-time.
陶德是兼職員工。

4705 My father is a **white-collar** worker.
我的爸爸是白領階級。white-collar 形 白領階級的

4706 Those employees are **blue-collar** workers.
這些工人是藍領階級員工。blue-collar 形 藍領階級的

4707 What are your work hours?
你的工作時間是什麼時候？

4708 What time do you get to work?
你幾點開始上班？

4709 We punch in at 9:00 a.m. and punch out at 5:00 p.m.
我早上九點開始上班，下午五點下班。

4710 I am a nine-to-fiver.
我是朝九晚五的上班族。

4711 Most staff in our company work shifts.
我們公司大部分的員工都要輪班。

4712 I am on day shift one week and night shift the

next week.
我一週上日班，一週上夜班，交替輪班。

4713 I live in the company dormitory.
我住在公司的宿舍。

4714 I rent an apartment near our company, and I walk to work.
我在公司的附近租了一間公寓，我都走路上班。

4715 I commute to work every day. I go to work by train and **MRT**.
我每天通勤上班，要換搭火車和捷運兩種交通工具。
MRT (= Mass Rapid Transi)

4716 I work in Taipei, but I prefer living in the **country**.
我在台北上班，但我比較喜歡住在鄉下。 country 名 鄉下

4717 I work at home.
我在家上班。

4718 I am a **workaholic**.
我是個工作狂。 workaholic 名 工作狂

4719 I love my job because it is interesting.
我的工作很有趣，所以我很喜歡它。

4720 My main responsibility is **trouble-shooting** between top management and the general employees.
我的主要職責是要調解勞資雙方的糾紛。
trouble-shoot 動 分析解決問題；為…解決困難

4721 My job is **terribly dull**.
我的工作超無聊。 terribly 副 非常 dull 形 乏味的

4722 I am getting used to my **repetitive** job.
我已經漸漸習慣這種重複的工作了。 repetitive 形 反覆的

4723 This is really a **demanding** job.
這份工作實在很吃力。 demanding 形 高要求的

4724 I often have to work **overtime** and even weekends sometimes.
我常需要加班，有時候甚至連週末也得工作。 overtime 名 加班

4725 Department managers need to **approve** staff overtime.
部門主管需要批准員工的加班單。 approve 動 批准

4726 Do you need to work overtime during the peak season?
遇到旺季時，你們需要加班嗎？

4727 We have **endless** overtime work in the peak season and we keep working **nonstop** for thirteen hours a day.
在旺季，我們有加不完的班，一天要持續工作十三小時。
endless 形 無盡的 nonstop 副 不休息地

4728 We also get lots of overtime pay.
我們也領不少加班費。

4729 I get paid on the tenth of every month.
我們公司每個月十號發薪水。

4730 I get the **minimum wage**.
我領的是最低工資。 minimum 形 最低的 wage 名 工資

4731 I get a basic salary, plus **commission**.
我的薪水是底薪加上佣金。 commission 名 佣金

4732 Besides basic salary, I get tips from customers.
除了底薪，我還能得到客人給的小費。

4733 I am a salesperson; I get a basic salary and commission every month.
我是業務員，我每個月可以領底薪加佣金。

4734 I get commission for every car I **sell**.
我每賣出一輛車，就能抽成。 sell 動 售出

4735 I've got a **raise**. It will start from next month.

我加薪了，從下個月開始正式調薪。 raise 名 加薪

4736 All employees will **receive** a five-percent raise next month.
所有員工下個月都可以加薪百分之五。 receive 動 得到

4737 This raise is due to an **increase** in our **profits**.
因為公司的獲利提升，所以這次才能加薪。
increase 名 增加 profit 名 利潤

4738 My boss just gave me a new **assignment**.
我的老闆剛剛給我一項新任務。 assignment 名 工作

4739 The **president** approved the **proposal**.
總裁核准了這個提案。 president 名 總裁 proposal 名 提案

4740 They turned down our offer.
他們駁回了我們的提案。

4741 I'll **collaborate** with my **co-workers** on this project.
我會和同事合作，完成這個案子。
collaborate 動 共同合作 co-worker 名 同事

4742 My co-workers and I **cooperate** very well together.
我和同事合作無間。 cooperate 動 合作

4743 We share the responsibility.
我們分工合作。

4744 The **clerk** is **inefficient**.
這名職員的工作效率很差。 clerk 名 職員 inefficient 形 效率差的

4745 Diana always **passes the buck** to me.
黛安娜總是將責任推託給我。 pass the buck 片 推卸責任

4746 Who is in charge of this case?
這件案子是誰負責的？

4747 We have some excellent people **on board**.

我們公司裡有一些很傑出的人才。 on board 片 在(船、飛機…)上

4748 Mr. Wu is our CEO.
吳先生是我們的執行長。

4749 He is also the **entrepreneur** and **founder** of our company.
他也是我們公司的創辦人。
entrepreneur 名 企業創辦者；企業家 founder 名 創立者

4750 He is an excellent and successful business person.
他是一位優秀又成功的企業家。

4751 Our general manager is our **policy** maker.
總經理是我們的決策者。 policy 名 政策

4752 Nicole is Mr. Wu's secretary. She is nice and experienced.
妮可是吳先生的祕書，她人很好，也很資深。

4753 She is always one step ahead of the boss.
思考事情的時候，她總會比老闆早一步設想到。

4754 Her supervisor **praises** her all the time.
她的主管對她總是讚不絕口。 praise 動 讚美

4755 Miss Kang is our CFO, and she is very smart.
康小姐是我們的財務長，她很精明能幹。

4756 Mr. Zheng is one of our four **vice presidents**.
四位副總當中，鄭先生是其中之一。 vice president 片 副總

4757 Ms. Yang just **assumed** the position of assistant manager last month.
楊小姐上個月才取得副理的職位。 assume 動 就任；取得

4758 She is really **efficient** in her job.
她的工作效率沒話說。 efficient 形 效率高的

4759 She's responsible for **coordination** among

departments.
她負責協調各部門之間的關係。 coordination 名 協調

4760 The IT director **heads up** the IT department.
資訊部的主管領導資訊部門。 head up 片 領導

4761 Mr. Chen is the supervisor of the sales department.
陳先生是業務部的主管。

4762 Kenny is one of the **old-timers** in the sales department.
肯尼是業務部的老鳥了。 old-timer 名 老資格的職員

4763 Miss Yen is bossy and **bosses her subordinates around**.
顏小姐很跋扈，常常使喚她下面的人。
boss sb. around 片 頤指氣使 subordinate 名 部屬

4764 She **dominates** over the whole team too much.
她對整個團隊的控制欲太強了。 dominate 動 控制

4765 She is not flexible enough, especially when she is making decisions.
她不懂變通，做決策的時候尤其如此。

4766 I **bet** that she gets very bad **peer** reviews.
我敢打賭，她在同儕間的評語一定很差。 bet 動 打賭 peer 名 同儕

4767 I think she really should change her **attitude**.
她真的應該好好改一下自己的態度。 attitude 名 態度

4768 I don't like **flatterers**.
我不喜歡愛阿諛諂媚的人。 flatterer 名 阿諛者

4769 He's a **brown-noser**.
他是個愛拍馬屁的人。 brown-noser 名 拍馬屁的人

4770 He always takes **the lion's share** of the **credit**.
他總是搶別人的功勞。
the lion's share 片 最大的那一份 credit 名 功勞

4771 He is a real **eyesore**.
他真的很令人討厭。 eyesore 名 看不順眼的對象

4772 I hate to say this, but there are two **cliques** in the office.
雖然很不想說，但我們辦公室有兩大派系。 clique 名 派系

4773 Patrick is on **sick leave** today.
派翠克今天請病假。 sick leave 片 病假

4774 You were lucky. We were terribly busy on your last day off.
你真幸運，在你休假的最後一天，我們忙死了。

4775 I have to **take** a day **off** tomorrow due to some personal stuff.
我有點私人的事要處理，明天必須請假。 take...off 片 休假

UNIT 4 電話響起的應對 When The Phone Rings

4776 Good afternoon, ABC Corporation.
午安，ABC 股份有限公司。

4777 Mr. Smith's office. May I help you?
史密斯先生的辦公室，我可以替您效勞嗎？

4778 Good morning. Lisa Huang speaking. / This is Lisa Huang speaking.
早安，我是黃莉莎。

4779 Who would you like to speak with?
請問您要找哪一位？

4780 Who did you say you were trying to **reach**?
您剛剛說要找哪位呢？reach 動 與…取得聯繫

4781 What's the name again?
可以再說一次名字嗎？

4782 Mr. Chang? May I have his first name? We've got two Mr. Changs here.
張先生？請問有他的全名嗎？我們這裡有兩位張先生。

4783 Please give me the name or **extension** number of the person you wish to speak with.
請給我名字或分機號碼。extension 名 電話分機

4784 May I know your name, please?
請問您的大名是？

4785 Could you tell me your name one more time?
可以再講一次您的名字嗎？

4786 Did you just say you are Tim? Or Jim?
您剛剛是說您是提姆嗎？還是吉姆？

4787 Who did you say this is? Robert?
您剛才說您是哪位？羅伯特嗎？

4788 May I get your full name, please?
請問您能給我全名嗎？

4789 Could you **spell** your name?
請問可以拼給我您的名字嗎？spell 動 用字母拼

4790 Could you please spell your **last name** again?
可以請您再拼一次您的姓氏嗎？last name 片 姓氏

4791 Should I tell him who is calling?
您希望我通報您是哪位嗎？

4792 May I ask what you want to speak to him about?
可以請問一下，您找他有什麼事嗎？

4793 May I ask what's your business, madam?
女士，可以請問一下有何貴事嗎？

4794 May I know what this is regarding, sir? / May I ask what this is about?
先生，請問有什麼事嗎？/ 請問有什麼事呢？

4795 Just a moment, please. / Just a minute, please.
請稍等一下。

4796 Could you wait for just a moment, please?
請稍後，好嗎？

4797 A moment, please. / Hold on. Don't **hang up**.
請稍候，不要掛斷。 hang up 片 掛斷電話

4798 This is Karen Wang. Could you put Dr. Chen on the line?
我是王凱倫，麻煩請陳醫師接電話。

4799 This is Vincent Lin of the accounting department. May I speak with Ms. Luo?
我是會計部門的林文生，我要找羅小姐。

4800 This is Emily calling from Chicago. Is Mr. Wang in?
我是從芝加哥打來的艾蜜莉，請問王先生在嗎？

4801 Is there a Mr. Lin there?
那裡是不是有一位林先生？

4802 Hello, this is Albert from Taiwan Bank. May I talk to you about an **investment opportunity**?
您好，我是台灣銀行的亞伯特，方便向您介紹一個投資機會嗎？
investment 名 投資 opportunity 名 機會

4803 Hello, sir. Have you heard of Longlife Insurance? I have just the plan for you.
先生您好，有聽過長壽保險嗎？我們有一項很適合您的計畫。

4804 Did I reach extension 2214?

請問這是分機 2214 嗎？

4805 Is this 933-180-926?
請問這支電話是 933-180-926 嗎？

4806 Am I talking to William? Ext. 1538?
請問是威廉嗎？分機號碼是不是 1538 ？

4807 Human **Resources**, please.
請轉接人力資源部。resource 名 資源

4808 Can you connect me to the **library**?
麻煩幫我轉接到圖書館。library 名 圖書館

4809 Please give me the extension number for the Health Center.
請給我健康中心的分機號碼。

4810 What's the extension number in the first **meeting** room?
第一會議室的分機是幾號呢？meeting 名 會議

4811 Could you check if Mr. Hu's office can be reached at extension 1214?
你可以幫我查一下胡先生的辦公室分機是不是 1214 嗎？

4812 Have I reached Holiday **Inn**? Reservations, please.
假日飯店嗎？請幫我轉訂房部門。inn 名 小旅館

4813 Hi, I need to talk to the person who is in charge of the production facility.
你好，請幫我轉接負責生產設備的人。

4814 I'd like to speak to someone about our order for an **air conditioner**.
我想找承辦空調訂單的人員。air conditioner 片 空調

4815 If I have any **delivery** questions, whom should I talk to?
如果我有運送方面的問題，應該找哪位談呢？delivery 名 運送

4816 I'd like to know more about the newest **SUV**. Can you transfer my call to a sales **representative**?
我想了解一下最新的休旅車款，能幫我轉接給負責的業務嗎？
SUV 縮 休旅車 (= sport utility vehicle) representative 名 代表

4817 Could you connect me to the **head** of your department?
請幫我轉接給你們的部門主管。head 名 首長

4818 I have been trying to get **hold** of your manager for days. Is he in?
我已經找你們經理很多天了，他在嗎？hold 名 抓住

4819 I am the person who called about ten minutes ago. May I talk to your manager again?
我是十分鐘前打來的那個人，可以再與你們的主管講個話嗎？

4820 May I speak to Amanda in marketing?
我可以和行銷部的阿曼達通話嗎？

4821 Mr. Wang, please. This is Charlie Zheng, and I am returning his call.
麻煩接王先生。我是鄭查理，他之前有打來找我。

4822 May I speak with Kenny? He's expecting my **call**.
請問我可以跟肯尼通話嗎？他在等我的電話。call 名 電話

4823 Could you please put me through to Mark, the sales manager?
可以幫我轉接給馬克嗎？他是業務經理。

4824 Is Mandy in? I called her this morning, and she said I could reach her this afternoon.
請問曼蒂在嗎？我早上有打來，她說下午可以找得到她。

4825 Mandy, this is Louise. Do you have a minute to talk? I **promise** I'll be **brief**.
曼蒂，我是路易斯，你方便講話嗎？我保證會長話短說。
promise 動 保證 brief 形 簡短的

4826 Is Annie **on duty**? Can I speak to her?

請問安妮有上班嗎？我方便和她說話嗎？ on duty 片 上班

4827 Is there a guy named David there?
你們那裡有個叫大衛的人嗎？

4828 I'm wondering if Evelyn is around.
我想知道伊芙琳在不在？

4829 Is there a Frank there?
請問你們那裡有一位叫法蘭克的人嗎？

4830 This is he. Who's calling?
我就是，請問是哪位呢？

4831 Yes, I am in charge.
是的，我就是負責人。

4832 Could I ask what I can do for you?
請問有什麼可以幫您的嗎？

4833 Speaking. But I am busy now. Could you call me back in ten minutes?
我就是，但我現在正在忙，您可以十分鐘之後再打給我嗎？

4834 I'm sorry. I have a call on the other line. Can I call you back?
很抱歉，我在講另一支電話，我可以等會兒回電給您嗎？

4835 I'm afraid I can't talk now. I have some **visitors**.
我現在有訪客，不方便講電話。 visitor 名 訪問者

4836 I'm just about to go out. Could you call me again after 4:00 this afternoon?
我正要外出，您可以下午四點以後再打給我嗎？

4837 I'm driving. Could you phone me **around** ten o'clock?
我正在開車，您可以十點左右再打給我嗎？ around 介 大約

4838 I'm on the way to my office. Can I talk to you at **quarter** to ten?

我正在去辦公室的路上，九點四十五分再與您聯繫可以嗎？
quarter 名 一刻鐘；十五分鐘

4839 I'm in a **conference** right now. Could I call you back in an hour?
我正在開會，可以一小時後再打給您嗎？ conference 名 會議

4840 I have a meeting in five minutes. Could you **cut it short**, please?
我五分鐘後要開會，您可以長話短說嗎？ cut it short 片 長話短說

4841 Sorry, I can't talk now. Could you leave your message with my secretary?
抱歉，我現在不方便講話，您可以留話給我的祕書嗎？

4842 I am sorry, but I really can't talk. Can we talk some other time?
抱歉，我現在真的沒辦法多聊，改天再聯絡好嗎？

4843 Is that Allen? I **recognized** your voice right away.
是亞倫嗎？我立刻就認出你的聲音了。 recognize 動 認出

4844 Oh, Miss Lin. This is Greg. I didn't recognize your voice.
噢，林小姐，我是葛瑞格，剛剛沒聽出你的聲音。

4845 So nice to hear from you. / I'm so happy to get your call.
很高興接到你的電話。

4846 It's good to hear your **voice**.
聽到你的聲音真好。 voice 名 聲音

4847 I haven't heard from you for a long time. How have you been?
好久沒聽到你的消息了，最近過得好嗎？

4848 Hi! I've been waiting for your call for **a while**.
嗨！我已經等你的電話好一會兒了。 a while 片 一會兒

4849 What a coincidence! I was just about to call you.

真巧！我正好要打給你。

4850 I will put you through to Linda. Hold on.
我幫您轉接給琳達，請稍等。

4851 Hold on, please. I'll put you through.
請稍等，我幫您轉接。

4852 I'll transfer your call to customer service.
我幫您把電話轉到客服部。

4853 A moment, please. I'll transfer your call to the person in charge.
請稍候，我替您把電話轉給負責人聽。

4854 Just a moment, please. I'll get an English **speaker**.
請等一下，我去找會講英文的人來聽。 speaker 名 講某種語言的人

4855 Hold the line, please. I'll get someone who can **answer** your question.
請不要掛斷，我去找能回答您問題的人來聽。 answer 動 回答

4856 Hold on, please. I'll put you through to an English-speaking **division**.
請稍候，我替你轉接至講英語的單位。 division 名 部門

4857 Hold on, please. Let me see if he is in.
請稍等，我去看他在不在。

4858 One moment, please. Let me get Mr. Lee.
等一下，我請李先生來聽。

4859 Hang on. Louise will be here in a minute.
別掛斷，路易斯馬上就來。

4860 Wait! He just **stepped** in.
等等！他剛好進來了。 step 動 踏進；跨入

4861 Certainly. Mr. Brown, Ms. Hu is expecting your call. Hold on, please.

當然可以，布朗先生，胡小姐正在等您的電話，請稍等。

4862 Mr. Chen, the manager of the accounting department is on line three.
陳先生，會計室經理找您，在三線。

4863 Ms. Chang is on line two. Are you available now?
張小姐打來，在二線，你現在方便接聽嗎？

4864 Laura, Mr. Lee is calling about our **offer**.
蘿拉，李先生打來要問我們的報價。 offer 名 報價

4865 Are you ready for the phone?
你現在方便接電話嗎？

4866 Danny, do you have a minute to take the phone?
丹尼，你有空接一下電話嗎？

4867 I am calling **on behalf of** Mr. Luo, the general manager of our company.
我是代表我們公司總經理，羅先生打來的。 on behalf of 片 代表

4868 I am calling to return Mr. Chang's phone call.
我打來回張先生的電話。

4869 I'm phoning to answer your **questions**.
我是打來回覆你的問題的。 question 名 問題

4870 I just got the message you left me earlier.
我剛收到你的留言。

4871 I am calling to ask if you could **do me a favor**.
我打來是要問你可不可以幫我一個忙。 do sb. a favor 片 幫忙某人

4872 I have been trying to reach you. I want to ask you a question.
我一直在找你，我想問你一個問題。

4873 Mr. Lin suggested I call you for **further** information.
林先生建議我打給你，以尋求進一步的消息。 further 形 進一步的

4874 I am wondering if you have time to **discuss** our new proposal.
不知道你有沒有空討論我們的新企劃案。discuss 動 討論

4875 I'd like to arrange an appointment to discuss our possible cooperation.
我想要約個時間討論我們的合作案。

4876 Do you have time to **go over** the details?
你有沒有空可以討論一下細節？go over 片 察看

4877 I'd like to introduce a new product to you.
我想要介紹一個新產品給你。

4878 I'm calling to ask you if it is **possible** to send you some **samples**.
我打來是要問一下，我方便寄一些樣品過去給你嗎？
possible 形 可能的；合適的 sample 名 樣品

4879 May I ask if you got my order?
請問你有收到我的訂單嗎？

4880 Just want to make sure that you got my fax this morning.
我只是想要確認你有收到我早上傳的傳真。

4881 I am just checking if you got my message.
我只是想確認一下，你有沒有看到我的留言？

4882 I just want to give you my email address. Could you write it down?
我只是要給你我的電子郵件，你可以寫下來嗎？

4883 I am calling to inform you that your bill is **due** today.
我打來是要通知您的帳單今日到期。due 形 到期的

4884 Just want to tell you that your boss has been looking for you for an hour.
只是想跟你說，你的老闆找你已經有一個小時了。

4885 I am checking to see if we are still meeting at 10:30 a.m.
確認一下，我們還是上午十點半碰面嗎？

4886 I was wondering if we could **put off** the appointment until this afternoon.
我在想我們是不是可以把約會延到今天下午？ put off 片 延遲

4887 Could we make it after 3:00 p.m. **instead**?
我們可以改到下午三點以後嗎？ instead 副 作為替代

4888 I want to let you know the staff meeting has been postponed to 5:30 p.m.
跟你說，員工會議的開會時間延到下午五點半了。

4889 May I confirm the time of the annual meeting?
我可以跟你確認一下開年度會議的時間嗎？

4890 I am calling to inform you that I can't **attend** the meeting.
我打來是要通知你，我無法參加會議。 attend 動 參加

4891 I am calling to cancel the morning meeting tomorrow.
我打來是為了取消明天的晨會。

4892 I'm calling to tell you that **I'm stuck in traffic**. I won't be there on time.
我打來是要告訴你，我塞在路上，無法準時抵達了。
be stuck in traffic 片 (某人)遇上塞車

4893 Sorry, I'd better go now.
抱歉，我得掛電話了。

4894 I have to go. Someone is **knocking** on the door.
我得掛了，有人在敲門。 knock 動 敲；打

4895 Nice talking to you.
和你談話很愉快。

4896 I'll call you again later, OK?

我之後再打給你，好嗎？

4897 That's all. Talk to you later.
就這樣了，之後再聊。

4898 I'll think about it and call you back soon, OK?
我考慮一下，會盡快回電給你，好嗎？

4899 I can't **reply** to you right away. I need some time to **think** it **over**.
我現在無法馬上回覆你，我需要一點時間考慮。
reply 動 回覆 think over 片 仔細考慮

4900 Please call me when you have more information about this.
如果有更進一步的資訊，請再打給我。

4901 Sorry. I'm having a meeting soon. Let's talk some other time.
抱歉，我馬上有個會議要開，改天再聊。

4902 I wish I had more time to talk, but I've really got to go.
我也希望有時間多聊一下，但我真的得掛電話了。

4903 Sorry, I'm **rather** busy. Can I call you tomorrow?
抱歉，我很忙，可以明天再打給你嗎？ rather 副 相當

4904 Do we have other issues to discuss?
我們還有其他的議題要討論嗎？

4905 Anything else we should talk about?
我們還有其他的事要談嗎？

4906 If there's nothing else we need to discuss now, can I talk to you next time?
如果沒有其他事要談，我們可以下次再聊嗎？

4907 I must keep the line free as I'm expecting a very **important** call.
我不能讓這電話佔線，我在等一個非常重要的電話。

important 形 重要的

4908 Let's talk more after I read your email.
等我看過你的電子郵件後，我們再談吧。

4909 Thanks for your call, Ms. Wu. I'll call you if I have questions.
吳小姐，謝謝你打電話來，如果有問題的話，我會打給你。

4910 Thank you for calling.
謝謝你的來電。

4911 Thanks for returning my call.
謝謝你回我的電話。

4912 Thank you for your time, Mr. Wang.
王先生，謝謝你撥冗和我談話。

4913 Thanks for your **patience**.
謝謝你有耐心聽我說。 patience 名 耐心

4914 It's been nice talking to you. Bye.
很高興能與你通電話，再見。

4915 Let's talk some other time. Say hi to your colleagues!
我們改天再聊，替我向你的同事們問好。

4916 I'll be waiting for your call.
我會等你的電話。

4917 I hope to hear from you again soon, Caroline.
卡洛琳，希望很快就能再和你講電話。

4918 Catherine is talking on another phone right now.
凱薩琳現在正在講另一支電話。

4919 The line is **engaged**. Can you hold?
電話忙線中，您要等嗎？ engaged 形 (電話)使用中的

4920 Will you call back or do you want me to **put you**

on hold?
您想晚一點再打，還是要在線上等候？
put sb. on hold 片 將某人置於(電話)線上等候

4921 I'm afraid she won't be finished for a while.
她恐怕要再過一陣子才會結束。

4922 Anthony is not in, sorry.
抱歉，安東尼不在。

4923 Jill is **dining** out with friends. Try calling her **mobile** phone.
吉兒和朋友出去吃飯了，您要不要打她的手機？
dine 動 用餐 mobile 形 可動的

4924 Would you like to call his mobile phone?
您要不要打他的手機？

4925 Our manager is **away** from his desk.
我們的經理不在位子上。away 副 離開

4926 Sorry, he hasn't come back to his office yet.
抱歉，他還沒回辦公室。

4927 I'm afraid he's still on the way, but he should be back soon.
他恐怕還在路上，但他應該快進來了。

4928 Ms. Chou is out for lunch, and will be back in thirty minutes.
周小姐外出吃午餐了，三十分鐘後會回來。

4929 Ivy is busy right now. May I take a message?
艾薇現在正在忙，可以替您留言嗎？

4930 Ms. Su has a visitor. Could you call her later?
蘇小姐現在有訪客，您可以晚一點再打來嗎？

4931 She should **be able to** be reached in an hour.
一個小時之後應該就能聯絡上她了。be able to 片 能夠

4932 Chad was transferred to the Personnel Department last week. Miss Lee is taking over his job. Shall I put you through?
查德上週調到人事部了，他的工作現在由李小姐接手，需要我幫您轉接嗎？

4933 Kathy retired last December. Would you like to talk to Ms. Wang who has taken over from her?
凱西去年十二月退休了，您想和接他工作的王小姐講電話嗎？

4934 I'm afraid Carter has left already.
很抱歉，卡特已經下班了。

4935 Mr. Hu is off today. Do you want to **leave a message**?
胡先生今天休假，請問要留言嗎？ leave a message 片 留言

4936 He works the **night shift**. Could you call after eight?
他上夜班，您可以八點以後再打來嗎？ night shift 片 夜班

4937 He's out for the rest of the day. Could you call him tomorrow?
他今天不會再回來了，您可以明天再打嗎？

4938 He's not in. I'll transfer your call to his assistant, Ms. Chen.
他不在，我幫您把電話轉給他的助理，陳小姐。

4939 Our manager won't be available until the conference is finished. I think his assistant can help you with this.
我們的經理在會議結束之前都無法接聽電話，他的助理應該可以協助您。

4940 I'm his secretary, Vivian. Would you mind telling me your name?
我是他的祕書，薇薇安，方便告訴我您的大名嗎？

4941 This is Grace, Mr. Chang's secretary. **Unfortunately**, Mr. Chang is in a meeting now.

我是張先生的祕書，葛瑞絲。真是不巧，張先生正在開會。
unfortunately 副 可惜

4942 She's in a sales conference now. Is it **urgent**?
她現在正在開業務會議，有急事嗎？urgent 形 緊急的

4943 What time will Professor Chang be in his office?
張教授幾點會回辦公室呢？

4944 Would he be able to be reached in an hour?
他一個小時之後會在嗎？

4945 Can he talk after the **teleconference**?
他的視訊會議結束後，方便講電話嗎？teleconference 名 視訊會議

4946 What's a good time for me to call again?
我什麼時間再打來比較方便？

4947 It's urgent. I'll try in an hour.
我有急事，那我一個小時之後再打。

4948 I really need to talk to Steven **as soon as possible**.
我得盡快聯繫上史蒂芬才行。as soon as possible 片 盡快

4949 Could you get Mr. Hong now? I am **leaving for** Japan soon.
你現在可以找到洪先生嗎？我馬上就要前往日本了。
leave for 片 前往

4950 I know she's on the other line. I only have a quick question, so could you please put me through?
我知道她在講電話，但我只有一個小問題要問她，很快就會結束，能幫我轉接一下嗎？

4951 Do you mind telling me his **number** there?
你介意告訴我他那邊的電話是幾號嗎？number 名 號碼

4952 May I have his cell phone number?
可以告訴我他的手機號碼嗎？

4953 Sorry, we can't give out his private number.
抱歉，我們不方便給您他私人的電話號碼。

4954 I'm wondering if you could tell me if she has another number.
我想知道有沒有其他的號碼可以聯絡她？方便告訴我嗎？

4955 Do you **happen to** know her home number?
你會知道她家裡的電話號碼嗎？ happen to 片 碰巧

4956 I know Mr. Chang is out of **town**. Can I talk to his secretary?
我知道張先生出差去了，我可以跟他的祕書講嗎？ town 名 城鎮

4957 Can you recommend a person whom I can **contact**?
你能推薦一位聯絡人給我嗎？ contact 動 與…聯繫

4958 I can't find Jeff. Could you tell him to call me back when you see him?
我聯絡不上傑夫，如果你看到他，可以請他回電給我嗎？

4959 When can I call again? Or, can I leave her a message?
應該什麼時候再打呢？還是我可以留話給她？

4960 Can you take a message?
你可以幫我留話嗎？

4961 Can you give Melissa a message?
可以幫我留話給梅麗莎嗎？

4962 I'd like to leave a message. You've got a **pen**?
我想留話給他，你手邊有筆嗎？ pen 名 筆

4963 Please tell her I will pick her up at 4:10.
請幫我轉告她，我四點十分會過去接她。

4964 Could you ask her to call me at 555-8989?
可以請她回電到 555-8989 這支號碼給我嗎？

4965 OK. Please tell her that Hunter tried to contact her.
好的，請轉告她杭特有打來找她。

4966 If possible, please tell Ray to call me back. This is Paul, his co-worker.
如果可以的話，請雷回電，我是他的同事保羅。

4967 Please tell him to call me at the Lela Hotel, room 1536. This is Zoe Lin from Taiwan.
請他回電到里拉飯店 1536 號房，我是台灣來的林柔伊。

4968 Could you tell her that I will be at this number for two hours? After that, I will be at another office.
請你告訴她，這兩個小時我會用這支電話，接下來我就會在別的辦公室了。

4969 I'm sorry. Mr. Hsu is **still** on the other line. Do you **still** want to wait?
很抱歉，徐先生還在講電話，您要繼續等嗎？ still 副 仍然

4970 Her line is still busy. Would you like to hold or should I have her call you back?
她仍在忙線中，您要在線上等，還是要請她回電呢？

4971 Do you want to wait or call again?
您要等，還是之後再打過來呢？

4972 I'm sorry to keep you waiting, but he still cannot be reached.
很抱歉讓您久等，不過她仍然在忙。

4973 Can you hold for another few minutes? He should be available soon.
可以再等一下嗎？他應該馬上就可以接電話了。

4974 Will someone else do?
找其他人接聽可以嗎？

4975 Mr. Tang is still in the meeting. Would you like to leave a message?

湯先生還在開會，請問要留話嗎？

4976 May I take your message?
我可以幫您留話嗎？

4977 Is there any message I can give him?
請問要不要幫您留話給他呢？

4978 Would you like me to tell her you've called twice already this morning?
需不需要我轉告她，您今天早上打過兩次電話呢？

4979 Don't hang up while I get a pen.
別掛電話，我去找支筆。

4980 Please wait. Let me get my pen.
請稍等，我去拿一下筆。

4981 Please tell Grace that I'll pick her up at 6:30 p.m. By the way, I don't have my mobile phone with me.
請轉告葛瑞絲，我晚上六點半會過去接她。還有就是，我今天沒有帶手機。

4982 Please tell Mr. Lee that I sent him an email ten minutes ago.
請轉告李先生，我十分鐘前寄了一封電子郵件給他。

4983 May I have him call you back? / Do you want him to return your call?
要請他回電給您嗎？

4984 Would you like Ms. Yang to **phone** you back?
要我請楊小姐回電嗎？ phone 動 打電話給…

4985 Do you want me to ask him to return your call when he's in?
他回來的時候，要我請他回電嗎？

4986 No, never mind. I'll call again this afternoon.
不用了，謝謝，我下午會再打給他。

4987 It's OK. I'll reach him some other time.
沒關係，我改天再找他。

4988 Don't **bother**. Thank you.
不用麻煩了，謝謝。bother 動 煩擾

4989 Just called to **say hello**.
只是打聲招呼而已。say hello 片 打招呼

4990 I can write him an email instead. Thank you, anyway.
我再寄電子郵件給他就可以了，不過還是謝謝你。

4991 What number should I write down?
請問您的電話號碼是幾號呢？

4992 Does she know your phone number?
她知道您的電話號碼嗎？

4993 Does she know how to **get in touch with** you?
她知道您的聯絡方式嗎？get in touch with 片 與…取得聯繫

4994 When should he call you back?
他應該何時回電給您呢？

4995 OK. I'll repeat it. Your name is William Baker. W-I-L-L-I-A-M, B-A-K-E-R.
好，我重複一次。您的名字是威廉．貝克，W-I-L-L-I-A-M B-A-K-E-R。

4996 I've got it all down. Let me **repeat** it to you.
我都寫下來了，讓我重複一次。repeat 動 重複

4997 I'll make sure Ms. Wang gets the message as soon as possible.
我會盡快轉告王小姐。

4998 I'll tell her that you are expecting her call.
我會告訴她，您在等她的電話。

4999 I'll tell him to call you back as soon as possible.
我會請他盡快回電給您。

5000 I'll let her know you called.
我會轉告她，您打過電話來。

5001 That would be nice. I'll be waiting for her call.
太好了，那我就等她回電給我。

5002 Hello, Helen, did you just call me?
嗨！海倫，你剛剛是不是有打給我？

5003 I am sorry I missed your call while I was in a meeting this morning.
抱歉，你今天早上打來時，我正在開會，所以沒接到電話。

5004 There's something wrong with this **connection**. May I call you back?
訊號有點問題，我可以重打一次嗎？ connection 名 連接

5005 The lines are **crossed**.
電話線受到干擾。 crossed 形 相互干擾的

5006 We have a bad connection. / The connection is bad.
收訊不良。

5007 I can't hear you very well.
我聽不太清楚。

5008 I can't quite **follow** you.
我聽不清楚你在說什麼。 follow 動 傾聽；聽懂

5009 Should I hang up? We've got a bad line here.
我應該先掛斷電話嗎？收訊不良。

5010 Hello? Hello? Can you hear me?
喂？喂？你聽得到嗎？

5011 Are you still there? / Are you still on the line?
你還在（線上）嗎？

5012 Are you having trouble hearing me?
你聽得見我的聲音嗎？

5013 I can't hear you at all. / I can't hear what you are saying.
我完全聽不到你說話。

5014 I'm having a **difficult** time hearing you.
我聽不清楚你在說什麼。 difficult 形 艱難的

5015 Is that your problem or mine? I really can't hear what you are saying.
是你的問題還是我的？我真的聽不到你在講什麼。

5016 I can't hear you very well. I'll call you back when I get home.
我聽不太清楚，我回到家再打給你。

5017 Do you hear the **echo**? Let me ring you back, OK?
你聽得到回音嗎？我再打一次，好嗎？ echo 名 回聲

5018 I am stepping into the **elevator**. May I call you later?
我要進電梯了，等一下再打給你可以嗎？ elevator 名 電梯

5019 I am on the **HSR** now. I'm not getting a **signal** here. I'll call you back later.
我在高鐵上，快要收不到訊號了，我晚點再打給你。
HSR 縮 高鐵(= High Speed Rail) signal 名 信號

5020 I'm on the elevator. If we get **cut off**, I'll call you back.
我在電梯裡，如果斷線了，我會再打給你。 cut off 片 中斷

5021 Please speak a little **louder**. / A little **louder**, please.
請講大聲一點。 loud 副 大聲地；響亮地

5022 Could you repeat what you just said?
能重複一次你剛剛說的話嗎？

5023 I'm sorry. I didn't **catch** that. What did you say?
抱歉，我沒聽清楚，你剛剛說什麼？ catch 動 理解；聽清楚

5024 Would you **slow down**, please?
可以請你講慢一點嗎？ slow down 片 減低速度

5025 Would you mind saying it over again?
你介意再說一次嗎？

5026 I just want to **make sure** I get the right information. Could you go over it again, please?
我只是想確認我剛剛聽到的資訊沒有錯誤，可以麻煩你從頭再講一次嗎？ make sure 片 確定

5027 What was the last part again?
最後的部份再說一次好嗎？

5028 Is this slow **enough**? / Am I speaking slowly **enough**?
這樣講得夠慢了嗎？ enough 副 足夠地

5029 Am I speaking loudly enough?
這樣說話夠大聲了嗎？

5030 Is that better?
這樣有好一點嗎？

5031 Much better. Thank you.
好多了，謝謝。

5032 Could you **speak up** a little? / Please speak a little louder.
你可以再大聲一點嗎？ speak up 片 大聲說

5033 Sorry about the **disconnection**. There are some problems with my phone.
抱歉剛剛斷線了，我的手機有點問題。 disconnection 名 切斷

5034 My **apologies**. I cut you off **by accident**.
對不起，我不小心切斷電話了。

apology 名 道歉 by accident 片 意外地

5035 We are breaking up. Could you repeat that?
剛剛斷線了，你可以再重講一次嗎？

5036 The **noise** is disturbing me. I can't **hear you clearly**.
有雜音干擾，我聽不清楚你在說什麼。
noise 名 噪音 hear sb. clearly 片 清楚聽見某人說話

5037 Your voice is too **low** to be heard.
你說話的聲音太小，我聽不見。 low 形 (量、度…等)少的

5038 I can **barely** hear you.
我幾乎聽不到你說話。 barely 副 幾乎沒有

5039 Where are you? It's **noisy** there.
你在哪裡？你那邊好吵。 noisy 形 嘈雜的

5040 Sorry, there's too much noise here. I'll call you back in three minutes.
抱歉，這裡太吵了，我三分鐘後再打給你。

5041 This is Mr. Ho's office. Not Mr. Hu's. You must have the wrong number.
這裡是何先生的辦公室，不是胡先生的，您打錯電話了。

5042 There's no one here by that **name**.
這裡沒有人叫那個名字。 name 名 姓名

5043 I beg you pardon? Ms. who?
對不起，您說哪位？

5044 I'm sorry, but I don't think I know that name.
抱歉，我不認識這個人。

5045 There's no one named Chris here.
這裡沒有叫克里斯的人。

5046 I'm sorry, but there's no engineer named Paul here.

抱歉，但這裡的工程師沒有叫保羅的。

5047 There isn't a Ms. Luo here, but there is one in the Finance Department.
我們這裡沒有羅小姐，但財務部有一位。

5048 Mr. Chen? I am sure there isn't a Mr. Chen in our department.
陳先生？我很確定我們部門沒有姓陳的先生。

5049 There are three Jacks here, but no Jack Lee.
這裡有三位叫傑克的人，但當中沒有姓李的。

5050 You must have the wrong number.
您一定是打錯電話了。

5051 I'm afraid you've **dialed** the wrong number.
您恐怕打錯電話了。dial 動 撥電話號碼

5052 This is extension 2105, not 2104. Do you want me to transfer your call?
這裡是分機 2105，不是 2104，需要我幫您轉接嗎？

5053 I'm sorry. I dialed the wrong number.
對不起，我打錯電話了。

5054 Sorry, I made a **mistake**.
抱歉，我打錯了。mistake 名 過失

5055 Sorry. Wrong number.
抱歉，打錯電話了。

5056 Is this 769-8796?
這支電話是 769-8796 嗎？

5057 No, this is 767-8796.
不，這裡的號碼是 767-8796。

5058 What number are you trying to dial?
請問你要撥打的是哪一支號碼呢？

5059 May I ask what number you are dialing?
請問一下你撥的是幾號呢？

5060 It's 555-1243. Isn't it?
我撥的是 555-1243，不是嗎？

5061 Yes, it is. But there is no one by that name here.
你撥的號碼沒錯，但這裡沒有人叫那個名字。

5062 I might have copied it down **incorrectly**, sorry.
抱歉，我可能抄錯號碼了。 incorrectly 副 錯誤地

5063 Will you check the number again, please?
請你再核對一下電話號碼，好嗎？

5064 I am afraid that the number has been changed.
恐怕這支號碼已經換了。

5065 I suggest you **look** it **up** in the phone book.
我建議你查一下電話簿。 look up 片 查詢

5066 Oh! I am sorry. Wrong number again.
真的很抱歉！我又打錯了。

5067 I am sorry to have disturbed you.
抱歉，打擾了。

5068 Thank you for calling 764-2222. No one can answer the phone right now. Please leave a message after the **tone**.
這裡是 764-2222，謝謝您的來電。目前沒有人可以接聽電話，請在聲響後留言。 tone 名 聲調

5069 Hello, you've reached the Smile **Dental** Office. Our **office hours** are 9 a.m. to 4 p.m. from Monday to Saturday. Please call back during our **office hours**.
您好，這裡是微笑牙科診所。我們的上班時間是週一至週六的上午九點到下午四點。請於上班時間再來電。
dental 形 牙科的　office hours 片 上班時間

5070 Hi, this is Hu's Law Firm. We're closed at this moment. Please call back during our office hours, which are from 9 a.m. to 5 p.m. Thank you.
你好，這裡是胡律師事務所。現在是下班時間，請於上午九點至下午五點的上班時間再來電，謝謝。

5071 Thanks for calling CC Electronics. All our representatives are not available right now. Your call is important to us. Please do not hang up, and our representative will be right with you.
這裡是 CC 電子公司，感謝您的來電，目前所有的服務人員都無法接聽電話。您的來電對我們十分重要，請不要掛斷，服務人員會立即為您服務。

5072 You've reached ABC Company. Please feel free to leave a message.
這裡是 ABC 公司，歡迎留言。

5073 This is Hannah Mills calling. Please call me as soon as possible.
我是漢娜．米爾斯，請盡快與我聯絡。

5074 Hi, it's Linda. I know you're busy, but I have some great news for you. Call me.
嗨，我是琳達，我知道你在忙，但我有一個好消息要告訴你，打給我吧。

5075 It's me, Patrick. Call me back at 807-2083.
是我，派翠克啦！回電給我吧，號碼是 807-2083。

5076 Hello, Jimmy. I just want to tell you I've changed my cell phone number. It's 0920-881-100. Oh, this is Anna.
嗨，吉米，我只是要告訴你，我換新手機了，號碼是 0920-881-100。對了，我是安娜啦。

通知！準備開會囉
At The Meeting

5077 The annual meeting is going to be held next month.
下個月要開年度會議。

5078 I've gotten **notice** of the **board** meeting.
我已經收到要開董事會的通知了。 notice 名 通知 board 名 董事會

5079 We have a **progress** review once a month.
我們每個月開一次會，檢討工作進度。 progress 名 進展

5080 The sales meeting has been postponed to next week.
業務會議延到下週了。

5081 Rick called a meeting for 6 a.m.; I wonder what he **has in mind**.
瑞克要在清晨六點召開會議，真不知道他在想什麼。
have sth. in mind 片 思考某事

5082 The manager wants to meet us in five minutes.
經理五分鐘後要找我們開會。

5083 I heard that it's a **crisis** meeting.
我聽說這是危機處理會議。 crisis 名 危機

5084 Is everything going well for the **staff** meeting?
員工會議都準備得差不多了嗎？ staff 名 員工

5085 Who are the **participants**?
與會者有哪些人呢？ participant 名 參與者

5086 What issues are going to be discussed?
要討論哪些議題呢？

5087 Before the meeting, the most important thing is to confirm the **agenda**.
開會之前，最重要的是得先確定好議程。 agenda 名 議程

5088 When will the **final** schedule be ready?
最終的議程何時會確定呢？ final 形 最終的

5089 I'd like to set the meeting schedule as soon as possible.
我想要盡快擬好議程。

5090 I'll try to **finalize** all the details.
我會設法把所有的細節定案。 finalize 動 完成

5091 We're looking for a **conference room** with multi-media facilities.
我們在找有多媒體設備的會議室。 conference room 片 會議室

5092 All the **audio-visual aids** should be ready in advance.
所有的視聽設備都要事先準備好。
audio-visual 形 視聽的 aid 名 輔助物

5093 Please check the **venue**, making sure the conference room will be available.
請確定一下場地，確保到時候會議室可以用。 venue 名 發生地

5094 How long do you **anticipate** the meeting will take?
這個會議預計會開多久？ anticipate 動 預期

5095 Will every participant be **announced**?
已經通知每一位成員了嗎？ announce 動 通知

5096 I've emailed the meeting notice.
我已經寄電子郵件通知大家開會的事情了。

5097 Everyone has been told.
已經通知大家了。

5098 How about the **presenters**? Have you confirmed

with them?
要報告的人呢？你有跟他們確認了嗎？ presenter 動 提出者

5099 I have confirmed with each of them **individually**.
我已經個別跟他們確認過了。 individually 副 逐個地

5100 Let's go over the conference schedule.
我們把議程從頭到尾看一遍吧。

5101 We should start with the **opening remarks**.
會議一開始，先進行開場的致詞。
opening 名 開始 remark 名 評論

5102 After the **presentation**, we are going to have a coffee break.
報告結束之後，會有一個中場休息時間。 presentation 名 表現

5103 After group discussion, let's have a **lunch break**.
小組討論之後，是午休時間。 lunch break 片 午休時間

5104 What's the first **item** on the agenda?
議程的第一個討論項目是什麼？ item 名 項目

5105 Who is the **chairperson**?
誰擔任會議主席呢？ chairperson 名 主席

5106 Mr. Chang is the most suitable person to be the **chair**.
張先生是最適合的主席人選。 chair 名 主席

5107 One of the chair's responsibilities is to keep things moving during the conference.
主席的任務之一是使會議順利進行。

5108 The chairperson should be a good timekeeper, too.
會議的主席也必須懂得掌控時間。

5109 Ms. Lin will be taking **minutes**.
林小姐會擔任會議紀錄。 minute 名 會議紀錄

5110 Shall we **begin** the meeting?
會議要開始了嗎？ begin 動 開始

5111 There are still some **latecomers**.
還有一些人還沒到。 latecomer 名 遲到者

5112 Should we wait for the latecomers?
要等遲到的人嗎？

5113 It's about time we **got started**.
我們該開始開會了。 get started 片 開始

5114 Mark, would you please open the discussion?
馬克，可以請你為討論做開場白嗎？

5115 It's my **honor** to **invite** Mr. Hill to open the discussion.
我們很榮幸邀請到希爾先生為我們今天的討論做開場。
honor 名 榮譽 invite 動 邀請

5116 To avoid wasting time, I plan to **stick to the point**.
為了避免浪費時間，我希望可以直接切入重點。
stick to the point 片 切入重點

5117 Does everybody have an agenda?
大家都有拿到議程表嗎？

5118 I believe that each of you has a **copy**.
大家應該都拿有到資料吧？ copy 名 複製品

5119 There are three main points on the agenda.
議程上要討論的主要項目有三點。

5120 We must **face** three issues.
我們必須討論三項議題。 face 動 面臨

5121 Why don't we **get down to** business?
我們進入正題吧。 get down to 片 開始做某事

5122 Let me bring your **attention** to what I see as the main issues.
我們先來談談我個人認為最重要的幾項議題。attention 名 注意力

5123 I'd like all of you to **brainstorm** about the issue.
關於這個議題，我想請大家集思廣益一下。brainstorm 動 集思廣益

5124 Let's put our heads together to solve the problem.
大家集思廣益一下，來解決問題吧。

5125 Please tell us what you think. / Please give us your **views**.
請告訴我們你的想法。view 名 看法

5126 I'd like to hear your input.
我想聽聽大家的意見。

5127 Let's **proceed** to the next item. / Let's **move on**.
讓我們進入下個議題。proceed 動 繼續進行 move on 片 繼續前進

5128 We should have a meeting about the **project** this weekend.
我們這個週末應該要針對這個企劃案開個會。project 名 企劃案

5129 We need to discuss our sales plan for next **quarter**.
我們需要討論下一季的銷售計畫。quarter 名 季度

5130 If we can communicate **effectively**, we can **iron** the problem **out**.
如果我們能有效溝通，問題就能解決了。
effectively 副 有效地 iron out 片 消除

5131 What's your **standpoint** on this issue?
對於這個議題，你的立場為何？standpoint 名 觀點

5132 I am in **complete agreement**. / I agree with you. / I couldn't agree more.
我完全同意。complete 形 完全的 agreement 名 同意

5133 That sounds like a good idea.
聽起來是個好主意。

5134 That's what I am thinking, too.
我也是這麼想的。

5135 We are **on the same page**.
我們都有共識。 on the same page 片 有共識

5136 What you said was very **productive**.
你所說的很有建設性。 productive 形 富有成效的

5137 I will stand behind you **without a doubt**.
我絕對會毫不猶豫地支持你。 without a doubt 片 毫不猶豫地

5138 I don't really agree with what you said. / I am afraid I can't accept your idea.
我不怎麼同意你的看法。

5139 That's not true.
事實並非如此。

5140 I hate to say this, but I really think you are wrong.
我實在不想這麼說，但我認為你的觀點錯了。

5141 Do not try to **distort** what I said.
不要曲解我的意思。 distort 動 扭曲

5142 It's situation-related rather than person-related.
這是對事不對人。

5143 That is your **bias**.
那是你的偏見。 bias 名 偏見

5144 Are you **challenging** me?
你是在質疑我的意見嗎？ challenge 動 懷疑；反對

5145 I don't think I can **go along with** you there.
我想我無法再跟你討論下去了。 go along with 片 與…意見一致

5146 Sorry for **interrupting**.

很抱歉，打擾一下。 interrupt 動 打斷

5147 May I come in here? / **Allow** me to say something, please.
我可以加入討論嗎？ allow 動 允許

5148 I am sorry, but I didn't hear you.
很抱歉，我剛剛沒聽清楚。

5149 Could you use the **microphone**?
你可以用麥克風講嗎？ microphone 名 麥克風

5150 Could you go over what you just said?
你可以把剛剛說的再講一遍嗎？

5151 What exactly do you mean by that?
你剛剛講的到底是什麼意思？

5152 I **understand** what you're saying, but the suggestion doesn't seem very suitable.
我了解你所說的，但這個建議似乎不太適當。 understand 動 理解

5153 I know what you meant, but could we discuss this issue later?
我懂你的意思，我們可以晚一點再討論這件事嗎？

5154 Sorry to interrupt you, but we really should move on to the next issue.
很抱歉，打斷你的發言，但我們必須討論下一個議題了。

5155 We're running late, so I'd like to move on to the main points of the meeting.
因為時間不太夠了，所以我想進入本次會議的重點。

5156 I am afraid it is **out of the question**. Let's get back on topic.
這恐怕離題了，我們還是回到正題吧。
out of the question 片 離題的

5157 I am afraid we're running out of time.
我們恐怕快沒有時間了。

5158 We will have to stop in fifteen minutes.
再十五分鐘，我們就得結束了。

5159 I am going to **sum up** and close the meeting.
讓我來做個總結，就結束會議吧。sum up 片 總結

5160 I'll ask the **executive** department to **follow up** on that.
我會請行政部門對這件事做後續追蹤。
executive 形 行政上的 follow up 片 採取進一步行動

5161 I will **forward** the final decision to all the departments by this Friday.
我會在本週五之前將最終決議轉寄給所有部門。forward 動 轉寄

5162 Any **feedback**?
有什麼意見嗎？feedback 名 反饋

5163 Can we all agree on this?
大家都同意吧？

5164 I appreciate the feedback.
謝謝大家的意見。

5165 We can **draw** the meeting to a close if everybody agrees.
如果各位都同意的話，會議就到此為止。draw 動 作出

5166 Let's **call it a day**.
今天就到此為止吧。call it a day 片 到此為止

5167 I will let you know the final decision next Monday.
我下週一會告訴你最後的決議為何。

5168 How do you feel about the meeting?
你覺得這場會議怎麼樣？

5169 I thought it was very productive.
我覺得很不錯，很有收穫。

5170 These conferences are great for business.
這些會議對生意很有幫助。

5171 We had some **effective** discussions in the conference.
會議中，我們有一些很有成效的討論。 effective 形 有效的

5172 Both **sides** reached an agreement in the meeting.
雙方在會議中達成共識。 side 名 一方；一派

5173 We've reached an agreement that is good for both sides.
我們達成對雙方都有利的協議。

5174 You bet. We have **benefited** from this one.
的確，這次的會議，我們獲益不少。 benefit 動 得益；受惠

5175 Mr. Chen and I have some **disagreements**.
陳先生和我的意見不同。 disagreement 名 爭論

5176 I thought it was a complete **waste** of time.
我覺得這場會議根本就是在浪費時間。 waste 名 浪費

UNIT 6 準備簡報&臨場表現
Giving A Presentation

5177 I'm going to give a presentation tomorrow.
我明天要上台做簡報。

5178 What's the **purpose** of the **event**?
是什麼場合啊？ purpose 名 目的 event 名 事件

5179 It's a product **launch** presentation.

是一個產品的發表會。 launch 名 發行

5180 Marian is an **expert** at giving presentations.
瑪莉安是口頭簡報的專家。 expert 名 專家

5181 She has some tips for a successful presentation.
她有一些讓簡報成功的技巧。

5182 What makes a good presentation?
好的簡報應該具備哪些條件呢？

5183 Be confident and look confident.
對自己要有信心，而且要讓這股自信散發出來。

5184 Before you even **open up** PowerPoint, **sit down** and really think about your presentation.
在製作簡報的 PPT 之前，先坐下來，好好思考一下你要做的簡報內容。 open up 片 開啟 sit down 片 坐下

5185 How much time do you have to speak?
你的簡報時間多長呢？

5186 You have to think about who your **audience** is.
你必須考慮聽眾包含哪些人。 audience 名 觀眾

5187 How much does your audience know about the **subject**?
聽眾對於你要講的主題了解多少？ subject 名 主題

5188 Don't waste time telling your audience what they already know.
對於聽眾已經知道的事，就不要再浪費時間贅述。

5189 Good presentations depend on **solid content** and great delivery.
成功的簡報取決於完整的內容以及巧妙的表達。
solid 形 充實的 content 名 內容

5190 You can **draw up** a draft and **rehearse** it.
你可以先擬草稿，再練講。 draw up 片 起草 rehearse 動 排練

5191 What should I do if I lose my whole **speech**?
如果我整份演講稿都不見了，該怎麼辦？ speech 名 演講

5192 Relax! Just wing it.
放輕鬆！就即興演講，自由發揮囉。

5193 After that, let's talk about making your **slides**.
接下來，我們來談一下如何製作簡報吧！ slide 名 投影片

5194 Are there any tips when making my slides?
在製作投影片時，有沒有什麼技巧呢？

5195 I would say that **choice** of color is the most important thing.
要我說的話，選顏色是最重要的。 choice 名 選擇

5196 The right color can help **persuade** and **motivate** the audience.
選對顏色，能提高說服力，並激發聽眾聆聽的意願。
persuade 動 說服 motivate 動 刺激

5197 Some **animation** is a good thing, but stick to the most professional **type**.
加一些動畫效果是不錯，不過切記，形式還是必須專業。
animation 名 動畫 type 名 形式

5198 Use the same **font** set throughout your **entire** slide presentation.
整份簡報都要使用相同的字型。 font 名 字型 entire 形 整個的

5199 A good presenter should use the visuals **properly**.
好的提報者會懂得運用視覺效果。 properly 副 恰當地

5200 Professional supporting visuals can help your presentation be successful.
專業的視覺輔助能讓你的簡報更成功。

5201 Visuals help me to deliver my talk.
視覺效果可為我的簡報加分。

5202 Don't use too many visuals.
但也不要使用太多的視覺效果。

5203 Make sure your slides are in the correct **order**.
要確認投影片的順序無誤。order 名 順序

5204 Be passionate about your **topic** and be confident.
要對你要講的主題充滿熱忱，而且要有自信。topic 名 主題

5205 Make the **first impression powerful**.
要給人強而有力的第一印象。
first impression 片 第一印象 powerful 形 強而有力的

5206 The first two to three minutes are the most important.
一開始的前兩三分鐘往往是最重要的。

5207 A strong speech opening can **definitely capture** the audience's attention.
強而有力的開場白絕對能吸引聽眾的注意。
definitely 副 肯定地 capture 動 奪得

5208 Try to **memorize** the first five **sentences** of your speech.
試著把講稿的前五句話背起來。
memorize 動 記住 sentence 名 句子

5209 Get closer to your audience and make a connection.
離你的聽眾近一點，和他們互動。

5210 Don't forget to face your audience; don't turn your back on the audience.
記得要面對觀眾，不要背對他們。

5211 **Avoid** reading directly from the slides.
避免看著投影片內容一字不漏地照念。avoid 動 避免

5212 I'm here to make a presentation about a **cutting-**

edge product.
我今天要介紹一個劃時代的產品。 cutting-edge 形 最前衛的

5213 I've divided my presentation into three parts.
我的簡報分為三部份。

5214 First of all, I'd like to **outline** the main points of my talk.
首先，我先介紹一下今天演講的綱要。 outline 動 略述

5215 I'll be happy to answer questions at the end of my presentation.
演講結束之後，我會很樂意回答各位的問題。

5216 Let's look at this **graph**. / Have a look at the **diagram**. / Just have a look at our chart for a moment.
我們來看一下這張圖表。 graph 名 圖表 diagram 名 曲線圖

5217 I'd like you to have a look at the **table**.
請大家看一下這個表格。 table 名 表格

5218 As you can see, the **chart** shows our growth.
從這個圖表可以看出我們的成長。 chart 名 圖表

5219 The graph shows our profits for the past six months.
從這張圖可以看出我們過去半年的獲利。

5220 If you look at it more closely, you'll notice a surprising **development**.
仔細看的話，就會注意到令人驚喜的進展。 development 名 進展

5221 This line graph shows that the price is **skyrocketing**.
從這張曲線圖可以看出，價格正在飆漲。 skyrocket 動 猛漲

5222 We can easily see the sales **figures** through the **bar** chart.
從這張柱狀圖就看得出銷售數據。 figure 名 數字 bar 名 條

5223 Before I go on to the next part of my presentation, are there any questions on what I've presented **so far**?
在我進入下一個部分之前，對我目前為止的報告，各位有什麼問題嗎？ so far 片 目前為止

5224 I'm now nearing the end of my presentation.
我的簡報已經接近尾聲了。

5225 Let me sum up the important points.
我來總結一下重點吧。

5226 I'd like to **recap** what I just said.
我扼要地重述一下剛才所提到的重點。 recap 動 重述要點

5227 If there are no other questions, perhaps we should **wrap** it **up** here.
如果沒有問題的話，我們就到此結束吧。 wrap up 動 結束

5228 I am sorry; I don't quite get your question. Could you please go through that again?
抱歉，我不太了解你的問題，可以再說一次嗎？

5229 I am **glad** you asked that.
很高興你的提問。 glad 形 高興的

5230 I think I answered that question earlier.
這個問題我之前似乎已經回答過了。

5231 I am afraid I'm not able to answer that question **at present**.
我目前恐怕無法回答你的問題。 at present 片 現在

5232 I'll have to look over the figures before I can give you an answer.
我得先看過數據，才能回答你。

5233 If you could leave me your email address, I'll try to get back to you.
你是否能留下你的電子郵件帳號？我會再回覆你。

5234 If you don't mind waiting, I'd prefer to answer your question later on.
如果你能等的話，我可以之後再回答你的問題嗎？

5235 That's the end of my talk. Thank you all for your attention.
我的報告到此結束，謝謝各位的參與。

5236 Thank you for listening.
謝謝各位的聆聽。

5237 I'm afraid we've run out of time. I think it's a good place to stop.
已經超過時間了，就到此結束吧。

UNIT 7 商務往來 & 收單
All About Business

5238 We are going to have a customer-supplier **negotiation** tomorrow.
我們明天將有一個客戶對供應商的洽談。 negotiation 名 協商

5239 I really need to talk about it with my client.
我實在必須和客戶討論一下。

5240 Negotiations are usually difficult and **tiring**.
協商通常既困難又累人。 tiring 形 令人感到疲倦的

5241 We need a **skillful negotiator**.
我們需要一個有技巧的協商者。
skillful 形 熟練的 negotiator 名 交涉者

5242 We'd better prepare and plan well before negotiations.

我們最好在協商前先擬好計畫。

5243 If possible, I prefer to meet on my own **ground**.
如果可以的話，我希望能在我們這裡進行協商。 ground 名 場所

5244 How about 3 p.m. in my office? I will arrange this meeting.
下午三點在我的辦公室怎麼樣？我會安排這次的會議。

5245 It'd be better if we met on **neutral** ground, like in a hotel **meeting room**.
在中立的場所談會比較好，比如在飯店的會議室。
neutral 形 中立的 meeting room 片 會議室

5246 We need those items **urgently**. If we can talk face-to-face, it would **expedite** the process.
我們急需這些產品。如果能面對面談的話，進度會快一點。
urgently 副 急迫地 expedite 動 迅速執行

5247 I'm glad you could meet with me today to discuss the details of your order.
真高興我們今天能見面，討論你們訂單中的細節。

5248 I'm interested in a couple of items in your new **catalogue**.
我對你們新目錄裡的幾項產品感興趣。 catalogue 名 目錄

5249 We would like to make an **inquiry**.
我們想要詢問一些事情。 inquiry 名 詢問

5250 Could you **quote** it in U.S. dollars, please?
可以麻煩你用美元報價嗎？ quote 動 報價

5251 If you can give me an idea of the **quantity**, I can quote you a more **accurate** price.
如果能告訴我大約的訂購數量，我就能提供更精確的報價。
quantity 名 數量 accurate 形 精確的

5252 Would you please **take a look at** our brochures? If you have any **preferences**, just let me know.
請參考一下我們的冊子，如果你有任何喜歡的產品，請告訴我。

take a look at 片 看一看 preference 名 偏好

5253 I have received your full catalogue. I'm very interested in your products.
我已經收到貴公司所提供的完整目錄，我對貴公司的產品非常感興趣。

5254 We'd like to know your lowest **quotations** for air conditioners.
我們想要知道貴公司冷氣機的最低報價。quotation 名 報價

5255 We would like to know the price **exclusive** of tax of your **tablet**.
我們想了解一下，貴公司平板電腦不含稅的價格是多少。
exclusive 形 除外的；排外的 tablet 名 平板電腦

5256 Please quote us your best offer based on FOB Taiwan as well as CIF Japan.
請以 FOB 台灣和 CIF 日本為條件，提供報價。

5257 Will you please send us a copy of the catalogue, with details of the prices and **terms** of payment?
請寄一份目錄給我們，並註明價格及付款條件。term 名 條件

5258 Certainly. I can fax or email the information to you this afternoon.
沒問題，我可以在今天下午把資料傳真或用電子郵件寄給你。

5259 We have received your **enquiry** and will give you a quotation soon.
我們已收到你們的詢價，將盡快報價給貴公司。enquiry 名 詢問

5260 We would love to quote you a price on our **vacuum cleaners**.
我們很樂意提供吸塵器的報價。
vacuum 名 真空 cleaner 名 吸塵器

5261 I will send you a copy of our price list as soon as possible.
我會盡快把價格清單寄給你。

5262 All prices are **subject to** change without notice.
所有的價格隨時會變動，恕不另行通知。 subject to 片 依照

5263 We hope you will be **satisfied** with our samples and quotations.
希望貴公司能對我們的樣品和報價感到滿意。
satisfied 形 感到滿意的

5264 What if we place an order? Would we still have to pay the sample **charge**?
如果我們有下訂單呢？這樣還需要付樣品費嗎？ charge 名 費用

5265 If you receive the sample and then later decide to **place an order**, the sample charge will be **deducted** from the cost of the order.
如果你們在收到樣品後決定下單，樣品費會從訂單的貨款裡扣除。
place an order 片 下訂單 deduct 動 扣除

5266 I'm afraid that the price is **beyond** my budget.
這個價格恐怕已經超出我的預算了。 beyond 介 (指範圍)超出

5267 Is that the best price you can do for me?
這是你能給我的最低價格嗎？

5268 I'd still like to see something a little **cheaper**.
我想看便宜一點的產品。 cheap 形 便宜的

5269 I just received your price for the product. Your price is too **high**.
我剛收到產品的報價，那個價格太高了。 high 形 昂貴的

5270 The price you quoted me before was 26 U.S. dollars.
之前你跟我報的價是二十六美元。

5271 I'm afraid it's higher than we expected. How can I get a discount?
價格比我們預期的高，我要如何才能享有折扣呢？

5272 Really? We think the offer is very **fair**.

是嗎？我們認為這個報價很合理。 fair 形 公正的

5273 Our price is **competitive**, and I hope that we can **establish** a relationship.
我們的價格極具競爭力，希望能與貴公司建立合作關係。
competitive 形 競爭的　establish 動 建立

5274 Could we get a bigger discount with future orders?
如果我們續訂的話，折扣可以再多一點嗎？

5275 Would it be possible for you to **lower** the price a little if we order more?
如果我們訂多一點，價格有可能再壓低嗎？ lower 動 降低

5276 What quantities are you looking for?
你們要訂多大的量呢？

5277 We were thinking about thirty thousand **units**.
我們打算訂三萬件。 unit 名 一個

5278 Larger customers get the larger discounts.
訂單量愈大的客戶，享有的折扣愈多。

5279 Could you **double** your order? I can give you more discounts.
您能將訂單加倍嗎？我可以給你更多折扣。 double 動 使加倍

5280 We may offer you an extra 10% off if you buy more.
如果買多一點，我們可以再給你們百分之十的折扣。

5281 I think we can **reduce** the price if you can increase the quantity.
如果你能提高訂購數量，我們就可以降價。 reduce 動 減少

5282 It would be to your **advantage** to sign the contract now because the price will **go up** next month.
現在簽約對你們有利，因為下個月就要漲價了。
advantage 名 利益；有利條件　go up 片 漲價

5283 The price you offered is **out of line** with the market.
你們的報價不符合市場現況。out of line 片 與…不一致

5284 The price we quoted is the lowest and will **likely rise** soon.
我們提供的已經是最低報價了，不久價格就會回升的。
likely 副 很可能 rise 動 上漲

5285 I am afraid your price is **above** our **limit**.
你們的價格恐怕超出了我們的上限。above 介 超過 limit 名 極限

5286 With the **exception** of the high price, it is really a good product.
除了價格太高以外，這個產品真的不錯。exception 名 除外

5287 Is it possible to **shave** a little **off** the price?
有沒有可能降一點價格？shave off 片 削去

5288 I think we could agree to that.
我想應該是可以的。

5289 By how much could you bring down the price?
你們能降價多少呢？

5290 It's the best we can do. Ten percent is our **bottom line**.
最多只能這樣，百分之十是我們的底線了。bottom line 片 底線

5291 We don't think we can cut our price to the **extent** you **request**.
我們無法把價格降到你們提出的限度。
extent 名 程度 request 動 要求

5292 I can't make a profit at that price. I don't think that's acceptable.
那樣的價錢沒有利潤可言，我沒有辦法接受。

5293 If you can make the price a little lower, we shall probably be able to place an order.

如果你能再降一點價格，我們就有可能下單。

5294 We might conclude a deal should you **knock** the price **down** a little.
如果價錢再低一點，就有可能成交。knock down 片 降低

5295 If you pay in cash, I can offer you a 15-percent discount.
如果你付現的話，我可以打八五折給你。

5296 If you book a further order, we have more **room** to bring down the price.
如果之後有續訂，就比較有議價的空間。room 名 空間

5297 That sounds more like what I had in mind, but I'll have to check with my office first.
這聽起來比較接近我原本預估的價格，但我還是必須先跟公司確定一下。

5298 Would you please tell us your final decision within seven days?
能請你於七天內讓我們知道最後的決定嗎？

5299 I think we're in business! I'll get back to you after I've reviewed the details.
就這麼說定了！等我把詳細資料看完之後，再給你答覆。

5300 But what are the terms of your payment?
不過你們的付款方式是怎樣的呢？

5301 Our payment terms are very flexible. We offer financing as well.
我們的付款方式非常有彈性，還有提供融資服務。

5302 The only requirement is an advance payment of twenty-five percent before delivery.
唯一的要求就是必須在交貨前，先付百分之二十五的預付款。

5303 When is the **balance** due?
那什麼時候要付清餘款？balance 名 結餘

5304 **Upon installation** of the equipment, for the cash option.
如果是付現，設備一裝好就要付清。
upon 介 在…之後就立即 installation 名 設置

5305 You pay the advance, and the balance must be **paid off** within twelve months.
先付預付款，餘款則須於十二個月之內付清。 pay off 片 償清債務

5306 We would also accept a **certified check** or a direct bank **remittance**.
我們也接受保付支票或直接由銀行匯款。
certified 形 有保證的 check 名 支票 remittance 名 匯款

5307 Could we place the delivery order for more than one **shipment**?
出貨單上的物品可以分批出貨嗎？ shipment 名 裝載的貨物

5308 Well, if you sign a confirmed-purchase order for the entire amount.
這樣的話，你們就必須簽訂一張訂購單，確認訂購總數。

5309 Once we receive your purchase order, we'll confirm the delivery dates quickly.
一收到訂購單，我們就會盡快確認交貨日期。

5310 Once the order is confirmed, we need you to give us 10-days' notice ahead of your order.
訂單經確認後，請於下單前十天通知我們。

5311 What payment terms will you accept?
你們的付款條件是？

5312 Could you pay it in a week?
您可以於一週後付款嗎？

5313 The payment term is Net 10. Could I pay Net 30?
付款條件是貨到十日付款，我可以貨到三十日才付款嗎？

5314 If you offer more flexible payment conditions,

then we will accept it.
如果付款條件能更有彈性一點，我們就會接受。

5315 Could you provide good **technical** support?
你們能提供技術支援嗎？technical 形 技術的

5316 We've settled the terms for the contract **in general**, and we are prepared to place an order.
合約條款大致上都已談妥，接著就要準備下訂單了。
in general 片 通常

5317 We still need to discuss the **specs** and the quantity of our order.
我們還需要討論一下所訂商品的規格和數量。
spec 名 規格(= specification)

5318 We are going to make an order.
我們打算下訂單。

5319 We are ready to place an order.
我們準備下訂單。

5320 We have decided to place an order for the products.
我們決定要訂購這些產品。

5321 Well, which **model** do you want to order?
那麼，你們要訂哪一型呢？model 名 型號

5322 Throw out a number!
開個價吧！

5323 We'll deliver the shipment on the **assigned** date.
我們會在指定日期送貨。assign 動 指定

5324 We **guarantee prompt** delivery.
我們保證會立即交貨。guarantee 動 擔保 prompt 形 迅速的

5325 Shipment will be late due to the **typhoon**.
因為颱風的關係，送貨會延遲。typhoon 名 颱風

5326 It will take at least fourteen days for delivery.
至少要十四天才能交貨。

5327 Our **factory** is **booked up** for the next season.
我們工廠下一季的訂單已經滿了。
factory 名 工廠　book up 片 把…預訂一空

5328 Maintaining the quality of our products has always been our top priority.
維持產品的品質一直以來都是我們的優先考量。

5329 No more orders, please, because our **inventory** is running a little low.
不要再接訂單了，因為我們的存貨有些不足。 inventory 名 存貨

5330 We will absolutely offer you free delivery if you can place the order now.
如果你們現在下單的話，我們會提供免運費的服務。

5331 It's a **deal**. I am glad we've got the **deal** done.
就這麼說定了，很高興我們能達成協議。 deal 名 交易

5332 I've asked the company **lawyer** to draw up the contract.
我已經請公司的律師擬合約了。 lawyer 名 律師

5333 All details are shown in the sales contract.
所有的細節都列在買賣契約上。

5334 I hope we can **commit** to a two-year contract.
我希望我們可以簽兩年合約。 commit 動 使表態

5335 I will hand you the contract **in person**.
我會親自將合約送到你手上。 in person 片 親自

5336 Do you agree to the terms of the contract?
合約上的交易條款與條件，您都同意嗎？

5337 I will get my lawyer to check it.
我會請我的律師看一下。

5338 Our **attorney** has read the contract.
我們的律師已經看過這份合約了。 attorney 名 (美)律師

5339 He doesn't agree with some terms and conditions.
針對某幾項條款和條件，他有不同的意見。

5340 We've **revised** it as you have asked for.
我們已經按照您所要求的做修正了。 revise 動 修改

5341 It's time to sign the contract. Please sign on the **dotted line**.
現在該簽訂合約了，請於虛線處簽名。 dotted line 片 虛線

5342 I hope we can do more business together in the future.
希望日後還有機會與你們做生意。

5343 We always enjoy doing business with your company.
與貴公司的合作一直以來都相當愉快。

5344 We will place more large orders if we are satisfied with this order.
如果我們滿意這次的訂購，往後會向貴公司下更多大筆訂單。

5345 We've **bargained** for an hour and finally got a good deal.
我們議價了一個小時，總算談到一個好價格。 bargain 動 討價還價

5346 Sometimes, it is necessary to make a **concession**.
有時候，讓步是必須的。 concession 名 讓步

5347 We've just had a successful negotiation.
我們的協商很成功。

5348 We've reached a win-win **solution**.
我們達到雙贏的局面。 solution 名 解決辦法

5349 We finally have reached a **mutual** agreement.
我們終於有共識了。mutual 形 相互的

5350 How are **promotions determined**?
升遷是如何決定的呢？promotion 名 升遷 determine 動 決定

5351 We determine promotions based on performance.
我們會依工作表現決定是否替員工升遷。

5352 I got promoted last month.
我上個月升官了。

5353 Our company announced yesterday that Mr. Lin has been promoted to general manager.
公司昨天宣布，林先生被升為總經理。

5354 He deserves it more than anyone I know.
在我認識的人當中，他是最值得被升的。

5355 I know that he will **go far**.
我就知道他一定會成功的。go far 片 有成就

5356 He worked his way up to the top.
他盡一切努力往上爬。

5357 We've **run into** a couple of problems at the main factory.
我們主要的工廠出了一些問題。run into 片 陷入

5358 I didn't notice anything out of the **ordinary**.
我一點都沒察覺到異狀。ordinary 名 普通

5359 What **sort** of problems are you facing?
你們碰到什麼樣的問題呢？ sort 名 類型

5360 The company recently had some problem with their **labor union**.
這家公司的工會最近出了一些問題。 labor 名 勞方 union 名 協會

5361 The workers are **upset** about the working conditions in the factory.
員工對工廠的工作環境很不滿。 upset 形 苦惱的

5362 The workers are **demanding** a 10% pay raise because they have to work in an **unsafe** environment.
因為要在不安全的環境中工作，所以工人們要求加薪百分之十。
demand 動 要求；請求 unsafe 形 危險的

5363 If something isn't done soon, I'm sure we'll have a **strike on our hands**.
如果不處理的話，一定會引起罷工。
strike 名 罷工 on one's hands 片 對…負責

5364 All the workers may **go on strike**.
工人可能會全體罷工。 go on strike 片 罷工

5365 We'd better do **whatever** we can to avoid the problem.
我們最好設法解決問題。 whatever 代 不管什麼

5366 A number of firms have been **downsizing** due to the financial **storm**.
因為金融風暴的關係，有幾家公司最近正在裁員縮編。
downsize 動 裁減人數 storm 名 風暴

5367 The **boom** in the industry **came to an end** last year. Now, it's hard times.
業界的好景氣只到去年為止，現在很不景氣。
boom 名 繁榮 come to an end 片 結束

5368 I heard our company is going to **lay off** twenty percent of the office staff.

聽說公司準備要裁掉百分之二十的員工。lay off 片 解雇

5369 **Administration** will be the first department to be hit.
行政部門是第一個面臨裁員的部門。administration 名 管理部門

5370 All the staff in the administrative department are so **anxious** about that.
行政部門的所有員工都很擔心這件事。anxious 形 焦慮的

5371 Many employees have taken long periods of leave without pay.
許多員工都休了很長的無薪假。

5372 Benson is on unpaid leave.
班森目前留職停薪。

5373 Downsizing could reduce our **operating** costs.
裁員可以降低營運成本。operating 形 營運的

5374 The company has reorganized and **restructured**.
公司內部已經重整改組了。restructure 動 改組

5375 We don't need too many employees, but we want productive ones.
員工不需要太多，我們只需要有生產力的。

5376 They needed to **narrow** their focus to stay competitive.
他們需要把重心放在「維持競爭力」這件事情上。narrow 動 縮小

5377 We are afraid our company will downsize.
我擔心我們公司會縮編。

5378 Our company is downsizing and we have to lay off some employees.
我們公司正在縮編，所以必須資遣部分員工。

5379 We did this to reduce costs.
這麼做是為了要降低成本。

5380 Downsizing increases **efficiency** and profits.
縮編能增加效率和收益。 efficiency 名 效率

5381 The company **reorganized**, and my department was **eliminated**.
公司進行了重組，我的部門被砍掉了。
reorganize 動 整頓 eliminate 動 消除

5382 I was **fired** because my company is downsizing.
因為公司在縮編，所以我被炒魷魚了。 fire 動 解雇

5383 I left them **solely** because they reduced the **scale** of their operation.
由於公司裁減編制，所以我離職了。
solely 副 單獨地 scale 名 規模

5384 I received notice that I was laid off this morning.
今天早上才被通知：我被解雇了。

5385 Karen got a **disciplinary dismissal**.
凱倫受到解雇處分。 disciplinary 形 懲戒的 dismissal 名 解雇

5386 Leah was fired.
莉亞被開除了。

5387 Do you know if I qualify for **unemployment insurance**?
問你喔，我這樣符合領失業救濟金的資格嗎？
unemployment 名 失業 insurance 名 賠償金

5388 You can get unemployment insurance for six months.
你可以請領六個月的失業救濟金。

5389 I am so **pessimistic** because I am **jobless**.
因為失業，我感到人生無望了。
pessimistic 形 悲觀的 jobless 形 失業的

5390 I heard that our company has been having financial difficulties recently.

聽說我們公司最近有財務困難。

5391 I heard that you have just **made a killing**, haven't you?
聽說你們剛大賺了一筆，是嗎？ make a killing 片 大賺一筆

5392 Don't believe that it's easy to make a killing in the **real estate** market.
別相信房地產能讓人一夜致富。 real estate 片 房地產

5393 Our last projects didn't make a profit.
我們前幾個案子都沒獲利。

5394 Our **operation** has been **in the red** since last year.
去年開始，我們的營運就開始出現虧損了。
operation 名 營運 in the red 片 赤字

5395 It is impossible to **break even**.
不可能打平收支了。 break even 片 不賺不賠

5396 We might have to **close up** unless we find a way to increase **revenues**.
除非找到增加收益的方法，否則我們就要關門大吉了。
close up 片 停業 revenue 名 收益

5397 Can we take a **loan** out from the bank?
我們可以向銀行貸款嗎？ loan 名 貸款

5398 The bank **rejected** our loan **application**.
銀行拒絕了我們的貸款申請。 reject 動 拒絕 application 名 申請

5399 They are talking about **declaring bankruptcy**.
他們正在討論要宣布破產。 declare 動 宣告 bankruptcy 名 破產

5400 Declaring bankruptcy is the only **option** for us now.
宣布破產是目前唯一的方法了。 option 名 選擇

5401 The company was forced to go out of business.
公司被迫倒閉。

5402 I lost my job because my company went **bankrupt**.
我們的公司倒閉，所以我失業了。 bankrupt 形 破產的

5403 Unfortunately, my employer has been forced to **liquidate** his business due to the worldwide economic **adversity**.
很不幸，由於這次的全球性經濟危機，我的老闆不得不結束公司業務。 liquidate 動 清算 adversity 名 (經濟方面的)窘境

5404 Our president has announced the bankruptcy to all the employees.
總裁已經向所有員工宣布公司破產的這件事了。

5405 The company will offer **severance** packages.
公司會提供資遣的配套措施。 severance 名 分離；切斷

5406 All the laid-off employees will get two-month's **severance pay**.
所有被資遣的員工都會領到兩個月的資遣費。
severance pay 片 資遣費

5407 I left the company due to the closing down of the company's business.
由於我的公司結束經營，所以我離職了。

轉換跑道 & 退休
Quitting & Getting Retired

5408 I am considering a **career** change.
我在考慮轉換跑道。 career 名 職業

5409 I've just decided to **rethink** my career.
我才剛決定要重新考慮我的生涯規劃。 rethink 動 重新考慮

5410 I have to **make up my mind**.
我不能再三心二意了。 make up one's mind 片 下定決心

5411 I don't want to work in sales anymore.
我不想再繼續做業務的工作了。

5412 I **resigned** from my position. / I am off the **payroll**.
我離職了。 resign 動 辭去 payroll 名 發薪名單

5413 Here is my **resignation**.
這是我的辭呈。 resignation 名 辭呈

5414 I finally quit the company.
我終於辭掉工作了。

5415 I heard that Sue quit **all of a sudden**. What happened?
我聽說蘇突然辭職，發生什麼事了？ all of a sudden 片 突然

5416 I understand she is unhappy with the **workload** and her supervisor.
我知道她對工作量和她的主管不滿。 workload 名 工作量

5417 I am just wondering what the **last straw** will be?
我很好奇到底什麼會是壓垮駱駝的最後一根稻草呢？
last straw 名 最後一擊

5418 I don't know why he **submitted** his resignation this morning.
我不清楚他今天早上為何會遞辭呈。 submit 動 提交

5419 All of us **regret** your resignation.
我們都對你的離職感到惋惜。 regret 動 因…而遺憾

5420 What made you decide to leave your job?
你為什麼要離職呢？

5421 Due to my health, I need to leave my job.
因為個人健康因素的關係，我必須離職。

5422 I'm leaving my **present** job just because of the **expiry** of my employment contract.
我離職是因為工作合約期滿。present 形 當前的 expiry 名 滿期

5423 I had a **quarrel** with my boss.
我和老闆發生口角。quarrel 名 爭吵

5424 I was commuting to the city and spending a significant amount of time each day traveling back and forth. I would prefer to be closer to home.
我每天花很多時間在通勤，因此想找離家近一點的工作。

5425 I think I need a rest to **take care of** my **elderly** mother.
我覺得我需要休息一段時間，照顧年邁的母親。
take care of 片 照顧 elderly 形 上了年紀的

5426 I'm sorry, but I've decided to study **abroad**.
很抱歉，我決定出國留學。abroad 副 到國外

5427 I left the position to **improve** myself.
我辭職是為了想自我提升。improve 動 增進

5428 I left the office because I don't want to **be stuck in a rut**.
我離職因為我不想像現在這樣一成不變。
be stuck in a rut 片 一成不變

5429 I hope to change to an environment where I can **broaden** my **horizons**.
我希望能換個環境，開開眼界。
broaden 動 使擴大 horizon 名 眼界；視野

5430 Losing you would be a huge **loss** to the company.
你離職，將會是公司的一大損失。loss 名 損失

5431 I know that you have always taken me under your wing.
我知道你一直都對我照顧有加。

5432 I'd love to stay, but my family is moving to the United States.
我也想要留下來，但我們全家要搬到美國去了。

5433 I'm experiencing a **bottleneck** with this project at the moment.
這份企劃進行到現在，遇上瓶頸了。 bottleneck 名 瓶頸

5434 I have been with my current company for four years, and I don't find the work as interesting as I once did.
我在現在的公司工作了四年，發現這份工作不像以前那麼有趣了。

5435 I found myself **bored** with the work and looking for more challenges.
我厭倦了現在的工作，想要更多的挑戰。 bored 形 厭倦的

5436 I have enjoyed my **tenure** at ABC Company, but it's time to move on to a new challenge.
我十分喜歡在 ABC 公司的工作，但現在差不多該接受新的挑戰了。 tenure 名 任期

5437 I am **desirous** of leaving the office to gain more experience in **advertising**.
我希望離職的原因，是想在廣告業取得更多經驗。
desirous 形 渴望的 advertising 名 廣告業

5438 I have accepted another position.
我已經接受了另一份工作。

5439 To be honest, I've got a better opportunity.
老實說，我得到一個更好的工作機會。

5440 I've decided that is not the direction I want to go in my career.
我想清楚了，那並非是我想走的職業道路。

5441 Changing jobs is not a bad thing. I just don't want to get into a rut.
換工作不是件壞事，我只是不想要這樣一成不變。

5442 I would like to have a job that is more **lively** than my present one.
我希望能找到一份更有活力的工作。 lively 形 活潑的

5443 I am looking for a company that I really want to work for so that I could settle down and make a **long-term contribution**.
我想找到一家理想的公司，使我能安定下來，並做出長遠的貢獻。
long-term 形 長期的 contribution 名 貢獻

5444 To be honest, I can't stand the **unreasonable** workload anymore.
老實說，我無法再忍受這樣不合理的工作量了。
unreasonable 形 不合理的

5445 I've had it with my **current** job.
我真是受夠了目前的工作。 current 形 目前的

5446 I don't want to accept a position that I don't think I will be happy in.
我不想接受一份會讓自己感到不快樂的工作。

5447 I think there is too much responsibility for me. I wonder if I can handle it.
我認為這份工作要承擔的責任太多，我不知道能否應付得了。

5448 I've been **trying my best**, but I don't think I'm qualified for this job.
我盡力而為了，但還是無法勝任這項工作。 try one's best 片 盡力

5449 I am working at a small company where further promotion is impossible.
我在一家小公司工作，所以不太可能有升遷的機會。

5450 It seems that I have no chance for advancement.
看來我是沒有升遷的機會了。

5451 I think it is time for me to leave.
我想該是離開的時候了。

5452 I won't be leaving **right away**; this is my one-month's notice.
我沒有要馬上離職，會再待一個月。 right away 片 立刻

5453 Most people at least give two-week's notice.
大部分的人都會在兩週前提出。

5454 Best of luck with your future career plans.
祝你未來的事業一帆風順。

5455 When are you planning to **retire**?
你打算什麼時候退休呢？ retire 動 退休

5456 I am going to retire next year.
我明年就要退休了。

5457 I've reached **retirement** age.
我已經達到退休年齡了。 retirement 名 退休

5458 I am five years away from retirement.
我還有五年就要退休了。

5459 Who will take over your duties once you retire?
你退休之後，誰會接任你的工作呢？

5460 The accountant is going to retire, and we'll need someone to fill that position.
這位會計即將退休，我們需要找人遞補他的位子。

5461 I'm having a hard time getting over Nancy's leaving so quickly.
南西突然離職，我還真不習慣。

5462 We are having a farewell dinner for Carl, who is retiring next month.
我們要替卡爾辦餞行餐會，他下個月就要退休了。

國家圖書館出版品預行編目資料

英文袋著聊：口語慣用句5,000 / 張翔 編著 -- 初版
. -- 新北市 : 知識工場出版 采舍國際有限公司發行,
2016.09 面；　公分. -- (Excellent ; 84)
ISBN-978-986-271-713-4 (平裝附光碟片)

1.英語　2.會話　3.句法

805.188　　　　105014022

知識工場 · Excellent 84

英文袋著聊：口語慣用句5,000

出版者／全球華文聯合出版平台 · 知識工場

作　　者／張 翔
出版總監／王寶玲
總 編 輯／歐綾纖
印 行 者／知識工場
文字編輯／何牧蓉
美術設計／蔡億盈

郵撥帳號／50017206 采舍國際有限公司（郵撥購買，請另付一成郵資）
台灣出版中心／新北市中和區中山路2段366巷10號10樓
電　　話／（02）2248-7896
傳　　真／（02）2248-7758
ISBN-13 ／978-986-271-713-4
出版日期 ／2016年9月初版

全球華文市場總代理 ／采舍國際
地　　址／新北市中和區中山路2段366巷10號3樓
電　　話／（02）8245-8786
傳　　真／（02）8245-8718

港澳地區總經銷／和平圖書
地　　址／香港柴灣嘉業街12號百樂門大廈17樓
電　　話／（852）2804-6687
傳　　真／（852）2804-6409

全系列書系特約展示
新絲路網路書店
地　　址／新北市中和區中山路2段366巷10號10樓
電　　話／（02）8245-9896
傳　　真／（02）8245-8819
網　　址／www.silkbook.com

本書全程採減碳印製流程並使用優質中性紙（Acid & Alkali Free）最符環保需求。

本書爲名師張翔等及出版社編輯小組精心編著覆核，如仍有疏漏，請各位先進不吝指正。
來函請寄mujung@mail.book4u.com.tw，若經查證無誤，我們將有精美小禮物贈送！